Praise for
SILENCE

"Perry is the grand poobah of the running-away narrative, with its trapdoor escape mechanisms, elaborate chase sequences and unsettling identity issues, and he's at the top of his cat-and-mouse game in *Silence*...His complex characters, including a pair of insanely appealing villains, are all the more attractive for being so devious and untrustworthy. Paul and Sylvie Turner...are inspired creations." —Marilyn Stasio, *The New York Times Book Review*

"Mr. Perry is known for good reason as a careful, incisive writer of psychological crime stories. And *Silence* is another prime example. As Mr. Perry spins an elaborate web of cat-and-mouse machinations, his story is driven as much by the characters' fears and neuroses as by ordinary motives...Perry renders these dynamics in his typically lean, perceptive style, to the point where none of the principals make a false move...Steadily surprising."
—Janet Maslin, *The New York Times*

"[Perry's] appeal lies in his intricate plotting and original, often irresistible characters. In *Silence*, he is at the top of his game...Paul and Sylvie Turner [are] two of the most interesting villains you never want to meet." —Associated Press

"Thomas Perry is one hell of a writer. *Silence* is an ingeniously plotted and tightly written novel of taut psychological suspense. This is catnip for true fans of the mystery/suspense genre."
—Nelson DeMille

SILENCE

THOMAS PERRY

SILENCE

AN OTTO PENZLER BOOK

A HARVEST BOOK • HARCOURT, INC.

Orlando Austin New York San Diego London

www.HarcourtBooks.com

Excerpt from *Fidelity* copyright © 2008 by Thomas Perry

The Library of Congress has cataloged the hardcover edition as follows:
Perry, Thomas, 1947–
Silence/Thomas Perry.—1st ed.
p. cm.
"An Otto Penzler Book."
1. Murder for hire—Fiction. I. Title.
PS3566.E718S53   2007
813'.54—dc22   2006026957
ISBN 978-0-15-101289-3
ISBN 978-0-15-603330-5 (pbk.)

Text set in Adobe Garamond
Designed by April Ward

Printed in the United States of America

First Harvest edition 2008
A C E G I K J H F D B

For Jo, Alix, and Isabel,
with gratitude to Robert Lescher

SILENCE

1

THE SMALL NEON LIGHT outside that said BANQUE was turned off. Wendy Harper armed the alarm system, flipped the light switch to throw the dining room into darkness, slipped outside, tugged the big front door shut, and locked it. David the bartender and the last three kitchen men loitered, leaning against the pillars beside the entrance of the old bank building, talking quietly while they waited for her. "Thanks, everybody," she said. "Eric and I really appreciated all of your work tonight."

Victor, Juan, and Billy, the three kitchen men, gave Wendy shy, murmured answers and began to walk toward their cars, but David stayed at her side as she walked to the far end of the parking lot where she had left her car. She was surprised at how hot the night was, even though it was after three o'clock. The dark fronds of the tall, thin coconut palms beside the Banque parking lot were absolutely motionless in the still night air, and it felt as though the asphalt was exhaling the heat it had stored during the day.

She got in her car, started the engine, and locked the doors. She backed out of her space and waited until David was in his car, then waved to him, pulled out of the lot to La Cienega, and turned to head toward Sunset. Wendy checked her rearview mirror frequently, and sometimes abruptly. Whenever she passed a car idling on a side street or pulling out onto La Cienega, she kept track of it until it turned and disappeared.

She felt gratitude for the patience of the restaurant crew. They seemed to be watching over her late at night. *Eric and I thank you,* she thought. *Eric and I.* That was a big part of what had changed. For all of the time since Banque had opened—in fact, for all of her years in the restaurant business—she and Eric had gone home together. It had not mattered to her if it was three in the afternoon or three at night because he had been there. But tonight she had seen Eric leave at midnight.

The kitchen had already shut down, but the bar was still noisy and active when she had crossed the dining room to oversee the end of food service. One of the busboys opened the kitchen door and held it open for someone to pass with a bin of heavy dishes. Beyond the door she could see the white-suited helpers and Victor, the kitchen-floor man, beginning to scrub the tables and scrape the grill. She saw Eric. He had already taken off his white coat and changed into a short-sleeved blue shirt.

When she looked at him, even from a distance, she felt a physical sensation, as if he'd touched her. She could almost feel his short blond hair, nearly a crew cut but soft as cat fur, a little wet after a night in the heat and steam and exertion. He was athletic and strong, a head taller than any of the cleanup crew working around him. He was moving away from her. As he passed Victor and Juan, he smiled and gave each of them a pat on the arm that turned into an affectionate shoulder squeeze, and said something to each of them. She could not read his lips, but she knew roughly what he was saying. Even though Eric was becoming a famous chef, he had started as a busboy not so many years ago, and it was too soon for him to forget. The door swung shut.

As she drove toward their house she began to feel her anxiety grow with each block. She went up above Sunset onto the narrow, dark and winding roads in the hills, and she began to look for danger without knowing what form it would take. Could a car follow her on these streets with its headlights off? For the past two weeks she had been going home by different routes, and leaving the restaurant at different times every night. It was probably Olivia's fault. She had been with Wendy since the opening of the restaurant and been her friend through everything, but she had lost her nerve. She had kept reminding Wendy of what could happen, how easy it would be to do, and how hard it would be to prevent. She had left town two weeks ago.

As Wendy drove past the houses in her neighborhood, she studied each one separately, looking for tiny changes. This was an area where every house was different, some of them three stories high and dug into the hillside, and others almost invisible beyond tall hedges. When she turned the last curve, she could already see the house that she and Eric had bought less than a year ago. One of the things she had liked about the house was that it had seemed so substantial, but now it didn't feel to her like a place of safety. Tonight the house would be big and empty, and most of it dark. But she had nowhere else to go.

She slowed and turned into the driveway. Recently she'd had automatic lights installed along the front and side of the house that went on when the night came, but they had not had the right effect. The bright beams under the floodlights left big spaces between them and beyond them that seemed much darker than before. She would have to remember to do something about that tomorrow. Maybe there should be more lights, or bulbs that were dimmer and more diffuse. She reminded herself that she was being foolish to keep changing things. She and Eric had once planned to stay in this house forever, but that was not going to happen.

She parked her car in the garage and walked toward the side door. She liked the Japanese-style natural wood timbers that jutted out from the eaves. She had patterned that look after the enclosed garden behind the restaurant. The garden was her little surprise for customers who had come in the front door between the Corinthian columns and walked across the marble floor of the bank lobby.

As she walked toward the door under the jasmine vine, she crossed the boundary of its perfume, and the air was thick with it. She looked down to separate the key from the others on her ring, and looked up to see the man.

She could see he was holding something as he took a step out from the dark pocket under the arbor, and then his swing began and the motion made her recognize that the something was a base-ball bat. Wendy threw up her arms and jerked back in a reflex to protect her face, but the man had not been swinging at her face.

There was an explosion of pain in her left thigh above the knee, and the bat swept her legs out from under her. She hit the pavement on her left hip, but she tried to scramble, to crawl away from him. The second blow hit her forearm. When it collapsed, she knew the small bones had been broken.

She could see him now, the broad shoulders, the dark sport coat, the face like the face of a statue in the dim light. "What?" she asked. "What do you want?"

The bat swung again, and it hit her just below the hip. The pain splashed a red haze over her vision for an instant, then faded. The blow obliterated her disbelief, her sense that this could not be hap-pening. She knew he was crippling her, and in another swing, she would be beyond hope. She would be immobile, and then he would kill her. He raised his bat again. She exerted a huge effort, pulled herself to her feet and tried to run, but all she could manage was a painful, limping hobble. In three steps, his strong hand grasped her arm and dragged her backward.

She tried to jerk her arm away, but his hand closed its grip on her blouse at the shoulder. He still had the bat in his other hand, but he swung her in a quick circle. The blouse tore, much of it came away in his hand, and her momentum flung her to the pavement of the driveway. This time she was in the center of a pool of light from a floodlight mounted under the eaves of the house.

The man knelt, held her down with the bat, and hit her with his free hand, delivering four quick punches to her face and shoulders. She was groggy. She tasted blood, and couldn't seem to spit it all out, and there was more in her eyes. She was in hot, throbbing pain. Both her arms felt weak and useless.

With the glare above and behind him, she could only see him in silhouette, raising the bat again. When he brought it downward, she flinched and half-rolled away from it. The bat hit the concrete beside her head with a hollow sound, bounced up and skinned the back of her head. This time he stood with one foot on either side of her, raised the bat above his head. She could see this swing was going to crush her skull.

The world ignited and burned with new light. The man, the bat, the house behind him, the concrete beside her face were all lit as though it were daylight. The man's face lifted to squint up the street, and he stepped out of her vision. She heard his footsteps, fast-running, going away from her. She heard the bang of a car door, and then another, and then voices.

2

JACK TILL STRAIGHTENED his necktie as he watched the paparazzi across the street. They had been calm and still for a time, glancing now and then at the hotel, but now they were up out of their cars and pacing, their eyes on the front entrance. He noticed that they devoted half of their attention to each other. They were competitors, and a photograph wasn't worth much if the others got it, too. Till was lucky that Marina Fallows was in the hotel tonight for the charity banquet. She had stood out in small parts in a couple of big movies, and fresh faces were always the favorite prey of the tabloids. He wondered what this week's issues would say she had been doing here.

The photographers stood still for an instant, as though they'd heard something. Then they all moved at once, a shift toward the front doors, where the doorman and parking attendants had suddenly been reinforced by a couple of dark-suited security men. In a moment a pair of dark limousines floated in from the parking lot around the corner, and veered close to the curb.

The show inside the reception room where Marina Fallows had been must be over, and now the show outside was beginning. The doors opened and the beautiful young woman appeared, dressed in a long strapless black evening gown and open-toed shoes that glinted in the light. She was accompanied by a man about her age in a dark suit who looked as though he had been chosen to look good by her side. The flashes began and Till was surprised once again by how small some actresses were in person, almost like children. The flashes became continuous like strobe lights, the photographers elbowing each other aside to get closer, shooting at the rate of three frames a second. Two of them stood in front of the lead limousine to block its path while their partners ran along beside the couple, pushing their flashing cameras into their faces until the two were inside and the door slammed.

Till kept his attention on the doorway. He saw two couples come out, then a third, all dressed in evening clothes. Till reached into his pocket, extracted a letter-sized printed sheet, studied the color picture on it for a moment, then began to walk as he put it away and then reached into the side pocket of his coat.

Till was six feet one inch tall, forty-two years old, with broad shoulders and an energetic stride. He was dressed in a dark suit that made him look as though he had attended one of the events in the hotel's reception rooms. As he approached the front of the building, the paparazzi and the security people seemed to sense that it was in their best interest to assume that he had nothing to do with their struggles, and pretend not to see him.

Till reached the curb while the third couple waited for the parking attendant to bring their car to them. They were in their forties, the wife very thin and blond, with freckles that melted together like a tan on her bare shoulders and collarbones. The husband was tall and fit, with an open, boyish face and eyebrows that looked almost white in the reflected light of the street lamps. As the couple's Mercedes pulled up to the curb, Till's eyes returned to the wife's neck.

Till took a small digital camera out of his coat pocket and snapped a picture.

The man laughed and held up his hand. "Hey! We're not famous!"

Till said, "Sorry, my mistake," and kept walking.

As he came abreast of the couple, he saw the woman turn away from him and whisper urgently to her husband, her hand clutching her throat. Till picked up his pace.

The husband ran after Till and tapped him on the shoulder. "I'm sorry, friend, but I'm going to have to ask you for that film."

"I'm sorry, too," Till said. "You can't have it."

"All right, I'll pay you for it. My wife really doesn't want to have her picture taken, and you can't sell it, anyway. We're not actors." He produced a very small, soft wallet, and extracted a bill. "Will a hundred cover it?"

"No," said Till. "You're welcome to tell her I exposed the film or something, but I can't take your money. I've got things in the camera that I want, so I can't help you."

"You have to." The man lunged for Till's hand to snatch the camera.

Till's left hand came up so quickly, it seemed to have been in the air waiting for the man's hand to arrive. He caught the hand and twisted it around so the man had to bend to the side.

"Let me go. Let go of my hand!"

"Okay." Till pocketed his camera and then released him.

The man straightened and backed away. When he was a few feet off, he turned and hurried back into the hotel entrance with his wife. He already had his cell phone out, and he was talking into it with animation. Till could see through the glass doors that several other men and women in evening dress were flocking around the couple. Three of the men came out and took a few steps in Till's direction, but they didn't seem to be able to decide what to do. Their friend didn't need to be saved, and Till wasn't running away. They withdrew to the front door of the hotel to look in the glass door at their friend and then back at Till.

The police car arrived in about four minutes, veered to the curb behind the couple's Mercedes, and rocked once on its worn shock absorbers. Two young police officers got out, one male and one female. The woman was short, with dark hair tied back in a bun, and she looked stocky in her bulletproof vest, but the man was tall and thin, like a basketball player. "Sir," the male officer said, "are you Mr. Mason?"

"No, my name is Jack Till. George Mason is inside the door over there. The tall, blond one with the tan."

"Officer! Officer!" George Mason rushed out of the hotel through the glass doors, followed by his wife and the rest of his party. "This man assaulted me. He took our picture, and then he twisted my wrist."

"Hold it, everyone," said the policewoman. "Everybody will get a chance." She said to her partner, "You take Mr. Mason's statement. I'll talk to this gentleman."

She led him a few paces up the street and stopped. "Are you the Jack Till who used to be a cop?"

"Yes," he said. He took out his identification and held it up, but she didn't look at it.

"I thought I recognized you. I was in the Hollywood Division when you were there in homicide. I'm Becky Salamone. I know you don't remember me, so don't pretend."

"Nice to meet you."

"What happened?"

"Since I retired, I've been doing PI work. I've been watching Mrs. Mason for about a week. She and her husband, George, reported a necklace as stolen in a burglary two years ago. Here's the insurance company's circular on it." He unfolded it and handed it to her.

Officer Salamone held it. "Sapphires and diamonds. Nice."

"Yeah," said Till. "McLaren Life and Casualty paid them three hundred fifty thousand. She's wearing it tonight."

"Oh?" Salamone looked around her. "Where is she?"

Till looked toward the hotel entrance. "She must have gone back inside. I took a picture, she got upset, and her husband came after me wanting the film. First he tried to buy it, then to grab it. I couldn't let him do that." Till took out his camera. "It's digital. You can see the picture." He turned the camera on so she could see the shot of the Masons standing beside their car.

Salamone compared the image with the photograph on the sheet. "Great shot."

"I got the car in because you can see the model and the plate," said Till. "The car wasn't built when the necklace disappeared. It's brand-new."

George Mason shouted from the front of the hotel, "Hold him! I want to press charges."

Officer Salamone handed Till's camera and circular back to him, then approached the group outside the hotel, took her partner aside for a few seconds, whispered to him, and then returned. "Mrs. Mason. Where is Mrs. Mason?"

Mrs. Mason came forward. "I saw all of it. This man was—"

Officer Salamone said, "Mrs. Mason, weren't you wearing a necklace earlier?"

"I don't understand."

Till held up the picture from the insurance company and unfolded it. "This one."

Mrs. Mason was beginning to look pale. "No, I wasn't wearing that. I don't have a necklace like that. What does this have to do with your attacking my husband? It's ridiculous!"

Till turned to the other people who had been at the event in the hotel. "Anyone see Mrs. Mason wearing a necklace tonight?"

None of the guests seemed to understand the question. Their expressions looked as though Till had been speaking a language they had never heard before. Till turned his left side to the group and gave a barely perceptible wink to Officer Salamone with his right eye. "I guess there's no choice. You'll just have to search all of them and charge the one who has it."

Salamone's face was unreadable. She gave a slight nod.

Till called out to the group, "Don't anyone attempt to leave. Extra units will be arriving in a moment to bring everyone down to the station so officers can take your statements under oath and perform body searches. Most of you will be free to go within a few hours."

All of the party looked horrified, but one of the women began to tremble, and then to cry. She looked at Mrs. Mason. "I'm sorry, Brenda, but I can't do this. Not even for you." She opened her purse, lifted out Mrs. Mason's necklace, and held it out to Officer Salamone as though it were a venomous snake.

THE NEXT MORNING Jack Till walked to his office. He almost always left his car parked in the space under his apartment building on the east side of Laurel Canyon, and walked to his office on Ventura Boulevard. The distance was no more than a half mile, and he liked being at street level, looking around and thinking.

He felt good this morning. The insurance company had already responded to the news that their necklace had been recovered. They would pay him enough to ensure that this year his detective agency would almost break even, and the year was only half over. And when he had come home last night, he had played back his voice mail and listened to a message from Dan Mulroney, a detective in the Hollywood Division, telling him he had referred a client who would probably come to see him today. It was only his second year as a private investigator, and he might actually make a profit.

He stopped at the open-air newsstand on the corner, bought this morning's *Los Angeles Times,* put it under his left arm and made his way along the boulevard with the morning sun at his back. He stopped in Starbucks to pick up a cup of coffee, and made his way to his building. It was a two-story complex with a big antique shop and a row of three stores that sold women's clothes, gifts, and eyeglasses on the ground floor. There was a narrow entry between the antiques and the women's clothes, a black felt directory under glass on the wall inside the door, and a staircase leading to a single corridor of offices on the second floor.

Till's office was the first on the right, a single room that held a telephone, a desk, two filing cabinets, and a couch, all from an office-furniture–liquidation dealer on Sherman Way. On the left side of the corridor were three offices held by three sallow young men who kept long, irregular hours and were always reincorporating themselves as different television-production companies. Till walked up the stairs carrying his newspaper and coffee, and found a young woman leaning against his door.

She was slight and blond, her hair fine and glossy as a child's, but it took him a moment to see what she really looked like because her face was discolored by purple bruises and distorted by swelling. She looked, more than anything, like some of the female homicide victims he had seen. As soon as she saw him, she pushed herself away from his door, and then grasped the cane he had not seen before. She used it to make way for him to unlock his door.

"Good morning," he said. "Are you here to see me—Jack Till?"

"Yes."

"Then come on in." He was sure he knew her story simply by looking at her. She must have been in a car accident. There was some kind of lawsuit, and she would hire him to investigate the other party. He set his coffee and paper on the desk and pointed to the couch. "Please make yourself comfortable."

She looked at the couch skeptically. "Do you have a regular chair? That kind of thing isn't good on my back right now."

As Till went to the other side of the room to retrieve a straight-backed chair, she edged closer to his desk, and at first he thought she was sneaking a look at the files on the surface, but then he realized she was staring out the window that overlooked Ventura Boulevard. He could see her pupils moving in small jumps, focusing on one person, then another. She was terrified.

He realized there had been no accident. He put the chair down in front of the desk. "Who did this to you?"

She held her arms out from her sides as though she were showing him her dress, but he could see the gesture meant her battered face, her injured body. "A man. Two men, really. They want to kill me."

"Who?"

"I don't know who they are."

"What would you like me to do—protect you? Find them?"

"Help me run away."

SIX YEARS LATER, Jack Till would still remember that moment in his office, when he had seen Wendy Harper for the first time. When he had listened to her story, he had reacted as though he were still a policeman. He had tried to get her to do all of the sensible things, to turn the problem over to the police and let them protect her. She had a rebuttal to every suggestion, a reason why the only hope she had of staying alive was to try to live elsewhere. She had already been to the police after she had been beaten, and they had suggested she see Jack Till. In the end, he had given in. He had taught her what she needed to know about the methods police departments used to track fugitives, on the theory that anyone searching for her would not be as good at it as the professionals. When he had finished teaching her and the injuries that were visible had healed, he left her in another city at the entrance to the airport.

For the first year he worried, scanning the newspapers for any news of her, waiting to read that her body had been found. Five more years passed, and he heard nothing more of Wendy Harper.

He hoped that the silence meant she had made it.

3

ARE YOU GOING to do it?" she asked.

"*You* are," he said.

Paul and Sylvie Turner made their way along Broxton Avenue with the unhurried grace of long-legged wading birds. They were both tall and slim, and their straight posture elongated them. Sylvie was pretty, with smooth skin, big eyes, and shoulder-length dark brown hair that shone in the late afternoon sun. They both wore large sunglasses, khaki slacks and dark-colored tailored jackets. As Paul and Sylvie walked past the windows of a bookstore, only Paul glanced in that direction to check their reflection in the glass. He liked being in Westwood because most of the people on the streets were UCLA students who paid little attention to a middle-aged couple. Ahead of Paul and Sylvie, dominating the intersection was a big old movie theater called the Regent.

They spoke, as couples like them often did, without looking directly at one another. "Why do you want *me* to do it?" she asked.

"I just do. It's your turn, and I think you would feel better if you did it. I'm just thinking about you."

"No, you're not," she said. "You like to watch me."

"Maybe I do."

They crossed the street, and Paul bought them tickets to the movie that was scheduled to start in five minutes. A young usher took their tickets just inside the door, tore them, and returned the stubs to Paul. Without speaking, Sylvie and Paul separated in the lobby and went into the restrooms. Sylvie gathered her hair into a ponytail and slipped a band over it. When they returned to the lobby they both had removed their sunglasses and jackets. They occupied themselves by looking at posters for coming attractions.

After a few minutes, the door of one of the screening rooms opened and a crowd of about a hundred people, many of them couples around the same age and description as the Turners, straggled out and across the lobby toward the street. The Turners waited until the first few stepped out into the sunlight and stopped to push buttons on cell phones or search their pockets for parking receipts. Then Paul and Sylvie allowed themselves to be swept out with the main body of the group. They stayed in the group all the way across the street and into the parking structure, where they walked past the black BMW that Paul had driven into the lot. Instead, they got into their second car, the black BMW that Sylvie had parked here.

The receipt for the movie tickets carried the credit-card number and the time of purchase. For eighteen dollars they had just bought two hours. Paul and Sylvie had become expert at bending and molding time in small ways. Paul slipped the two ticket stubs into his wallet, and Sylvie retrieved the parking receipt for her car and handed it to him.

Paul stopped at the parking attendant's cubicle while Sylvie looked the other way, but she knew it would not be necessary. There would be a different attendant later who had never seen her before. Paul drove out to Wilshire Boulevard and onto the San Diego Freeway. He followed it to the Santa Monica Freeway, took it to the Fifth Street exit, and parked in the structure there. Paul and Sylvie joined the pedestrians walking past the open promenade of Fifth Street toward the Santa Monica Pier, but when they reached the corner, they let the group go, turned, and walked along Ocean Avenue. Paul looked at his watch for the second time, but Sylvie touched his forearm. "That's getting to be a nervous habit," she said quietly.

"Sorry."

"It's okay. Just watch the pretty sunset on the ocean. There's plenty of time, and if you keep checking, then people will start watching you to see what the hurry is."

"You're right," he said. "I'm just still not sure yet that this is the very best place and time."

"It's the best for him," Sylvie said. "It's the only time when we can be really sure he's alone. He'll do all the checking for us. She lives right up there. It's the third building, fourth balcony from the end on the fourth floor. See it?"

"It's open. Maybe he's watching the same sunset through those white inner curtains," Paul said. "Have you thought about that?"

She smiled patiently. "No, he's not. That's the bedroom. He's there, he's with her, and he's not interested in the sunset."

"He could have left already, too."

"He never leaves until after it's dark."

"Just this once he might."

"No, never," she said. "You have to remember it's not about him. It's about her. She has a reputation. She has a husband."

"I suppose you're right. He's a gentleman."

"You're a gentleman," she said. She clutched his arm with both her hands, pulled it to her body, and looked up into his eyes. She was trying to gauge whether he had noticed that she had known he was feeling the impulse to look at his watch and she was holding his arm down.

"Thank you." He squinted at the sun, just touching the ocean to the right of the south-facing bay. "We should probably start moving. He'll come out the back." The sun looked soft and distended, like the yolk of an egg on the flat horizon.

She looked at the sun, too. "You're right. It's getting to be time."

"Do you have everything ready, so you could do it right now if you had to?"

"Yes."

"Are you getting excited?"

"Yes. Always. No matter how many times."

"Let's go meet him."

They strolled away from the ocean, then turned into the alley behind the row of apartment buildings west of the pier. They walked slowly, lingering now and then in dark alcoves and shadowy places where the last light of the darkening sky did not reach.

They both saw him come out a rear door of the next building in the dusk, stop on the low step for a moment, then turn to walk toward them. Sylvie felt the gentle pressure of Paul's hand on her back, the firm touch she felt when they were dancing. She yielded and took a step forward.

And then she was alone.

JIMMY POLLARD kept his head down, looking at the uneven, cratered pavement of the alley as he walked. People insisted on keeping dogs in the city, and there was a certain group of them who didn't want to walk their dogs out front where they had to obey the ordinance and dispose of their messes. They walked them in alleys, so a person had to watch where he set his feet.

The thought pushed Jimmy Pollard into one of the moments, once rare but now becoming disturbingly frequent, when he stepped outside himself and saw himself from somewhere above, as an objective observer might see him. His past was all stretched out behind him and leading here, to this moment.

He was sneaking out the back door of a woman's apartment building in the twilight and making his way up an alley. It was the time when other men were coming the other way, arriving from their day's work, opening the front door and seeing the women they were doing it for, some of them even smelling dinner cooking. But maybe that was a dream image left over from his childhood. Maybe nobody did that anymore. The women were mostly out all day, too, because nobody had any children now. The ones who did put them in some kind of day care and picked them up around now. Maybe the whole world was sneaking along some alley. "Here I am," he said to himself. That was all.

Jimmy had a wife, three kids and a job. He and Connie had grown apart over the years, a pair of roommates who had things they held against each other. But Emma, Ben, and Melissa were on his mind every hour. Thinking about them made him feel happy and terrible and lost all at the same time. And here he was.

He heard the light sound of footsteps on the pavement, looked ahead in the dim light, and saw the shape of a woman—the hips, the narrow waist, the shoulders. He drew in a breath—Connie? Would she come here?

The woman's strides brought her closer, and as she stepped into a strip of light that reached the alley between two buildings she was illuminated for a second. No. Even from this distance, it wasn't Connie. Thank you, Lord. He knew that confrontation was going to happen someday, but not here and not now. He still had time. Even as he thought that, he knew he would not use the time, if it were fifty years. He would never be a faithful husband again. He would never break off the affair, or use the reprieve to go to Connie and tell her. He quickly recited the reasons, an inventory that included the children, the house, the job, the money.

Unexpectedly, in the inventory was something new; a piece of unintentional clarity. One of the reasons why these afternoons with Sally were so irresistible was that they were forbidden and secret.

Jimmy kept his head down, concerned to be sure this woman in the alley didn't get a look at his face. Women didn't walk alone in alleys. If she was walking a dog, he hadn't seen it. She was probably a neighbor who had come down to toss something in the

Dumpster. She could be one of Sally's friends who would remember seeing him here, and could easily be present some other time and recognize him. Still, he couldn't resist the impulse to look.

He glanced up and then down again, and brought back an impression that was favorable. She was tall—too tall for him, but very slim and graceful, like a dancer. If she could afford a beachfront condo in Santa Monica, she was more than a dancer. She was probably a party girl who lived with some rich guy. He took another glance, and he found he didn't want to take his eyes away. He began to think about her. She wasn't really that tall, just straight.

He was about ten feet from her when he met her eyes, and smiled respectfully. He said, "Hello," with just the right combination, he thought, of friendliness and perfunctory politeness to reassure a woman alone in an alley. She reached into her purse, probably to put her hand on her canister of pepper spray, but she smiled. Was that mischief?

"Hi, Jimmy," Sylvie said.

He gaped. Who was she? She took her hand out of her purse. There was a gun. He knew he didn't have time to turn around and go back, so he kept walking. If she was scared of him, then in a few seconds she would see he'd meant her no harm. There was a flash-bang, he felt pain, and he began to run. He ran hard, past her. He heard the gun again, but he could still move, still make his legs take step after step toward the opening to the street. There would be people. He could run to them and yell and make a scene.

A man stepped out of the shadows ahead, already aiming a gun at him.

He knew he would never get there.

4

PAUL AND SYLVIE TURNER took the crowded elevator to the eighth floor of the tall gray-white office building on Wilshire Boulevard. The building housed busy lawyers, accountants, and medical specialists, so the Turners had to stand in the back of the elevator and sidestep out when they reached their floor, and then pass several people in the carpeted hallway. They entered the door marked DOLAN, NYQUIST, AND BERNE, ATTORNEYS.

The waiting room was empty. Behind the glass in the reception window was a woman in a stylish gray skirt and jacket. She displayed her professional smile to the Turners when they entered. "Mr. and Mrs. Turner. Good afternoon." Then she glanced at the appointment sheet on her desk and said, "Come in." She pressed a switch and there was an audible click as a bolt in the big wooden door disengaged.

Paul opened the door and held it for Sylvie, then let it click shut again behind him. The woman said to Sylvie, "He's in Four." They went farther into the suite past doors with numbers on them until they came to Four, a conference room with natural-wood chair rails, credible-looking antique portraits on the walls, a long table with twelve padded chairs around it. Michael Densmore sat in one of them.

Densmore was vain about his clothing. He was wearing the pants from a charcoal suit, but the coat was draped on the back of the chair beside him so the shoulders were filled out and the arms hung naturally, like a headless scarecrow. His shirt was pure white with a starched collar and a fine silk tie with a subdued pattern of very small blue squares. He stood when Sylvie walked in. He had a slight belly that caused him to make nervous, ineffectual attempts to tuck his shirt in to cover it. His smile was youthful, but showed wrinkles at the corners of the eyes and the forehead. He closed the door after them and flipped a lock lever below the brass knob. "Sylvie, you look lovely." He grasped her hand, and then shook Paul's. "Good to see you both." He sat down, so his belly would be hidden by the table. "Everything's okay?"

"Sure," said Sylvie.

"Very smooth," Paul agreed. "I'm sure you saw it in the paper."

"Of course. I was very interested to know."

"Nice little .32s. Pop-pop-pop," Sylvie said.

Densmore held his hand up. "No details, please. Nothing specific. I don't want any information. I represent the widow, and I'll be talking to the police. I don't want to have something incidental slip out in conversation, and then find out I've incriminated myself."

"Sorry," said Sylvie. "Forget I said anything. He died of infidelity. Did Mrs. Pollard happen to leave anything for us?"

"Yes, I have it right here." Densmore lifted a briefcase from under the table, opened it, and displayed a row of stacked bills.

"The money is clean, right?" Paul asked.

"This isn't her cash. I deposited her checks and took the cash from several of my own accounts as I always do, so there's no chance bills are marked or anything like that." He smiled. "I'll get my cut by overcharging for settling the estate."

"I'm sure you'll be fine," Sylvie said.

"What about her? Is she a problem?" Paul said.

"No."

"What did you tell her?"

"The usual warnings. She knows that if she and I go to jail, her children will still be out there somewhere, and so will you. She doesn't know who you are."

"Very good. It's always a pleasure to do business with you." Paul rose, took the briefcase, and held out his hand for Densmore to shake.

Densmore remained seated. "Don't go yet." He pushed a folder across the table and opened it so they could see two packets of paper that had been produced on a computer printer. "Can you sign these papers for me, please? They're just duplicates of the wills we made out two years ago, with a new date. I need to have something to put in the file so the office staff won't wonder why you came in. But you know, while you're here, there is one other thing I'd like to discuss with you both, if you've got a minute. Do you?"

Sylvie shrugged, opened the folder, and signed in one of the designated spaces. Paul sat down in his seat again, and took his turn. He held the briefcase on his lap.

"I have something else that's coming up, and I wondered if you would like to be part of it." He opened the folder that was at his elbow on the conference table and took out a photograph. "It's this woman."

Sylvie snagged the photograph and slid it to the space between her and Paul. "She's pretty. Isn't she, Paul?"

"Oh, I don't know."

"Yes you do. She's pretty."

"Yes, but nothing special. Not like you, for instance."

Densmore watched the couple in silence. Sylvie Turner was ten years older than the woman in the picture. Whenever Densmore saw Sylvie, he thought she was attractive. But compared to this woman, Sylvie's features seemed coarse and her skin flawed. Sylvie's face was thin, her nose and mouth projected forward subtly, and her eyes had a cruel glint that made him uncomfortable.

"Who is she?" Sylvie asked.

"Her name is Wendy Harper. She was the part owner of a restaurant called Banque. Do you know it?"

"Banque? Sure," Paul said. "We've been there a couple of times. A big, beautiful room—I guess it was actually a bank lobby—good food, good service. Give me a minute, and I'll think of the name of the chef. Eric something. Fuller?"

"Right. Fuller."

"Darn," Sylvie said. "I remembered, too, but you beat me to it." She glared at her husband. "Paul is always showing me up in the domestic stuff. He makes a better woman than I do, don't you think?"

The skin of Paul's face lost its flexibility and his black eyes were like dots. Densmore wondered what she thought she was doing. Densmore would never have said anything that might offend Paul Turner. He tried to push them past the awkward moment. "They started the restaurant together about ten years ago. He was the chef, and she was the business head. The place was a success right away."

"And?" Sylvie said.

"They had a romantic relationship, I'm told. At some point that ended. Love is temporary, but a successful business is forever. They broke up, but kept the partnership and worked in the business together. After about four or five years, she disappeared."

"How very odd," Sylvie said. "Imagine his surprise."

"That was how the police looked at it six years ago. They had the crudest kind of partnership. The agreement was written out by the two of them in their own handwriting and signed in front of a notary. They owned everything in common, and if one died, the other got all of it. They had two identical life-insurance policies, each with the other partner as beneficiary. It would have made sense to insure him for more because he was the chef, but they didn't, probably because insuring young women is cheap. Anyway, she disappeared, he collected, and the restaurant went to him. The police found nothing."

"Thank God I've ordered only the seafood at Banque," said Sylvie.

Densmore was careful enough to laugh with them. After a moment, he said, "The real situation is more complicated than that. A client of mine wanted her dead. He made an attempt on her six years ago. He failed, but she hasn't been seen since. He still wants her dead."

"He's trying to hire someone to do it now? After she's been gone for six years?" Paul asked.

"He's asked me to make an arrangement. The money would be very significant. I've spent some time working on it, and I've decided that the best hope I have of succeeding is you."

"Us?" Sylvie said.

"Yes," he said. "There's a way to find her, but it seems to have a potential for mishandling, and it could be dangerous. You're the only ones in whom I would feel any confidence. Let me show you what I've got to work with." He got up, walked out of the room for a moment, then returned carrying a nylon bag about a yard long, with two handles. He set it on the table.

"What's that?" asked Sylvie. "Your bag of tricks?"

Densmore looked at her and nodded. "I guess you could call it that." He opened the bag and showed them a baseball bat and a torn piece of white cloth caked with dried blood.

"Are we supposed to do something with that?" Paul asked.

"You bury it. Then we wait a few months and make it turn up again."

5

CHEF CHARGED IN PARTNER'S MURDER

Jack Till sat in his office and stared at the newspaper article for a long time, his mind brushing the sentences aside to find the detail that had caused a homicide detective to arrest Eric Fuller, and a DA to charge him. The article just repeated that Eric Fuller was a well-known chef, that Wendy Harper had been his partner, and that when she disappeared six years ago, he got richer.

Till put the newspaper on his desk, locked his filing cabinets, and put his gun in the safe. He went down the stairs to Ventura Boulevard, walked to his apartment on Laurel Canyon to get his car, then drove downtown on the Hollywood Freeway.

He parked in the underground structure on Spring Street and walked to the District Attorney's office at 210 West Temple. It was only as he was passing the courts complex that he realized that he should have called ahead, found out which of the 938 Assistant DAs had been assigned to prosecute Eric Fuller, called him, and arranged an appointment. But an appointment had not occurred to him, any more than it would have if he'd been driving a heart-attack victim to a hospital. This was the sort of visit that obliterated the slow, careful broaching of topics.

He entered the main reception area of the District Attorney's office impatiently, waited his turn in the line of visitors, then showed his wallet to the middle-aged woman behind the counter. On one side it held the unofficial ID that showed he was a retired police officer, and on the other his private investigator's license. "My name is Jack Till," he said. "I need to know which Assistant DA is prosecuting the homicide case against Eric Fuller. Would you be able to help me?"

"*People* v. *Eric Fuller.* Not listed here," she said. "You said homicide? What's the victim's name?"

"Harper, Wendy A."

The woman looked down at a directory, then dialed four numbers on the phone in front of her. "This is Nell," she said softly. "Can you direct me to the prosecutor who's in charge of the homicide of a Wendy Harper? Thanks." She hung up. She took a sheet from a message pad and a pen, leafed through a notebook, and then wrote a name and office number on the sheet and handed it to him. "You must know your way around this building, right?"

"Yes, ma'am. Twenty years on the force. Thank you very much." He went through the metal detector, then waited his turn for the elevator while he deciphered the note. The prosecutor's name was Gordon something. No. Gordon was the last name. Linda Gordon. He rode upstairs, then walked along the hall past the offices of other Assistant DAs working on other cases. He knew some of them, but fewer and fewer each year as they retired or accepted offers at private law firms. When he found the office, the door was closed, but he saw beneath the door that a light was on, and heard a woman's voice, so he knocked.

A moment later a young woman with long blond hair that looked as though it had begun as brown opened the door. She looked startled when she saw him. "Yes?"

"Are you Linda Gordon?"

"Yes." She looked impatient. He could see that she had left her telephone off the hook and the receiver was on her desk. Till recognized the expression. She was waiting for him to deliver a subpoena.

Half the lawsuits in existence were convicts suing prosecutors and cops.

"My name is Jack Till. I need to speak with you for a few minutes. I can see you're on the phone. I can wait out here until you're finished."

She looked suspicious. "What's this about? Who are you?"

"I'm a private investigator, and I have some important information about the case you're prosecuting against Eric Fuller."

"Just hold it a minute." She stepped quickly to the phone and lifted it. "Carl? I've got to call you back. Two, three minutes. Honest." She set the telephone in its cradle. "Come in."

Till entered the small, cluttered space and looked for a place to sit. There was one chair, but it appeared to be the permanent place for a stack of files. She saw the direction of his eyes and started toward the chair, but he held up his hand. "Don't bother. I'll only be here for a few minutes. I saw the newspaper a little while ago. I came to let you know that there's been a mistake. You can't prosecute Eric Fuller, or anybody else, for the murder of Wendy Harper."

She bristled. "I can't?"

"No. Wendy Harper is alive."

Linda Gordon leaned against the wall behind her desk with her arms folded. "Go on."

Jack Till recognized the gesture. She was protecting herself unconsciously—from him? She was blocking what he was saying. All he could do was keep trying. "The reason you don't have a body is that she's still using it."

"Have you talked to the police?"

"Not yet. I came straight here."

"Well, that's the normal way to do things when you have information. The detective in charge is Sergeant Max Poliakoff at Homicide Special in the Parker Center. If you'll just—"

"I know him. I was the one who trained him when he was in Hollywood Homicide."

"Trained him? You're a police officer?"

"Retired."

"And you want to give me this evidence?"

"Yes. I can go over and talk to Max Poliakoff first, if you'd prefer it."

She stared at him for a second, and he could see that she was thinking far ahead. "All right. At this point I'd better stop you. I want to record what you're saying on my tape recorder. Is that all right with you?"

"Okay."

She took a small pocket recorder from her purse, slipped a new tape cassette into it, and clicked a button. "This is Linda Gordon, Assistant District Attorney, and I'm interviewing a gentleman who has come to my office on Wednesday, May 13. It's now eight-fifty-three A.M. And your name is?" She held out the recorder as though she were challenging him to run.

"John Robert Till."

"Spell it?"

"T-I-L-L."

"Now, you have not been placed under oath. But you have told me that you're a retired police officer, so you know that it is a crime to lie to a law-enforcement official about a homicide case. You are, of course, aware of that?"

"Yes. I am."

"Then say what you wish to say."

"I'm here to advise you not to pursue a case against Eric Fuller for the murder of Wendy Harper because I know that she's not dead."

"How do you know that? Have you seen her?"

"Not recently. I saw her six years ago, after the last time she was seen in Los Angeles."

"So you were the last one to see her alive?"

"Not at all. But I was the last one to see her *here*. I'm a private investigator. She hired me. She had been attacked by a man one night when she was coming home from her restaurant. He beat her up in a way that sounded to me as though he intended to disable her and then kill her."

"How can you know what he intended to do?"

"He used a baseball bat. He started with her legs and arms, then hit her a glancing blow on the head, but he was interrupted by a couple of cars before he could keep her still long enough for his big swing."

Till could see the description had elicited an expression of pure revulsion in Linda Gordon, and that she had not intended him to see it. She set her recorder down on the desk and resumed the pose with her arms folded and the desk between them. "What was the purpose of this attack?"

"I believe it was to murder her and make it look like a predatory, opportunistic killing rather than a practical sort of homicide. Somebody was after her, and she knew it."

"Who was after her?"

"She said that a friend—a woman who sometimes worked at her restaurant—had a boyfriend she thought might be dangerous."

"Dangerous in what way?"

"The woman had told her some things about him, some things he had done to her."

"Why would he be after Wendy?"

"One night Wendy was outside the restaurant after closing. She saw the guy when he came to pick up the friend, and he saw her. A few days later, the friend was gone. She stopped coming to work. Her apartment was empty. Wendy believed she was dead."

"What was the boyfriend's name?"

"I don't know."

"What was the waitress's name?"

"I don't know."

"Why don't you know? Didn't you ask?"

"Sure. She wouldn't tell me the woman's name, and claimed not to know the man's name."

"That's it? That's all? You gave up?"

"I was no longer a police officer, and had no way of compelling her to tell me anything. A responding officer had interviewed her the night of the attack and a detective talked to her afterward, in the hospital. If I'd had a month or so, I might have persuaded her that telling me more would make her safer, but at the time, she was too terrified to listen. She wanted to leave Los Angeles immediately. She was convinced that if she stayed in Los Angeles long enough for this boyfriend to find her again, she was going to die."

"Was she right?"

"I honestly don't know. I don't know who her friend's boyfriend was, or who the man he'd hired to beat her was. I offered to protect her, to act as contractor to get her some bodyguards, or to put her house and her restaurant under surveillance. But if this man wanted her badly enough—"

"So what did you do?"

"I gave her the help she wanted, the help she was willing to take."

"Which was?"

"I drove her to a hotel in Solvang. I hid her there for a few days. We stayed in her room most of the time, and I told her how I would go about finding a person who didn't want to be found."

"Explain."

"I told her the methods professionals might use to find her. And then I taught her ways to avoid those methods."

"And then what?"

"Then she left."

"Just like that. She left. You never saw her again, or heard from her."

"No. That was one of the things I warned her about. If you have contact with people you used to know, you'll get caught. She had not told anyone she was going to hire me, but if someone had already been watching her, then he might know. We were definitely not followed to Solvang. But later on, a potential killer might monitor my mail or my phone and wait for her to write or call."

Linda Gordon was finding his clear, unemotional delivery maddening. "Let me ask you something. What evidence can you give me that any of this ever happened, or that you ever met her?"

"I tried to be sure there wasn't any. Keeping evidence could have endangered her. I wouldn't be telling you any of this now if you hadn't charged someone with killing her."

"Did Eric Fuller know she simply went away voluntarily?"

"No. She wanted him to believe she was dead, and go on with his life. She felt there was nothing to be gained by telling him anything. She believed that if he knew, he would try to find her and possibly get them both killed."

"I thought she was in love with him. That's the story we've been told. I'm sure that's going to figure in his defense. You expect me to believe she would leave him like that?"

Jack Till looked at her, beginning to lose his optimism. She wasn't really listening to what he said. She was formulating arguments against it. "They were a couple when they came to Los Angeles. They had gone to college together and had been close friends. At different times, that friendship took a lot of different forms. They were roommates, and they were engaged to be married, and they started a business together. When the romantic relationship went away, nothing else changed. They were still closer to each other than they were to anyone else, and they trusted each other. They stayed partners and the restaurant did well."

"Well enough so he killed her to get her half of it?"

"What I came to tell you is that he didn't kill her, and neither did anyone else. I sent her away."

"Maybe you did. That was one day, one moment in time. You admit you have no way of knowing what happened to her after that day six years ago. Isn't that right?"

"It's right. I haven't seen her. I haven't tried to see her. I taught her how to keep from being seen, and then sent her off to do it."

"And you think a week of lessons from you was that effective? That she just heard your advice, and then she could stay hidden forever?"

"It's not as simple as that. Nobody was looking for her until she had been gone for at least a month. She told Fuller she was going on a trip to recuperate from the beating, and nobody else cared where she was. When she didn't come back, he tried to find her by calling mutual friends, who hadn't heard from her. By the time the cops were involved, there was no place for them to start looking."

"And you planned that, too?"

"Yes. I did. I taught her what I knew, and that was enough to get her started. But now she's been at it for six years, and probably knows more than I do. She's a very bright woman."

Linda Gordon pushed off from the wall and stepped closer to her desk. Till could see her eyes lower for a second, and he knew she was looking to check that enough tape was left in her recorder without reminding him that it was running. She leaned on the desk. "You know, you'll be in serious trouble for telling me all this."

"I know."

"You've admitted that you're a party to insurance fraud, that you helped a person get false identification, and I don't know what else. You used to be a cop. You know there will be quite a list."

"I had a choice. I could go to bed every night for the next thirty years knowing that Eric Fuller was going to spend another night in prison, or I could go to bed knowing I was the one who prevented that."

"You could go to jail."

"The choices aren't always good."

"Very stoical. Let me show you something." She walked around her desk to the chair with the stack of files, moved a few to the desk, found the one she wanted, and opened it. There were ten-by-twelve-inch color photographs. She selected one and handed it to Jack Till.

There was a white cloth torn like a rag and covered with dark stains. It was stretched out on a lab table. He could see the ruler on the table in the corner of the shot to give it scale. "What is it?"

"It's her blouse, with her blood on it." She handed Till another photograph.

"And what's this one?" he asked.

"It's a bat like the one you were talking about, also with her blood on it." She glared at him. "Interesting, don't you think?"

"Where did you get this stuff?"

"It was found at Eric Fuller's house."

"Where—the front porch?"

"No," she said. "Buried in the back yard in a rusty metal box. There was a gas pipe leaking, and the gas company dug it up while they were looking for the leak."

"Just as good."

"What do you mean?"

"It's planted. That rag may have been a blouse once, and it may even have been the blouse Wendy Harper was wearing when she was attacked. I assume you have a lab report that the blood is a match for hers."

"She had herself genetically tested for a breast-cancer gene a couple of years before she was murdered. There isn't any doubt that this sample belongs to her, and that means she's dead. I've got a significant amount of her blood on a piece of her clothing, and murder weapons."

"Weapons? Plural?"

"There was also a knife that once belonged to a set in Eric Fuller's kitchen. We have proof that Eric Fuller bought the set eight years ago. I'm sure by the time we go to trial, we'll get something similar on the bat."

"The evidence is faked."

Linda Gordon said, "I don't know if you're telling the truth about what you did or not. If you're telling the truth and you tried to help her save herself, I'm truly sorry for you. But it certainly looks to me as though sometime around the period when she disappeared, Eric Fuller caught up with her. She hasn't been seen for six years. How can I look at that blouse and that bat with her blood on them, and do nothing?"

6

JACK TILL LEFT Linda Gordon's office and walked to his car, thinking about all the reasons Linda Gordon had not to believe him. He had no way of explaining to a young, ambitious prosecutor why an old homicide cop would make the decisions he had made: why he would help Wendy Harper disappear, and why he would go to the DA's office six years later and admit it. Linda Gordon just hadn't lived long enough yet.

He sat in his car, took out his cell phone, and punched in the phone number of his old office in Parker Center. "I'd like to speak to Sergeant Poliakoff, please. This is Jack Till."

In a moment, Poliakoff's voice said, "Jack?"

"Yeah."

"How's it going?"

"I can tell from your voice that you heard already. Did Linda Gordon just call you?"

"Yeah. She wanted to know if you were a good guy or a bad guy. Have you decided yet?" Till could picture him sitting behind the old dented steel desk he had inherited when Till had retired. He was three inches taller than Till, so he had to adjust his chair low and sit in a crouch to fit his knees under the desk.

"After you told her I was the best of the best, did it sound as though she would consider dropping the charges?"

"I'm sorry, Jack. The way I read it, there's zero chance unless Wendy Harper walks into her office. She doesn't think you're lying, so your record isn't the issue. She just thinks you're wrong about what happened after you weren't around."

"I had to ask."

"I know. At the moment, I agree with her, but one of us is going to be surprised, and it could just as easily be me. Maybe we can share leads, like the old days."

"Can you give me some help finding Wendy Harper?"

"That I can't do. That suggestion just got covered. The defense will have to pay you to do it."

"Who is Fuller's attorney?"

"Jay Chernoff of Fiske, Chernoff, Fein, and Toole. I'll give you his number."

Till listened to the number, then said, "Thanks, Max. See you."

Till made the call to the law office, then drove to Beverly Hills and parked at the end of Brighton, past where it met Little Santa Monica. He walked past the shops along the street until he found the small red-brick building where Fiske, Chernoff, Fein, and Toole had their offices. He entered the narrow lobby and glanced at the directory on the wall, then stepped between the polished brass doors of the elevator and pushed the button for the third floor.

The law office was decorated with framed papers and trimmed with maple, so it had the atmosphere of a courtroom. He stepped toward the desk of the woman who presided over the waiting room intending to introduce himself, but before he got there, a short, middle-aged man with curly red hair and a severely receding hairline came out of a door behind the woman, and said. "Mr. Till? I'm Jay Chernoff." He held out his hand and Till shook it. "Thank you for coming."

"Thanks for seeing me." He let Chernoff lead him inside, then around a corner to an office. When they arrived, Chernoff pulled a chair away from the wall, set it in front of a couch, and motioned for Till to sit on the couch. Till sat, and waited until Chernoff had settled in the chair, leaning forward with his elbows on his knees.

Chernoff said, "You said you have information about the Wendy Harper murder?"

"Yes. It's not a murder. The reason I'm here is that she's not dead."

"Not dead?"

"No." Till held up the wallet with his private detective's license and the card that showed he was a retired police officer. "About six years ago, she wanted to disappear. I helped her do it."

"Oh, my God, I can't believe it!" He looked elated. He actually leaned back in his chair and chuckled. "Have you told the police yet?"

"When I got to my office this morning, I looked at the paper and saw that Eric Fuller was being charged, so I went straight to the DA's office and told Linda Gordon. I just came from there."

"You saw Linda Gordon? What did she say?"

"She recorded my statement, then showed me police photographs of what she thinks are Wendy Harper's bloody blouse and a couple of murder weapons belonging to your client. She hasn't decided yet whether or not she believes I really did help Wendy leave town. She thinks that if I did, then Fuller found Wendy a short time later and killed her."

Chernoff took a deep breath and let it out in disappointment. "I might have known. Why did you help Wendy Harper leave town?"

"Somebody beat her up. She thought it had to do with a man who had been dating one of her waitresses at the restaurant. The girl disappeared, and Wendy thought he might have killed her. She looked into it, and one night when she came home, there was a different man waiting for her with a baseball bat. When she got released from the hospital, she came to see me."

"Of course Eric told me about the waitress and the beating, and that Wendy had been in the hospital. All this time he's thought that man must have tried again and killed her. Why didn't Eric know she was leaving voluntarily?"

"That's the way she wanted it. She believed there was nothing he could do to protect her, but he would try, and it would get him killed."

"There was a police report filed after the attack, but I didn't see anything in it about a second man she believed was really behind it. Why not?" Chernoff's frustration was beginning to show.

"She thought she was being practical. In a way, she had a point. If she didn't know the man, then the police had nobody to look for, and waiting around was just giving him another chance to kill her. She felt the only way out was to get beyond his reach."

"So the victim is alive and I have an innocent client."

"Yes."

"And the evidence in Eric's yard. Do you have a theory on how it got there?"

"The guy who attacked her had the bat, and he must have torn the piece of cloth off her. I don't know why he kept them. Maybe he was supposed to kill her and then use them to frame Eric Fuller at the time. Maybe he hid them and remembered them later. I would guess they were planted within the past few months—just long enough ago so the ground didn't seem disturbed."

"Do you have any way of proving what you did?"

"No. Six years ago I tried not to leave any evidence that I had ever seen Wendy Harper. We traveled by car, mostly late at night. I made cash transactions when I could. I burned receipts. I didn't want somebody to search my office someday and find papers that would tell him where I took her. I taught her how to get a new name, but made sure I didn't know what it was. When I left her, I wouldn't let her tell me where she was going."

Chernoff pursed his lips and stared past Till for a few seconds. "What do you think we should do?"

"Linda Gordon has physical evidence, and I have nothing to counter it. The only way Linda Gordon will drop the charges is if Wendy Harper walks into the police station."

"Do you think she would come back?"

"I think if she learns what's happening, she'll try to save Eric Fuller. She cared a lot about him six years ago. But remember that the only one who could have planted evidence in Fuller's yard is the person who had it. I think the man who wanted Wendy dead six years ago is trying to lure her back."

Chernoff looked worried. "We can't expect the DA's office to help us. They're trying to make a case against Eric Fuller."

"Max Poliakoff, the detective in charge of the case, is an old friend of mine, but he can't help with this. We've got to proceed without help," Till said.

"Proceed to do what?"

"Get word to her that Eric Fuller needs her, and hope we can keep her alive when she comes."

7

TILL LOOKED OVER the copy for the ads as he walked away from Jay Chernoff's office. "Eric Fuller has been accused of the murder of Wendy Harper. Persons having information about this matter may contact Mr. Fuller's attorney, Jay Chernoff, c/o Fiske, Chernoff, Fein, and Toole, 3900 Brighton Way, Beverly Hills, CA 90210."

The second ad was an attempt to use Till's name to reassure her this wasn't a trap. "Wendy Harper, Eric needs your help after six years. Please get in touch with Jack at Till Investigations, 11999 Ventura Boulevard, Studio City, CA 91604."

The third ad purported to be from Eric. "To Wendy Harper: I've been accused of your murder. Please call me so we can prove you're alive. Love, Eric." She would still remember that address because the house had once been hers too. This ad was a bit of a fraud because Eric knew nothing about it yet.

The difficult question had been where to place the ads. Till had noticed six years ago that Wendy Harper was one of those people who read the *New York Times* whether she was in New York or Solvang, California. Till had noticed a hundred times over the years that fugitives seldom changed small habits that struck them as safe. The ads would run in the *New York Times* in rotation beginning in two days.

The *Los Angeles Times* seemed to him to be another obvious choice. Wendy Harper had once been a part of the food scene in Los Angeles, and the restaurant she and Eric had owned together was more popular than ever. Till guessed that she checked on the restaurant from time to time, or read about people she had known. Jay Chernoff had suggested the *Chicago Tribune,* just because it was the big regional paper for the center of the country. She and Eric had gone to college in Wisconsin, so the Midwest might be an area where she would have felt comfortable enough to settle.

In about two weeks the ads would also run in *Gourmet* and *Saveur,* on the theory that a person who had made her living in restaurants might still read about food. Till also remembered that Wendy had mentioned something she had read in the *New Yorker,* so he added the magazine to the list.

The advertisements were going to be spectacularly expensive, but Till had talked Chernoff into including them in the cost of Eric Fuller's defense. And unless they could prove that Wendy Harper was alive, there was no defense.

Till had been in Chernoff's office for much of the day, and now rush hour was beginning and his progress north and east was slow. He had one other stop to make this afternoon, and it was one he longed for and dreaded at the same time. As Till drove, he wished he were visiting Garden House for a different reason.

Till had always liked to think that Holly had thought of the name because that was the way her mind worked. She was not always cheerful, because her life had never been easy, but she took delight in things that were good or beautiful. She named them and she pointed them out to other people whenever she saw them.

Garden House was a two-story residence in South Pasadena, a vintage Craftsman bungalow with a big front porch and an old, established garden with bleeding heart and flowering shrimp plants that had gone out of style, and bright orange Joseph's Coat roses on trellises. The lawn was always a bit overtrodden and dusty, because there was always something going on out there—a badminton net had been up all spring, and before that one of the kids had decided it was a good spot for a horseshoe pit. Till had to remind himself not to call them kids aloud, because that irritated Holly. They were adults. Holly was twenty-one already, and she could cook and drive a car, and she had been almost self-supporting for three years. Till smiled to himself. That was better than he had done during his first three years in the detective business.

Whenever Till visited Garden House he drove around the block once, doubled back to be sure he had not been followed, and then parked his car in a different spot at least a block away and walked. He had been a homicide cop for a long time, and now he often took cases that left people angry with him. He had always dreaded the possibility of leading anyone to Garden House, and he knew that beginning today, his precautions would need to be more elaborate: He had just made sure that a potential killer knew his name. He took a last glance behind him as he walked up the sidewalk to the porch and rang the doorbell. Even though Till and the parents of the five other kids had formed a trust that paid for Garden House, the idea from the beginning was that it belonged to the kids, and the parents were guests.

The door swung open and there was Bob Driscoll, his face already in a grin. "Hi, Jack," he said, his voice loud and happy. "Come on in, Jack." He pulled the door open wide, and Till followed him into the living room.

"Hi, Bob. How have you been?"

"Great. Just great. I got a different job. It pays a lot better than the car wash. I'm working at this little organic vegetable store on Foothill called Darlene's Farm. Come in and see us. You're here to visit Holly, of course."

"Sure am. Seen her around?"

"Not in a while. She and Marie went to buy groceries. And Nancy, maybe. Yeah. I think the three of them went. Holly, Marie,

Nancy. Hey! I bet you could stay for dinner. They were going to get some stuff to make an Italian dinner together."

"No, I don't think so, thanks. I just dropped by for a little visit with her. You know I have to see how my little girl is."

"She's great, Jack. You'll see." He sat quietly for a moment. "And how about you? How have you been?"

"Not so bad, I think. I'm pretty much always the same. How are your parents?"

"I saw them last week. They're getting old, but they're still happy."

As Till looked at Bob Driscoll, he could not keep himself from seeing the distinctive features of a person with Down syndrome— the rounded head and body, the slightly protuberant eyes and small nose. The young people who lived in Garden House all resembled each other more than they resembled their relatives. It was as though Garden House were a family. The young people also seemed to share things that were more fundamental, a set of attitudes and mannerisms that they picked up from each other, and an outlook that often made them seem to him to be like half-wise, unspoiled children. But they were no longer children.

The birth had been in December. During the pregnancy, Rose had decreed that the baby would be Christopher if it was a boy, and Holly if it was a girl. Her obstetrician had not seen any reason to insist on amnio, because all was going well, and Rose was healthy and twenty-four. There had been no warning that something had happened on chromosome twenty-one, and that Holly had Down syndrome.

By the next December, Rose had already walked out on them, and Till was making his first Christmas celebration for his only child, Holly. Her first birthday, on the tenth, had been a quiet two-person affair, with Holly asleep at seven, and he had resolved never to let any celebration be quiet again. Every birthday and every Christmas after that had been big and boisterous, with the house full of people. Till had noticed with satisfaction that since Holly had come to live at Garden House, her three birthday parties had been long, raucous, and messy.

He heard the car come in the driveway, then a couple of doors slam. He stood to look out. Holly and the two other girls were laughing and chattering as usual, and then, as though she had felt his gaze, Holly looked toward the house. "Dad!"

He came out onto the porch. "Hi, Holly. Can I help with the groceries?"

"Sure. I was looking to see if Bob and Randy would help, but I see they're hiding until all the work is done."

"That's how men are," he said. "I warned you."

"You're not that way, Jack," Marie said.

"That's because Holly trained me."

"Hello, Jack," said Nancy. "Long time no see."

"I was here on Wednesday, Nancy."

"I know. I just like to say that."

"Okay, then." He lifted some of the grocery bags, went inside with the others and set the bags on the counter.

When their arms were free, Holly threw hers around his neck and they exchanged their usual exuberant hug. "Can you stay for dinner?"

"I don't think so tonight. I'm in the beginning of a hard case, and I've got to do some things tonight. But thanks. I really just dropped by because I wanted to talk to you a little."

"Really? How come?"

"Because I like to talk to you."

"That's because you love me," she said. "It's good."

"I know."

"Come on, then," Holly said. "Let's go for a walk while we talk."

"Okay."

She called to the empty doorway to the hall, "Don't stand there, Bob. You can start the water boiling while I talk to Dad."

Bob emerged from the hallway, unabashed. "Okay."

Till and Holly walked out across the porch, down the steps to the sidewalk and strolled up the street past more old houses, all of them refurbished during the past few years. Till said, "How are things this week, Holly? I know it didn't go too well last week."

"It's better. Work has been more fun since I got Nancy hired. We've been doing a big cleaning to get ready for the summer sales. We may even paint the place. Mrs. Fournier and I are thinking it over."

"Sounds ambitious."

She looked over her shoulder. "We're far enough from the house now to talk. What's up?"

"It's this case."

"You got it today?"

"Not really. It's something that happened six years ago. You were about fifteen then. I don't know if you remember. I was gone for a bit over a week. You stayed with Grandma."

She shrugged. "I don't know. I remember staying with Grandma a few times. Usually you just had a girlfriend and you were sleeping with her."

He smiled uncomfortably. That was part of it, too. To Holly there didn't seem to be any special categories of things that weren't for discussion. "It's possible," he said. "But this was something else. It took over a week. It was a girl who was hurt and scared. I took her far away and taught her how to stay hidden from some bad men."

"Good for you, Dad. You're the best!"

"Well, it may be that I'm going to get in trouble for helping her hide. I found out that an innocent man—an old boyfriend of hers—is being accused of killing her. So I had to go to the District Attorney's office and admit that I took her away and she's living somewhere else."

"Why?"

"So the DA would tell the police to let him go."

"Couldn't you just tell the police yourself? They know you."

"No. It had gone too far for that. There's going to be a trial."

"So you told, and saved him. Now what's the problem?"

"I may have to go away myself, because of it. What I did to make this girl hard to find wasn't all perfectly legal. I helped her get false identification papers and so on. I helped her to lie."

"Are you going to jail?"

"I don't know."

"When will you know?"

"Sending me to jail would take a long time. They would have to charge me and then have a trial, and I would get my turn to tell the judge why I did it, and show that I didn't mean any harm, or really hurt anybody."

"So you probably shouldn't worry yet."

"That's exactly right. It may never happen. I'm only telling you about it right now because that's always been our arrangement, our deal. You and I tell each other things as soon as we know them."

"What can I do to help you?"

"Nothing yet. Maybe if I *do* have to serve some time, you can store some of my stuff for me."

"I would visit you. too. And write you long letters."

"Thanks, honey. I knew I could count on you to think of something nice to do."

They were walking around the block, and Till could see the back of Garden House between the two houses behind it. He watched Holly staring at the house, as though she were deciding what to plant next, or what color to paint it.

He wondered what her mother would think if she could see her and hear her. Holly was visibly a person with Down syndrome, but she was also beautiful and strong. He wished that Rose could have foreseen the possibility that someone could be all of those things at once. Rose had been living in Florida for twenty years already, re-married for eighteen of them to Dr. Timothy Zyrnick. It had always seemed strange to Till that she had married a doctor. He had never been able to tell whether Dr. Zyrnick knew about Holly. In the letters Till had sent her over the years—usually once a year—he had never asked, and in her replies, she had never mentioned anything that passed between her and her new husband. Till had enclosed pictures of Holly at first, but then one of his letters got an answer asking him not to. A few years later, Rose asked in a letter that he stop writing to her and allow her to go on with the new life she had built. She had added that if she and her husband moved, she would keep him informed in case there were some legal or medical reason for his knowing. Since then she had moved about three times to houses in fancier-sounding neighborhoods around Naples. She'd never had any more children.

He walked along beside Holly, made the last turn toward Garden House, and felt a deep sadness. He had a lot to do this evening, but he hated stopping for ten minutes, having a quick conversation, and then leaving her.

She looked at him slyly. "It's spaghetti, you know. You can always add enough of it to the boiling water to invite another person."

He put his arm around Holly's shoulders and squeezed. "Okay. Now that you've coaxed me, I'd love to stay for dinner."

8

LATE THAT NIGHT, Jack Till sat in his car on Vignes Street, watching the lighted space outside the gate of the county jail. Even though it was after midnight, the slit windows of the big concrete building were brightly lighted and at least forty people sat in their cars or stood beside them at the curb outside, waiting They looked like people at the harbor waiting for a ship to dock. There were young women with children who were too tiny to be out at this hour, old ladies who were obviously waiting for sons or daughters. On the other side of the street there were three low-rider cars with candy-flake paint jobs and lots of chrome, all sitting nose-to-tail. The young men who had brought them were out walking back and forth, talking and waving their heavily tattooed arms for emphasis. Till couldn't tell from here what gang colors were on the tattoos, but he knew that if he moved closer, he would recognize the symbols. He had seen all of them before on corpses and on suspects. The friend they were waiting for must have been popular to rate a convoy to take him home.

The door of the building opened and a group of inmates was released into the area just inside the gate. The jail was crowded and understaffed, so the guards always seemed to process the prisoners in batches. Till saw a few arms wave, a few of the people in cars get out and walk toward the fence. A guard went to the gate and unlocked it, then let the prisoners out one at a time.

Till got out of his car, stood beside it and spotted the prisoner he had been waiting for: Eric Fuller was in his early thirties, as tall as Jack Till, and he had hair so short and blond that the eye had trouble telling where it began or ended. His face was reddish and slightly lined for his age, as though he had spent time squinting. As he came out the gate, Till intercepted him. "Hello, Mr. Fuller. I'm Jack Till."

"Jay Chernoff told me about you. Where is he, anyway? I thought he'd be here."

"I asked him to stay on the other side of the building, in case there are reporters or something worse waiting for you. We agreed that I would take you home, because I wanted to talk to you. All right with you?"

Fuller looked up the dark street. The other prisoners had all gotten into cars and driven off. "I don't have much choice."

He followed Till to his car and got into the passenger seat. Till got in and drove. "I know you have a right to be mad at me."

Fuller turned to look at him. "I'm happy to know that Wendy's alive, and I guess I should thank you for that, and for coming forward now. That doesn't mean I like you. You took Wendy away, and let me think she was dead for six years. Wendy was—is—the most important person in my life. I've thought about her every day since she disappeared. Sometimes I've wished I had died with her. And about twenty-four hours ago, I got arrested and hauled down here and thrown in a cell that smells like piss and vomit, and charged with murdering her. I can't help thinking I owe you some of the thanks for that, too."

"I was trying to save her life. I apologize to you for the parts of this that got you in trouble. As soon as I found out about it, I went to the DA."

"I know you didn't intend to do me any harm. But what made her do that? I loved her. What the hell was she thinking?"

"I was under the impression that you two had broken up."

"Broken up? That term doesn't apply to us. We had been together so long that getting married seemed like the obvious thing to do. When we realized it wouldn't work, we admitted we'd been more attracted to other people from the beginning, but didn't see how we could be apart. We weren't mad at each other. It wasn't like her not to tell me what she was doing. Why didn't she tell me?"

"She thought it was the only way to protect you. She believed that her time here was over. Yours wasn't. She had helped start your restaurant and turn it into a paying business, but you were the real force behind it. She said, 'Nobody comes to a restaurant because there's a good MBA in the back office.'"

"That isn't a reason to let me think she was dead."

"She also thought you would try to protect her, maybe go after the people who were trying to hurt her."

"It was a stupid thing to do. I could have helped her. Instead I get accused of killing her."

Till took a deep breath and let it out. There was no reason to hold anything back now, and he had no right. "She also felt that at some point you two had to separate. You would never find a woman who could tolerate having someone like her in your life. If she was around, you wouldn't even look. The same was true for her. The reason she left was the danger, but the killer wasn't the only thing she needed to escape."

Eric Fuller was silent for a few seconds, his body leaning forward in the seat and his eyes on the dashboard. It looked to Till as though he might lunge toward him. His face was reddening, and looked almost swollen, and Till could see moisture welling in the blue eyes. "She didn't even think it through and prepare. She left everything—her half of the restaurant, her half of the house, everything we had built together."

"She thought you had more right to it than she did, and there was no way to hold on to things like that and disappear. I know you're mad at her tonight, but I can tell you that she cared about you and wanted to be sure that her trouble didn't destroy you."

He leaned back in the seat with his eyes closed and rubbed his forehead. "God. I'm sorry. It's just that everything is happening at once. To be honest with you, I'm afraid. I'm just out on bail. Nobody dropped any charges. I don't want to go to jail for the rest of my life. Jay told me about the advertisements. I keep wondering what happens if Wendy doesn't see them. What if she's living in another country? I could be convicted of murder, and she would never even know it. I could get the death penalty."

Till drove in silence for a few seconds. "That's one of the reasons I wanted to talk to you. I need to know anything you can tell me that might help me figure out how to reach her."

"I don't know. When she was missing at first, I called everyone we knew, searched our house and our restaurant for any clue about where she might have gone."

"Was there any other city she ever talked about where she wanted to live someday?"

"Here. L.A. She was the one who chose it as the place to start the restaurant."

"Is there anywhere that she said she wanted to go on a vacation, but you never did?"

"Oh, God. Everywhere. When we were really young we were too poor to go anywhere, and when we were older, we were too busy. At one time she wanted to go to France, but it was mainly so I could apprentice in a great restaurant. When we were in school in Wisconsin, we would talk about Tahiti in the winter and the Rocky Mountains in the summer. We were never serious about any of it. She could be anywhere."

Till said, "I told her that if she wanted to stay hidden, she should never try to get in touch with anybody she knew again. But that's not an easy rule to follow. If she weakened and decided to talk with someone, who would she choose?"

Fuller shrugged. "The person she would choose is me."

"That's what I thought. That's the other reason why I wanted to talk to you right away, tonight. What you've got to understand is that six years ago people like me gave her lots of sensible advice and tried to talk her out of it, but she was the one who was right—there really *were* men determined to kill her. The only person who could have planted the evidence to frame you now is the one who attacked her. They're trying to get her to show herself. When she does, they'll try again. They'll be watching you, and if it helps them get to her, they'll kill you, too."

He drove Eric Fuller to the house that he had once shared with Wendy Harper. When Fuller got out, Till handed him a business card. "If she calls or writes or tries to get in touch with you in any way at any time of the day or night, you've got to call me immediately. And if you notice any kind of surveillance on you, I'll come and check it out. It may just be the cops, but if it's somebody else, I'll arrange a surprise for them."

"Why would you risk your life to help me?"

"Maybe I'm not helping you. Maybe I'm helping her."

After that night, Till waited a month for an answer to the advertisements he and Jay Chernoff had placed in magazines and newspapers. At the end of the month, he paid a visit to Garden House, even though it wasn't the day of the week when he usually came. He drove past the house five times at ten-minute intervals, parked in the lot beside a supermarket, and walked a half mile to the house, searching the neighborhood harder than usual for any sign of change. Later that evening, he took Holly to a movie, then had a long, serious talk with her and left her at her door.

When he got home, he called Chernoff. "Jay, Wendy's not coming in. It's time for me to go after her."

9

SYLVIE LOVED the evenings at the dance studio. The studio's exterior was deceptive. It was one of the best ballroom dancing studios in the city, but it was on a block that contained both a plumbing-fixture showroom and several middle-class houses, on the upper level of a long wooden building that consisted of two galleries of suites.

Tonight was Tango Night, and she and Paul were especially good at the tango. Eight years ago, they had gone to Buenos Aires and spent two months studying with the noted dance mistress Renata Gomez La Paz. The dance mistress was less than five feet tall and bony and was reputed to be in her seventies, but she had worn a black leotard, high heels and a scarlet skirt to demonstrate the steps to her disciples. Her makeup was thick, with blood-red lipstick and dark eye shadow. Her hair had been dyed coal black and tied in a bun. Enormous gold hoops hung from her ears, and on each of her hands had been three glittering diamond rings. Sylvie had kept thinking that, given her age, the diamonds were antique, probably the kind that would not be found anywhere again.

When Señora Gomez La Paz spoke, she bit her words with bared teeth. Although Sylvie did not speak Spanish well, she knew that the señora had said she danced like a cow. Paul had lied to her about it, but Sylvie had not minded. That was part of it, wasn't it? The tango wasn't about cuddling. The dancers held themselves in tension. The dance was about lust and jealousy and suppressed hatred.

The experience had conferred on her and on Paul an implied authority at the dance studio. They had learned the dance from one of the legendary choreographers in Buenos Aires, not from some little cutie in Van Nuys who had learned it as an elective class at Oklahoma State.

Paul backed the black BMW into the lot and parked it nose-out, far from the others. Then he leaned suddenly toward Sylvie in the shadowy car and kissed her. She leaned to him, letting the kiss go on for a long time. It was hard and passionate, not exactly affectionate. Then Paul was out of the car, around the back to open her door. He offered his hand to help her out, and she took it, placing the lightest, most graceful touch on the back of his hand as she stood.

She moved toward the building, heard the car door slam shut and then Paul's long, rapid strides to catch her, and felt his hand on her waist. Already she was excited, ready. As they climbed the stairs to the upper gallery she could hear the music behind the door at the end of the walkway. Paul took a half-step ahead in the last yard to swing the door inward for her, and she stepped inside. Sylvie was conscious of making an entrance. She strutted across the polished floor and tossed her black-fringed shawl over a chair negligently, knowing that all of the other dancers were watching her movements and watching Paul hover at her shoulder attentively, maybe possessively. She held herself erect, able to emphasize her height and slenderness when she stood with Paul, because he was a few inches taller. She dressed for Tango Nights the way Señora Gomez La Paz had dressed, knowing that on Sylvie, the costume was elegant and exotic.

She had already completed her survey of the other dancers in the room by looking at the mirrored wall where Mindy stretched at the ballet barre. Mindy lifted one leg to the barre and rested it there and then touched her forehead to her knee. Mindy raised her blond head and gave a flash of bright white teeth and a long welcoming gaze in the mirror, but her eyes didn't seem to be focused where they should be. Sylvie half-turned her head to follow the trajectory of Mindy's stare off the mirror to Paul. Sylvie raised her right foot to the seat of the chair where she had draped her shawl and examined her shoe, as though she had not seen.

Mindy had made a foolish miscalculation. She had a pretty little figure that stayed in shape because she had to work as an aerobics instructor during the day. She had a cute round face with wide blue eyes and bleached teeth and hair. She undoubtedly got plenty of attention from older married men every day, but she had made a misguided assumption in picking out Paul. Mindy had no idea who Paul was. She had no idea who Sylvie was.

Paul had a very thin waist, fine features, a complexion that was smooth, and big eyes with long lashes. The look was probably what the attraction was for Mindy. She was like those teenaged girls who had crushes on boy singers who looked like other teenaged girls. Paul seemed docile and unthreatening: He was the sort of man who went to the door and bought cookies from the Girl Scouts and sent them off feeling charmed. But Paul was other things, too.

A faint smile formed on Sylvie's lips at the thought of Mindy's error, and her jealous feeling went away. She felt the warm-up music in her stomach and in her spine, and she put her foot on the floor and began to do a few steps by herself. Instantly Paul recognized them and was with her, dancing the beginning of a routine that Señora Gomez La Paz had taught them.

Several of the other couples were drawn to them and stood nearby watching, and a few others stopped and tried to learn the steps by imitating them. Paul held Sylvie and spun her around. She could see Mindy for a second, pretending to finish her warm-up by doing stretches and paying no attention.

Sylvie was whirled the other way, and she could see their admirers again. They were mostly married couples in their late thirties or early forties like the Turners, with just a few who were older. They had all taken dance lessons, and a few had some competition experience, so it was an advanced group. They were businesspeople or professionals, and a lot of pairs arrived in two cars, even though the class started at eight-thirty.

At exactly eight-thirty, Mindy turned off the music and called out, "Good evening, señors and señoritas. I see you all remembered it was Tango Night, and really got into the spirit of it." She surveyed the group of twenty people and gave the women time to look critically at each other's outfits, which were heavy on blacks and reds, with black fishnet stockings. "Tonight we have a lot of work to do, because I want to show you three great steps I just learned myself. Here is the first one. I'll do the woman's part." She put the music on and danced a slow, stately passage, made a turn as the music changed, and stalked forward. "See? Four steps, a procession. Then pirouette, and then the lioness, hunting, comes forward." She repeated it three more times, and then watched the women in the group attempt it three times. Now and then she rushed to one of them and adjusted the student's posture or raised an arm higher.

Next she demonstrated the male part, and watched the men try to imitate her. They were less convincing than the women, and their movements were calculated to make Sylvie remember that all of them except Paul spent their days locked in offices. Mindy called out, "Now we put the two together and make magic." There was some appreciative laughter, and the uncertain set of partners moved out to the floor, clinging to each other.

She said, "By the way, we should welcome the Turners. They've been away for a month or so in Europe. It's always good to see them, especially on Tango Night, because they're our experts. Paul, can you come up and be my partner for this demonstration?"

Paul gave a perfunctory smile, glanced into Sylvie's eyes and then went to stand beside Mindy. He put his arm around her shoulders as they stood in front of the group. She spun her body and her right hand grasped his left. Only then did she remember to lean down to the CD player to begin the music, so her move turned into a dramatic dip.

Most of the class smiled or chuckled at the sight, but Sylvie's jaw clenched. It stayed clenched as she watched Paul and Mindy perform the short passage with the new step. They didn't stop, but kept dancing, Mindy looking up into Paul's eyes and smiling, dancing overdramatically for the next five bars before they stopped.

Sylvie felt a soft tap on her shoulder, not like the touch of a hand, but the feel of a small animal trying to crawl onto her shoulder. She shivered and whirled in involuntary repugnance and saw the grinning face of Grant Rollins. She knew he was a lawyer who lived in Tarzana. He was five feet seven and weighed at least two hundred and thirty pounds, and whenever he took his coat off, sweat defined his armpits. "Phyllis is running late tonight. Can we team up for this?"

Sylvie nodded, stunned. She and Grant Rollins stepped out to join the others, and as she began to dance, he stepped on her foot. "Sorry." She glared down at him, and saw the top of his head. He was watching his feet.

She was acutely, painfully aware that she must look ridiculous with him. She was a head taller than he was. She stiffened her arms and held him away from her. He danced haltingly, off the rhythm and unmoved by the passion of the music. She hated this. When they came to the dip, Sylvie had to just lean back slightly and perfunctorily, to avoid having little Grant try to hold her up and fail. She wasn't going to end up on the floor with Grant on top of her.

At last the demonstration was over: Her ordeal had ended. Paul came back to stand beside her, his expression sympathetic. She could barely look at him. Mindy danced the rest of the practice with Grant. He was an inch taller than she was, so they looked only like two generations, not like two different species.

The music stopped again and Mindy blocked out the next step, first the female side, then the male. When all of her students had learned to move in imitation of what she had done, she said, "Sylvie, can I borrow Paul again to demonstrate?"

"No." Sylvie had not been aware that she was going to say it, but once it was out, she felt hot, defiant.

Mindy thought it was a joke. "Please?"

"Next time he wants sex, you come over and help me out. Then I'll let you dance with him."

Mindy's face turned pale, except for a reddening spot on each cheek. She laughed, looking faint. "What a generous offer, but I'm afraid I have a boyfriend."

"Then bring him and make him dance with you."

The red spots on Mindy's face were growing, about to reach her neck. "Okay, Grant. Then it's up to you." Grant hesitated, then stepped close to her. She took his hand and assumed the dance position. "Ready? One-two." Mindy carried on her demonstration, holding Grant Rollins as far from her body as she could. After she finished and the students were taking their places to dance, she restarted the CD and let them dance as they would, while she retreated to the farthest corner of the room and observed in silence. When Phyllis Rollins came in looking breathless and flustered, Mindy took a few minutes to show her the two new steps. She did not make any attempt to teach the class her third step, and never spoke to the group again until ten, when she stopped the music, smiled a false smile, and called out, "Marvelous, everyone. You've all learned it so well! Now remember, next Tuesday will be Samba Night. Good night. Drive carefully." Then she walked the length of the mirrored wall to the back of the building where the dressing room and storeroom were, and closed the door.

As the others filed out, Paul leaned close to Sylvie. "Was that necessary?"

Sylvie faced him, her hands on her hips. "I was left to dance with a troll. I looked big and clumsy."

"It was just for a couple of minutes."

"She humiliated me, and you helped her."

"She made an innocent mistake."

"If it were innocent, it wouldn't be a mistake." She picked up her purse and shawl from the chair and let him escort her to the door. When she got there, she verified that the other members of the class were all far along the upper gallery now, and many were already down the steps, getting into their cars or standing on the asphalt and talking. They were alone with Mindy. Sylvie stopped in the doorway. "Maybe I'll kill the little bitch."

"Brilliant, absolutely brilliant!" Sylvie could see that Paul was getting angry. She wasn't sure why his displeasure was making her sexually aroused, but it was. She had felt the excitement of dancing to the passionate music, then felt so totally bereft and alone, and now she had his attention, all of it. His eyes, his mind were focused only on Sylvie.

She said, "She's all alone."

"Twenty-five people know that we're here, the last ones, and saw you get jealous. You made a joke out of it, but they knew." As he spoke, he held both her arms in his hands, his face less than a foot from hers.

She lifted her face to him and kissed him. "You're right. Bad idea." She went out the door and he followed. It was only when they were outside that she heard the page. "Oh God!" she muttered, and reached into her purse, pawing things aside.

"What?"

"The pager. It's been vibrating in my purse. I wonder how long that's been going on." She looked at the telephone number on the display. "Let's get to a pay phone."

They hurried along the second-floor walkway, the heels of Sylvie's shoes making a *pock-pock* sound. They were down the stairs and in the black BMW in a moment.

Three minutes later Mindy was still standing inside the storeroom that she used as a dressing room, her ear to the door. She wanted to be sure all of the members of the class had departed before she came out. She could not bear to look at them or hear them talk again tonight. She didn't bother to analyze her sudden reluctance. She just felt through with them for now. After a few more minutes of silence, she took her purse and costume bag, opened the door a crack and verified that all of them had gone. The outside door was propped open and the hot night air had come in to stimulate the air conditioning system, so the fans were humming, blowing a frigid breeze onto the empty dance floor.

A HALF MILE AWAY, Paul sat in the car with the engine running, watching the mirrors and windshield while Sylvie stood outside at the pay telephone beside the gas station. He didn't need to look directly at her, because he felt her position automatically. In a moment he felt her beside him again. She slammed the door.

He looked at her and saw the puzzled, thoughtful expression. "Well?"

"Jack Till is on the move. Densmore thinks he's going somewhere to pick her up."

Paul smiled as he put the car into gear and drove. "Finally," he said.

10

JACK TILL DROVE HARD in the summer night, still driving the way he had when he had been a cop, pushing the speed limit just enough to move him past the trucks that were pushing it, too, but letting the future organ donors flash past him. To his left was the endless dark ocean, with only the ruler-straight row of lighted oil platforms in the channel to relieve the blackness. On his right were the high sand hills that in daylight seemed to be held there by goldenrod and wildflowers, but at night were only looming shadows. He had the air conditioning on high, so the interior of the car was cold and kept him alert. Twenty minutes later, he began to pass the Santa Barbara exits. He waited until he had reached the Storke Road exit, took it, and then the second ramp onto Sandspit Road. He went past the airport entrance to the row of car rentals, pulled into the first lot and stopped.

He got out of the car, stepped around to the trunk and removed his suitcase. As he stood there pretending he was searching the trunk for something else, he kept his eyes on the road he had just driven, watching for headlights. When he had satisfied himself that he had not been followed, he closed the trunk and walked into the long, low car rental building.

He had made the only deadline that mattered. The car rentals here would close ten minutes after the last incoming flight of the evening at eleven. He went to the desk and he knew the young man behind it was probably as pleased to see him as he looked. He was alone and undoubtedly had been for most of his shift.

Till showed his rental club card and a set of keys. "I rented a car in L.A., and I'd like to trade it for another model."

The young man said, "What kind of car would you like, sir? Compact, full size, luxury?"

Till said, "What have you got that's luxury? Cadillacs and Town Cars?"

"Yes, sir."

"Have any out there and ready to go?"

"Yes, I believe we do."

"I'll take a Cadillac."

The young man tapped his computer keyboard and looked at the screen, quickly produced a rental form from a shelf under the counter and checked the lines Till was to sign, then went to a cabinet to get a set of keys. "Here you are, sir. A Cadillac DeVille. The third space from the right in the second row."

"Thanks." Till stepped outside. He went to the car quickly, tossed his suitcase into the trunk, and drove the Cadillac onto the road.

Till had been a private detective for seven years now, and a police officer for twenty before that, and he knew that this was the kind of job that required him to submerge, to go beneath the surface and emerge looking slightly different. He needed to be part of the background, undifferentiated and maybe a bit out of focus. But first, he had to give himself time to be sure nobody was watching.

On the way to Santa Barbara there had been lots of traffic, but no single vehicle had seemed to stay with him for long. Since he had left the freeway, there had been only empty highway behind him. It was disconcerting, because he had expected that there would be people watching him. Whoever had gotten Eric Fuller charged with Wendy Harper's murder had forced Jack Till to the surface. From the moment when Till had put his name on the advertisements for Wendy, they should have been watching him.

He had made only a halfhearted attempt to hide his departure from Los Angeles, because he wanted to see who was following. Tonight he had given them opportunities to reveal themselves, but there still was no sign of them. He had stopped once for coffee and once to change cars, but no other car had stopped, too.

He turned the car onto Hollister Avenue and doubled back into Santa Barbara. He took a couple of turns onto small streets, parked for a few minutes and waited, but there were no cars that showed any inclination to follow. He returned to Hollister and kept driving. Hollister turned into State Street, and brought him into the center of town to Figueroa. He parked near the police station.

Till stepped into the front entrance and up to the counter and said to the female officer behind it, "I'm Jack Till. Sergeant Kohler was going to leave something for me to pick up."

She said, "May I see your identification, please?"

He removed his LAPD identification card from his wallet and held it with his index finger over the word "retired."

She looked at the picture on it, then at his face, and said, "Come with me." She came around the counter, opened a swinging door, and called over her shoulder to a male officer at a desk, "I'll be right back."

Till followed her to an open office with five desks, where several plainclothes police officers were at work. She stopped at one of the desks, picked a manila envelope off the blotter and handed it to Till. "He said you were welcome to look at it here, if you'd like. You can use his desk."

"Thank you," said Till. He sat down, opened the envelope, and extracted a packet of papers. The heading on the first page was "Southwest Airlines Flight 92, Departure Santa Barbara 7:05 A.M., arrival San Francisco 8:35 A.M." Each sheet recorded a different flight. Kohler had requested the passenger lists for all of the flights that had left Santa Barbara on August 30 six years ago.

Till had known Kohler slightly in the old days. He had been one of the young detectives coming up in the department, and Till had spoken to him only a few times, but he had left a good impression. Till remembered he had been big, with an open expression and a reputation for hard work. When Till had called Max Poliakoff to ask about the passenger lists, Max had mentioned that Kohler was in Santa Barbara, and that a request for lists from flights out of Santa Barbara would raise fewer questions if it came from a Santa Barbara cop. Till had decided to presume on the acquaintance.

As Till went through the airline-passenger lists he remembered something Wendy Harper had said on the day when she had come to his office.

She had said, "Why did you quit the police department?"

He had said, "Because of the money."

What had really happened was that Till had simply looked up from the body of a fourteen-year-old boy lying on the street as the morning light was almost imperceptibly altering the deep darkness of night, thought about how many bodies he had seen like this, and realized that it was time. He had not told Wendy Harper about that, but remembering it had helped him understand the decision she was making. She not only believed that leaving Los Angeles was necessary, but as soon as she had begun contemplating it, she had realized it was time. That part of her life was over.

He finished sorting the passenger lists. He had set aside all of the flights that had taken off before noon on August 30 because he had left her at the airport right at noon that day. He studied each of the later flights: three to San Francisco, three to Las Vegas, five to Los Angeles. Those were all possibilities because in any of those airports she could have switched to a plane to anywhere in the world. If she had changed planes, she would have stayed up on the second level past the security checkpoints and not gone down to the ticket counters and baggage areas, where it was dangerous. He had taught her that if she had to wait in an airport, she should stay in a ladies' room because the people she had to fear would almost certainly be men.

His problem now was that he had also taught her a few ways to get false identification papers that weren't exactly false. People loitering in MacArthur Park every afternoon could produce a fairly good-looking California driver's license for two hundred bucks, but the license would be too crude for a person to use to start a new identity. She needed *real* documents.

Till had gone with her to take out a marriage license. Then he had taught her to forge the last name of her husband to give him—and herself—whatever new name she wanted. Almost nobody ever tampered with the names on marriage licenses, so they had not been made difficult to alter. All she had to do was take the marriage license and her driver's license to the DMV and pay a fee to get a new license in her husband's last name. As soon as she was settled somewhere else, she could exchange the California license for a driver's license in her new state. She could repeat the process there, and end up with a second new last name. Any artifice could be unraveled, but no conceivable inquiry about Wendy Harper was likely to lead a hunter through two states and three names to her new identity.

The Social Security number was just as easy. She had to obtain a genuine birth certificate for herself, change the surname and birth date, and apply for a number for a newborn daughter with a name that was a variant of her own. Since the card didn't carry a birth date, she could use it.

Once she had the major documents, there were hundreds of ways of bolstering her new identity: Open a bank account, rent an apartment, and pay her utility bills for a month, and she would be a new person. Applying for a library card, a health-club membership and a few other easy cards would fill out her identity. She didn't need to fool a squad of FBI agents, just the kid handling the desk at Blockbuster Video or the lady who worked part-time at the gift shop.

Till could still see her face, giving the incredulous look. "It's that easy?"

"The key is avoiding resistance."

"What kind of resistance?"

"You don't just go around in a flurry applying for things. You wait until somebody asks you and then sign up. You wait for those letters that say 'Your acceptance is assured.' It's not, but they're hungry for your business. Deal with people who want to help you fool them."

"Then what? Am I going to have to lay low and go out only at night or something? Live some kind of half-life?"

He said, "At first you will have to lay low. It won't be pleasant or easy. After a while, you'll feel safe enough to be with people. Stay out of hip restaurants and bars. Go where nobody is going to be looking for you—get a job that keeps you out of sight in the day, go to night classes. From the first day, you've got to have a story about yourself, and you've got to stick to it. Once you have a friend or two, they'll help keep you safe. You'll go places with them instead of alone, and that will make you look different. They'll introduce you to their friends and tell them your story, and the new people will believe it because they heard it from them, not you."

He had made sure he didn't know the name she chose for her first doctored marriage license, so now he had no idea what she had called herself on her airline ticket. He sat in the Santa Barbara police station at his borrowed desk and examined the passenger lists for flights that departed between 12:01 P.M. and 11:59 P.M. He began by crossing off the names of men and boys. That eliminated more than half. Then he went through again and found the names of women and girls who had seats beside people with the same surname. That was another third. The remaining names belonged to women traveling alone.

There were no Wendys. He had been expecting a Wendy. The method that he had taught her was to appear to have had her surname changed in a marriage, but that would still make her a Wendy. As he went over the lists again, wondering if he had missed one, he thought of another possibility. He took out his cell phone and looked at the card he carried in his wallet, then dialed Jay Chernoff's home phone number. When he heard Chernoff's voice say, "Hello," he said, "What's her middle name?"

"What?"

Till said, "Sorry to call you at night. But I never heard her middle name, or if I did, I forgot it."

"It's on some of the court papers. The indictment will have it, if nothing else. Let me get my briefcase and look." He was gone for at least a minute, and then he returned. "It's Ann, with no e."

"A-N-N. Got it. Thanks, Jay. I'll try not to bother you again for a while."

"Where are you?"

"I'd rather not say on the telephone, just in case they put something on your line. Let's make them work for it."

"All right. Then good luck."

"Thanks."

Till disconnected. As they were speaking, he had already begun running his finger down the lists of passengers looking for Anns. He knew that he had been right. She would have been able to use whatever new surname she had put on the marriage license, but her driver's license would still say Wendy Ann Something. She could call herself Ann and still use the license as identification to get on the plane. There were plenty of people whose parents had inflicted names on them that they hated, so they used their middle names.

He found three women named Ann who had flown out of Santa Barbara that day traveling alone. There was Ann Mercer, who had flown to San Francisco. There was Ann Wiggett, who had flown to Los Angeles, and Ann Delatorre on a flight to Las Vegas.

He tried to put himself inside Wendy's mind. The name Ann Wiggett sounded like Wendy Harper looked. Wendy was white-blond, with fine hair and very light skin that sometimes seemed transparent. She could easily be the sort of woman whose ancestors all had names like Wiggett and Hemsdale. But would Wendy choose that name?

Ann Mercer sounded like a practical name for Wendy Harper. Mercer was common enough to be unsurprising to the people she met, and it was the same length as Harper, easy to fit into documents she wanted to alter.

He swiveled in his chair and looked at the cop behind him, a young detective who was reading something that looked from a distance like an autopsy report. Till said, "Excuse me. I'm Jack Till, from Los Angeles. Kohler is helping me on a case."

"I figured," said the cop. "I'm Dave Cota."

"I wondered if you had a phone directory I can use."

"Sure. It's up there on the table."

"Thanks." Till had intentionally not said he was a private investigator. He stood at the table and leafed through the book quickly. Regular telephone books had been useless for years because most people paid to keep their numbers unlisted. He had to use the special police directory that listed everybody while he was here in the station. He started with the name Wiggett.

There were three numbers, all under the name Howard Wiggett. He dialed the first Wiggett number, and a man who was probably Howard Wiggett answered. Till said, "May I speak with Ann Wiggett, please?"

"I'm sorry," said the man. "Mrs. Wiggett has already retired for the evening. May I help you?"

Till decided to go for complete verification. "I'm calling from United Airlines. I have a record that on August 30 six years ago,

Mrs. Wiggett flew from Santa Barbara to Los Angeles. Was there a piece of luggage belonging to her that was misplaced?"

The man hesitated. "Six years? That's a long time. It's quite likely that she was on the flight. She used to visit her parents in New York, and the flights usually stopped in Los Angeles. But I can't recall her ever losing any luggage. Can I take your number and call you back tomorrow?"

"Certainly," Till said. "800-555-0600. I'll make a note that we spoke. Thank you." Then he hung up.

He tried Mercer. There were four Mercers, including one Ann. He dialed her number and when a woman answered, he said, "Is this Ann Mercer?"

"Yes, it is."

"I'm calling from Southwest Airlines, and there's something I'd like to check with you. If you don't remember, we'll certainly understand. On August 30, six years ago, did you fly from Santa Barbara to San Francisco?"

"Wow. That's a long time ago. Let's see. I probably did. I fly up there a couple of times every summer. What's the problem?"

"No problem at all, ma'am. We're cross-checking our reservation system right now to match it with our security system, and using old flight information as a test. Thank you for your cooperation."

"But what—"

Till hung up. He called long-distance information for Las Vegas, and asked for Ann Delatorre's number. A recording came on: "We're sorry, but that number is not listed."

He stood up, gathered his passenger lists, waved good-night to Detective Cota, and walked out of the office to the lobby and the street.

He felt pride in Wendy Harper. She had done well.

11

S YLVIE TURNER had been staring at the lighted display on her laptop computer screen for two hours, watching the line of bright blue dots appearing on the map in their predictable progression, and her eyes were getting tired. She closed them for a moment, then turned her head to watch Paul drive. She still felt lucky whenever she looked at him. He was tall and slim and graceful, but he was also strong, the perfect dance partner, and for Sylvie, the dance was the sign and physical expression of all of the complex relations between a man and a woman. It was flirtation, shyness, flattery and affection, celebration, sharing, demand and compliance, and even possession by force. Dance projected all of her feelings, and let her act them out. She owed that to Paul, too. Dance was something she had lost, but he had restored it to her life.

Long before she met him, she had been a good dancer. Her mother had taken her to ballet class from the time when she was three until she was sixteen. She had loved it, but the discipline had been inhuman, an exercise that seemed to punish her body rather than build it. The toe shoes deformed her feet, and there was the look. A dancer was not a personality, but a fiction that had to do with the idea of perfection. Nobody had ever told Sylvie that she could not be a dancer if she ate, but it was obvious even to a small child that she shouldn't eat. She stayed so thin that she had not begun her period when she was fifteen.

It had not bothered her particularly. Her slender flat-chested body had made her seem more like a dancer. She had kept training, practicing, dancing. She had outgrown four ballet schools by then, each one farther from home. Her mother had been driving her from Van Nuys to Santa Monica every day after school for her class at the latest and best school for nearly a year when Madame Bazetnikova had subjected the girls to her annual evaluation.

The first few girls who had gone into Madame's office had come out smiling and crying at the same time, hugged each other and then collapsed. Madame was a difficult woman. She had been a dancer in Russia, not for the Kirov, but for a lesser company in Minsk. Her dancing career had ended in the 1960s, and by the time she defected she had been only a chaperone in a company touring Norway, and her government didn't bother to protest her loss. But she had moved to Los Angeles and built a fanatical following among the ballet mothers of the city. As she reached old age, she had begun to look dramatic, the way they thought a ballet mistress should look. Each year she took a corps of twelve girls from all of her classes and toured the state for a week during Christmas break, presenting them in excerpts from *Swan Lake* and *The Nutcracker.*

After most of the other girls had been called into the office and come out, she called Sylvie. By then Sylvie expected to hear that she would be Odette in *Swan Lake,* or Clara in *The Nutcracker.* The others had come out happy, but none of them had said anything about being the lead. When Madame Bazetnikova had said, "Sylvie, come sit by me," she had been certain. Madame had never spoken so kindly to her, or to any of the other girls in her hearing. She had been particularly fond of showing contempt with the mere raising of an eyebrow. This time her voice was soft and motherly. "Sylvie."

"Yes, Madame."

"You are a serious, hardworking girl. You have studied your labanotation, learned your steps, and practiced." She stared at Sylvie for a second. "How long do you practice at home each day?"

"Two hours, sometimes more."

"I'll bet a lot of times it's more. I've watched you, and so I know. And you know that in each girl's fifteenth year, I make a decision about her. You are over fifteen now, but I needed more time for you. Now I've decided. You will never be a ballet dancer. It's not your fault. You tried as hard as any girl, but your body is wrong. You don't have the look. You're nothing but bones, but you're still too big."

"I'll try harder," she protested. "I'll practice. I'll stop growing and—"

But Madame was shaking her head. "That's the wrong thing to do. Stop trying. Dance for pleasure, for the joy of it. Eat. Or don't eat and go be a model. I know the world of dance, and I can tell you that you have gone as far as you can go."

"Can I still come and take lessons?"

"No."

"Why not?"

"Because it would make us both unhappy."

Sylvie went out of the room slowly, took off her ballet slippers slowly, put them in her bag slowly, all the time hoping that something would happen to keep her from leaving. Nothing did. She went outside, walked alone to a diner down the street and used a pay telephone to call her mother, then waited in a booth for her mother to arrive.

For a year after that, she did nothing except go to school and do her homework. She ate and she grew. In a very short time, she stopped looking like an emaciated child and began to acquire curves. She grew taller, had her first period. Her resentment and sense of grievance seemed to be what transformed her into a pretty young woman over six feet tall.

Sylvie glanced at Paul again. He was driving with his usual graceful aggression, cutting in and out among the other cars, never making the others nervous, never attracting attention from the police because his coordination seemed to make his speed justified. His driving was like his dancing. When they met, she had not danced for almost ten years.

She had graduated from high school in Van Nuys and gotten a job as a receptionist at a company that sold ceramic tiles for bathrooms and kitchens. She still went out with her high-school boyfriend, Mark Karsh. She had been in love with Mark Karsh from the age of sixteen. Mark Karsh had curly black hair and brown eyes that promised intelligence. Mark had decided not to go to college because he had an uncle who was a film editor. After graduation, the uncle drew heavily upon old friendships and got Mark a job at a company that used computers to make special effects for television shows. After a few days at work, Mark was shocked: He was expected to start at the very bottom of a strict hierarchy. All he had been given was a chance to learn difficult technical skills, and to prove himself by working harder and longer than he was paid to.

Sylvie accepted his complaint that his employers were exploiting him. If they had appreciated his true worth, then he would already have been promoted, and his real movie career would have begun. But after a few months, he still had not learned to operate the machines with any skill, and he had grown sullen and lazy, so he was fired. Sylvie paid for their dates while he searched unsuccessfully for a new position. Finally he accepted the job Sylvie had gotten him in the tile factory.

One night after about a year at the tile factory, Mark asked Sylvie out to an early dinner at Il Calamari. He said he was celebrating something that he wanted to be a surprise. She had always wanted to go there, and she had waited a long time for Mark to take her on a real date, where he invited her somewhere and drove her there and paid. All through dinner he teased her, refusing to tell her what the surprise was. After dinner he drove her to her apartment. She had thoughts of special new careers for Mark, and in unguarded moments, a vision of a ring for her.

Once inside, he told her the news. "You're not going to believe this. When I was working at the digital-imaging studio, I met a few industry people. One of them was a guy named Al Molineri. He's known in the business." Mark was artful in the way he underplayed it. "He's not a major player or something. He's just a guy who has connections. He's written a few scripts, done some editing, video and sound, produced a movie or two. He knew my uncle's name and he introduced me to some other guys who can get a movie made. They liked me. While I was at it, I showed them your picture, too."

She began to feel a difficulty in her breathing. He was keeping something back—no, keeping a lot back—and she was afraid she knew what some of it was. "What picture?"

"Well, just the one I carry in my wallet at first, but then a few other things." He hurried past that topic and into his news. "They were really interested. They want to meet with us and put us in a movie."

"What did you show them?"

He shrugged. "I don't remember everything. What difference does it make? Didn't you hear what I said? We're going to be in a movie."

"You showed them the pictures you took of me that time. The ones you said you would never let anyone see." She began to cry.

He rolled his eyes. "We'll both be stuck working all day every day in the fucking tile company for the rest of our lives unless we do something. I'm trying to give us a future."

"It's a porn movie!"

"There's a love scene. There's one in just about every movie. It's nothing we haven't done a million times, and nothing I'd be ashamed to have anyone see."

"Then do it yourself with somebody else."

"They want us both, not one of us. Both. Look, just come with me. We go to a restaurant tomorrow night, have dinner with them, and hear what they have to say. That's all. If you think it's a bad idea, we'll say, 'No, thanks.'"

They met the two producers at a coffee shop in Reseda that wasn't too far from the part of Van Nuys where Sylvie had grown up. The producers were a man in his forties named Eddie Durant with a beard so short it just looked as though he had forgotten to shave, and a woman named Cherie Will. They were sitting together in a booth near the back drinking coffee and looking over a stack of papers from an open briefcase.

When Sylvie and Mark approached their booth, Eddie Durant didn't stand up or shake hands, but Cherie Will smiled and reached across the table to each of them. She didn't seem exactly attractive to Sylvie, because she was twice Sylvie's age, and there were some wrinkles on her forehead and, oddly, her upper lip. Instead, she seemed athletic, with tight bulbous young breasts that were too high on her chest. She said, "Hi, sweetie" to Sylvie and called Mark "dude."

Sylvie was fascinated by Cherie Will. Cherie looked into Sylvie's eyes when she spoke. "Why don't you two order something to eat?"

Sylvie and Mark ordered and ate, but all the waitress seemed to bring Eddie and Cherie was more coffee. Eddie said, "The story is that you're a young housewife who has an argument with her husband before work in the morning."

"Is that Mark?" Sylvie asked.

"No. Not sure who it is yet. But it's another guy about your age. You get mad. You both go to work. You work in an office, as a receptionist."

"I do. I really do."

"Then it's not a big stretch. This delivery boy, played by Mark, comes in. He's delivering a box of paper or something. You like the look of him, so you offer to show him where the storeroom is. You take him in there, close the door, and have sex. Then you've gotten back at your husband, and you're not mad anymore."

Cherie smiled. "It's an old, simple story, but it always works. Men have fantasies that the pretty receptionist will fuck them in the storeroom, and women have fantasies of getting even with their husbands by fucking the pretty delivery boy, who will appreciate them. I've been in that story about forty times myself, in some variation or other."

Mark Karsh said, "How much would the gig pay?"

Eddie Durant said, "A thousand dollars each for one day's shooting." He smiled. "If you find you like the work and you're good at it, the pay goes up. There's a lot of work for people who can do it. The Valley is the adult-cinema capital of the world. About eighty percent of the adult features shown anywhere are shot within four miles of here."

Mark looked at Sylvie, tried to fathom what she was thinking, but failed. "I think we have to talk about it first."

"Okay. We shoot day after tomorrow at eight A.M. sharp. Call me by noon tomorrow." He held out his hand and Mark shook it. As he and Sylvie walked up the aisle toward the front entrance, two women in their early twenties came in and stood in the entry, blocking their way out while they craned their necks looking for someone. Sylvie couldn't help feeling jealous for a second. She instinctively moved closer to Mark and put her hand on his, even though she was furious at him.

When she and Mark were outside, she turned back and looked in through the glass. She saw that the two girls had made their way back to the booth where Cherie Will and Eddie Durant sat. She could read Cherie Will's lips as she said, "Hi, sweetie," to both of them, and this time Eddie Durant half-rose to shake their hands.

Later on, Sylvie looked back through the years and realized that what had really caused her to make the decision she had was not anything that Mark had said to persuade her. She had been angry with him, and not inclined to do anything drastic to make him happy. It had not been what Eddie Durant or Cherie Will had said. It had been the two girls.

One of them had been short and blond, with blue eyes and a size-two figure with good breasts, a tiny waist, and a perfectly rounded bottom. Girls like that had always been cruel to Sylvie because she wasn't like them. The other was tall and willowy like Sylvie, and that infuriated her, because that girl seemed to be competing for the same spot in the universe as Sylvie was. As Sylvie stared in the window of the diner, she realized that she had to have the job, simply because those two wanted it.

She tortured Mark for a couple of hours before she announced to him that she would do it. She could still see him, all these years later, looking as though he had struck it rich. He was sure that doing this one dirty movie would get him discovered. All he had to do was grit his teeth and smile through one day as a porn star, and then he would be a real star.

The next day, Sylvie and Mark arrived for work at seven-thirty. The studio was a small warehouse that Cherie and Eddie had insulated to cut the echoes and lit with floodlights. Cherie was already waiting "We've got to go get you tested."

Sylvie thought Cherie meant a screen test. They got into Cherie's car, a black Mercedes with dirty leather upholstery and signs of wear. Mark sat in the front beside Cherie, and Sylvie was in the back by herself. When Cherie stopped the car and they got out, Sylvie followed her into a small office that looked like a clinic. She asked, "What's the test?"

"Blood test," said Cherie. "You have to be checked for STDs every thirty days if you want to work in the industry."

Sylvie dutifully sat in the chair while a nurse punctured a vein at the inside of her elbow, took several small vials of blood, then said enigmatically, "We'll let you know." When Mark had done the same, Cherie drove them back to the warehouse.

Sylvie entered as Eddie Durant finished shooting a scene for another movie. Somehow she had assumed there would be a couple of people in a closed room and maybe a cameraman. But there was no room, just a couch with a pair of fake walls held up by wooden struts. Men adjusted lights and camera angles, while others stood in small groups drinking coffee and talking, or making notes on scripts and schedules. Eddie Durant saw Cherie bring Mark and Sylvie in, and he took them off the set to see a man in his mid-thirties with hair so black that Sylvie thought it must be dyed. This was Bill. He wore a pair of jeans, T-shirt, and sandals. "Megan?" he called, and a woman in her early twenties wearing jeans and a huge Winnie the Pooh sweatshirt ambled over, smoking a cigarette.

Cherie said, "Now we have all the principals. Bill is Sylvie's husband, and Megan is the husband's girlfriend. We're on a tight schedule, so we've got to move quickly. Eddie is going to shoot Bill and Megan's scenes in here this morning. Rather than striking the set with the couch, we'll re-dress it as Megan's living room. I'll shoot Sylvie and Mark's scenes in the company office. When we're done, we'll come back in here and do the rest with the set for Bill and Sylvie's house. Everybody got it?"

Cherie took Sylvie and Mark to a corner of the soundstage, where a harried woman with big hair put makeup on their faces, asked them what sizes they wore, and handed them two hangers with clothes on them. They followed Cherie to the company's office, where a tall, thin man named Daryl had set up a big video camera on a tripod in the reception area, and had a big reflective hoop of white cloth just above frame height to diffuse the bright lamplight. Sylvie put on the receptionist outfit, a skirt that was made for a shorter woman and a blouse that was made for a bigger one. Sylvie managed to learn and repeat her lines while seated at the reception desk, even though the telephone rang twice and she had to answer it and hand the phone to Cherie. Her line was "Package? Come into the storeroom and I'll show you where to put it." Then Cherie unplugged the telephone and the camera rolled. There were three takes, one close-up on Sylvie, one on Mark, and one that showed both of them at once.

The next shots were in the storeroom. Cherie explained the scene: "All right, Sylvie. You're the one who drives this scene. You're pissed off at your husband, and you lured this handsome guy in here. Now you've got to make him glad he came in."

"How do you want me to do it?"

"I want this to look natural. Real. You come in, you lock the door, and then you do what you would do. If I want something changed, I'll say, 'Cut,' and have you do it differently."

Sylvie had spent twelve years as a ballet dancer. She was accustomed to having people look at her closely and impersonally, as a body assuming poses, so she didn't feel as though stripping off her clothes was a big step. She had spent all of those years learning to move and to place her body in positions that were graceful and beautiful, and to set her face in expressions to convey feelings and attitudes she didn't necessarily feel. That was about all the acting that was required.

Mark was her boyfriend and they were used to each other. The only part that was disconcerting to her was when Cherie stopped them and told them to change positions, or Daryl the cameraman moved into her field of vision to remind her that they were not alone. When Cherie decided that they had exposed enough tape, she said, "Cut." Then she took Sylvie into her own office and let her use it as a dressing room. She said, "You've got a gift, honey. This is going to be a good movie—as these things go—and you'll get all the work you can do from now on."

"Thank you." Sylvie was still feeling breathless and a bit addled, trying to concentrate on what had happened and what was happening.

"It's not a compliment," Cherie said. "I'm telling you that you're going to get rich." As they walked back to the soundstage, Sylvie said, "Aren't we going to wait for Mark?"

"No. He's not in the next couple of scenes, and we've got a tight schedule." When Sylvie got to the soundstage, she saw the re-dressed house set and the nightgown that the costume and makeup girl had on a hanger, and understood. The scene with her husband Bill wasn't going to be just an argument at the breakfast table before they both left for work. She was supposed to have sex with him, too.

Sylvie thought about everything as she sat down and let the makeup girl work on her. She stared at herself in the mirror. She stole a few curious glances at Bill as he stood talking to Eddie Durant on the set. She could get up and walk out the door. Nobody would stop her, and probably nobody would even blame her. She was a twenty-year-old girl who had been talked into something. There was no reason for her to go on. This was all about Mark's ambitions, not hers. There were hundreds of other girls just like her, waiting for this chance.

"Sylvie?" Cherie called.

She stared at herself in the mirror. Her face was beautiful in this light. She could never have made her skin look so radiant, her eyes so big. Her hair was shining. She was amazing.

"Sylvie!"

"Coming." She stood up, took a few hurried steps to join the group, and said to Cherie, "Where do we start?"

That night the production wrapped at nine, and Sylvie went outside to find Mark. His car wasn't where she remembered it. She went to the office and found Lily, the receptionist. She was just returning from the inner offices, where Eddie Durant had been signing the day's payroll checks. Lily leafed through them quickly and handed one to Sylvie. She said, "Uh, Mark? He's been gone for hours. Where do you live? I can give you a ride."

When Sylvie got home, she waited for Mark's call, but it didn't come. At ten-thirty, she tried calling him. He answered after a few rings. She said, "Where were you?"

"Where were *you*? I waited for a couple of hours after I was done."

"I had some more scenes to shoot."

"I heard."

Those words had the end in them. The day's experiences had changed his plans. He was not going to be a star. He was not happy that he had been at the studio or that he had brought her there. He was not going to see her again.

Call-waiting signaled a few times that she had another caller. She said to Mark, "I'm tired. I'll talk to you another time," knowing that she wouldn't. She clicked the flash button to get the other call. "Hello?"

"Sylvie, it's Eddie Durant. Cherie and I just went through today's tapes to do a director's cut, and I've got to tell you, we couldn't keep our eyes off you. We're writing you into a movie we're starting day after tomorrow."

"Gee, I hadn't really thought about that. I just got home a while ago."

"We'll pay you two thousand—double the last time—for a day's work."

"Can I have time to think about it?"

"Sure. Call me later tonight. We'll be here editing until at least one or two."

That was the beginning. On Thursday she drove to the studio and listened while Cherie Will explained the script to her in the five minutes it took to have her hair and makeup done. Then she spent the day having sex with three different men she had never seen before.

Eddie and Cherie had her working three days a week for the next month. Sylvie kept telling herself that she ought to call the tile company to tell them she had found another job, but she didn't. She didn't want to tell Martha, the middle-aged office manager, that she was acting. Martha would instantly sense what sort of movies they were, and she would talk. Sylvie didn't want the men in the company hurrying into video stores to find a tape with a picture of her on the box. The tile company still owed her about three hundred dollars, but going in to pick up the check didn't seem worth it.

Now nearly twenty years had passed, and Sylvie felt so different that she could only reconstruct some of the young girl's feelings. Many of the faces had faded in her memory and lost their clarity. As Sylvie stared ahead through the windshield, thinking about the distant past, something startled her. The display on the laptop computer's screen had changed. "Paul! The car is right up ahead. It's not moving."

The idea of tracing Jack Till's car this way had been a revelation to Sylvie. She knew that the car-rental companies had been using the global-positioning units installed in rental cars to catch customers violating their contracts by speeding or taking their cars out of state. Paul had gone to the rental company where Till had rented his car, and given a thousand dollars in cash to a mechanic in exchange for teaching him how the company found a lost car. They simply went online to the service that monitored the global-positioning system, typed a code, and watched the display on their own computer. The code for Till's car had cost another thousand.

Till appeared to have parked in the lot at the end of Castillo Street, at the Santa Barbara Harbor. Paul pulled into the lot and searched for the blue sedan, driving up and down each aisle as though what he was looking for was an empty space. Sylvie was the one who spotted Till's car. "There. Right near the entrance."

"I see it," said Paul. He drove up the next aisle so he could pull out and follow if Till and Wendy Harper came back and got into the car. "You get out and check the dock and the shops."

Sylvie got out of the car and walked toward the docks. A few stores along the wharf sold bright-colored kayaks, wet suits, or expensive clothes for people who hung around beach resorts. Sylvie checked each of the stores. There was nobody in any of them who remotely resembled Jack Till, even from a distance. She walked out onto the dock and stopped at the jetty where the commercial fishing boats unloaded. There were big turnbuckles where they tied off, and an electric winch on an armature for lifting the heavy wooden boxes that were piled on the back of the fish packers' trucks parked nearby.

She saw a bored-looking blond boy with a tan so deep that the whites of his eyes glowed as though he were looking out of holes cut in leather. He sat on the back of one of the trucks listening to a radio and waiting for a boat to come in. Sylvie considered the chance that the boat would contain Wendy Harper, then dismissed the idea. She walked farther out along the dock and studied the row of fishing boats, each with its net rolled up on a big drum near the stern. Some of the boats looked deserted, worn and dirty, as though they hadn't been out of port in years, but she supposed that was probably the sign that they were out often. It was possible that Till was retrieving Wendy Harper from one of the hundred or so yachts that were anchored in the harbor, or moored along the next set of docks, but if so, there was no sign of a dory going to or from any of them.

She went back the way she had come, and got back into the car beside Paul. "I couldn't find him. He could be meeting her in a boat. I've been everywhere else. They could be on the beach, but I figured it was best to come back here so he didn't slip by me or something."

"That was smart," Paul said. "We'll just wait and then follow when he leaves."

Once again, for the ten thousandth time, Sylvie wondered: When Till finally showed himself and got into his car, would he look up, see her, and recognize her face from one of the movies she'd made? It had happened twice in supermarkets and once at the bank just two years ago, and it had humiliated her terribly. If it ever happened when she was working, it could get them caught. She looked at Paul, wanting to tell him what she was thinking, but knowing that she had better not. She took the 9mm Beretta out of her purse, released the magazine to be sure it was fully loaded, pushed the magazine back in until it clicked and held, and made sure the safety was on. She arranged the things in her purse so the flimsy scarf just covered the gun.

"Shit," Paul said. "Oh, shit!"

"What?" She looked out the windshield and saw a potbellied man in his late thirties wearing a Hawaiian shirt and khaki shorts. He was opening the doors of Till's rental car. She could see the white plastic rental-company key tag dangling from the keys in his hand. "Oh, no." Then, from around the side of the building where the restrooms were, she could see Mom coming along with two kids about five and eight. The kids got into the car, and Mom knelt while she put more sunscreen on their little faces. Sylvie whispered, "How could we have the wrong car? How could we?"

"We didn't. Till must have turned it in, and these people rented it."

"But how?"

"Please don't keep asking me how. Probably when it stopped last night near the airport, he was turning it in. They must have cleaned it, filled the tank, and rented it to these people."

Sylvie and Paul watched as the parents got in and the father carefully backed out of the parking space. He drove out and turned right onto Cabrillo Boulevard. The mother was half-turned in her seat. She seemed to be coaxing the kids to look out at the blue expanse of the Pacific, but the little girl reached out and punched her brother, then pretended he had hit her and began to cry.

12

JACK TILL SAT BACK in the driver's seat of the Cadillac and watched the miles of road roll under it. There was a hard wind in the high desert today, and it had blown any suspicion of cloud away. The sky was an unchanging deep blue, and the sun glinted off any piece of metal like a camera flash. Since Till had come down out of the pass into Nevada, he had been able to look out over the emptiness now and then to see dust devils swirling in the distance.

As he drove, he revisited the days before he had taken Wendy Harper away. He had tried not to learn too much about her. He had barely listened even to her volunteered confidences because he had not wanted to figure out where she would be and carry that information in his mind for the next twenty years.

But there had been one question he had asked her repeatedly: "Who is the guy you saw with the waitress? I used to be a homicide detective. I still know nearly everybody in Homicide Special, and a lot of people in Hollywood Homicide. If he killed her, we can get him. They'll lock him up."

"I didn't say she was a waitress. And I only saw him with her once, at night. He didn't do anything to me. I think he *hired* the one who did, but that one didn't say he did. He didn't say anything."

Till said, "You know the identity of a person who is missing and maybe dead, at least a description of the murder suspect, and had a good long look at an assailant who is probably working for him. We could do a lot with that, probably connect the two and put them both away."

"I thought about it all the time in the hospital. I don't know enough to identify him, much less get him arrested, but he thinks it's worth paying people to kill me. I'll run out of blood before he runs out of money. So I'll go away."

"I think you know more about him than you're saying. His name is enough. I can get it to the homicide people without having you hauled in."

"Here's the joke. I don't know his name. She never told me that."

"Then how do you know he's behind any of this?"

"When I saw him with her in the parking lot, he was trying to hide his face. He carried himself funny, to stay in the dark part where the shadow of the building hid him. While I watched him, he went to his car to check something inside, but he didn't open the door because it would turn on the dome light. Don't you see? It's a hundred small observations in two or three minutes, and I've forgotten sixty of them by now. It's degenerated into an intuition, and an intuition isn't good enough. All I can do is get away."

"Getting out is a huge thing to do," Till said. "It means giving up your career, and all of the people who care about you."

Then she had said the most surprising thing to him. "In a way, it's probably a good thing. My life here has reached a kind of paralysis."

"So running will solve your personal problems?"

She smiled. "I didn't ask for this. I had two ribs broken with one swing of that bat. I'm just saying that when something like that happens, it changes your life—everything in your life."

"Are you one of those women who gets sick and thinks it's good because she loses weight?"

"No. I didn't say the change was for the better, and if it were, it wouldn't be worth it. I know I'm trading old problems for new ones. What I'm really telling you is that I would never have had the guts to walk away from this life unless something big and ugly was chasing me. I've got a half-interest in a successful restaurant, with investors begging us to open more locations. It's worth millions, but I can't sell it. I also own a half-interest in a million-dollar house with Eric, but I can't sell that, either. I don't even have a real career. My career is handling Eric Fuller, keeping him productive, solvent, and supplied with fresh produce and linens."

"You're willing to leave him forever?"

"Leaving Eric is the part I hate, but it's the thing I should have done, anyway. Eric doesn't need me anymore. He's a great chef, and he's got the loyalty of a whole staff of good people we found and trained. He's got a national reputation now. He's made. But if I don't leave, his chance for a real personal life is going to pass. If I'm with him, my chance will pass, too."

Jack Till fought through the fog of years and brought back details. She had said her mother was dead. Her father had apparently been out of the picture since she was a child. Was he dead, too? She and Eric had grown up in upstate New York. Poughkeepsie. They had gone to college—where? Wisconsin.

Just from the way she had handled her new name, he believed she was too smart to return to the place where she was raised, or the place where she and Eric had gone to college. She would know that there were people who had known her well—teachers, neighbors, friends and the parents of friends, doctors. Even if she could have been sure nobody like that was left, there would be others who knew her by sight or reputation. She would try to stay away from any of the cities where she had lived before.

As he drove through the desert, he kept picturing her, listening to her voice in his memory. It was an uncomfortable feeling, because at the time he had caught himself feeling a strong attraction to her. He had told himself at the time that he had to hide the affection he felt for her: She was running for her life, and he couldn't go with her. After it was over, he had thought of her often, always reluctantly, and with a sense of loss. But thinking about her now made him feel almost certain. Wendy Harper had changed her name to Ann Delatorre and flown to Las Vegas on August 30 six years ago.

Las Vegas was garish and vulgar and extravagant. It was an endless river of people who thought the rules of the universe were about to change, so this time they would end up with the money and the casino owners would end up with a hangover. Wendy Harper wasn't a gambler. She had saved most of her money and worked seven days and six nights a week for years. The ambience of Las Vegas didn't fit with anything Wendy Harper had ever liked. But she had come to Jack Till to learn how to stop being Wendy Harper. She was Ann Delatorre now. Who knew what Ann Delatorre liked?

When Till took the exit from Route 15 at the Mandalay Bay complex, he was once again amazed at the traffic. Ten or fifteen years ago, he and Jimmy DeKuyper had driven here a number of times to pick up fugitives being extradited on L.A. homicides. He had always taken this exit so he could drive up the Strip, and couldn't remember ever being delayed on the way uptown. Now, going a couple of blocks on the Strip was a project. He decided to check in at a hotel and let a cabdriver do it for him.

He pulled his rental car into the circle at the MGM Grand and saw the valet arrive to drive it away. He got out, and it was as though the door to a blast furnace had opened. The hot, dry wind seemed to take the moisture from his skin and dry his eyes. He walked inside, found his way to the front desk, and stood in line. There were about twenty-five women in gray uniforms along the desk at stations where they were checking people in as quickly as they could, but the lines were still growing behind him. He had been consciously keeping his moves random, always deciding at the last minute according to whim, and now he wondered whether he had made a mistake. But when he reached the front of the line, the woman asked for his reservation but showed no reaction when he said he didn't have one, and gave him a folder with a set of key cards in it.

He put his suitcase in his room and then went to work. The telephone company had told him Ann Delatorre's number was unlisted, so he would have to find it another way. He called the offices of unions, and the personnel offices of all the large companies he found in the phone book. When he found nothing, he went back to the telephone book and looked at the ads for local private detectives.

He found plenty of agencies that looked honest and reliable: "All our investigators are former police officers, fully licensed and bonded," or "Offices in New York, Dallas, and Chicago." He didn't want anybody like that, so he kept searching the pages. He found one that had a suite on the second floor of a building with an address that sounded like a strip mall. The small, cheap ad said: FRAUD DETECTION, MARITAL, DEBT COLLECTION.

He took a cab to the address. The building was in a part of the city that Till thought of as Daylight Las Vegas. Tall hotel buildings poked up like fingers in the distance, but in the foreground there were only one- and two-story box structures with stucco on the front sides and tinted windows that the eye could not penetrate. The address was on a strip with a low-end store that sold discount clothes, a tattoo parlor, a chiropractor, and a small storefront offering tae-kwon-do lessons. Up on the second level there was a door with a sign that said Lamar Collection Services.

He opened the door, heard an electronic bell ring, and waited at the counter at the back of the small reception area. He looked around and saw three plastic lawn chairs and a laminated table that held year-old car magazines. In a moment he heard some shuffling sounds from a back room, and a woman in her forties with bright red hair came through the door. She placed her hands on the counter, and Till could see a set of long blue fingernails painted with tiny white flowers. "How can I help you?" she said without enthusiasm.

Till took out his identification. "My name is Jack Till. I'm a private investigator from Los Angeles. I'm searching for a former client of mine. I'd like to find out if she's living in Nevada."

She shrugged. "We're skip-tracers. We can do that."

"Her name is Ann Delatorre."

"You haven't said you represent a company she owes money, or that you're trying to deliver money they owe her, or anything. There are laws."

"Oh. Did I forget to mention that? She hired me and didn't pay. What do you charge?"

"Depends. Just to see if we've got her under our noses is forty bucks. That includes a search of the two biggest databases. If you want us to collect for you, then you're talking about quite a bit more."

"I think I'd like to start with the easy stuff. For now I'd just like an address and, if possible, a phone number."

"Okay." She pushed a pad of paper to him with a pen. "Write down the name. You pay in advance, then come back in an hour."

He took out two twenty-dollar bills, wrote down the name. "I can wait here."

"Suit yourself."

She went away for no more than ten minutes, and returned with a skip-trace sheet she had printed out. She set it on the counter and turned to walk toward the back of her store. She said over her shoulder, "There you go."

Till got up from his plastic chair and took the paper. It had the name Ann Delatorre, a home address, and a Social Security number. Under occupation it said "Sales," and the employer was a company called "Karen's" on Paradise Road. It occurred to Till that it was possible Wendy Harper had found a way to have another extra identity. She could be Ann the salesclerk and also Karen, the absent owner who hired her, paid her salary and verified her ID papers. Till said, "Thank you," but the woman with the blue nails was gone.

As he walked to the street and took out the card with the cab company's phone number on it, he glanced at his watch. It was still early. Karen's would probably still be open. He called a cab, rode to Paradise Road, and found that the address was a mailing center that rented mailboxes. He reminded himself that Wendy Harper had stayed invisible for six years. He had expected her to be good at it.

13

SYLVIE SLIPPED OUT of the airplane's aisle into the window seat, then lifted the armrest up to open the space between her and Paul as he sat down and fastened his seat belt. Then she wiggled her hips once to establish contact with him. He looked down at her and smiled.

It was interesting to Sylvie to see Paul moving back and forth so easily between the extremes of his personality. Just an hour ago, he had been speaking with the boy in the car-rental office and smiling almost as warmly as he was now. He had said, "I really would appreciate your help in this situation. Jack is my oldest friend, and my wife's brother. We've got to locate him just as soon as we can."

The boy had not returned Paul's beautiful smile. He had simply played at being a heartless bureaucrat. "I'm sorry, sir. But company rules prohibit us from using the locator on a car just because somebody asks."

"But this is an emergency. My wife's mother is very ill: Jack's mother. We think this could be the end. She's a dear old lady, and she's asked for Jack. With the help of people from your company in Los Angeles we managed to trace him to Santa Barbara. We know he made it this far, and turned in the car. We need to know if he rented another car from you and is still in town, or if he got on a plane. I can't even conceive of what harm it would do to tell us. I'll pay you very well for your trouble."

"I'm sorry, sir."

"What's a day's pay for you? I'll give you that just for a little help."

"I don't know, sir. I'm paid once a month."

"All right. A week's pay, in cash. Divide your paycheck by four."

"I'm sorry, sir. Company rules." The boy held his hands up in a shrug.

Paul's long arm shot out, and before the boy could step backward, Paul had gripped his right wrist, spun him around, and had the arm twisted behind his back. Paul was as quick and graceful at jujitsu as he was at dancing. He held the boy's arm with no apparent effort. The boy was bent over, his face almost to the counter, his eyes watering, then almost closed in pain. His body tilted to the side while Paul was steering him around the counter and into the open.

Paul said to Sylvie, "Would you please give him three hundred dollars?"

"Sure." Sylvie opened her purse, took out the three bills, held them up like a magician's assistant, folded them once, and placed them in the boy's breast pocket.

Paul applied some more pressure, and the boy went to one knee. "I'll do it. All right. Stop. Stop it."

Paul released him and said, "Thank you." He watched while the boy pushed on his knee with his good hand to raise himself. The hand that Paul had held was pressed to the boy's stomach, as though held by an invisible sling. The boy went around the counter and Paul went with him. He used his uninjured hand to tap on the computer's keys while Paul looked over his shoulder. Paul took a pen off the counter and wrote on a map the code number for the locator on Till's car and the license number.

The boy said, "He's got a white Cadillac DeVille. It's in Las Vegas, parked at the MGM Grand Hotel."

"Thank you." Paul reached into his own wallet and added two more hundred-dollar bills to the boy's breast pocket.

Now, as Sylvie sat beside him on the airplane, she leaned into the space between them and snuggled, then leaned back to wait for takeoff. "I like Las Vegas."

"Me. too. Too bad it's got to be for work."

"I don't care. It's still exciting. I love going with you."

She was telling the truth. Paul had changed her life in the way that she had imagined when she was a little girl that a man would. Her mother had usually been without a man in her life, but she had always been trying, flirting with men in grocery stores and at school events. She had invited men from work over for dinner. Sylvie could still remember sitting in awkward silence while her mother talked to one of these men, her conversation false and bright and quick, her voice more strained as time went on. After a time, the man would always find a way to leave. None of the men had seemed very promising to Sylvie, but she had observed at other times that her mother was not a stupid woman. If her mother was so desperate for a connection with a man, then they must have value.

When Sylvie had been dismissed from the world of ballet and grown into a healthier-looking girl, she began to share her mother's interest, but she had some disappointing experiences with boys. She grew too tall at first. Boys she liked were a head shorter than she was. Once, when she was waiting at a dance for a boy to come up and ask her to dance, she saw two boys talking. The loud music drowned out their voices, but one of them mouthed the word "freak," and they both looked at her. She did not have time to look away, and they saw her eyes focused on them. She experienced nothing but contempt from boys at school. But after school each day she worked as a stock girl at a big pharmacy on Sepulveda, and the men who came in saw her differently. They seemed to assume that she was much older and more sophisticated than she was. In the first month, two men in their twenties asked her out.

In her junior year, she met Mark. He was one of the few boys who was taller than she was, and he was so handsome that looking at him when he was unaware made her want to reach out and touch him. When he finally approached her in the hall near her locker at school, she was barely able to speak. She smiled and blushed and looked at her feet through much of the conversation, but she agreed to go to a movie with him. A week later, he invited her to a party.

The party was at the house of a friend of his whom she didn't know, and she hated it and loved it at the same time. She loved being out, being Mark's date. But at the party there was too-loud, pounding music that hurt her ears, a lot of drinking and clouds of resiny marijuana smoke that made her eyes water and seemed to stick to her hair. The girls at the party were from a clique of popular tenth graders, who in spite of being a year younger than Sylvie looked down on her. She could dance better than they did, but Mark didn't like to dance, so she didn't even get the chance to make them jealous.

But the party had a surprising aftereffect: She noticed within a week that her status had changed remarkably. Girls who had never talked to her suddenly appeared beside her in some class and complained about their boyfriends or their rivals, the only two pertinent topics of conversation. In physical education, she had always been one of the strivers who ran their laps on the sun-heated tarmac while the popular girls lingered in the shade and brushed each other's hair. Now *she* was one of the girls in the shade, and she sat under a tree while Charlotte McClellan made her a French braid.

She was overwhelmed with gratitude at the way Mark had transformed her life, but for the first time she was constantly worried and anxious, afraid that he would disappear and her life would instantly go back to the way it had been. One Friday night she waited until they were in his car and away from her house, then spoke. "Mark?" She tried to say more, but didn't know what to say. She opened her purse so he could see inside. "While I was at work today I picked these up." She had a box of condoms. "I mean, just in case we ever want to."

He wanted to. They drove to a new street that had just been paved, in the northern edge of the Valley where it met the mountains. There were eight or nine skeletal frames of houses, their white-yellow two-by-fours gleaming in the moonlight, and stacks of plywood sheets and packs of shingles sat behind chain-link fences. Mark drove nearly to the end, then turned his car around so it was aimed outward toward the highway, and then they had sex.

Sylvie did not like it much. The back seat of Mark's car was cramped and uncomfortable, and she had not expected that there would be pain. But Mark liked it very much, and so she decided that she had made a reasonably good decision. Mark would not leave her for someone else. She was set from now until graduation. As she sat in the seat beside Mark, watching him driving back toward Van Nuys, she was surprised at how easy it had been.

Things continued in a satisfactory way past graduation, and then through that final summer, when the classmates who were going to go off to colleges were slowly severing their ties with the ones who weren't, and then for the year after that.

The day Mark got her into the movies and the relationship ended, he faded from her sight and her memory, just as her job at the tile factory did. Soon she was making four to six thousand dollars a week at Cherie Will's studio, Ma Cherie Seductions. One of the other girls told her that she could make money by having a 1-900 telephone number and charging her fans to talk to her. She didn't mind the calls. When her phone rang in the evening she would turn off the sound on her television set and watch the silent picture while she talked. After a couple of weeks she had the girl's boyfriend come to her apartment and take three dozen pictures of her naked, then sold the prints to her callers over the phone.

A year later, a promoter left a message for her. She called him back and agreed to a meeting at a restaurant in Burbank. His name was Darren McKee. He wasn't the type she had expected when she had talked to him on the telephone. He had sounded like a fifty-year-old truck driver she had known at the tile factory, but when she entered the restaurant, she found he was thirty-nine and attractive. He had reddish hair that seemed to be a single cowlick, and a boyish smile that she liked. He led her to a booth and they ordered drinks.

He said, "You just passed my test."

"What's your test?"

"It's whether I'd pay to be in the same room with you."

"What do you mean?" Sylvie was already on the edge of her seat, the strap of her purse in her hand, ready to leave.

"You look even better in person than on film. You've got a special quality that very few people have, and now you're getting famous. You've got to find as many ways as possible to capitalize on the few years when you're at your peak."

"Oh, I'm doing pretty well."

"Adult-film stars make a fairly good living for a limited period of time. But the minute they're not getting better, it's already over. Some of them, like Cherie Will, are able to do something afterward. She went off with Eddie Durant and started her own shop. That's about as rare as race-car drivers starting their own car companies. Chances are, you're not going to do that."

"Don't be too sure."

"I remember working with her on the set years ago. After the director set up a shot with other actors, she'd get up off the bed naked and look through the camera lens. After getting fucked all day by four or five guys, she would go sit with the editors all evening to learn how to cut the scenes together."

"Okay, she's smarter than I am. So what are you trying to get me to do?"

"I'd like to arrange a twelve-city tour of the very best gentlemen's clubs in the country."

"Stripping? I've never done that, and I don't want to." She slid over another few inches and stood. "Thanks for the offer, though."

"What if I guarantee ten thousand a night?"

She sat on the edge of the seat for a moment. "Just stripping? Nothing else?"

"That's right. You're not just a girl taking her clothes off, you're a movie star, a celebrity. Even if they never heard of you, saying that makes all the difference."

She stared at him and listened. The voice was still a mystery. He sounded like an old man who had smoked cigars all his life. She couldn't make a decision about him, but she agreed to let him see what he could arrange, and then went home. When she found herself alone again in that small, partially furnished apartment, she wondered why she had not simply turned him down. She had no desire to go into strip clubs to take her clothes off. She liked money, but she wasn't sure why she liked money. She did little more than buy the same kind of inexpensive clothes she always had, and leave the rest in bank accounts. But she was aware that the numbers were getting larger, and dollars were the only measure she had of the days that were passing or the life she was using up.

When she went in to work the next Monday, she talked to Cherie Will about Darren McKee. Cherie looked at her for a moment, then said, "I don't know what to say. A lot of girls do the clubs. It's a lot of extra money, and most of it is in cash. When I started to get offers like that, I took them for a year or two. I did three tours in that time. I hated the travel—which, by the way, is not first-class—and I hated the customers and the noise and the smoke. I guess they probably can't smoke in those places anymore. But the rest of it has to be the same—a few hundred horny, drunk guys drooling out there at the tables while you try to ignore them and hear the beat of the music over the noise. Do you even dance?"

Sylvie lied. "No," she said, then wondered why.

"Well, you can learn as much as you need to, I guess. The key to this is to get the money in your hands and invest it. Buy a house. Start a retirement plan, if you haven't already. Then keep putting the rest in stocks and bonds. That's why I own a movie studio with Eddie Durant, and the girls from my day who were better looking and better actresses and better everything are, well, wherever they are. Just make sure I always know your schedule."

Sylvie took everything Cherie said seriously, so she took this seriously, too. She had been saving her money, but now she began to invest it. At the end of the next week, McKee called her again. "Hello, baby," he said in his strange raspy voice. "I got you booked. We do fifteen cities in three weeks."

The first club was in San Diego. On her first night, she stood behind the curtain on the stage and looked out at the men in the bar while the lights were still up. She realized that they weren't scary. They weren't anything. They had nothing to do with her or what she was going to do up onstage. When she came out, the room was too dim to make out their features clearly. She began to dance. She was in a blue spotlight, and as she moved her body the dance was no more personal, no more Sylvie than it had been when she was assuming the classic poses of ballet.

At the end of each night, she was tired and covered with sweat, but the crowd of men had given her so many bills that each time her set was over, she had to gather the money and pile it in stacks in her dressing room. Darren McKee insisted on staying at her side and having one of the club bouncers take them to the hotel so she wouldn't get robbed.

Darren was better to her than she had expected him to be. For the whole tour, he went with her so she wouldn't have to make any travel arrangements or haggle with the management of the clubs.

Sylvie formed the theory that there had been earlier girls who had arrived late or gotten lost, and that he was determined never to let it happen again. He talked to her while he drove her from city to city, telling her funny stories about people in the business, and about others he met in hotels. He ordered healthy food for her when they were in restaurants, and even gave her vitamins after meals. He booked hotel rooms adjoining hers, and made sure she turned off the television and switched off the lights in time to get eight hours of sleep every night. He was reliable and strong and in control, and she felt safe and protected.

After all these years, it seemed to Sylvie that what happened was partly her fault. She was on the tour because she had been in a couple dozen adult movies, and the reason she was on the tour was to take her clothes off onstage. It would have seemed idiotic to close doors and make a point of hiding herself from Darren. She would have been embarrassed to put on clothes just because he was around.

The part that was Darren's fault was that he had effectively taken over her life. It had not occurred to her that at twenty she was almost exactly half his age. She didn't think of him as being her mother's age, and he didn't look it. She just thought vaguely that he was older and wiser, and therefore it was logical that he was in charge. He was always walking from his room to hers and back, handling her clothes, her luggage, or something. It became so un-surprising after a few days that one time when he came in while she was coming out of the shower she didn't bother to get dressed, and he began to make love to her. She accepted him without giving the change in their relationship as much thought as she might have a year earlier. She had become used to men, and used to Darren, and had figured that everything he did was good for her, and this prob-ably was, too.

It made their relationship unambiguous, and now she knew how to behave: how to interpret his touch, how to respond to things that he said to her and did for her. They weren't boss and employee, or star and manager, or dancer and agent. They were a man and a woman. She knew how to do that. She had never traveled with a man before, but she liked it. She liked living with someone who paid attention to her.

At the end of the tour, while they were driving toward Los Angeles, he said, "You made a lot of money this trip."

"Yes," she said. "More than I ever imagined I would."

"I think the clubs aren't good for you."

"It's not fun," she said. "But I liked traveling with you, and it's safer than working for Cherie and Eddie in the movie business. I'm not going to catch some disease and die from stripping."

"I want you to quit the movie business, too. Especially that."

She looked at him for a few seconds. "I don't get it. Why do you have an opinion?"

"Because I love you. As soon as we get back home, I want you to marry me."

Sylvie looked at Darren and considered his offer. Thinking about it meant allowing herself to acknowledge what she had decided not to feel—that she hated her life. There had been particular moments of humiliation and hurt and revulsion that she had known would make her want to die if she let them, so she simply hadn't. As she sat in the car beside Darren McKee that day, she found herself remembering all of it. "Yes," she said. "I'll marry you." As Sylvie considered that moment, all these years later, she realized it was the last big decision she had ever had to make.

The plane reached its apogee and the pilot began to mutter into the microphone in the cockpit. Sylvie looked at Paul, gave him a quick, perfunctory smile, squeezed his hand once, and looked out the window at the jagged brown rocks below. In a few minutes, they would be on the runway in Las Vegas. All they had to do was find Jack Till's car and follow it to Wendy Harper. Once the woman was dead, maybe Sylvie could get Paul to spend a few days here.

14

IT WAS LATE AFTERNOON when Jack Till took a cab back from the mailbox rental to the MGM Grand and went up to his room. He showered, unlocked his suitcase, and dressed in fresh clothes, then retrieved the parts of his gun. It was a black 9mm Beretta M92 pistol like the police-issue sidearm he had carried when he was a homicide detective. He had dismantled it so the slide, the recoil spring, barrel, frame, and the loaded magazine were in different parts of the suitcase. He laid the pieces out on the bed and assembled them. He had picked that particular gun because it had the right presence. It was blocky and utilitarian, and it was the model that civilians like Wendy Harper had seen strapped to cops a thousand times. He hoped it would make her feel safe.

He had to make her feel that she would be protected, or she might be reluctant to go with him. There was also the fact that the trouble she was hiding from was not imaginary. The men who had buried the bloody bat in her best friend's back yard had been trying to get her to show herself.

Till laid out the other items he had brought with him. He had a very good quality women's brown wig made of real hair cut in a short, wavy style that was not at all like Wendy Harper's long blond hair. Her figure had been very thin and small, and the quilted jacket he'd brought would add twenty pounds. He had chosen glasses for her: one set with dark-tinted lenses for the ride in the car, and the other clear for walking in the halls of the DA's office and the police department. Till was sure he would have to take her to both places. Assistant DA Linda Gordon would be predisposed to believe she was being hoodwinked, and would insist on having Wendy finger-printed, photographed, and positively identified. Till supposed he would have to prepare Wendy for the hostility and suspicion she would face. But the fact that nobody except Till would be planning to protect her once she was in Los Angeles he would keep to himself for now.

Till searched his suitcase, found a small battery-operated trans-mitter, switched it on, and used the receiver to test its battery. He planned to leave it in Ann Delatorre's apartment and telephone to listen to anyone who entered after he drove away with her.

He put the bug into his coat pocket, and slipped the gun into the belt holster at the left side of his body where he could open his coat and allow Ann Delatorre to see it. Then he gathered a few of the newspaper articles about the arrest of Eric Fuller into an enve-lope and locked his suitcase again.

He went downstairs to the casino, made his way through a crowd of people standing in front of an enormous glass case where a family of African lions draped themselves over a real-looking out-cropping of rock on a veldt on the hotel floor, stepped into a shop beyond it, and bought a map of Las Vegas and its suburbs. He went to the front entrance, stepped into the evening air and studied the map while the parking attendant went off to bring him his car. It took him only a few seconds to plot the route to Ann Delatorre's address, but he kept his head tilted toward the map for a minute while he scanned the area around him through his dark glasses. From the lot entrance he could see the windows of the San Remo Hotel, cars and pedestrians walking along Tropicana Boulevard, and if he looked to the right, he could see the permanent traffic jam on the Strip. He could see a thousand people right now, but there was no way to spot anyone who might be watching him.

He accepted his rental car, drove out Tropicana to Rainbow Boulevard, turned right on Charleston Boulevard to Jones Boulevard, and then north to Cheyenne Avenue, keeping watch on the cars behind him. He pulled into a grocery store parking lot, studied the cars that went by for a few minutes, then went inside the store to buy bottled water and snacks for the trip back to Los Angeles. Then he stood for a moment inside the doorway to see whether any of the cars he had seen on the road behind him had appeared in the supermarket lot or any of the other parking lots within sight, but none of them had.

Till got into his car again and drove aimlessly for a time, watching for followers and waiting for night to come. It came in a way that he had forgotten, a sky of blue and pink deepening into purple as the huge banks of moving, sparkling lights joined the billboard-sized television screens with shimmering videos of beautiful women, tables covered with food, and flutes of bubbling champagne to fight back the dark.

Jack Till drove past Cheyenne Avenue, then came back and parked. He got out and walked into a large condominium complex and then came out the other side, went around the block and returned to the car. Till was of the opinion that the way to keep from being followed was not merely to watch for followers, but to provide them with a plausible false destination and lead them there.

When he was positive that nobody could have followed him, he drove through the city to Boulder Highway, and drove south away from the tall hotels into the flat suburban landscape to the south, and then into Henderson, where Ann Delatorre lived. As he drove, he kept having the same thought over and over: Ann Delatorre might not be Wendy Harper. He had chosen her out of all of the women who had flown out of Santa Barbara on August 30 six years ago, but that didn't mean he was right. It would not be the first time when he had made a logical guess based on the soundest evidence and been utterly wrong.

The address was a house on a clean, quiet, broad, well-ordered street, one of a long row of similar one-story houses. Each house sat on a small patch of well-tended green lawn, and had a two-car garage to one side of it. After passing a few houses, he detected that there were three styles—Mediterranean, Southwest, Colonial— alternating so that no house was beside one just like it.

He found the house, drove past it slowly and studied the pattern of lights in the windows. The suburban street seemed an unlikely habitat for the Wendy Harper he had met, and that made him uneasy in a new way. It had been six years since Wendy had seen him. She might not even recognize him. He continued along the street for a distance before he turned around. If she was still nervous, still taking a precautionary look at every car that went by, then he should try to keep from alarming her. He could have made a telephone call to warn her that he was coming, but there was no way of knowing whether someone was monitoring her line or even his cell phone. He brought his rental car to a stop at the curb near her house, walked to her front door, and rang the bell. He heard footsteps.

He stood straight on the front steps, keeping his face up so the light would catch it and she would have a chance to recognize him. The door opened an inch, then clicked. There was a deadbolt in the floor with a second receptacle for the steel bar, and she had engaged it. He stared at the two inches of open doorway, and saw that the face staring back at him was black.

"Can I help you?" The woman's question was a challenge, a carefully polite message that she was not glad to see a stranger on the doorstep.

"Yes," he said. "My name is Jack Till, and I came to see Ann Delatorre. Is this the right house?"

There was a second of hesitation that told him it was.

"What can I do for you?" He could see her better now, as she moved her head from side to side in front of the open slice of doorway to see whether there was anyone with him. She was in her late twenties or early thirties, with a pretty face and large brown eyes.

"I'm a private investigator who helped her once, a few years ago. I know that she'll want to see me."

"I *do* see you," said the woman. "I'm Ann Delatorre."

"Oh. I'm terribly sorry to have bothered you like this. I was looking for someone else." He turned as though to leave, then stopped. "Oh, one more thing. Do you know any other Delatorres in the area? Delatorre is her married name. Her original name was Harper."

"I'm the only one I know about. Good night." She closed the door, and he heard the bolt click, and then a second one.

Till walked away from the door, turned at the corner of the house and made his way quickly along the side of it. When he reached the first window, he looked in. It was a dining room, but he could look through it to see the front door, where the woman stood, staring out the peephole in the door. She pulled away from it and Jack Till ducked down and bent low to sneak along the side of the house. He stopped at the next window and cautiously looked in. It was a kitchen.

She was at the counter across the room, reaching for a telephone. He knew that she might be calling the police to tell them he was lurking around, but he had to stay. She pushed eleven digits: long distance. He felt in his pocket and found the small microphone he had been hoping to plant inside the house. He looked for an opening on the outer wall of the house, and found a rounded metal awning that jutted a few inches from the wall, about six inches wide, with a metal flap. He could tell from the position high up and at the windowless portion of the kitchen that it must be the opening for the ventilation hood over the stove. He looked around for a way up, and saw three wheeled plastic garbage bins. He moved the heaviest one under the vent opening, stood on it, attached the thin power cord from the receiver to clip on the tiny microphone, and lowered it into the ventilator duct in the kitchen.

The duct seemed to amplify the sounds. He could hear the woman walking around, her footsteps sharp and heavy, as she listened to someone on the other end of the call. Then she said, "What he said was, 'My name is Jack Till. I'm here to see Ann Delatorre. Is this the right house?'" She listened. "No, he didn't say that right away. It was later, when he was about to leave. He asked me if I knew anyone else named Delatorre around here. He said it was your married name—that your maiden name was Harper."

Jack Till lifted his wrist close to his face. The call had been placed at 8:07. It was July 20.

The woman said, "He's sort of tall. Maybe six feet one or two. He's in good shape. I don't know. Yeah, he could be forty, I suppose. He said he helped you six years ago. Did he? I mean if he's for real. Is he telling the truth?" Jack Till could hear frustration in the woman's voice. As soon as she hung up, staying here was going to get very risky. He pulled the vent open and held it while he gently pulled up his microphone and pocketed it. He quietly climbed down from the garbage bin and rolled it back to the other side of the driveway, then hurried to his car and drove toward his hotel.

On the drive back into Las Vegas, Till had a few minutes to think. Watching the door of the house open and seeing the wrong woman inside had brought disappointment. Only a moment later had come the shock, the recognition that his disappointment was so painful because it was personal, not professional. He had been allowing himself to think about Wendy Harper again, to picture her and remember her voice, but he had not realized how much emotion he had invested in the prospect of seeing her again. In his mind, she had always been the woman he had met in the wrong way at the wrong time, the wasted chance.

Maybe the shock had been a corrective. He needed to see what was happening, not what he wished would happen. He went to his room and looked at the skip-tracer's printout for Ann Delatorre and found the account number and company she used for telephone service. He called the company's billing department and said, "I'm calling because I'd like to cancel our long-distance service. We're going to be moving to another city. We don't have a new address yet. We'll be in hotels at first, so I don't have a place to transfer the number to. But I'd like to get a final bill as soon as possible so I can take care of it before I leave. How soon do you suppose you could do that? Wow, that's wonderful. Thanks."

Till drove out to Henderson again the next morning. He spotted the letter carrier on her route, and then drove past her a couple of times to check her progress until he saw her delivering mail on the block where Ann Delatorre lived. He checked his watch: one-fifteen. He spent most of the day and evening watching the house to see if Wendy Harper had come, but there was no sign of a visitor. The next two mornings, Till drove by again, but there was still no unfamiliar car in the neighborhood.

On the third day at two-fifteen, he pulled his car into Ann Delatorre's driveway, went to the door, and pretended to press the doorbell. With his other hand, he reached quickly into the mailbox, took out the telephone bill he had requested, and slipped it into the inner pocket of his sport coat. After a moment, he turned, walked to his car, and drove away.

He parked at the Crown Pointe Promenade, opened the telephone bill, and scanned the list of toll calls. On July 20 at 8:07 P.M., Ann Delatorre had made a call to a number in the 415 area code. That was San Francisco. He wrote the number in the notebook he carried, tore up the bill, and threw it into a trash receptacle in the mall. At eight-thirty, he returned to Ann Delatorre's house.

He parked in the driveway again and knocked on the door. This time the door did not open a crack. It swung open abruptly, and

Ann Delatorre stood in front of him, aiming a revolver at his chest. The barrel was short, and from his point of view, the muzzle looked cavernous. He said, "It's only me again. Jack Till. If you pull the trigger on that thing, bits of my heart and lungs will be sprayed all over your entry."

"I know that. I'm glad to hear that you know it, too." She took three steps backward. "Come inside and close the door."

Jack Till stared into the woman's eyes. It was a risk to step inside with a woman aiming a gun at his chest. He wasn't quite sure how the law worked in Nevada, but in California, if a stranger like him was shot inside a woman's house, his murder was likely to be called self-defense.

"I know what you're thinking," she said. "But if I wanted to kill you, it wouldn't matter if you were in or out. I'd leave town."

He took a step forward, his eyes still on hers, and she took another step backward to maintain the distance between them. He looked down at the gun in her hand. He could see the dimpled gray noses of the bullets gleaming dully in the cylinder, waiting.

He closed the door and she moved the gun to the side so it was aimed at a spot to the left of his chest. "Thank you," he said. "I hate to see you walking backward with that aimed at me."

"I can still kill you."

"But at least now you'll have to want to."

"That way, into the living room." She pointed with her free hand. "Sit on the couch."

He stepped in and sat down, leaned back with his arms stretched out and became still. He wanted to keep his hands in sight.

She sat in a chair ten feet from him and rested the gun on the arm so she could keep it ready without getting tired. "You said that you were a private detective. Who are you working for?"

"I'm working for myself. Finding her was something that needed to be done, so I'm doing it."

"Are you after me?"

"No. I don't know you. I'm searching for a woman whose name was Wendy Harper."

"Why?"

"She came to me because somebody was after her. I helped her to get lost. Now a man who used to be her boyfriend is being charged with her murder."

"What if she's dead?"

"I don't think you would let me in and talk to me like this if she were dead. I'm trying to let her know that Eric Fuller is in trouble because of what we did."

"What do you want her to do about it?"

"I want her to come back to Los Angeles with me, just long enough to prove to the District Attorney's office that she's alive. They'll drop the charges, and she can go back to wherever she is now."

"*If* she's alive. And if she's *still* alive at the end of it."

Jack Till reverted to the tactic he had used as a homicide detective, trying to become the friend who understood and forgave. "Look, I'm on her side. I'm sure if you know anything at all about what happened, you know that already. I kept her alive once. And I can see you're on her side, too. I can tell you're scared, but you're trying to protect her and do what's best for her. So am I, but protecting someone can be tough, and it can be dangerous. You're not wrong to worry." He shook his head slowly, as though he were thinking about specific threats that she didn't know about yet.

"Go on."

"That gun isn't a bad idea. If anything, it's not enough. If you and I could just cooperate on this, I think we'd all be safer. Now, I know you called somebody right after I left here the other night. Was it Wendy?"

"It was my mother."

He let his disappointment in her show. After a moment he said, "I taught her how to hide. I thought that would be enough to keep her safe, but things have changed. The man she was running from before seems to have put out some serious money to get her. That means high-end killers. Why won't you help me?"

"I owe her."

"Then you should want what's best for her."

"I do. I'm not sure I know what that is, and I'm not sure you do, either."

"How long have you known her?"

She stared at him in silence, thinking for a moment, then shrugged. "All right. There's no reason not to tell you, so I will. I met her six years ago. It must have been about two weeks after you left her at the airport in Santa Barbara. I was walking along a hallway in my apartment building. I was crying, so I didn't see clearly where I was going, and I came around a corner and bumped into her. We looked at each other, and I could see she was crying, too. It was so stupid that we stood there thinking about it for a second, and started to laugh."

"Did she live there, too?"

"Yes. It was a terrible place, a whole building full of losers and people who were running away from something. It was a couple of miles north of town, and nobody talked to anybody, but after that, the two of us were friends."

"What were you doing there?"

She narrowed her eyes for a moment, then seemed to change her mind. "Boyfriend troubles."

"What kind?"

"He was looking for me. I left; he wanted me back."

"Where was that?"

"Another city. It doesn't matter to you which one unless you want to hurt me. You say you don't, and anyway, I'm not going to tell you anything that will give you the power. I met him, and I went with him. My mother was religious. She put all my stuff on the front steps and locked the door and the gate. I stayed with Howard, and that was hard. He wanted a lot from me, and I did it. I cooked for him and his friends and did all the work around the place. He would sell crack to cars that pulled up to his corner. I held the money and the crack and his gun. See, if you got caught, they wouldn't charge you as an adult until you were sixteen."

"He told you that?"

"That's right."

"Did he tell you that you couldn't get shot?"

"He didn't talk about that. But you've got him right. That's what he was. He was the one who got the money and I was the one who got the trouble."

"What kind?"

"Howard got into a fight with the guy who sold him drugs. It wasn't the kind of fight where you lay low for a while and then patch it up. It was the kind where you don't even go back to your place to get your clothes. You leave town."

"Is that when he turned you out?"

Her facial muscles seemed to slacken, so she had no real expression. "Yes." She watched him for some particular reaction that she must have seen before, but she seemed not to detect it. She started again slowly. "He said it was just going to be once, and then we would be safe, and he would always be grateful. It was a town where we had never been, and nobody would know me or anything, so once it was done it would be over."

"Was it?"

"What do you think?"

"I don't think so."

"It went on for about a week, until we had enough money to move on to another city, a bigger one. But Howard couldn't make a connection. The man who was supposed to be in that city and willing to help him get set up was gone. He had to go out and spend money to get to know people who would introduce him to the people he needed to meet." She sighed. "And the money ran out."

"He turned you out again."

She nodded. "This time it was different. The first time, we were both out, and I was dressed up and made up, and we would see a man and Howard would ask me if that one was okay, and I would either say, 'Please, not that one,' or 'Okay.' If I said okay, then he would ask the man if he was interested, and they would talk prices. Then I would talk to the man and take him up to our room. Howard would follow and stand outside to make sure nothing terrible happened. This time he set it up differently. I had to go out alone on the street where the men came to find girls. I didn't want to. I was cold. I was scared of the men and the cops, and the other girls out there who looked like they wanted to beat me up or chase me off.

"Howard told me that if I didn't go with anybody who didn't have a really nice car and nice clothes, I would be safe. I turned a few down, and then a man came by in a Jaguar. He was maybe sixty years old and dressed in a black sport coat and blue jeans. When he held the steering wheel with his left hand, the coat sleeve slipped down a little and I could see a fancy watch. He leaned over to talk to me through the open window on the passenger side. He said, 'Miss? Are you working tonight?' I remember how polite he was. I was amazed at my luck. I could get into the car and off the street and not be cold or afraid for a while. I was so relieved that I really did have feelings for him, a little bit. I got in and he drove to the place where I was staying, and we went in. When we got there, I expected Howard would be around, but I didn't see him. I had to unlock the door and turn on the light so we could go in. But Howard had been in the room, looking out the window and waiting. He had heard us come along the hall to the door, heard me get the key out to unlock it, and then hid. I locked the door after us and started to do my job, what I had promised this older man.

"All of a sudden, out of a closet came Howard, holding a knife. He scared the man with it, stole his wallet, his watch, and his car keys, and left him there tied up. Howard took me with him, drove out of that town to the next one. He stripped the car and left it, used the credit cards for a few hours to buy stuff, and kept the cash. The next night, when he got a room and sent me out on the street again, I went out and just kept going."

"You ran to Las Vegas?"

"Not at first. All I did was get out of that city and go to another one. I got a job in a women's clothing store. After a couple of months, I came home one night and I saw that the lights of my apartment were on. I saw him in the window, waiting. He was sure I was stupid enough to go right in. I wasn't."

"What did he want? Did you figure that out?"

"Me. Sometimes I thought he wanted me back, and sometimes I thought he showed up only after I'd been on my own for a while because he knew if he gave me a couple of months I would save some money and he could take it."

"He doesn't seem to have found you after that. What happened?"

"Ann Delatorre. We got to be friends. We told each other everything. After about a year, she gave me a present."

"The name?"

"It's more than a name. It's a life. She stayed in that apartment building for only a few months. By the time I met her, she had already put a down payment on this house. She was getting ready to move in. She brought me with her."

"Just like that?"

"She knew I had to have a place to live where he wouldn't look for me. This is Ann Delatorre's house. We both knew that if he thought I might be in Nevada, then a suburban tract in Henderson wouldn't be the place. He'd think I would be in a crummy part of the city turning tricks."

"How did the two of you get by?"

"She set up the name and used it for a while, bought this house, and let me stay with her. She started a mail-order business that she ran off the Internet, selling overstocks of name-brand clothes. I worked with her, handling the packing and shipping and a lot of the hours online. We never said it was permanent, either of us. But we both knew that staying safe meant staying hidden, and that the longer we lived quietly in this neighborhood running a mail-order business, the less likely we'd be found."

"And then she just walked away from it, didn't she?"

"You think she wouldn't do that?"

"I know she would. She did it once before."

"I think she just got anxious, worried that she hadn't run hard enough, or far enough. She gave me everything: the birth certificate, her credit cards, the deed to this house, the incorporation papers for the business. She withdrew the money from the business account at the bank and helped me start a new account at another bank that would know me as Ann Delatorre. She went with me to New Mexico so I could apply for a driver's license in the new name. Then she left."

"Where is she?"

"I don't know."

"She gave you her name. You know that somebody is after her, too, don't you?"

"Of course. We told each other everything."

"But you kept the name, anyway—Ann Delatorre. That was part of the deal, wasn't it? You could have the house and the mail-order business, but it had to stay in the name Ann Delatorre. You're her early-warning system. If somebody came for her, the mostly likely way they would do it was the way I did—by tracing the name change and then finding this address. If anyone came here, you would warn her."

"It's not like that. Neither of us believed anyone would ever come."

"I mean nobody any harm. I'm only trying to save her best friend from going to trial for her murder."

Ann Delatorre looked defiant. "He's not her best friend anymore. I am."

"Then you'll let me talk to her. Where is she?"

"I don't know."

"You do know, or you could never warn her. You're here for that. You have something. Is it just a phone number?"

Ann Delatorre looked at him, puzzled. "You're so smart, but you're not so smart."

"No?"

"If somebody comes for her here, either they'll kill me, or I'll kill them. Either way, it will be in the newspapers, won't it? All she needs to do is type the name Ann Delatorre on the Internet once a day, to see if it's been in the news."

He stared at her. She was still holding the gun on the arm of the chair. It was not aimed nearer to his heart, but no farther away, either. "You aren't going to trust me."

"I can't."

"I'm going to stand up now." He leaned forward slowly and raised himself from the couch without making any rapid or abrupt movements. Ann Delatorre rose, too, and retreated around her chair to keep it between them. As he walked toward the door, he said, "You're a good friend. I can see that. But somebody else is searching for her now. The man who's after her hires people to do his killing. They're pros, so as long as he can pay them, they won't stop looking. Sooner or later, they'll trace her this far. Expect them."

As he opened the door, he turned to look at her. She still held the gun on him. "I do."

15

I**T WAS NEARLY** ten o'clock in the evening when Paul Turner drove the rental car to the corner of the street where Ann Delatorre lived. "He's gone. He's been to that house twice today," said Paul. "I'll bet he set this up six years ago: If he ever needed to get in touch with Wendy Harper, he would come here, and Ann Delatorre would know where she was."

"Till's amazing," Sylvie said. "He never let anybody know that he had even met Wendy Harper, let alone taken her away. But he still bothered to set up a woman nobody ever heard of to act as a go-between."

"You know, this could easily be the meeting place. But we can't assume that."

"What do we do?"

"It's like watching a magic trick. You keep your eye on the hand that holds the ball, and ignore everything else." He looked at the notebook computer on Sylvie's lap, and watched the blue dots appearing on the map. "We follow Till's car."

He pulled out from the curb and drove out to the Boulder Highway toward Las Vegas. When he reached the city and turned left toward the Strip, he saw bright spotlights and construction machinery ahead. He took three quick lane changes, moving in and out of traffic. Then he made a wide turn. There were pockets of road construction everywhere in Las Vegas, constant revision and replacement. This road was being widened to accommodate the expansion of a hotel, but tonight all but one of the lanes were blocked by big yellow machines hauling asphalt or stirring up clouds of dust. Paul's hand was always sure and steady as he swerved to achieve position.

Sylvie wasn't worried about catching up with Till's car. She watched Paul's dark eyes shine as he looked ahead, and she knew he was looking ahead in time, too. He was working out details.

"We're going to need the two .38s, and also the rifle. Make sure they're loaded and lying where you can reach them, so we can pick one up and fire."

"Okay." Sylvie released her seat belt, knelt on her seat, and reached between the bucket seats to the floor behind her. She carefully pulled the SKS rifle between the seats to the front. She had to keep it low and covered with her jacket because the drivers of trucks and bulldozers they passed could see down into the car.

Sylvie was comfortable with the .38 revolvers they had picked up from Paul's gun dealer. Revolvers were simple, and the differences between them were mostly cosmetic. But the SKS rifle had a nasty profile like a black wasp, with a folding metal stock and a pistol grip that made it short enough to swing around inside a car. The SKS was Russian, so the markings that hadn't been drilled off meant nothing to her, and the action felt stiff and unpredictable. The spring-operated moving parts seemed likely to pinch her fingers. She held it carefully under her coat and reached behind her to the floor for the ammunition clip. "Do you want me to crank a round into the chamber of this thing?"

"Go ahead."

"Okay. Just so you know it's there." She clicked the magazine into the underside of the receiver, then held the rifle by its pistol grip and pulled back the charging lever. She checked the safety catch and then carefully placed the rifle between her seat and the door with the barrel upward so any accidental discharge would only blow a hole in the rented car's roof. Then she reached into the glove compartment and took out the two .38 pistols, careful not to bump the threading on the ends of the barrels against anything. She checked the cylinder of each, put them both on her lap under the coat and waited for Paul.

The SKS would punch through the sheet metal of a car without slowing down very much. The .38 pistols didn't have the same piercing power, but they would be lethal fired through glass at short range. Paul must be planning to take Jack Till and Wendy Harper in Till's car and kill them both at once, without any preliminaries. He always seemed to know what he wanted and how to get it. That was one of the things that she had always loved about him.

When they had met, she had still been married to Darren McKee. After all this time, it was hard to remember what it had felt like being married to Darren. He had been short, and had come up to a spot about even with the middle of her ear. She could remember embracing him and feeling his hair tickling her earlobe. She could still recall how bristly his mustache had felt on her skin, but that wasn't a feeling anymore, it was just information. She couldn't bring back his smell or hear his voice or feel his shape on her hands or her body. He had no weight or volume in her mind anymore.

Darren pampered and controlled her. He allowed her to buy all the clothes she wanted, but he would look at them when she brought them home, and if he disapproved of them he made her take them back to the store. He scheduled her days, so there was a two-hour period for exercise, then an hour for hair and makeup. Darren believed it was beneficial for her to leave the house every afternoon, so from one to five she was free to shop, see friends, or go to matinees. She had a cell phone, but she almost never made a call. Darren would call her several times a day to see if she was on schedule. If she wasn't, he would adjust the schedule to give her more time.

The money had been a big surprise to her. Darren had been managing the stripping tours of adult-film stars for about fifteen years by then. As a group, his clients required a great deal of managing—some were addicted to drugs, some were not very bright or practical, some were lazy—but they were good at attracting male audiences. Darren acted as producer. The club paid to book a show, and Darren paid the women salaries. So instead of taking ten or fifteen percent as a manager would have, he took about sixty, and let the women get rich on tips.

Before she had learned that Darren had money, he had talked her into signing a prenuptial agreement. "Honey," he said. "It's to protect your money and my pride. I can't have people in the industry thinking I married a hot young star so I could live off her money. It's emasculating. If we sign the agreement, our assets stay separate. I can say I support my wife, and haven't touched a cent of her money." She had signed. Shortly afterward, she realized how he had stayed rich through three marriages. But it had not bothered her.

What eventually did begin to bother her was that she was twenty-one and he was forty. She was bored. He was busy, obsessed with business, and not much fun. Then one day she was at the gym finishing the exercise class that Darren had put into her schedule, and on the way into the locker room she saw a sheet on the bulletin board. It said "DANCE CLASS: BALLROOM DANCING." The small print said the class was to take place in the aerobics workout room later that afternoon, so she stayed to look through the glass wall into the room.

When Sylvie heard the music and saw the woman who was running the class demonstrate the dance, Sylvie began to move to the music, unconsciously imitating the steps. But the instructor—she had introduced herself as Fran a moment earlier—noticed, and beckoned to her through the glass.

Sylvie didn't see Paul at first. She came into the room, keeping her eyes on the instructor and taking a few tentative steps of a samba, and then he was there beside her and they were dancing together. That was all. They had become partners. When the class was over, Paul stood with her for a few minutes in the big room outside where there were stationary bikes and treadmills and Nautilus machines. They exchanged names and the short versions of their histories that people constructed and carried around like calling cards. When she said, "I've got to go," and he said, "I'll look forward to seeing you on Thursday," she walked off and noted that the capsule autobiography she had given him was a newly revised version. She had not mentioned that she had a husband.

On Thursday they simply walked in when the aerobics class ended and stood together but apart from the rest of the dance students, waiting to begin. At the class she wore her hair in the chignon she had worn all those years in ballet. Fran, the dance instructor, was a skinny middle-aged vegan who had been a physical-education teacher at one time. She moved like an anthropologist demonstrating the dances of a tribal culture. The steps were all mimicked with technical accuracy, but the passion and the grace were what she had not been able to bring back with her. She had to evoke them with words, exhort the better dancers to supply the missing qualities, and the best dancers were Sylvie and Paul. Paul was the sort of man that Madame Bazetnikova had called *un danseur noble*. But it wasn't about him. It was, as in ballet, about *her*.

When she danced with Paul, Sylvie felt herself become beautiful and wild and somehow triumphant. After years of slouching, she held herself erect and was still not nearly as tall as he was. She had tried since she was in high school to look small, so she wouldn't be noticed. Now she wanted to be noticed, to be admired. She felt light and graceful, as though she could float a foot above the floor.

When the music ended for the last time, and Fran put on her oversized sweater to leave, the rest of the class followed. Paul simply placed his hand on the small of Sylvie's back and exerted the same gentle pressure that had been there since the dance had begun.

They talked as they walked, mostly about the dancing, the parts they liked the most, the parts they wanted to work on and improve. But Sylvie was not thinking about the words. She was thinking about the large male hand on her back.

She thought about what he might mean by placing it there, and what it meant when she let it stay, and when she obeyed its pressure, walking where he guided her instead of turning to go into the women's locker room to dress for her workout. He conducted her to the passenger side of his car, opened the door, and drove her to his apartment. On the way, they talked about the traffic, the summer heat, the houses on his street, and not about where they were going. She told herself it was faintly ridiculous for her to have been in those movies, but now to feel the tension of this moment, to feel the delicate ambiguity of each word or touch or glance.

She let him lead her into the apartment as he led her in the dance. She let him undress her, and she felt, for the first time, a sense of rightness. This was the way she had always wanted things to be. Later, when it was over, she lay in Paul's bed for a few minutes, then sat up, walked into his living room, putting on her clothes as she found them on the floor. On the way back, they talked as they had before, about the songs they loved and the dance class.

The next Tuesday, the same thing happened, and Sylvie realized that it hadn't been an isolated event, a mutual lapse that they would each silently wonder about forever. That had been the lie she had told herself. Soon she was lying to Darren about the exercise sessions she missed at the gym and about her partners in the dance class. Sometimes she would describe for him men who really were in the class, and sometimes, because there were more women than men, she would say that she had danced only with women that day.

After a few weeks, she told Paul that she was married. He said, "I saw the mark on your finger where you took off your ring."

Two months later, Paul said, "We should be married. It's time to get your divorce."

She told him about the prenuptial agreement she had signed. "If I divorce him, I won't have much money—only what I could save before I got married."

"Does he have a lot of money?"

"Yes."

"Then he's made a mistake."

"Why?"

"Because he's only left you one way to get your share of it."

Sylvie let the moment pass. She never asked, "What do you mean?" She said nothing. For two more months, she thought about what Paul had said. She knew he had meant it at least a little, because he had said it the way some men made jokes—the kind that really weren't jokes, but questions. She detected certain feelings in herself that she should not be having. She resented Darren for having caught her at a weak moment and holding out marriage as the alternative to a bad part of her life. She began to wish that Darren were dead.

But Paul took care of Darren by himself. He waited for Darren to go out on one of his tours with a couple of women who had used the names Ray-Lee and Kay-Lee in their last few films. All actresses in adult cinema liked to do girl-on-girl scenes because they were so much easier, less dangerous and strenuous than regular sex. These two had temporarily captured the imaginations of the segment of the audience who liked to watch that sort of thing.

Paul flew to New York, drove to Philadelphia, and waited for Darren and the women to reach town. He took a room in the hotel where they would be staying, then waited until a morning when the women left the room beside Darren's to go to the hotel's spa. He stood outside Darren's door holding a grocery bag and knocked. When Darren opened the door, he pushed his way in and closed the door. Paul's bag held a .32 revolver with a plastic one-quart water bottle taped over the barrel to suppress the sound. Paul fired once into Darren's chest, then stood over him and fired into his head. He walked out with the gun still inside the bag, and closed the door. If anyone heard the noises, they did not interpret them as shots. The women found Darren two hours later, when Paul was already in the airport waiting for his plane home.

Sylvie was awakened abruptly that morning by a ringing doorbell, and opened the door to a pair of police officers. Since this was only four hours after Darren had been killed, the visit ended forever any suspicion that she'd had any direct role in his death: No flight from the East Coast could have brought her home that quickly.

Even so, when Paul paid his respects before the funeral, he told her that they must not call, write letters, or meet each other again for three months because police often kept family members of murder victims under surveillance. Ninety-one days later, they met, apparently by chance, at the Ritz-Carlton Hotel in Chicago. They returned to Los Angeles on different days, Sylvie started going to the dance class again, and Sylvie and Paul had a period of simulated courtship.

Sylvie watched Paul driving the streets of Las Vegas, and felt a light-headed tingle of excitement about him. There was nothing in the world as erotic as being with a man who had killed her husband to take her. The breathless feeling was still there after fifteen years. But as she watched, she could see his face was changing, taking on a new expression. "What is it?"

"Look."

She looked ahead. As she did, the big red-striped shape of a Southwest Airlines jet glided over them and onto a distant runway. "Is he at the airport?"

"His car is at the airport. I think he turned it in."

"Then how are we going to find out where he went?"

PAUL WALKED CAREFULLY along the side of Ann Delatorre's house in the darkness, keeping his shoes from making any noise. There were no security-company signs on the lawn, no stickers, and no keypads visible through the windows, and he wasn't surprised. People on the run didn't want any conversations with the police officers who responded to false alarms, or even minor burglaries. They wanted everything quiet and undisturbed. He liked that. What he didn't like was that many of them made up for it by arming themselves.

Paul peered around the corner of the house and saw Sylvie waiting outside the back door. In the darkness behind the house he could just see that her right hand was down at the side of her body, and he knew she was holding the pistol beside her thigh, where it would not be seen if a light came on. She had screwed the silencers on the threaded muzzles of the two .38 revolvers. Paul liked to use the lower-caliber, low-velocity cartridges for jobs like this. If Ann Delatorre could be intimidated by a gun, a .38 with a silencer on it would scare her as much as a .44 magnum, and if she couldn't, then it would be big enough to kill her.

Sylvie gave Paul a silent wave, and Paul moved back toward the front of the house. He was searching for the room where Ann Delatorre slept. He had looked in at two dark bedrooms, and seen only the smooth, tight bedspreads and undented pillows on the beds. At last he found what he had been looking for. The third bedroom had its blinds closed, but he was able to put his eye to the corner and make out the shape of a sleeping person on the bed.

He stood still for a few seconds and listened. The night was quiet out here in the suburbs. He knew that Route 215 swung through Henderson, but it was too distant for him to hear the cars. He went around the house to a spare bedroom where the door was closed. Any incidental sounds he made getting in would be less likely to reach Ann Delatorre's ears from there.

Paul used a glass cutter to etch a small half-circle in the windowpane just at the latch. He ran a strip of duct tape across the semicircle, then put on his leather gloves and pounded it once with his hand. There was only a dull thump and a click as the semicircle of glass was punched inward and held by the tape. He peeled back the tape carefully and brought the small piece of glass with it, then reached inside, unlocked the latch, and slid the window open six inches.

He put his head to the opening and listened. When he heard nothing but the hum of the air conditioner, he lifted the window all the way, and climbed inside. Then he crouched on the floor for a few seconds, letting his eyes adjust to the deeper darkness. Paul had killed several people at night while they were asleep in their beds, and he had come to enjoy it. He moved quietly to the door, stood still for a few seconds, then turned the knob and pulled the door inward.

The sudden bang made him jump in alarm, and the muzzle-flash blinded him. He had leaped to the side instinctively, so he was behind the wall again, and he squatted there. He heard footsteps dash out of the bedroom across the hall, already past him and around the corner before he was able to get his gun out of his jacket.

Paul leaned around the doorway and fired, but he knew that the shot was at least a whole second late. It was just a way to fight his paralysis and do something. He ran down the hallway, knowing that if she were waiting to shoot him, the place she would aim was at the corner. He ran past it into another doorway and aimed up the next hall. All he saw was an open door, and the night beyond.

She had made it outside. He dashed to the back door and heard Sylvie's voice rasp, "Drop it at your feet. Now turn around and go back inside."

The woman's shape appeared in the doorway, and then Paul could see Sylvie's taller silhouette. She stepped in and closed the door, and Paul turned on the light.

The woman was black. She was barefoot, wearing a pair of gray sweatpants and a white T-shirt that said UNLV. Paul stared at her. "Who are you?"

"My name is Ann Delatorre."

"Where is Wendy Harper?"

"Who's Wendy Harper?"

Paul lunged forward and punched her in the ribs with his free hand. He suspected that he had broken a couple of them, because when she tried to straighten, the pain overpowered her for a moment.

Paul grasped a handful of her hair and shook her, then wrenched it to the side so her head hit the wall. "You know her. Say it."

"I know her."

He held her hair and jerked her head up so she had to look at him. "If you tell us where she is, I'll give you ten thousand dollars. You can get on a plane and take a vacation, then come back and nobody will know how we found out. You'll never see us again."

"I don't know where she is."

Paul swung her head against the wall again, harder this time. It hit, then she slid and collapsed onto the floor. He waited a few seconds until she seemed to regain consciousness, then kicked her.

Sylvie began to worry. The woman on the floor was getting hurt, maybe incapacitated, but she didn't seem to be afraid. Sylvie whispered, "Don't kill her, or she can't tell us."

He said, "Miss Delatorre. Can you understand what I'm saying?"

"Yes."

"Then think for a minute. I want something small and simple. I'll pay you money for it. If you don't tell me, I'll inflict suffering. Don't answer now, automatically. Just listen and think." He turned to Sylvie. "Go to the kitchen and bring me back a butcher knife."

Sylvie walked into the kitchen. She didn't want to turn on another light, but she didn't see any knives on the counter, so she'd have to look in some drawers. She heard a growling cry—not of pain, but anger and hatred. She pivoted and ran back to the hallway.

When she emerged from the kitchen she was horrified. It was the woman who was making the noise. Somehow she had tripped Paul and now she was on him, scratching and biting. He was using his left hand to hold her off, and his right forearm to protect his face, but he couldn't get a grip on her, and she kept reaching for the gun, and when he pulled it away, she would go for his eyes.

Sylvie rushed forward and poked her gun against the woman's head. "Stop it! Stop!" she shouted, but the woman whirled suddenly, her eyes alive, almost joyful as she snatched at Sylvie's gun.

Sylvie fired into her head. The woman's body fell where it was, straddling Paul in the narrow corridor, while he lay on his back. He pushed at her body, then rolled and kicked himself free of it. "Shit," he said. He stood up with difficulty. "This is a fucking disaster."

Sylvie stared at him, the horror undiminished since the instant when she had heard that growl. Paul was wet with the dead woman's blood. Her blood had spattered the hallway, even a few drops on the ceiling, but the wound had emptied onto Paul's chest and neck, so his clothes were soaked. He had three long red scratches on his left cheek, where the woman's nails had raked him, and a nail mark under his right eye. He pulled his shirt away from his chest and opened it a couple of buttons, then looked at the skin beneath.

"Oh, God, she bit you!"

"Yeah. Bit, scratched, tried to get my eyes."

"She was crazy."

"Yeah. I just looked away from her for a second when you went toward the kitchen. She was waiting for it, I guess." He looked down at the body. "I sure wish you hadn't killed her."

"What?"

"That was what she wanted, not what I wanted. Sylvie, you knew we needed her alive to answer questions."

"What could I do? She was hurting you."

"It doesn't matter. It's over. No use in arguing."

"But what did you want me to do?"

"You could have shot her anywhere, but not in the head. She would have been in pain and too weak to cause trouble. We could have kept her alive and made her talk."

Sylvie walked into the kitchen.

"Wait. Where are you going?"

"I don't want to think of you as an asshole. I'm going to give you a chance to stop being one."

"Sylvie, this isn't the time. We need to do some searching. Find some rubber gloves and get started while I get her out of the way."

"What do you want me to look for?"

"Anything that would tell us where Wendy Harper is—a stub from a plane ticket, an address book, a letter. Use your imagination."

Sylvie fought her sense of injustice. She had saved his life, and now he was blaming her for losing what the woman knew. She opened the cabinet below the sink, found a box of disposable rubber gloves, and put a pair on. She searched drawers and cabinets, leaving them open so she wouldn't look in the same place twice.

She passed by the entrance to the hallway and looked at Paul without letting him see her. He was cleaning up—wrapping the body in a blanket. She kept moving. Let him do it by himself. She had tried to do something nice for him by killing her, and he had not appreciated it. Let him think about that for a while.

Sylvie moved through the house, opening drawers and cabinets, feeling her way through stacks of folded linens, moving cans and bottles aside to see if something was hidden behind them. She found a drawer where old bills were kept, but none of them seemed to contain any information that she could use. She found a sheet of names and addresses printed out beside the computer in one of the spare rooms, but then another sheet below it, and another, a whole stack of dozens of pages. They seemed to be mailing lists of customers for some kind of business.

Sylvie woke up the computer and tried to sign on, but the password had not been stored. She had started typing passwords like "Ann" and "Ann's computer" and "Open sesame" when she saw the purse. It was a reddish brown Coach shoulder bag with a small silver clasp, and Sylvie's first thought was that she liked it, but she pushed that thought out of her mind and picked it up.

She looked inside, and found an address book. She didn't have much hope it would say "Wendy Harper," but it might contain the computer password or something else she could use. She searched through every page, but found nothing that she could identify as useful. She found Ann Delatorre's cell phone, turned it on and began to scroll through the stored phone numbers, then the recently called numbers. They were all local.

She looked inside the wallet. There were a few credit cards, a library card, a couple of business cards from companies around Las Vegas. The driver's license looked real, but it didn't say Ann Delatorre. It said L. Ann Delatorre. She found no passwords or out-of-town addresses, but in the back of the wallet, she found something that made her draw in her breath suddenly. It was a printed card that had come with the wallet. It said, "If found, please call" and in a woman's handwriting it gave a telephone number and the word "Reward."

Sylvie looked at the number on the desk telephone. That was a 702 number. She checked Ann Delatorre's cell phone. The little screen showed a 702 number, too.

She understood Ann Delatorre, without knowing her at all. She had been a woman who had been absolutely resolved to protect Wendy Harper. She would never have written down her phone number for herself. She had memorized it a long time ago and would remember it forever. She had known that she wouldn't lose her wallet. But she had also known that someday she might be killed. There would be police, or at least someone who found her body and would go through her purse. They would call the number. And on the other end, Wendy Harper would learn that Ann Delatorre was dead. "Paul?" she called. "I'm pretty sure I found the phone number. It's a 415. Isn't that San Francisco?"

16

IT WAS PROBABLY the last flight of the night—certainly the last flight to San Francisco. The long-distance number Ann Delatorre had called was in the 415 area code, so now Jack Till was in an airplane looking out the small plastic window at the lighted maintenance area beside the flight line. The ten minutes or so while he waited for the seats beside him to fill always guaranteed a low level of suspense. The seats on Southwest were not assigned, so anybody could sit anywhere, and night flights usually had a few empty seats.

Till watched attractive women walking up the aisle clutching their purses and oversized carry-ons, their big, liquid eyes narrowing in pure self-interest as they hunted for the seat they considered the best. He was sometimes amused in a cold way when he saw what they chose. They did not often choose to sit beside Jack Till.

Till was tall but thin, and didn't have the sort of frame with elbows and shoulders that encroached on a neighbor's space. He always wore a good sport coat and crisply pressed shirt when he was working, and travel was work. He knew he wasn't ugly. But he supposed he looked like what he was: a retired cop whose face showed some wear.

He watched the next woman's eyes zigzag from one side of the aisle to the other, reading faces. They passed over his quickly, not quite afraid of him, at least not in an airplane, but not comfortable near him, either. He supposed it was because after all of those years protecting people like her, he had picked up the look of the people he'd been protecting them from. It didn't matter. He wasn't interested in company.

His mother would have been offended on his behalf, but his mother had been a difficult woman who was offended regularly. She married his father in an act of speculation, like buying a piece of land cheap on the guess that any chunk of the planet might have something valuable on it. Ray Till had already been drafted for the war when she met him, and she might easily have been a young widow. But he returned from Europe a couple of years later a captain, with three battlefield promotions and a silver star. He was a quiet man with blue eyes that had beneath them an underlying toughness, and maybe the toughness had been what had attracted her. He became an electrician and wired whole developments in the San Fernando Valley during the building boom, when vast orange and lemon groves were cut down and incinerated in bonfires to make room for the new houses.

Till's parents became mildly prosperous, but there were some times when Helen Till was unkindly reminded that her husband wasn't a doctor or a lawyer. Even a minor executive in the movie business held a higher social standing than an electrical contractor, no matter how many men he sent out in trucks each day to wire people's swimming-pool heaters and electronic-gate openers.

When Jack decided to go to the police academy, his parents did not understand, because he had never given them the reason. They never exactly accepted his decision, but they became used to it. Helen and Ray both lived long enough to see their only son make Detective Sergeant, when no likely scenario involved anybody shooting at him. But his mother had strong opinions on every aspect of his life.

When Jack brought a girl named Karen home from college to meet his parents for the first time, his mother greeted her warmly and then retired a distance, pretending to be arranging places on the table, but really to observe Karen while she talked to Ray and Jack. No, there was someone else present, too. Who was it? Aunt Nancy, his mother's younger sister.

Jack remembered seeing them talking in the kitchen, and then he saw his mother give one of her shrugs. Helen Till was not a woman who spent much time in a state of uncertainty. When she shrugged, it never meant "I don't know." It always meant "I can't imagine why *everybody* doesn't know."

Later, Jack left with Karen. He spoke with his mother the next day, when he came by to thank her for the elaborate dinner. He said, "Well? What did you think of Karen?"

She said, "As a date, or as a candidate for governor?"

That did it, saying it that way. She had directed his attention away from Karen's beauty and the extreme care she gave to dressing and grooming herself, and onto the sparse and oddly assorted furniture of her mind.

His mother looked into his eyes, and then shrugged. "If she loves you, the nicest, smartest girl in town will do everything the biggest whore will do. And she'll mean it."

Years later, when he married Rose, it was without the benefit of his mother's advice. But she liked Rose and approved of her. Rose was cheerful and eager to have fun, the sort of pretty woman who had sun-induced freckles, an athletic, lithe body and a sort of buoyant energy. She didn't mind that Jack was a police officer. In retrospect, he supposed that she thought of police work as a sport, like hunting. The way things turned out was as surprising to Jack's mother as it was to Jack. He still believed that if the trials that had fallen to them had been different ones—maybe bankruptcy or a chronic illness instead of Holly's problem—she might have held up, might even have been heroic. But she did not hold up. She ran away from Jack and from Holly. She left a note that said she needed to spend some time alone and think, and that she would be in touch as soon as she was ready. The way he learned her new address was by reading the divorce papers that arrived in the mail.

After Rose, there had been a series of relationships with women, but he had never been tempted to marry again. After a few misunderstandings and disappointments, he developed a talent for recognizing women—mostly widows and divorcees—who liked male company but had no more interest in marrying anybody than he did.

Holly was the center of his life. He had never kept the women he dated from meeting her, but he had never rushed the meetings, and he had never given Holly the impression that any of the women would be around for a long time. He had needed desperately to protect Holly from loss. He thought about Holly now, and wondered what she was doing tonight. It was late, so he pictured her asleep in her bed in the room she shared with her friend Nancy in Garden House. In a few hours she would be up again, bustling around in the kitchen and getting ready for another day at the shop.

Till felt uneasy. He looked out the plane's window along the flight line, where he could see the rounded shapes of four other planes nosed up to the terminal. He could see the lights of the hotels, and beyond them the dark of the desert. Leaving Henderson felt wrong. There were too many things he did not know, too many questions he had not asked, too many possibilities that he had left untested. He was still bothered by the telephone call that Ann Delatorre had made to Wendy Harper after his first visit. He'd heard what Ann had said, but what had Wendy said? Had she told Ann Delatorre not to let Till know where she was? Had Wendy told her to find a way to get rid of him?

Maybe Wendy had heard what was going on in Los Angeles and was already making her way there on her own. That would make a great deal of sense. If Wendy had become adept at hide-and-seek over the past six years, then she might have decided that her best use of Jack Till was to leave him wandering around trying to develop leads to places where she wasn't. Maybe her plan was to slip into Los Angeles alone and unnoticed. If that was her plan, then he was blowing it for her right now. He was on an airplane that was about to take him straight to her.

He couldn't fly to San Francisco without knowing whether he was helping her or hurting her. The only way to find out was to talk to Ann Delatorre one more time. He stood up, opened the overhead compartment, and took out his small suitcase.

"What are you doing?"

Till turned his head and saw that it was the flight attendant. "I'm leaving. I'm not going to be on this flight. You can give my seat to somebody else."

"Why? Is something wrong? Are you ill?"

"Nothing's wrong. I just forgot something I have to do."

"Sir, I don't know if you'll be able to get a refund."

"That's okay," he said, and manufactured a reassuring smile. "By the way, this is my only bag, so nobody has to take anything else off the plane."

She decided to believe that he wasn't a terrorist and he wasn't insane. She moved up the aisle past him, weaving through the passengers who were still boarding. "Excuse us, please. Excuse us." She stayed ahead of him to secure a few feet of aisle leading toward the front of the plane, so he could step into it after her. When they reached the end of the aisle, and he stepped out the hatchway, she said, "I hope everything works out for you."

"I'm sure it will be fine. You've been very helpful. Thanks."

He moved quickly out into the concourse and then to the moving walkway, found the baggage area, then made his way through crowds of people to the car rental counters. This time he chose a different rental company to throw off anyone who might be watching him.

Till drove out of McCarrran Airport and took the 215 south to Henderson. He was cutting back to cross his own trail, but he was sure it was the right thing to do. He knew he had missed something when he was talking to Ann Delatorre. She had said she was Wendy Harper's closest friend. What would her closest friend do if Wendy was in danger? Maybe she would join her, or maybe she would summon Wendy back to Las Vegas from wherever she was living. Maybe she had been eager to invite him in and tell him her story to get rid of him before Wendy arrived.

Till drove up Ann Delatorre's street looking for cars parked along the curb that he had not seen before. There were none, but he kept going past the house to see if there were any other changes. There was a light on in the back of the house. He had driven past several times on different nights, but he had never seen that light on.

Till pulled over and parked a distance from the house, and then walked back, staying on the garage side, where the view from the house was limited. When he reached the house he could see that the light was coming from the hallway that led from the living room to the kitchen. He took in a deep breath and slowly blew it out through his teeth. She must have left already. She had gone to meet Wendy Harper. When he had watched the house before, she had never left lights on this late at night. Till supposed she had probably forgotten it, or plugged a light into a timer, then set it to go on and off at the wrong times because she was in a hurry to get on the road.

Till walked to the rear of the house where the light was on, and looked in through the window of the back door. He took out his cell phone and dialed 9-1-1 as he walked along the house to look in the bigger window.

A woman's voice came on after a few seconds. "What is the nature of your emergency?"

SILENCE

"I just found a woman's body at 93117 Valerio Springs in Henderson. She's wrapped in a blanket on the kitchen floor of her house. Her name is Ann Delatorre."

"Your name, please?"

"Jack Till."

"You know that she's dead?"

"I can see she's been shot in the head."

17

IT WAS AFTER TEN in the morning. Ann Donnelly did not dare to dial the Henderson number again. Ann Delatorre had said that she would call again this morning, but she had not called. Ann Donnelly had suspected from the start that the man who had gone to the house in Henderson was not Jack Till. Six years ago, when Jack Till had taught her how to escape, he said that he did not want to know where she was going, or what name she was going to give herself.

He had said, "You know what a secret is?"

"Tell me."

"It's something that only one person knows. Giving it to someone else is like trying to pass a handful of water to a friend. The best part of it gets spilled."

"That's why you don't want to know? *You're* not going to spill it."

"If the people who want you have found out about me, then they'll be watching me. They'll watch until one of us tries to communicate. It's not you or I who will give up the secret. It's the empty space between us."

"You don't sound like a cop anymore."

"That's how I learned it. I caught a few people by watching their friends and relatives. More than a few. It takes a very special kind of person to cut off all contact with everyone, because it goes against instinct. Most of the people who can do it easily aren't people you'd like."

She remembered saying, "There are certain people who will be hard for me. I'll think about Eric every day. My friends from college in Wisconsin will be a loss, and the ones who built up the restaurant with us."

"There's still time to come back to L.A. and help the police find these guys. Even if you change your mind later, you can come home."

"I don't think I will." How had she known that? Was it because she had decided nothing could depend on other people—their decisions, their assessments of what she was feeling and thinking and capable of doing? She had made a decision to act, to leave nothing up to anyone else.

After that conversation, she had looked up at Jack Till and experienced an odd temptation. She could remember the surprise of it even now, six years later. He was completely wrong for her, a mismatch. He was older, his eyes already acquiring that hooded look that at first glance seemed sleepy, but then was sad and very wise. He was tall and thin and hard, with narrow feet and hands. The hands were, oddly, part of the attraction, because they weren't thick and clumsy like the hands of a cop. They were long and thin, and when they moved they seemed to have a grace and exactness, like the fingers of a pianist. Watching them when Jack Till did things— wrote or picked up a key or dialed a telephone—revealed the intelligence that animated them.

She had observed him on the beach with her, the two of them pretending to be a couple of tourists while they waited. Perhaps by pretending to be a couple they were asking for those feelings to develop. So much of what happened between people in ordinary life was induced by their roles, and roles were pretending. It was how doctors and ministers and bosses and—yes—policemen existed. It wasn't a good idea to examine how much of love was induced by the two opposite roles that two human beings tried to play when they paired off. But she had already known by then that sometimes love was that way. People pretended until they believed.

She had stepped close to Jack, put her arms around his neck, and kissed his cheek. Then she had lingered with her arms around him and her face turned up in case he wanted to turn his face to her, put his arms around her and kiss her, too. That was all it would have taken to have her—either then or anytime afterward. But Jack Till had chosen to misconstrue the kiss to preserve his conscience or her pride. She had been the right kind of woman for Jack to dismiss that way. She was demonstrative, and kissed everybody on the cheek—male, female, old or young—when they showed up at a party, let alone saved her life. At the restaurant Eric had once said she was a health hazard, kissing fifty customers a night, transferring germs from one to the next.

Jack had pretended not to get what she meant, but later on he had said things that made her know that he had understood. "You're in the scary part right now," he said. "You've jumped off the side of the chasm you were on, and your feet haven't touched the other side yet. It can make you feel alone and desperate. Pretty soon you'll be in a new place with new people, and you'll begin to feel better."

What he had not known—had not seen because she had not let him—was that she had already taken that into account. She had wanted to get involved with Jack to make the break with the old life final. It was something Wendy Harper would never have done, and Jack Till would have helped her stop being Wendy Harper.

She supposed he had learned his resistance by being a cop. Cops were used to seeing women at moments of their lives when they were most vulnerable and frightened. At those times, a big strong male who was sworn to protect them was what some primitive lobe of their brains craved. It was a bit too easy for someone like Jack.

She remembered the moment hours later when he stopped the

car just outside the Santa Barbara airport and sat with her for a moment. She kissed him a second time, but his posture remained stiff and unyielding. She said, "Thanks for saving my life, Jack." Did she actually add, "If you need a friend, or there's anything I can ever do for you..." or was she imagining it? Yes, she said that. There could be no reality unless she told herself the truth. She threw herself at him.

In response, he said, "Just take care of yourself. If you need me, you know where I am. Later, if somebody calls or comes looking for you, remember that I don't know where you are. It isn't going to be me."

She'd had no choice. "I'll never forget you." She got out of the car, took the small suitcase that contained her few carefully selected belongings and the shoulder bag that contained seventy thousand dollars in cash, and waved to him one last time. Then she walked into the terminal and caught her plane.

Now, as Ann Donnelly was packing to leave again, she was just as frightened as she had been then. Her movements felt unreal. She watched her hands doing things automatically. She reached up to the pole in her closet and selected outfits that she knew would be useful and passed over the rest. It occurred to her that what she was doing now was exactly what Jack Till taught her.

Ann Delatorre should have called her by now. She was afraid. The man Ann described sounded a bit like Jack Till, but Jack Till would never have come after her. Ann should have called. That was the arrangement. The only conclusion she could draw was that Ann Delatorre was dead. Not Ann Delatorre. That was a made-up name. She deserved to be thought of under her real name: She was Louanda Rowan.

Ann Donnelly found herself crying again as she finished packing. She had been crying about Louanda on and off for hours, but now she had to control herself. She closed her suitcase and latched it, then looked around. The bedroom seemed comfortable and reassuring. The big king bed with its high walnut headboard and antique quilt looked so safe and secure. It was terribly hard to leave this room.

When she had run away from Los Angeles, she had looked for a chance to invent a new and better self. She worked on being Ann Delatorre for a time, and then realized that she needed another layer of distance from the past. She conceived the idea of giving Louanda Rowan the identity she had invented, and the business she had built and the house she had bought. It was a chance to repay Louanda for her friendship and help. It was also a way of keeping tough, fearless little Louanda between her and her troubles. She had to acknowledge that now and accept it. She had befriended a woman who was poor and desperate, used her as a surrogate—a double—and put her in terrible danger. She had never intended the danger to be real, but that was how it had worked out. Now, as the minutes went by, it was becoming surer and surer that Louanda was dead, and that she had died trying to protect Ann Donnelly.

Trying. That was a word that raised other problems. If Louanda had been hurt or running, she could have called this house and told Ann Donnelly what to do to help her. But if she had been caught in Henderson and had not been able to keep Ann Donnelly's name and address from her captors, then waiting for her call was wasting the only time left to escape.

Ann walked slowly through the house again. As she walked, she absentmindedly corrected things that had been left out of place. She straightened the oriental rug in the living room, then used her foot to push the strands of fringe at the ends into place. She gathered a pile of magazines into a stack on the coffee table, picked up a plastic dump truck with a Barbie doll in it, carried it into the playroom, and set it on a shelf. She looked at her watch. It was after eleven. She had given Louanda all the time she could spare. She went back into the hallway, picked up her suitcase, and walked toward the back door.

It was as though she had awakened suddenly. Once she had begun to move, the insanity of waiting here for her executioner to arrive began to seem obvious. She stepped outside, looked up and down the street for signs of unusual activity, then locked the door behind her, went into the garage by the side door, and put the small suitcase into the trunk of her beige Nissan Maxima. She started the car, backed out of the driveway, and noticed again the flat of strawberries that she had bought three days ago, before the call from Louanda, but never planted. She pressed the remote control to close the garage door.

She drove up the street, made a few turns randomly in case somebody had arrived in time to follow her, and then turned onto a pretty street with big trees shading her car. She parked, then dialed her cell telephone and waited.

Dennis's voice came on, but she recognized the recording instantly. "This is Dennis Donnelly. I'm not available at the moment, but please leave a message, and I'll get back to you as soon as I can."

"Den, this is Ann. I'm sorry, but the thing I told you might happen someday has happened. I left the kids—you know where I left them, so I won't say it on the phone. I told them I had to go away for a long time on business, so that's our story. Don't try to add details. We'll just contradict each other. Don't even think about bringing them back to the house. That goes for you, too. Tell your partners as soon as you get this message that something has come up and you've got to take a trip. Pick the kids up and go from there. I'm sure you remember that the kit I put together for this is in the trunk of your car. I love you." She turned off the telephone and put it back into her purse. She was crying so hard that it took her a minute before she could wipe away enough tears to look behind her and be sure she hadn't been followed.

18

JACK TILL got off the plane in San Francisco and made his way to the car-rental counters. While he waited for the keys to a car, he kept turning his head and scanning the changing, moving crowds of people behind him, looking for some constant, some person who stayed in sight.

His search for Wendy Harper was different now that Ann Delatorre was dead. Till had not been able to stay in Henderson to wait for the crime lab and the autopsy, but he had seen enough bodies to know that she'd been beaten before she had died. Probably her assailant had been trying to get information. It had ended with a shot to the side of the head near the back from less than a foot away—close enough to singe her hair a little. He hoped it had been a shot taken out of anger and frustration at a failure to make her talk.

The angle of the shot to her head hinted at more bad news: Judging from the marks on the wall in the hallway where the blood was, and the marks on the right side of her forehead, he believed that the person who had beaten her had used his right hand to hit her head against the wall. A shot to the left side of the head at the back meant a person holding a gun in his left hand. To Till, the difference raised the possibility that there had been two people involved in the killing.

Till had to go to the baggage-check office to pick up his gun in its locked carrying case before he went to his rental car. A day ago he would probably not have opened the case, but now everything had changed. Now that Ann Delatorre had been killed, he knew that the danger wasn't theoretical or distant. He drove his car out of the airport onto the 101 freeway, then took the next exit and pulled into the first big open-air parking lot near a Costco store. He unlocked the case, loaded the gun, put it into its holster, and clipped it to his belt.

He drove into San Francisco with the last of the morning traffic. He had called Max Poliakoff from Las Vegas to convert Wendy Harper's telephone number into an address in San Rafael. He had been hoping to get to the house before Wendy Harper went off to work or whatever she did, but it was already past eleven, so he had probably missed her.

Till headed northward into the city and through its center, across the Golden Gate Bridge to San Rafael. After Max Poliakoff had given him the address, he had used a computer at the hotel in Las Vegas to go onto a real-estate site where he had found the name of the legal owner and a description of the house. The house had been bought four years ago. It had four bedrooms, four bathrooms, and a pool, and was 4,500 square feet on a half acre of land.

Wendy Harper's luck seemed to have improved. She had apparently started badly in Las Vegas, floundering, living in a cheap apartment building among people who were essentially transients and fugitives. She had made a very lucky meeting in the woman she renamed Ann Delatorre, but a big part of her luck was that she didn't meet anyone who would hurt her or make an effort to find out what betraying her might be worth.

Till drove along the streets of San Rafael, watching the signs for the right one. The listing had said the house belonged to Dennis Donnelly. That was a ploy that Till admired. Wendy Harper must have converted herself to Ann Donnelly, put a bid on the house, and invented a husband who was too busy to come to the escrow office to sign the papers, so she had to take them to him and get them notarized. Or maybe she had simply bought the house in one name and transferred ownership to the other to make her nonexistent husband the owner.

Jack Till found the street and coasted past the house, looking in his practiced way at every aspect of it without letting his foot touch the brake, and then studying the mental image of it he had filed away. It was long and low, with a lot of expensive wooden detail work along the eaves and windows and the front door. The big pieces of natural wood gave the place a look that was somewhere between Craftsman and Japanese. It was the sort of architecture that had characterized the house she had owned with Eric Fuller and the enclosed area at the back of their restaurant, where the tables began inside the dining room and spilled out through an open glass wall onto the stone patio with groves of dwarf evergreens. That had been in Los Angeles, where bad weather was mostly theoretical, and the sun shone three hundred and fifty days a year. He supposed that up here in the Bay Area, things like rain and cold wind weren't unusual, and the doors would be more substantial.

He had also spotted two signs on the lawn and one on the gate that said "NATIONAL PACIFIC SECURITY—ARMED RESPONSE." He stopped the car around the corner and called 4-1-1.

"What city, please?"

"San Rafael."

"Go ahead."

"Do you have a number for National Pacific Security?"

There was a pause. "There's no number for San Rafael. No listing for Marin. Nothing for San Francisco. Nothing for Oakland. You could try San Jose."

"Thank you very much." Till disconnected. If there was a security company that responded when its alarms went off, it would have to maintain an office nearby. The sign was a fake, one of those signs that people picked up to fool burglars into thinking the place was wired when it wasn't. Everything that Wendy Harper did showed a growing knowledge of how to stay hidden. Putting up signs probably gave her most of the protection an alarm system would.

Till left his car where it was, walked to the front door of the house, and rang the bell. There was no answer, no sound of movement inside, so he tried the bell twice more and waited. There was still no sound from inside, so he walked around to the back. There was a high wooden fence that ran from the house to the garage. He reached over the gate to feel for the latch, and opened it. He waited for a few seconds, scanning the yard for a sign that Wendy Harper owned a dog.

There was no dog. He was mildly surprised. Wendy had seemed to him to be a person who would see a dog as a cheap form of security. He stepped along the stone path from the gate, glanced at the pool, and felt her presence: She'd had it landscaped with a lot of rocks and a fake waterfall that reminded him again of the gardens outside the restaurant in Los Angeles.

He stepped close to the sliding glass door at the rear of the house and looked in. He could see a grand piano with framed photographs on it, and a few more on the mantel over the fireplace. He strained his eyes, hoping to pick out a picture of the woman of the house. He could see a few of a man and some small children, but none of a woman. He supposed that having no pictures of herself around confirmed that this was Wendy's house. She was also certainly capable of getting some pictures of a man and some children to leave around and make her seem even more like other women her age.

Till saw something else, and he felt his breathing deepen and his muscles tighten. There was a frame lying flat with its back opened. The glass lay beside it. Someone had removed the photograph. Till hurried along the back of the house, looking in windows and doors. He wanted desperately not to find broken windows or forced doors. If everything was intact, then maybe she had taken the photograph with her.

But he saw it as soon as he turned the corner: a broken window that led to the master bedroom. The sash had been opened and left that way. He moved closer, his gaze automatically drawn to the bed, and then to the floor. There was no body. He used his handkerchief to touch the outer edge of the window where he would not be destroying fingerprints, lifted it higher, and then stepped over the sill into the room. He took out his gun and began to move forward cautiously, listening for sounds that would indicate the intruders were still in the house.

Maybe he had been unrealistic about Ann Delatorre. She had not been able to resist the beatings, and had given the killers this address. He moved from room to room listening and looking. There were two children. One looked from her picture to be about seven and the other about five. There was a man—not just a name on a deed, but an actual man who left his shoes lying on the floor and had coats hanging in the closet and shirts in the laundry hamper.

The kids had the same kind of thin blond hair that Wendy Harper had had six years ago, but they were too old to be her biological children. He scanned the collection of pictures on the piano and found a snapshot of a wide beach with big rocks, with Wendy kneeling there, hugging the kids and grinning. Biological or not, they were hers. He found a good picture of the man standing in front of a brownish Nissan Maxima that was no more than a year old.

The man was a shock to Till. When he realized that there was a real Dennis Donnelly, he felt an unexpected heaviness in his stomach. He tried to tell himself that what he had done six years ago had led her to this pleasant place and given her a life with a wonderful family. It was futile. Six years ago, Till had not wanted to take advantage of a desperate woman. He had not wanted to risk his daughter Holly's safety by bringing home a woman who was a target for murderers. He had reminded himself that Wendy Harper was a client. Six years ago, he had resisted his strong attraction to her for the best reasons, and he had regretted it a thousand times since then.

He knew she'd given him plenty of reasons not to care about her. She'd had knowledge of a probable murder, but wouldn't tell anyone who the murderer was, or even who the victim was. He had given her his standard ex-cop lecture about her responsibility to the community to help get a killer out of it. He had told her she would have a share of the guilt for the killing of the next woman this man met.

She had listened, she had agreed with the premise, but she had not told him anything he could use. She'd said she didn't know the man's name, couldn't even describe him very well. In the end, Jack Till had accepted the argument that she had a right to leave town, and acknowledged that if she didn't she would probably be killed. She had not done anything to invite the danger, and she had a right to get out of it.

Till looked hard at the man in the photograph, at Dennis Donnelly. He was young—maybe thirty-one or -two, but with a square-jawed, open face that seemed good-natured and pleasant. Till tried to decide whether he would have liked it better if Donnelly had looked ugly or stupid, but he realized he wouldn't have. He had wanted Wendy to succeed, to have a happy life, and he supposed the man was part of what he should have wanted for her.

Till went through the rest of the house, but nothing had been disturbed except the empty picture frame. He knew that they had taken the photograph to use in their search for her. He avoided moving or even touching anything else, and left the house the way he had come in.

The hunters had gotten here first, but Wendy Harper was out, and she was alive.

19

I'M SORRY, Mr. Till is not in the office. This is the answering service. Would you like to leave a message?"

"Do you know when he'll be in?" Ann Donnelly tried to keep the fear out of her voice. It was almost noon. Maybe he was just out to lunch.

"I'm sorry, but I don't. He's on an assignment out of town right now."

Ann Donnelly took a couple of deep breaths, thinking hard. "My name is Wendy Harper. He's been trying to get in touch with me."

"Yes, he has." The woman sounded different, as though she had just awakened. "He left a cell-phone number that we were to give you if you called. Do you have anything to write with?"

"Yes."

"Then here's the number." She recited it.

"I have it. Thanks. I'll try him right now."

Ann hung up the pay phone and moved away from the brick front of the 7-Eleven store. She had not realized how much the visibility of standing in front of a building had contributed to her unease. Jack had taught her that pay telephones were the safest, but standing in the open was too unnerving.

She hurried toward her car, got in and began to drive. She was afraid to stop the car, so she dialed the number on her cell phone while she drove.

The telephone rang once, twice, and she realized she was holding her breath. Then she heard "Yeah?"

She recognized his voice in that single word, and all of the feelings about him seemed to flood her consciousness unexpectedly. That voice meant strength, safety, hope. "It's Wendy. I heard that you were looking for me. Is it true?"

"Yes. Listen. I've got to see you right away, in person. Do not go anywhere near your house. The people who are hunting for you have been there."

"Oh, God! I figured that might be next. I've already cleared out, but no more than half an hour ago."

"Do you have a car?"

"I'm in it."

"Can you meet me somewhere?"

"Yes."

"You name it."

"Pier 39. I can be there in maybe half an hour."

"I'll be there waiting for you."

Jack Till was already on the Golden Gate Bridge, so it took him only twenty minutes on the freeway and the Embarcadero to reach Pier 39. He parked his car in a public lot and joined the crowds of tourists walking from the souvenir shops across the street toward the pier. He moved close to the knots of people getting off tour buses near the buildings where they sold tickets for boats to Alcatraz and admission to the aquarium.

Till marked the passage of time carefully. He was even earlier than he had expected, so he needed to find a vantage point. He moved onto the pier, where there were two levels of stores and restaurants that were not very different from any crowded mall except that the view through the windows showed a bright, choppy ocean. He climbed some wooden steps to the second story, stopped to lean over a railing and stare at the broad concrete entranceway and the parking lots near the street. He had noticed a brownish Nissan Maxima in one of the pictures at the house, so that was the car he watched for.

In five more minutes, he saw it swing into the parking-lot entrance. There was a lone woman in the driver's seat, but he didn't have time to see her face before she turned up the first aisle and was lost to view. He came down the stairs and moved toward the lot, then saw her coming toward him. She was striding along quickly and then almost trotting, holding the long strap of a big purse on her shoulder as she came.

He couldn't help remembering that when he'd last seen her she'd still had a noticeable limp, a hitch in her step that had begun at the hip where one of the blows from the bat had landed. Now her steps were strong and smooth, keeping just below a run because she didn't want to draw attention to herself. Her hair was still long and blond, as it had been six years ago. Seeing her brought a sudden rush of old feelings that he'd had to repress when he had last seen her. He resisted the temptation to run to meet her, and instead hung back in the crowds near the shops. He took his attention off her and scanned the street, the parking lot, the spaces behind her to see if he could detect anyone who was interested in her, or anyone he had ever seen before. He saw nothing, but he was aware that the crowds that kept Wendy from standing out could as easily be protecting enemies.

He let her come all the way to him, but said quietly, "Pass by me up to the first store on the upper level and wait inside for me."

He waited another two minutes to see if anyone came after her, but nobody did. There were no odd movements by anybody he could see. When he was satisfied, he went up the stairs and into the shop.

She came to him instantly. "Hi," she said quietly.

"Hi yourself. Let's go." They stepped outside and he used his high vantage to see if he could detect anything new. "Did you see anyone following you here?"

"I don't see how they could. I left home, stopped on another street for a few minutes, drove to a 7-Eleven a mile or two from my house, and called your office on the pay phone. Then I drove off and called your cell phone, and here I am."

"Why didn't you call me sooner? Didn't you see the ads?"

"Ads? What ads? I heard someone had come to Henderson looking for me, but I thought at first it couldn't be you. You said you would never come."

"Well, things have changed. Now we've got to be sure we can get to L.A. without being spotted."

"Get to L.A.?"

"Don't you know? That's what this is about."

She looked frightened, almost sick, the fear clutching her and making her stop walking, as though she couldn't get her legs to move. "I heard what the problem was. I said I'd meet you. I never said I was going back to Los Angeles."

He held her arm gently. "Wendy."

She looked at him with despair that made her eyes squint.

He said, "If we do it right, nobody will see you except Assistant DAs and cops. It won't take more than a day."

"I just don't see why I have to do this at all."

"Because if you don't, then Eric Fuller is probably going to be convicted of killing you and cutting you up with a kitchen knife. We just have to prove that you're alive, and that will be that."

"Why would anybody think he did anything to me? I still don't see any logic in that. I've been gone for six whole years."

Till kept his eyes on her. "I don't want to go into a long discussion of this while these people catch up with us. I met with Eric's attorney and talked with the Assistant DA who filed the charges.

The case they've built against Eric isn't a sure thing, but I've seen people convicted on less."

"Then he's being framed."

"Of course."

"If you know that, then stop it."

"I am."

"Another way."

"There *is* no other way."

"How can there *not* be?"

"I've already told the Assistant DA what happened—all of it: how I met you, where I took you, why you left. She's not—"

"*She?* Oh, Christ!"

"That's right. I think she's striking a blow for all of the young women who have turned up half-buried in fields somewhere."

"Good for her! Just tell her I'm not one of them yet."

"I have. You need to prove it in person. You always cared about Eric. He was the most important person in the world to you once."

"That's just it. He's not anymore. When I went away I left him with everything he wanted, and that's over. Now I have a real honest-to-God family. I'm a mother with two little children. Right now I've got their father taking them out of town to keep them alive. Don't you see? *They* have to be my first concern, not Eric Fuller."

"Are they gone?"

"Yes."

"Then you've done what you can for them. You've got one more thing to do."

"I know. I know what you want. And anybody would say, 'Why is she even hesitating?' But it isn't that simple. I have young kids, a husband. Nobody can tell me for sure that Eric would be convicted. If he were acquitted, he would be just fine. If he were convicted, I could come down then and show that I'm alive. You say, 'Why put him through a murder trial for nothing?' I say, 'Why put my family in danger? Why make me disrupt their lives, give them false identities, abandon our house, and destroy my husband's career, if Eric is just going to get off anyway?' "

"Because *we* did this—you and I—and we have to do the little we can to fix the consequences. Eric is an innocent victim."

"That's another thing." She looked desperate now, a person caught in a rip current and fighting it. "You say, 'Of course he was framed.' Well, who do you think did that? The man who couldn't kill me six years ago. He couldn't find me, so now he's devised a way to make me show myself. How can you ask me to do that?"

"Most of the damage is already done. The hunters have been in your house. They stole pictures—I think one was of you, but I'd be surprised if they didn't steal a few to help them identify your husband and kids. No matter what, you're going to have to stay away from that house. Whether you save Eric or not, you're going to have to take your family into hiding. There's a chance you'll get some witness protection from the authorities this time. If not, I'll certainly help you." He could see that she was barely listening. She had been resisting the knowledge that the life she had invented in San Rafael was finished.

"You're sure they've found my house already?"

"Yes."

"How could they?"

He waited. She seemed to look around her at the buildings, the pier, the stretch of water near the dock where the boats to Alcatraz were taking on passengers, as though she had not seen them before.

She said, "You haven't said a word about Ann Delatorre."

"You haven't, either."

"Is it what I think?"

"It looked as though she fought. She probably didn't see the gun, and it would have been quick."

Ann Donnelly's eyes were shut tightly and she moved her head from side to side as though she were saying no, but she did not cry.

When she opened them, Jack Till said, "You know what you have to do."

She began to walk. Jack Till walked with her toward the parking lot, and when he turned toward his car instead of hers, she was with him.

20

SYLVIE SAID, "You think she's prettier than I am, don't you?"

Paul glanced at her, then back at the car's side mirror. He used the button inside the car to adjust the mirror's tilt to keep the man and woman in sight. "Hardly."

"You're certainly staring at her."

"I've never seen her before. I want to get a good look."

"You always like those petite women with the little-girl shapes, and all men like blondes."

"I'm not in the market. And men don't all like blondes. Men don't even all like women."

Sylvie laughed. "That's a thought, isn't it? You do still like women, don't you?"

He took his eyes away from the mirror. "That's an odd thing to say."

"I didn't say it. You did."

He looked at Sylvie. She sat in the passenger seat of the rented sport utility vehicle, her body pulled away with her back to the door and facing him, as though she were planning to fend off a blow. He said with exaggerated patience, "I'm trying to keep my eyes on the woman because Densmore is paying us good money to kill her, not because I have some personal interest in her. I'm trying to be sure we can kill her without getting caught." He looked into the mirror again and saw nothing, so he tried the other mirrors, then turned around in his seat.

He saw them again walking along an aisle of cars. Wendy Harper moved away from her Nissan Maxima with a suitcase, and let Till guide her to a different aisle. The next few seconds were crucial. Paul needed to see the car they were going to take, and be sure it was the car he had already seen, and not some new one Till had planted here. He craned his neck, but they moved out of his view behind an SUV that was even bigger than his. Till was a pro. Paul couldn't take the chance of driving close enough to let Till see his face, but he couldn't let Till drive off and move out of his sight.

"I'm sorry."

"Huh?" he said.

"I said I was sorry. So you don't have to sit there freezing me out in absolute silence for the next few hours like I was a criminal."

"Fine. I don't think you need to apologize, but I'll accept your apology. Damn. I need to get a good look at the car they're getting into, but I don't dare let him see us."

"Why not just pull up behind him so he can't back out of the space, and open fire on them?"

"Because there are a thousand people who would turn around and see us."

"That's the idea. When there are a thousand people, there may as well be no people. There will be hundreds of conflicting stories, and half of those people will see somebody else drive off and say it was them."

"That may be true, but we could easily shoot them and then get stuck in this lot behind somebody and not be able to get out." He was getting irritated. He turned the ignition key and started the engine, began to back out of his space, and then was startled by the blare of a horn behind him.

Paul stomped on the brake and the SUV jerked to a stop and

rocked. He turned in his seat. It was a pair of teenagers, the boy driving and the girl glaring at Paul as they went past along the aisle.

As Paul resumed his attempt to back out of the parking space, he thought about the pair. They could easily have waited for just a moment to let him back out, but they had the aggressive mentality that was getting to be an epidemic. These kids couldn't imagine how close to the grave they were treading. It was difficult for even Paul to guess how much more provocation it would take right now for him to forget the caution he had urged on Sylvie and put a bullet through each of their heads. He got the big SUV out into the aisle and followed the two teenagers' car toward the exit.

He could see past their small car to the end of the aisle now, where Jack Till was opening the door of his beige Lincoln for Wendy Harper.

Sylvie said, "There they are."

The superfluity of her observation was an affront to Paul's consciousness. Of course he could see them. The fact that Sylvie was here to see them was entirely his doing. When he and Sylvie had broken into Wendy Harper's house and found it deserted, Sylvie had simply assumed they would rush off to be long gone before the burglary was discovered. It was Paul who had insisted on parking down the street and watching the house. He had known he had been right to insist when the first person to arrive was Jack Till. And when Till left the house, Paul managed to follow him all the way to Pier 39 without being discovered. He fought the urge to remind her.

"This is where things really start," he said. "We've managed to stick with him while he found her for us, and neither of them has seen us yet. That's huge."

"Okay," Sylvie said.

"Just concentrate on getting a clear view of their car, the license number, and where they go. We're going to have to leave the lot first and wait for them to pass."

"All right."

"Don't take your eyes off Till. He's a pro, so he probably has something in mind."

"I *said* all right."

"What's the matter with you?"

"I don't know. Could it be because you treat me like shit?"

"When was this?"

"Well, let's see. Ever since we went to Vegas, you've been snapping at me."

"No I haven't. I've just been trying to keep us both focused on this job. I have more experience, so maybe I give more directions. That's all."

"You were really nasty to me after I shot that black woman. I heard the commotion, then ran in and saw her biting and scratching you and going for your eyes, so I did it. That's all. And since then you've been hurting my feelings. Is it because a woman was about to kick your ass, and I'm the witness? Or is it because I'm a woman and I saved you?"

Paul's consciousness alternated between the sting of her accusation and a hollow amusement at the irrationality of it. When he was able to stabilize his emotions for a moment, he said, "I wanted to scare her, not kill her."

"You scared her, all right."

"If I had wanted her dead, I would have shot her myself. I had a gun. You knew that."

"I knew it, and so did she. I didn't want her to get her hands on it and kill us both."

"Okay," he said. "You fired because you didn't have confidence that I could keep her alive long enough to get her to talk. So I had to spend an hour cleaning up, and then another hour taking the house apart to find out what she could have told us."

"We're here, and it's because I found the phone number."

"Yes, we're here—about an hour too late to have caught her

packing and killed her before Jack Till got to her. Those two extra hours in Henderson start to look bigger now, don't they?"

"So I finally think I understand."

It was a battle for clarification. Their fights were always like this, the anger of the struggle forcing each of them to reveal the resentments they had resolved to hide, but finding they needed to use them as ammunition. His sense of structure told him that the fight was nearly at its core now, and soon he could know what it had been about. "What is it that you understand?"

"You haven't been romantic since we left home. Are you just angry at me for shooting her, or are you losing interest?"

"I'm not losing interest in you. I'm with you practically all the time, aren't I? Maybe that's the problem."

"I don't mean being around. I mean—you know."

"Sex?" It always astounded Paul that she had such a hard time saying even the word, given her history.

"Yes. You've been so cold and distant. You haven't been very interested in me for a long time."

"We've been working every minute. I'm interested, but I don't know when anything could have happened. When we haven't been on an airplane, we've been in a car." He took his eyes away from the cars ahead of him moving slowly toward the gate. "I love you. Don't ever forget the trouble we went through to be together. That's how much I wanted you."

"Wanted?"

"Want."

She leaned over to throw her arms around his neck and put a soft kiss on his cheek. "Let's kill them now and rent a room."

There was the sound of a horn behind them, and Paul glanced into the rearview mirror. This time it was a middle-aged woman who had noticed that he had let five or six extra feet of space open up between his bumper and the trunk of the two teenagers' car. "Just keep your eyes on their car," he said.

It still rankled Paul that Sylvie had accused him of being defeated by that young black woman in Henderson. Sylvie had killed her and left him no way to defend himself from the accusation of weakness. He had been just about to incapacitate the young woman when Sylvie had rushed in, hysterical, and shot her. He knew a dozen ways to immobilize a smaller opponent like that woman. He had been training in martial arts since he was a teenager.

He had been without any sense of direction as a boy. It had seemed to him that the gravity that held most other people to some path had no effect on him. People around him, even his own brothers and sisters, seemed to have some image they were growing into, some template that they were learning to fit.

Paul had balance, control, and coordination, so he thought he might be good at sports, but he had a difficult time finding the right one. He was tall and thin, so the basketball team had seemed a possibility, but he found that the countless hours of shooting a basket, rebounding, and shooting again that made other boys good players made him bored. He tried football, but it was like the punishment for some forbidden act that he had not even had the pleasure of committing. Then he found a karate class in a storefront on his way home from school. In karate he could use everything about himself—his long reach, his high kick, his coordination, his energy, his anger.

By the age of fifteen, he had already become a dangerous boy. He had little to do with the other students at school, but when he walked down the hall, he cut a path through the crowd like an icebreaker, straight and undeviating, bumping aside anyone who didn't see him coming and forcing those who did to go around him. One afternoon a boy pushed back, hard. Paul spun with the push, held the boy's arm and broke it, then delivered a series of quick blows that left the boy unconscious and bleeding in the hallway.

That evening after his mother came home from work, the police arrived and took Paul to the station. They asked him a lot of questions, and then locked him up for the night. Paul's mother went to the station and tried to get him out, but the police weren't yet sure how serious the charges would be, so they stalled. Finally he had been sent to a juvenile facility in the mountains for thirty days. That was where he had gotten his first paying job.

When he had been there for about two weeks and won four fights, three boys from the North Valley came to him and explained that they had a problem. They had been working as street pushers for a marijuana dealer. They had been in a feud with boys who worked for a rival dealer, and it had given one of them an idea. They would rob their own dealer's house, and then blame it on their competitors. The flaw in the scheme was that when they had broken into the house, a neighbor had seen them. The dealer they worked for was terrifying. He had several plantations in remote parts of national forests, tended by small groups of armed men. Each time a crop was ripe they picked it, bagged it, and packed it out on foot. The dealer had plenty of men from these crews to find and kill the boys if he learned what they had done. They needed to kill the neighbor before he saw them again and recognized them, but they were all going to be in the juvenile camp for at least two months.

They knew Paul was getting out in a couple of weeks. They were willing to tell him where they had hidden a gun and pay him a thousand dollars each to kill the neighbor. Paul said, "All right." As soon as he was out of juvenile camp, he went to the address they had given him, found the gun, went to the neighbor's house, and shot him while he slept. Paul had finally discovered his sport.

Paul had been doing paying jobs for a lot of years before he'd ever met Sylvie. It was incredible to him that she would attack his competence just to win points in some stupid argument. He forced himself to be calm. Nobody ever said women fought fair, and nobody ever sought out women because they were logical.

Behind him a horn sounded again, this time a long, loud blare.

21

J ACK TILL SWIVELED in his seat to see what the honking was about, but all he could determine was that it had come from one of the cars in the line behind him. A car had stopped in the aisle to let him out so it could take his parking space. The boy with a black baseball cap who was driving made Till uneasy because he was talking to his girlfriend instead of watching, but Till backed out and moved off.

Till turned out of the parking lot and drove west, away from the harbor. He wanted to be on a freeway heading south before the afternoon rush hour. He knew the importance of momentum to a witness like Wendy Harper. If things seemed to be stalled and faltering, she would begin to rethink her choices. He watched her closely whenever he was forced to stop at a traffic signal or wait for an obstruction to clear, and he could detect the nervous mannerisms he feared: looking out the side window at familiar buildings, her thumb running back and forth along the door handle. San Francisco was still home. He hadn't gotten her out of town yet. She could open the door at any stop, slip out, and know her way around.

"Don't be nervous," he reassured her. "You made the right decision."

"It was made for me."

"So much the better. You don't have to second-guess yourself."

"What I wonder is why you couldn't have brought a video camera and taken a shot of me talking and holding a newspaper or something. Maybe draw some blood for DNA tests."

"I thought of that," he said. "We know the crime lab has samples of your blood. The Assistant DA would have objected, but I think Jay Chernoff—he's Eric's lawyer—could have made it work in court."

"Why didn't you, then?"

"Because by the time I got to talk to you, Ann Delatorre was already dead and her killers had found their way to your house. There was no secret left to protect. The only option left was to get you out of town."

Her impatient expression let Till know that she had thought of that herself, and hearing him repeat what her own mind had told her was not soothing. "See that building down Geary toward Market?"

"The big gray one?"

"No. The brown antique-looking one. My husband works there. His office is right up there on the fourth floor, this side. I can see his window."

"What company?"

"Pan-World Technical Commerce. It started as a trading company to bring hard drives and things from Asia, but now the finance arm is what makes most of the money."

"It sounds like a good job."

"He's one of the owners. The partners. It took him about ten years to build it into anything. They started out working from a house in Oakland. I feel terrible that he'll lose it all because of me."

Till could see the building's magnetic pull on her as they waited for the light to change. She was feeling a strong urge to jump out of the idling car and run inside the building. He knew that distracting her was impossible, so he tried to keep her talking. "Maybe we can get his partners to buy him out."

"Probably not. I suspect that when they know he has to liqui-date, he'll get his next lesson in business. They'll keep him hanging until he has to walk away and leave his share to them."

"They'd do that?"

"That's the way I read them, but I might be more cynical and pessimistic than most people."

"I'll tell you what. I'll try to get some serious legal talent in-volved, and I'll serve as the go-between. We can sell his share of the business, your house, and your cars. I can collect your money and make a transfer to your next identity through intermediaries. If necessary, I can deliver it to you in cash."

She smiled. "I'd forgotten. You have a talent for that."

"For what?"

"For making people think that everything will be all right. You would have been a good general, sending soldiers on suicide mis-sions and things. It's a con game."

"I won't ask you to do anything I don't."

She shook her head. "You're the one who jumps across the chasm and then turns to the rest of us and calls, 'Come on. You can do it!' Only we can't. Or most of us can't."

The light changed and only one taxicab was caught in the in-tersection to block the traffic. Jack Till accelerated and then swerved into the left lane to avoid it at the last moment. He kept going on Pine Street and turned south onto Van Ness to head for the 101.

"Are we going to the airport?" she asked.

"I'm not sure."

"Why not?"

"I haven't seen anyone following us. If nobody is, then what they're probably doing is betting that we'll try to fly out."

"And?"

"And then they'll be waiting for us at the airport, so we don't want to go there."

"But you once told me airports are the safest place. How could they hurt us with all that security?"

"The system is designed to detect objects that blow up or people who might shoot into a crowd. There are a lot of other ways to kill a hundred-and-ten-pound woman and walk away."

"Jesus!" she said. "I can't believe that after six years I'm back to this again—running, just like the first day."

"If you've got anything new to tell me, I'd love to hear it."

"I had six years to think about this, but you know what? I didn't. I mean, not in any useful way. I went about my life, and I thought about what I had to do each day. I met Louanda after a few weeks, and—"

"Louanda? Is that Ann Delatorre?"

"Yes. Her name was Louanda Rowan. Without her, I don't think I would have made it this far."

"I'm sorry about her. If only I had been able to convince her to let me help, she would be alive. Somebody found her after I did."

"It's not your fault. You didn't know she existed. If I had been there to open the door as you expected, it never would have happened. *I* was the one who got her killed. *I* put her there." Tears began to well in her eyes and drip down her cheeks. She took a tissue out of her purse and tried to dry them.

"I can tell you that kicking your own ass doesn't leave much time for anything else."

"Have you done a lot of that?"

"Enough for the moment." Till drove aggressively like a cop on duty, moving along in a lane for a time, gaining steadily on the cars ahead and then switching lanes. He kept staring into the mirrors, trying to catch another car changing lanes to keep him in sight. After a few minutes, he said, "How are you doing?"

"Not so great. I'm so terrified, I can hardly breathe."

"We've got to be scared, but only enough to stay alert and do the little things we can do. *Use* your fear. Look out the rear window every couple of minutes and see if the same car is in the same spot three times in a row. And talk to me to keep me alert. Tell me what you think now about what happened six years ago."

"I suppose I have figured out some of it in the last six years. Not the important parts—about the man who is killing people or anything. Only the personal parts, the things about me, me, me. So it's not worth saying aloud."

"Yes it is. I'd like to hear it."

"Why?"

"Because your life—and mine—might depend on it. We can drive fast and try to be inconspicuous, but that won't stop the people who killed Louanda from trying to kill you."

"I don't know what to tell you."

He said nothing. After a few seconds, she said, "Why aren't you answering me?"

"Does that SUV back there look familiar? The dark one. It kept coming up a while ago, then kind of fell back, and now here it is again."

She stared at it through the back window. "I don't know. They all look alike."

"I'm trying not to be an alarmist, but I've got a feeling about it. Have you ever fired a gun?"

Her eyes widened. "Not really. Not the way you mean. When I was at camp, they taught us riflery. And I fired a friend's pistol once."

"Here's the problem. If the people in that SUV are the killers, they'll pull up on your side of the car and slightly behind us. The first few shots will get you. Then they'll pull forward to try for me."

"What can we do?"

He reached to his belt and took out his gun. "Here is the safety. If I tell you to, flip it off with your thumb, keeping your finger outside the trigger guard. You hold the grips tight, aim out the window with both hands. You fire four shots into their windshield—two rounds at the shooter, then two rounds at the driver."

"What?" She was shocked. "Shoot them?"

"If you hit anybody, it's over. If you just scare them, I can probably build up some distance and lose them."

He allowed the dark vehicle to gain on them, glanced at the freeway signs and took the next exit. He coasted to the end of the exit ramp, turned right, and pulled into the first parking lot he saw on the new street. It was the big lot for a Home Depot store, and the aisles were full. He pulled to the end of the first aisle, stopped, and looked back to watch the street in the direction of the exit ramp. He waited for a few minutes, but he saw no sign that the SUV had come down the ramp.

"What now?" she asked.

"You can give my gun back, I guess." He accepted it, put it back in the holster and covered it with his jacket again. He looked out at the street. "This is the way to the airport, isn't it?"

"It's one of the ways. The airport is just a few miles down the road that way. You stay parallel with the 101."

"Then it might be another opportunity to throw some more confusion in our trail. I rented this car at the airport. I'd like to turn it in and get a different one."

"Are you still against flying?"

"When you get on an airplane, people know exactly where you're going and exactly what time you'll arrive. If we go by car, we make them work to stay with us, and we get a chance to see who they are."

22

PAUL GOT OUT of the black SUV and opened Sylvie's door so she could climb out. As he watched her long legs swing out and straighten, and then saw her slide lightly off the seat and hop to the ground, he realized that the sight made him like her better. He had been seething, his jaw clenched much of the time since Sylvie had shot Ann Delatorre, and the nasty irrational remarks Sylvie had made in the parking lot at the pier had made things much worse. She was stupid and childish and completely unable to keep her mind focused on anything except herself. But the sight of those long legs and the graceful hop to the pavement dissipated his anger.

Paul was an aesthete. Other people could have said his response was not aesthetic but sexual, but that kind of statement would have shown that these people knew nothing. They didn't understand that the two were the same: the response of the human mind to beauty.

He glanced toward the car rental building and took Sylvie's arm, confident that he was pursuing the right strategy. Jack Till had left the freeway several miles before the airport. Till was fond of pulling tricks around airports, sometimes turning in his car and flying out, and sometimes turning in one car and renting another. Either way, the airport car rental was the place where Jack Till would be this afternoon.

"Why are we stopping here?" Sylvie asked.

"We've got to trade this SUV for a different vehicle." He removed the two small suitcases from the SUV and shut the back door.

"Why?"

"It's a tactic. Just like chess. I think he may have spotted us behind him. If he didn't pick this out as the vehicle to worry about yet, he certainly saw it, so now is a good time to change. We'll also block his move."

"What move?"

"He rented his car here. He got off the freeway a few miles back, so we're ahead of him. But he's on his way here to turn in his car. Either he'll just dump it and try to get on a plane to Los Angeles—which I doubt—or he'll rent a new car, too."

"And?"

"He'll still be looking for the black SUV, and we'll know what his new car is."

Paul walked into the car rental building. At the counter, he took out his keys and the papers he'd been given when he'd rented the SUV. "I'd like to trade in my SUV for something smaller, please," he said to the young woman behind the desk. She reminded him of a girl named Beth he had dated about twenty years ago. She had the same red-brown hair and the same light skin and blue eyes. This girl could be a close relative of Beth's. He wished he could say something. Sylvie was too prickly and difficult to listen to even neutral observations about women. Pointing them out made her want to kill them. The girl handed his keys to a man in blue overalls and watched him disappear out a back door.

As he watched the girl turn to her computer to tap in some information, he was tempted to say something to her; but he had dated Beth under his real name, so he couldn't. Anyway, Sylvie was a few feet away at the magazine rack near the door watching for Jack Till's beige Lincoln to come up the access road to the rental buildings.

Sylvie's jealousy was ridiculous, and that seemed to be part of her reason for it. The jealousy was her way of denying that she had done what he had seen her do in about fifty movies with at least a hundred men. When he first met her, he pretended that he didn't recognize her, and never let the topic of pornographic movies enter a conversation. He waited patiently, and when she made a big event out of gently, gradually telling him about her two-year career, he brought in a box from the garage to show her that he had already bought copies of all of her films. He said little more than the fact that he knew, and that it made no difference to him. That fantastic claim had struck Sylvie as entirely true.

The truth was that her film career had intrigued him and added to his attraction to her. What he had found to be a more difficult topic was *his* profession. For a time he tried telling her he was an entrepreneur who had made some money selling an Internet start-up business, then that he acted as a business consultant, and sometimes traveled to other cities to solve clients' problems.

In those days, he received most of his referrals from Bobby Mosca, the bartender at the Palazzo di Conti restaurant on La Brea. The Palazzo was a landmark where well-known people sometimes went, partly because it served good southern Italian food, and partly because it had a reputation. Sometimes the story was that it was a remote outpost for members of the Balacontano family who came west on business. A competing story was that Bugsy Siegel had once been the silent owner, and that when he was shot in the bungalow on the other side of town, one of the unintended consequences was that the apparent owners became the real owners.

One night Paul's telephone rang, and Sylvie answered and handed it to Paul. When the call was finished, he looked up and saw her in the doorway. She said, "I know."

Paul sat back in his chair with his hands folded on his stomach. "You know what?"

"I know who Bobby is. I know what you do for a living."

Paul nodded, keeping his eyes on her.

"You killed Darren so you could have me. Surely you must have expected me to know that much. When the police came here, they told me it was a professional execution. And after living with you for months, how could I *not* know?"

"So now what?"

"Are you asking me what I'm going to do about it?"

"No, I'm asking you what you feel about it."

She threw her arms around him and buried her face in his chest, then kissed him, hard. "I love you."

He had left late that night to complete the job Bobby had called about. He came home to find her waiting up for him.

She said, "How did it go? Tell me everything that happened."

"Why?" he said. "Why would you want to hear about that?"

"How else am I going to learn?"

As he looked away from the counter at Sylvie, he forgave her for the arguments and the idiotic defensiveness and lack of confidence. She was everything he had ever wanted. If he could just keep her convinced of that, then things would be tolerable. He heard the rental agent behind him, and turned.

He accepted the keys to the new car and looked at the tags. The car was a blue four-door Ford. That was acceptable: It wasn't anything like the SUV. "Thank you," he said. He turned and walked to Sylvie, picked up the two suitcases, and let Sylvie hold the door open for him. He walked to the car and put the suitcases into the trunk. Paul was pleased to see that the mechanic had already driven the black SUV around to the back of the building to clean and service it.

He and Sylvie got in. "Have you kept watching for Till's beige rental car?"

"Of course. There's only this one road for rental return. So far there have been fourteen cars since we got here. Two were beige or brown, but neither went to the Cheapcars lot, and neither had Till or the girl in them."

"Good watching." He reminded himself that he had thought of her as stupid, but Sylvie was absolutely not unintelligent. She could make all sorts of calculations and computations without engaging the major parts of her brain, and then announce them as though they were self-evident. It had been imprecise of him to let the word *stupid* float into his mind.

He felt his affection for her surge. He would never be able to separate what he saw from what he felt or what he thought. She was beautiful, therefore she was enticing, therefore he wanted her. The beauty itself was even more complicated because it was not perfection—Sylvie would never leave a flawless corpse—but depended upon an expression of the lips and a look about the eyes and a way of moving.

Paul understood his long attraction to her, but had never fully accounted for the moments when he reached the other extreme and felt rage. This gave his perceptions of her a tentative quality that made him uncomfortable. He watched the road, looking to the left and then the right, then pulled out of the lot.

"There it is," she said. The beige Lincoln Town Car popped into Paul's rearview mirror. He lifted his foot from the gas pedal and let the car slow down so it would stay on the straight section long enough for him to see the Lincoln turn into the Cheapcars lot. "Hurry up! You've got to make it all the way around the loop past the terminals and come by again in time to see."

"I will," he said. "Calm down." He sped up again and went around the corner out of sight of the rental lots, and toward the airport. He went past the terminals, maneuvering patiently among the shuttle buses, cars, and taxi vans. He kept to the left so he could take the rental-car loop again. When he came to it he took it and went slowly along the road until he could see the Cheapcars lot, and then pulled the car over to wait. He watched as a maintenance man came out and took charge of the beige Town Car, reaching toward the steering wheel shaft to turn on the engine and check the gauges.

Suddenly there was a movement in Paul's peripheral vision. The unexpectedness of it made him jump. He looked up and saw the front of a police car growing to fill the rearview mirror.

Paul noted that the cop had not turned on his blue-and-red flashers. The cop got out of the driver's seat instantly, which meant that he was not calling in the stop yet. He appeared at the side of the car beside Paul's window. He was less than thirty years old, with a chubby boyish face that didn't seem to go with his trim body, and black hair that seemed to start too low on his forehead, like a knit cap. Paul noticed the squared-off surface of his torso that revealed the body armor under his uniform.

Paul looked ahead through the windshield. This was just the kind of thing that Paul could not permit to happen. He had done everything right, followed patiently when a less-clever person would have made some premature, impulsive attempt that would have alarmed Jack Till. Now, when Till had finally come together with Wendy Harper, this fat-faced cherub of a cop was here to ruin everything. Paul read the metal tag on his right pocket: Rodeno.

The cop leaned on the car so he could look in at them. "Afternoon, folks."

"Afternoon," Paul said.

In the periphery of his vision, he saw Sylvie give the cop too much of a smile, and heard her voice become false and musical. "Hello, officer."

Paul stifled his irritation. She was trying to get control of the situation in the way that had always worked for her, and that was probably good. Even a cop would respond to a friendly smile from a pretty woman, even if she was fifteen years too old for him. Paul could see that the tension in the cop's arms relaxed a bit as he leaned to speak to them.

"Are you having car trouble?"

"No," Paul said. "Not exactly. I just rented this car and drove it out of the lot, but I needed to pull over, adjust the seats, and get to know the controls a little better before I get on the freeway with it."

"That's the kind of thing you should do in the lot before you drive out. What agency did you rent it from?"

"Miracle Rent-a-Car." Paul looked ahead again. He could see Jack Till and Wendy Harper coming out of the rental office. Time was passing, the moment of opportunity getting wasted.

"May I see your rental papers, please?"

Paul had not yet put them away, so he was able to snatch them out of the well in the door. The name he had used to rent them was William Porter. He supposed the name was going to be worthless after this. "Sure." He jabbed them out the window of the car, practically in Officer Rodeno's face. "Here they are."

Officer Rodeno had been startled by the abrupt movement. He accepted the papers and straightened. "The problem is, this isn't a place where you can park and make adjustments. It's a no-stopping zone. You should have gone around the loop and back into the Miracle lot, or off the loop onto a street where you could stop legally. Then you could make whatever adjustments were necessary to drive safely."

Paul said, "I'm sorry. I didn't realize that I couldn't stop here. I guess I missed the sign." He was intensely aware of everything going on around him. He felt the car move microscopically as Sylvie's back muscles contracted to make a slight shift in position. He knew she was looking ahead at Till and Wendy Harper, and he moved his eyes to see what had affected her.

There was an airport-shuttle bus at the Cheapcars lot with its doors open. A couple of customers who must have turned in cars climbed aboard. Paul strained to see whether Jack Till and Wendy Harper were among them. This was agony. Were they going to the terminal?

"May I see your license, please?"

Paul turned toward Officer Rodeno. "Look, I haven't blocked any traffic or done any harm. I was just getting ready to pull out when you arrived."

"May I see your license, Mr. Porter?" Rodeno repeated.

Paul sighed and took out his wallet. He had needed to use the Porter license to rent the car, so it was still in the pocket under the clear plastic. He slipped it out and handed it to the cop.

The license was good. He had bought a doctored Arkansas license two years ago in the name of William Porter and used it as identification to apply for a California license. As he thought about the trouble he'd gone through, his irritation grew. Officer Rodeno studied the license and then Paul's face. After a moment he turned away from Paul and stepped toward his car. The cop was going to run a check on William Porter.

Paul felt Sylvie move again, and then felt her put her gun in his hand. He could feel that the silencer had been screwed onto the barrel. He stuck it under his arm beneath his sport coat, got out of the car, and followed Officer Rodeno to his police car. Officer Rodeno sat behind the wheel with the door open, looking down at the license. He reached for the radio microphone. Paul moved to the open door of the police car, used his body to block any observer's view, and in a single, efficient movement, pulled out the gun and fired. There was a spitting sound, Rodeno's head jerked to the side an inch or two, then bowed, and his body followed it to rest on the wheel. Paul leaned in the open door and toppled Rodeno's body onto the passenger seat, got in and closed the door, then used his legs to push the body the rest of the way to the passenger side. The engine was already idling, and he threw it into gear and drove.

Paul adjusted the rearview mirror, and he saw Sylvie pull out onto the road to follow him in the rental car. He looked around for witnesses, but to his relief, he could detect nobody looking in his direction. Nobody seemed to have seen how the traffic stop had ended, or at least interpreted it as a killing. Shooting the cop and driving off had been quiet and taken no more than three or four seconds.

Instead of taking the loop to go through the airport again, Paul took the entrance to the freeway, then pulled off at the first exit and parked the police car on the lot of a big Sears store. He took a moment to retrieve his William Porter license and rental papers from the floor, and wipe off the door handles and steering wheel. By then Sylvie was pulling to a stop beside him. He got into the passenger seat and sat in silence for a few seconds while Sylvie drove off.

"What's the matter?" Sylvie asked.

"I still can't believe that happened. Did you see if they went to the airport?"

"They didn't get into the shuttle bus."

"Where are they, then?"

"They rented another car, just like we did. It's a Lincoln Town Car, like the other one, only charcoal gray. I have the license number, and they were just getting into it when we left. We can catch them in a few minutes."

23

JACK TILL THREADED the gray Town Car in and out of the heavy traffic in the airport loop, then took the entrance to the 101 South, glancing in his mirrors with nervous alertness.

"What's wrong?" Ann Donnelly asked. "Did you see something?"

"Nothing that stands out. This is just the time when we can get out clean. If there are no problems now, then there won't be later." He looked into the mirror again as he merged with the traffic on the freeway. "Back there near the car rental there was a cop who had pulled someone over to write a ticket. Maybe we were lucky and he scared off anybody who might have followed us."

"I hope there was nobody to scare."

"I've got to think that if these people were in San Rafael this afternoon, then they'll be somewhere near here now."

She frowned. "If we lose them, they'll catch up in Los Angeles, won't they—or fly there and wait? That's the part that keeps scaring me. I'm coming back to them, and they know it."

"I wish I could say you're wrong. I don't think you are. The trick is to get them to reveal themselves."

"How are we going to do that?"

"We make finding us as hard as we can, and see if we can spot someone searching. We pull off the road now and then and see who follows."

"That's all we can do?"

"Unless you can give me something to go on."

She straightened. "I don't know what you mean."

"We talked years ago about who was trying to kill you. At the time, you said you didn't know."

"Are you saying you didn't believe me?"

"I believed the bruises and the limp."

"Then what are you saying?"

"That was a long time ago. There might have been details that you didn't notice at the time that have surfaced in your memory—coincidences or unusual events. Maybe people said things that you heard, but didn't recall right away."

"I made a conscious decision after I left not to spend my life thinking about that. I thought about the way I wanted things to be in the future and what steps I should take to make it happen."

"Then make a conscious decision to remember now. Think."

"About what?"

"Try to bring back what you saw and heard at the time, or impressions you had. Have you remembered anything about the attack in the years since then?"

"No. I told the police everything, twice, and then I told you. A man I didn't know was waiting for me when I came home from the restaurant and hit me with a bat. When other cars came, he ran."

"Would you recognize him if you saw him again?"

"I don't know. I think I would have right after it happened. When the cars came their headlights lit him up for a second. But I was half-conscious with a concussion, and six years is a long time. He could have changed a lot." She made a fist, and pounded it on her knee. "Why ask me about all this now? Can't you see how scared I am?"

"Of course you're scared." He searched the mirrors behind him again. "What I find helps most is to try to do something about it."

"What? Try to remember things that happened in the dark years ago?"

"Not this minute." He had planted the idea, so it was time to back off and let her think about it. "For now, try to see if you can detect anybody following us. In an hour or two it will begin to get dark. If anyone is following us, I'd like to spot them before the headlights start coming on. It's a good idea to take roll so you can keep track: white pickup, green Bug, gray Volvo, blue Ford, red Cherokee."

She looked out the rear window. "I see them."

"Sometimes when people follow you, they'll do it in teams. For a while there will be a black SUV behind you. Then it disappears, so you don't think about it again. But then up comes a green car. You've never seen him before. He's been back too far, not even keeping in sight of you. He hasn't had to because the guy in the black car has been keeping in touch with him on the phone. Now it's *his* turn to follow you. Maybe they'll switch again in a half hour. Tag team. That's the way we did it when I was a cop."

"You're just trying to distract me, aren't you?"

"No, I'm not. You're still trying not to get caught, aren't you? If we stay alert, we'll have an advantage."

"All right. At least I'll be doing something." She half-turned in her seat and leaned on the door while she watched.

Till glanced at her and then away, his mind rapidly filling with unrelated observations. In six years, she had become more attractive. Her eyes had acquired a stronger, wiser look, and her features looked finer and more defined. He supposed maybe when he had left her at the Santa Barbara airport, her face had still retained some of the swelling from the beating.

Something else had changed since he had seen her last, but maybe the change was in him. Years ago she had been a pretty young woman who had been hurt and terrified and needed his help. He had been able to tell himself that she was dazed and dis-oriented, and that she probably hadn't seen anything anyway.

This time, Till could see that she was lying to him. She knew something that she had not been willing to tell anyone six years ago, and was not willing to tell him now.

24

I **T WAS GETTING DARK,** and the cars all had their headlights on. Sylvie leaned close to Paul and touched his cheek as he drove, then rested her hand on his thigh. "Are you okay?"

"Huh? Sure. Why?"

"When you kill somebody like that, there always seems to be a big rush of adrenaline—heart pounding, sweating, really happy you're alive—but then afterward there's always a kind of bad feeling, a letdown. I always get tired."

"I'm not tired," he said. "I'm just trying to do five things at once. We need to hear the radio, so we know if the police start looking for this car. I need to keep Till's car in sight, but stay back far enough so he doesn't notice us. I need to pay attention to the road ahead so we don't hit somebody, and the road behind in case the police *do* come after us."

She moved her hand up his thigh only an inch or two. "That's only four. Want something else to think about, so you're not short?"

"I don't think that's a good idea."

She withdrew to her side of the car.

"I'm sorry," he said. "I'm not annoyed. I'm trying to—" He stopped. "Look. Maybe you're right. Maybe I *do* have a delayed reaction to the cop. I had no intention of doing that, no plan about doing it. He just came out of nowhere with his helpful Boy Scout face and gave me the choice of letting him run my license or killing him. Maybe he put me in a bad mood, but I don't want to take it out on you. I'm just preoccupied, that's all."

She shrugged. "I was just trying to cheer you up. Let me find a better radio station."

"Thanks. It's almost the half-hour, and I want to be sure we pick it up if they've identified this car."

Sylvie held the button down and let the radio find the next strong signal, then listened to a commercial about somebody's "giant shopping mall of cars," and then found a news report. There was no mention of their rental car, not even any mention that a cop had been killed. Here it was, hours later, and nobody seemed to have looked inside the parked cop car yet.

Sylvie was impressed with Paul's timing. Killing the cop a minute earlier would have been foolish: There was still a chance he would go away. Killing him ten seconds later would have been too late.

She started to smile, but something stopped her lips, choked off the affection. Paul wasn't behaving right with her. Earlier in the day she had provoked him a bit to explore the question, but she had not yet satisfied herself. She had accepted his explanation of his coldness and distance, but her acceptance had been only tentative. It was only talk, but here was that feeling again. Were his conciliatory words more real than her feeling? She loved him, had given herself to him all these years, and he was rejecting her, shutting her out.

She felt pained. She was over forty now. The first time she had noticed a change in the way she looked—a decline—had been when she was only twenty-five. Until then every change had been an improvement. But at twenty-five, there had been a slight change in the texture of her skin. There had not been any wrinkles yet, just a loss in the elasticity of the skin beside her eyes and on her forehead.

That had been a mild, tiny warning that things were happening. She had been married to Darren then, and she had not mentioned it to him. She had needed to think about it and see whether creams and lotions would restore her skin. She'd thought maybe it was because she was working out in the gym so much and taking hot showers afterward. The air in Los Angeles was so dry, and maybe her soap was too harsh.

Then she had blamed Cherie Will. Just before Sylvie had quit, there had been a series of movies that Cherie had decided to shoot outdoors. One, Sylvie remembered, had been about a picnic, and the other had been a thing about cowboys and cowgirls. Sylvie had gotten terribly sunburned, and sunburn was the worst thing for skin. Cherie had told everybody she was shooting so many movies way out on a ranch because the actors looked so much better in natural sunlight. The truth was that she had bought the ranch and was charging her own production company location-rental fees to help pay for it. All she had needed to dress the set was a checkered tablecloth for the picnic and two bales of hay for the cowboy stuff. Cherie had told her that her makeup would protect her face from sunburn.

That had been when Sylvie was twenty or twenty-one, and now she was over forty. How could she have gotten so old? She had always looked younger and prettier than her age, but now time was catching up to her. The dancing and the exercise had fought off the years for a long time, but now she was beginning to see a bit of extra fat on her bottom in spite of the work. Maybe even her tummy was beginning to soften.

She watched Paul without moving her head. He was resenting her. The resentment always was officially for being annoying or making a mistake or something, but it was really for letting herself go. Being a less-desirable woman was to be less respected, less wanted. For at least the past couple of weeks, he had been making the situation increasingly clear to her.

Sylvie could feel a suspicion slowly revealing itself to her. As she had been getting older and less desirable, Paul was becoming older and more desirable. He was still trim and hard. The extra years had given his skin a tan, sculpted look. The bulging muscles of his arms and legs had been giving way to a sinewy leanness. His thick dark hair had grayed a bit at the temples. He looked distinguished and seasoned. On her a gray hair was a blemish, a revelation that her youthful look was an imposture.

Paul had to be cheating on her. She tried to think of who and when. It could easily be that little dance instructor Mindy, the puppy dog. She had been flirting with Paul for at least a year, and lately she'd been overtly trying to get between them by using Paul as her partner, almost a second instructor. The woman could be any woman, or lots of women. There was no way to catch Paul after the fact, or know whether he had even started cheating yet. He was emotionally separating himself from her, and that was the big step.

How could Paul be so disloyal? She knew the answer to that, too. He would consider himself justified—all the work was done for him in advance. It wouldn't matter that Sylvie had been completely faithful to him for fifteen years, and shared his difficulties and dangers—literally killed for him. He would believe that because of those two years in her life when she was very young and naïve, she had no rights. The fact that she had stopped doing films four years before she met him and already been a respectable married woman would be irrelevant. She simply had no right to be jealous.

Arguing with Paul's justification was a meaningless activity. Justification was meaningless. What he wanted to do, he would do. *Was* doing. She was aging, and that was enough. When Paul had spent enough time searching and holding auditions for the next woman to assume her role, he would replace her.

Sylvie looked at Paul again, driving along the dark highway. He had such a strong, appealing profile. The slight upturn of his lips and the arched eyebrows gave him a special expression, the look of a perfect partner. The expression had always struck her as the look of a flamenco dancer, dangerous in a sexual way—jealous, aggressive, maybe just on the edge of violence.

Her breath caught in her chest and stayed there for a moment. She forced it out slowly through pursed lips and waited a moment before she took another, just as slowly, to calm herself. She looked at him again. Paul wasn't some fat, soft-minded little business executive. Was he likely to file for divorce and then wait quietly for six months while Sylvie's lawyers stripped the meat off his bones?

If Paul had made the decision that he was finished with Sylvie, then she would have a problem. "I love you, Paul."

"What?

"I was just thinking about what a difference meeting you has made in my life. If it were all over now, I wouldn't regret it."

She studied him. He seemed genuinely puzzled, but not quite daring to be pleased, as though he were waiting anxiously for something unpleasant to follow. "What brought this on?"

"I don't know. Just being here with you, I guess. I was just thinking that things in life—even ones that seem permanent—are temporary."

He glanced at her with a look of amusement. "Are you trying to kiss me off?"

She laughed once, with no conviction. "Of course not. I just said I loved you. But since you brought up kissing people off, I guess it applies to that, too. If you did decide to leave me someday, I love you too much to make it hard for you." She had been listening to her own voice to hear whether the lie sounded convincing, but she wasn't sure how well she had done. He seemed merely confused.

"What do you mean?"

"You know. All of those women who get dumped think they have to get revenge in court and leave their husbands in poverty. I've heard them at lunch in restaurants laughing about how much they took, like harpies or something. They gossip about the ex-husband and the new woman, and try to sabotage them any way they can." Her eyes stayed on him as she talked. "You know. They turn him in to the IRS for hiding income or something like that." With some effort, she softened. "I just want you to know I'm not like them. If you want somebody younger and don't find me attractive anymore, I won't punish you for that."

"Oh. So that's it." He sounded tired and annoyed. "I had no idea what you were talking about. I should have known, I guess, but I didn't. I never said you weren't attractive, or that I wanted somebody younger."

"No. Please don't be mad. I'm not trying to start a fight. It's just the opposite. I'm trying to tell you that I've thought about you in all kinds of ways. And what I feel most is gratitude. I've had such an incredible time with you. I've learned so much—even that. You're the one who taught me to make all the decisions I can in advance."

"Okay." His voice sounded tight, as though he were holding back anger. He was reacting as though she had said the opposite of what she had said. She took a breath to speak, then held it. She was getting herself in deeper. She let out the breath and sat in silence, staring ahead at the red taillights. The cars went around a long, slow curve and she could see the ones ahead of her better. The headlights of the car directly ahead shone on the side of the next, and she could make out the head of the driver. "There. That's Jack Till."

Sylvie turned in her seat and squinted through the rear window at the configuration of headlights behind their car. As their car began the long curve, the headlights of the cars behind aimed off to the left, and she could see them better. There seemed to her to be none in the pack that were troublesome. There were an overdecorated white SUV with gold trim, a Volvo station wagon, and two Japanese cars that were too small for cops to use. She looked ahead again. "I don't think any of those cars can be searching for us, and I don't see any of them that could be a backup for Till. That's what

I would have done if I were Till. I'd have a second car following me with a couple of cops in it, just in case."

"This isn't a presidential motorcade," Paul said. "And Till isn't even a cop anymore. He was just trying to sneak her into L.A., and he's failed."

She watched Paul's expression of concentration, and his eyes moving from the rearview mirror to the highway ahead and back. It occurred to her that for the moment she was in no danger. Paul was an expert strategist, and he knew that his biggest advantage over his adversary right now was Sylvie. With her he had double the firepower, an extra set of eyes and hands and an extra brain.

Paul said, "Okay, here we go. He's pulling off the freeway, taking the exit up there."

"It's about time. I was wondering if those people ever had to pee." Sylvie took the silencer out of her purse and screwed it onto the barrel of her pistol.

"Get ready."

She resisted the impulse to say, "What do you think I'm doing?" Instead, she said, "Hand me your gun."

He pulled the gun out of the well in the door beside him and handed it to her. She took the second silencer out of her purse and screwed it on, then ejected the magazine and looked at it. "You didn't reload after the cop."

He looked mildly surprised, but he was busy trying to get off the freeway at the right speed and distance from Till's car. Sylvie could see he was staying barely within sight, only close enough to see which way Till turned before he disappeared. Till's car turned left and drove under the freeway overpass.

She wanted time, and the time was speeding up, slipping away. She rested both guns in her lap, one in each hand. She wondered for a moment whether in the long run she wouldn't be wise simply to wait for Paul to pull the car off the exit and put it in neutral, and then fire his pistol into his right temple. She would be able to squeeze the gun into his right hand and walk away. Then she could get a flight home, clean up the house, and await the visit from the quiet, respectful police officers. The tears would be real. That was the problem with the idea.

No, she decided. She wouldn't act now to prevent him from acting later. As long as this job was occupying him, he wouldn't harm her. She checked to be sure the safety was on and handed him the gun. "There's a round in the chamber."

"Good. Thanks. You're thinking better than I am."

"A pretty good compliment." She leaned over and gave him a soft, wet kiss on the cheek, then sat up in her seat, her eyes on the windshield again.

Paul followed Till's car at a distance, the taillights so far ahead that they looked almost like one red spot instead of two. The car swerved into the driveway of a big hotel on the hillside. Instead of following Till into the parking lot, Paul stopped at a gas station down the street. He coasted up to a gas pump but stayed in the car watching the hotel parking lot. Paul said, "He's parking in front of the hotel restaurant."

Jack Till got out of his car and stood beside it to stretch his long body and twist his torso a couple of times. Sylvie could see that he was standing guard with his coat open and his gun in easy reach while Wendy Harper got out and walked toward the restaurant entrance.

When Jack Till and Wendy Harper had disappeared into the restaurant, Paul got out of the car, went into the gas station, and gave the teenaged boy inside some money. Then he returned, inserted the nozzle into the car, and began to fill the tank.

Sylvie pressed the button to lower her window. "Why are you doing that now?"

He shrugged. "After we get them, I'm not going to want to stop for gas."

She shook her head in mock disapproval. "I hope you didn't smile into the surveillance camera, because I intend to go in that restaurant and get her right there."

"Oh? Don't you want to eat dinner first?"

"Not in that place. If you hadn't stopped for gas, I'll bet I could have bagged her by now."

"Don't get too eager." He wasn't sure how much of her impatience was an interest in getting the job done, and how much was wanting to kill a woman who was younger and prettier than she was. The nozzle on the hose clicked and stopped, and he took it out and hung it on the pump. He looked at the total on the pump, touched the screen to indicate he didn't want a receipt, and got back in beside her. "I want to do this right, so we need to be a little bit careful." He started the engine, looked at the gas gauge to be sure it was full, then turned out into the road and down the street into the parking lot between the hotel and the restaurant. He found a space among the cars of hotel guests, far from the one where Jack Till had parked. "Are you sure you can do her by yourself?"

"If you can get me out of there afterward."

"Okay. You get her when she's in the ladies' room. If Till moves when you come out, I'll shoot him. Then we'll just step outside with everybody else in the confusion."

"All right. Let's go in before I get nervous." Sylvie took a couple of deep breaths to calm herself as she walked toward the restaurant. She could see people sitting at the window tables along the front, but none of them was Till or Wendy. She wasn't surprised that they would want to avoid sitting in a lighted window. Wendy Harper had probably not lingered in front of a window in six years. Sylvie approached the front door and she could feel her excitement building.

She did not have time to hesitate in front of the door before she sensed the displacement of air to her right as Paul's hand appeared and opened the door for her. The closeness reassured her. It was the old unspoken certainty that she felt while they were dancing, the knowledge of where his body was in relation to hers.

Sylvie moved into the entry, where a fake wood sign said "PLEASE SEAT YOURSELF." She scanned the interior of the restaurant. Till and Wendy were to the left at the far end of the room, so she quickly turned right to find a table as far away from them as possible. Sylvie slid into a booth beside a large window overlooking the hotel and its parking lot. She could even see the gas station where she and Paul had stopped.

Paul sat down across the table from her. She could see his eyes focus on the part of the room where Till and Wendy sat. He let his eyes stay there too long, so she became more and more tense until he looked away. Then Sylvie tilted her head down and pretended to look at the menu while she surveyed the restaurant. She could see a counter along the back wall, and beyond that, the kitchen. There was about sixty feet of open floor between Sylvie and the far end of the counter where the hall began that led to the restrooms and telephones. Jack Till and Wendy Harper were on that side of the room, and she calculated that Wendy's walk to the restroom would be no more than thirty feet.

Sylvie would have to see Wendy get up and move toward the ladies' room, then get up herself and follow. She would reach the restroom after Wendy, put a bullet in Wendy's head with the silenced pistol, turn, and walk back the sixty feet to the front door, where Paul would be waiting. It would all work fine if Wendy didn't see the gun and scream.

Sylvie looked hard at the people sitting along the counter. When it was over, she was going to have to make it back here past all of them. Usually when bad things happened in public places, the people who were present stood with their mouths open, not able to move or even think. But sometimes there would be somebody who understood what he had seen and who acted instantly. She couldn't shoot Wendy and then have one of those four big men at the counter reach out and grab her. She would have to keep her gun in her hand so if one of them tried, she could pop him. She would carry it in her right hand, because the seats along the counter would be on her left. The gun would need to be concealed. She supposed the only natural-looking way was to carry it with her jacket over her forearm to cover it.

Far across the restaurant, Wendy Harper pushed back her chair and rose. "She's up," Sylvie whispered. Wendy Harper pushed the chair in, turned toward the ladies' room, and began to make her way past the tables. "Are you ready?"

Sylvie slid out of the booth, stood up, arranged her purse and jacket so her right hand was free, and took a step, but Paul's hand shot out, clutched her arm and pulled her down onto the bench on his side of the table. He was smiling as though he were teasing her, but his face was close to hers, and he whispered, "Look. Outside in the parking lot. Careful."

She kept her face close to his, but leaned to the right slightly so her right eye was clear of him and could see. There was a police car outside, stopped behind their rental car. The police officer inside had his radio microphone to his mouth.

"What are we going to do?"

"We've got to get out of here before more of them show up. They must have the license number."

"How?"

"Who cares? Somebody saw what happened at the airport."

"I mean how do we get out?"

"The hotel."

She looked in the direction of Jack Till's table, but Paul pushed against her with his hip. "Get up and go. Now." She got up and walked toward the door. He opened it quickly and was out after her.

Paul guided Sylvie around the front of the restaurant away from the direction of the rental car, and they walked quickly toward the main hotel building.

Paul held the door at the hotel entrance for her, and she slipped in and turned while he caught up. All their motions were smooth and familiar. They weren't nervous people fumbling to evade the cops. They were dancers again, a couple stepping gracefully into their hotel after a dinner date. She forced her anxiety to become excitement. She moved across the floor at Paul's side, aware of the danger gathering behind her. Cars were on their way in answer to the lone policeman's call.

Paul led her through an alcove and into a corridor lined with guest rooms. He moved along the hallway, turned twice until he reached a spot where the passage ended in a fire exit. He stepped to the door and looked out, then beckoned to Sylvie.

She could see the police cars arriving from the direction of the freeway. There were three of them already, all with lights on their roofs revolving and flashing. Paul put his hands on her shoulders. "Stay right here," he whispered. "If the cops come in here, talk to them loud. If they come for me, open fire. I'm just waiting a second to give these people time to see the flashing lights outside." He stood there, glanced at his watch, and gave her a pat. "Time."

He stepped along the hall listening at doors. It was early evening, and the first few rooms seemed to be empty. Finally he knocked on one of them. There was a muffled voice that Sylvie couldn't quite hear. Then Paul said, "Police. Open up." He held his wallet in his hand, and passed it quickly in front of the peephole in the door.

The door opened and Paul pushed the door inward. "What the hell?" said a man's voice, and then Sylvie heard the spitting sound of Paul's suppressed pistol. The door closed.

There was a long wait, and then the door opened and Paul beckoned to Sylvie. She hurried to the door and slipped inside to join him. At first the room seemed empty, but on the far side of the bed she could see a man's bare feet sticking out. She moved closer, and saw the body. It seemed to be the size of a walrus, a big, rounded torso beached on the floor. Paul said, "Help me find his car keys. Hurry."

The flashing lights from the police cars blinked through a crack between the curtains, so she tugged them closed, then began to go through the pile of dirty clothes on the floor of the closet while Paul searched the drawers of the nightstands, the dressers, and the desk.

She looked up to begin searching the pockets of the clothes hanging above, and noticed that some of them didn't belong to the dead man. "Paul," she said. Someone in the hallway tried the doorknob.

"Shit!" Paul muttered under his breath.

Sylvie shook her head and pointed to the bathroom. Paul stepped into the bathroom and closed the door. Sylvie picked up her purse, slung it over her left shoulder and arranged her pistol in it so she could reach it quickly. Then she opened the door to the hallway.

Standing in front of her was a woman about fifty years old. She had a pizza box and a six-pack of beer in her hands, and dangling from her fingers was a set of keys. "Ray?" she said. "Oh, my God! Do I have the wrong room?"

"No, ma'am. Come in, please." Sylvie watched the woman enter and closed the door gently behind her. She remained at the door so the woman would have to look at her instead of toward the bed. "I'm a police officer. Are you Ray's wife?"

"Yes. I saw all your cars outside. What's going on?"

"It's a search for some fugitives. May I see your license, please?"

The woman set her pizza and beer on the dresser and opened her purse to take out a wallet. She slid a license out of a plastic sleeve and handed it to Sylvie with a shaking hand.

Sylvie held the license up to compare it with the woman's face. She seemed satisfied, but held on to it. "Your car. Can you tell me the make and model, please?"

"It's a green Toyota. It's the one parked right near the door."

"Are those the keys?"

The woman held the keys up where Sylvie could see them. Sylvie took them and the woman's license and set them on the bed. "Thank you. Now, I'd like you to turn around and hold both arms out from your sides."

The woman turned and lifted her arms like wings in an absurd flying posture. Sylvie pulled out her gun and fired once into the back of the woman's head, and she toppled to the floor.

Paul opened the bathroom door. "Sylvie?"

She said clearly, "Yes, Paul," then picked up the woman's license and keys from the bed. "It's a green Toyota, parked right outside the door."

Paul looked down at the woman's body, nodded to himself, then walked to the door, opened it to let Sylvie out first, hung the DO NOT DISTURB sign on the knob, and closed it, then wiped the fingerprints off the knob with his sleeve.

Paul and Sylvie stepped outside into the parking lot. They could see four police cars in the lot now, and several cops were gathering around the blue car they had rented in San Francisco. The cops looked at Paul and Sylvie as they walked toward the green Toyota. Then Sylvie saw another green Toyota one row farther off. She clicked the plastic switch attached to the key ring, and watched the dome light in the second Toyota come on and the lock buttons pop up. When they reached the car Paul opened Sylvie's door for her, and as she stepped beside him to get in she saw the cops turn away and look at the blue rental car again.

Paul got in and she handed him the keys. He started the engine and drove slowly toward the nearest exit from the lot. As he pulled out onto the road, he laughed.

Sylvie laughed, too, then she realized that she was trembling. The release of the tension was making her giddy.

Paul turned the car into the lot of the restaurant they had just left.

"What are you doing?"

"They're still inside," he said. "See? There's Till's car."

"Don't we have to get out of here?"

"Not until *they* do. Until checkout tomorrow, this car is clean and we've got nothing to be afraid of."

25

JACK TILL TOOK one more sip of his coffee and scanned the customers in the restaurant. They all had the weary look of people who had spent the day driving. Some were probably staying at the hotel across the parking lot, but many would probably be back on the road as soon as they paid their checks. He selected the four or five who looked to his practiced eye like potential shooters. He studied their faces for signs that they were interested in Ann Donnelly, and their clothing for places where they might be hiding weapons.

"Have I changed a lot?"

The question startled him. He considered Ann Donnelly. "No. You haven't aged at all that I can see. You haven't done a whole lot to change your looks, either."

"I did at first. I put away my contacts and got clear glasses for night, tinted for day. My hair was short and dark. I wore different clothes. In Las Vegas I used to lie out beside the pool to get a tan."

"When did you stop worrying?"

"I always worried. I just handled it differently. I think I had been living at the Royal Palms Palace for months before I got careless with the hair dye and Louanda noticed the roots. By then I was pretty well established as Ann Delatorre. Not once had anyone shown up looking for Wendy Harper. There had been no scares. So after we moved to Henderson, I slowly started to let myself look like me again."

He shrugged. "How would you know if there were close calls?"

"What do you mean?"

"You told me you couldn't identify the waitress's boyfriend, and the one with the bat was a hired hand. How would you know if they were getting close to you?"

She seemed irritated. "I suppose I didn't. Maybe it was just hard for me to stay scared of everyone forever."

Till looked at his watch. It was after eight. "I'm ready to get on the road again if you are."

"Okay," she said. "I guess I am, too."

They rose and he said, "Don't go outside alone. Wait for me while I pay."

Ann Donnelly stood a couple of paces behind Till while he paid for their dinner at the cash register. Till used the time to look around the restaurant once more. He had scanned all of the faces when she and Till had entered, and now he was doing it again. None of them seemed ominous.

Till put away his wallet and walked with Ann to the doorway. He pushed the glass door open and went outside with it, so he could scan the area while he held it for her.

"Wait," he said. "There are cop cars. I wonder what's up."

"It can't be about us."

As they walked toward their car, Till handed her the car keys. "Drive across the lot toward the hotel."

"What for?"

"Just do it. Stop near the farthest car and let me out. Keep the motor running."

She did as Till asked, then watched him unfold his long body and then stroll up to the cop who seemed to be in charge, a bald, forty-five-year-old man wearing a black nylon jacket and a pair of black lace-up boots. Ann pushed the button to lower her window so she could hear what Jack was saying, but the conversation was too low and ended too quickly. She heard him say, "Good luck," and then his long strides brought him back to the car and he got in. "Let's head for the highway."

She aimed the car toward the exit from the parking lot and slowly accelerated. "Well?"

"This is a good time to get out. In a few minutes, it will get a lot more crowded around here. That blue car they were all looking at was the one used by some guy who killed a cop near the San Francisco airport a few hours ago."

"So it has nothing to do with us?"

"It could. We were near the airport at about that time, and we're here now. The sergeant said nobody seems to have seen the car arrive, but the hood is warm."

"What are we going to do?"

"Keep driving." As Ann Donnelly pulled onto the street and drove toward the freeway entrance Till leaned back in the passenger seat, crossed his arms on his chest, and appeared to relax.

She accelerated onto the freeway and took a spot in the second lane. "When this is over, I suppose I'll have to go back to all that, won't I?"

"Go back to what?"

"Cut and dye my hair, wear sunglasses and hats everywhere."

"You're looking at this whole situation backward," he said. "If you can just give me something more to go on, then maybe these men will be the ones who have to worry about being caught, not you."

"I told you. I didn't see enough, I didn't hear enough, I don't know enough."

"Keep trying to remember."

"It isn't a question of remembering. There's nothing to remember."

"Then until these guys get caught for something else, you and your husband will just have to be careful to stay invisible."

"That's over." She said it quickly, but in a calm, unemotional way.

Till wasn't sure at first that he had heard right. He was accustomed to hearing that kind of announcement delivered with emotion, or even false bravado, so he waited for them. Then he said, "Your marriage? You're ending your marriage?"

"Yes, because I have to. I didn't think this was going to happen, or I would never have married Dennis." At last she had begun to sound unhappy. "I wasn't planning on doing this to his kids."

"So why are you?"

She ignored Till's question, and went on as though she were talking to herself. "When I was a little girl and my mother left, I said 'I'll never do that to my daughter.' This is the comeback, the big voice saying, 'Oh, yeah?' It isn't going to be easy for them. I know. Even my inadequate mothering is better than none."

"I don't think you have to make any decision right now."

"The decision is already made, Jack. It was made before Dennis and I ever got married."

"How did you manage that?"

"Dennis had the kids before I met him. Their mother had died in a car accident a couple of years earlier. Dennis and I were dating for a time, and he asked me to marry him. I had been dreading it. Once he asked, everything was different. I had to say yes, or tell him to go away."

"It must have been a hard decision to make."

"I wasn't ready. All I knew in advance was how I would decide. I invited him to go with me on a trip to Las Vegas, and took him to Henderson. He and I and Louanda sat down in the living room of the house I had bought. I introduced her as Ann Delatorre and explained to him how she had gotten that name. I told him everything.

Then the three of us spent a couple of days talking about it. From time to time, I sent Dennis out to buy food and supplies, and Louanda and I would talk alone. Louanda would tell me things she thought about Dennis, and about the idea of marrying him."

"What did she think?"

"She was protective of me. We were the ones who kept each other's secrets. We were—no, I was going to say 'like sisters,' but it's not like that because we weren't alike. We were like two men who have been through a war together. Each of us was a part of the other's life forever. She didn't think I should marry Dennis. When I told her I was leaning toward doing it anyway, she forced me to talk about things I probably wouldn't have."

"Such as?"

"Such as what would happen if we were married and the killers came for me. What would I do to protect his kids? We tried out all of the possibilities, followed them all the way through to their logical conclusions."

"So what did you decide would happen if today came—if you were married with kids and the killers came for you?"

She took her eyes off the road long enough to look at him for a second. "I couldn't sit still in San Rafael and wait for them. My husband and kids couldn't stay there because those people might kidnap them and make me trade my life for theirs, or simply kill them. And I couldn't run away and bring them all with me, a family of four. I knew that then—or Louanda did, and made me think it through. So before anything happened, I made other arrangements. Or Dennis, Louanda, and I did." Her face seemed to squint and compress itself in pain. He could see that the tears were coming now, without any way for her to stop them. "Oh, shit," she said. "Oh, shit!"

He wanted her to cry. He needed to obliterate the false composure she had perfected over the years if he was going to get her to tell him anything, but he had to be patient, or she would resist. "Maybe it was the wrong decision, the wrong arrangement."

"No, it wasn't."

She drove on for a few minutes, slowly bringing the sobs under control while Till waited. He kept looking back at the headlights on the road behind them, wondering which set was the one following them.

"We made a plan. It's just that long before we made it, I was sure we would never need it. Don't you see?"

"Sure I do."

"It was like making a plan for a nuclear war or something. You know the only responsible thing you can do is make a plan, but your little plan is only half-serious because you don't *feel* it. The threat isn't real. I would never have put us in this situation if I had felt that I would need a plan."

Till watched her fighting back the next wave of tears. He saw her eyes, her face in the flash-glow of the headlights on the northbound cars across the margin. "You have a place—a safe house—picked out for them, don't you?"

"Yes. How could Dennis be expected to take the kids and do everything by himself? He doesn't know anything about new identities or hiding or anything. He would be found in a day, and the kids would be dead. So I set up everything I could in advance."

"The two of you went somewhere and arranged for a place where they would live?"

"The two of us, yes. But not Dennis."

"Of course not. It had to be you and Louanda."

"It was really mostly her. We found a house. It's in Pennsylvania, about thirty miles outside Philadelphia. We bought a small farm. It was really just a corner of a much bigger place, but the owner had died and his kids needed to pay off some debts to keep the rest of the place clear, so they sold us that little bit. It's only about five acres and a house. Dennis will be on the way there right now, tonight."

Till needed to force her to revisit every decision. "I'm sorry for him," said Till. "It's not going to be easy taking two little kids across the country and into a place that's been unoccupied for years."

"It hasn't."

"A woman. There's a woman."

She was crying harder. "Of course there is."

"Who? A nanny?"

"Do we have to talk about every little detail?"

"Who is she?"

"She's somebody Louanda knew."

"How about you? Did you know her?"

"I got to know her. I spent time with her in Philadelphia, and she came to stay with us a few times in San Rafael, so if something really did happen, she wouldn't be a stranger." She glared at Jack Till with something that looked like hatred. "You're the one who taught me. You're the one who told me to make sure I had thought of everything, prepared for everything. 'Never let yourself get more than two steps in the front door if you can't already find the back door.' That's what you said. So I did it. I did it a hundred times in a hundred ways, and this was one of them. Of course there's a woman. Without her the plan would have been a fake."

"But who is she?"

"She and Louanda knew each other for years. She's a couple of years younger than I am, and she even looks a little bit like me. Louanda used to kid me about that at first, before it wasn't funny anymore. Dennis is capable of getting the kids to the farm without telling anybody his real name. Then Iris will step in and start taking care of things."

"Taking care of things?"

"She'll take care of the children. She'll take care of the house.

She'll cook for them. She'll be sure they're enrolled in a local school, and get there every day with clean clothes and a lunch."

"What are people supposed to think she is?"

"The identification papers are in the names Donald, Linda, and Timothy Welsh. There are also some papers in the house that say Kathy Welsh."

Jack Till said nothing. He looked back at the highway behind the car, trying to discern a set of headlights that might have been there too long. His experience as an interrogator told him he needed to keep pressing her now, trying to learn more, trying to force her to remove the next layer of half-truths. He had found her first real vulnerability, and he needed to probe it. But it was also his vulnerability.

There were several minutes of silence while Ann Donnelly stared ahead at the highway, thinking. When she spoke again, it was as though her thoughts had simply become audible. "She'd had a rough life, even by Louanda's standards. Louanda swore that Iris would be good to the children no matter what. After we had all spent time together, I was sure that part was true, and it was the only part that mattered. The kids know her and like her."

"How did Dennis feel about this arrangement?"

"He'll be just fine."

"Is that what he said?"

"He promised he would go through with this. He knows that the kids' lives might depend on his following the plan."

"There's a lot you're not saying. What is it?"

"I don't know. What is it? Do you want to know how it feels to walk off and give your life to another woman? Bad. Really bad. Now my family is headed for a place where I can never go. I've lost them."

Till tried to keep his mind on forcing his way to the next reve-lation. But he kept thinking of what it would be like to have to leave Holly forever. He had a memory of her looking up at him and smiling, then turning away to go back into Garden House when he had last seen her. He could hardly bear it. "I told you before that you don't have to make any big decisions tonight."

"And I told you it's over. It's been the arrangement from the beginning, from the day when I told him the truth in Henderson the first time. If he wanted to get married, he had to agree to the plan. He'll keep his word. She'll do the rest."

"She's not just an employee, is she? And she's not just for the kids."

"No."

"Does he know?"

"No. Yes. He's just a guy—a good, kind, ordinary guy with a business that keeps him busy all day, and a few things like golf and watching sports that keep him occupied the rest of the time. And the kids. He adores the kids. He doesn't require an oil well to come in before he considers it a good day."

"So why did you hire this Iris?"

"Hire her? I suppose I did, in a way. But hardly any money ever changed hands. All I had to do was take the life that I had built for myself, show it to this woman whose life was crummy, and say, 'If anything ever happens to me, will you please take over?' Of course she would. A couple of times a year we would talk on the phone, and I would say, 'Still available?' and she would say, 'You bet.'"

"And did Dennis seem satisfied with her?"

"I told you, he'll be fine."

"Did he say that?"

She glared at him. "During the month or so at a time when she came to stay with us, I arranged lots of times when I would take the kids somewhere for a day or two, and leave Dennis in the house with her to see if they would be able to get along and agree on things. Then I would come home and talk to each of them alone."

"What happened when he cheated on you?"

She glared at him again. "If you're smart enough to know that happened, then you can't be so dumb as to think I didn't expect it. Louanda and Iris and I sat down together beforehand and talked about that possibility on some of the trips to Philadelphia. Louanda thought I was foolish, letting go of my husband when there might never even be a reason."

"What about Iris?"

"She wasn't sure what she wanted, at that point. She had met Dennis by that time and she admitted she'd been attracted to him. She was afraid that maybe I would turn my faithful husband into an unfaithful one, and I would never feel the same about him."

"But you persuaded her?"

"No. No. I didn't. I just made sure everybody had every chance to get to know one another—Iris, the kids, Dennis—and left them alone as much as I could. Don't you see why?"

"Why don't you tell me?"

"Everybody's objection was that the killers would never come after me. Well, now they have, and it turns out that I'm the one who was right."

"But what advantage was there?"

"For me? None. Not then, certainly. Not ever. It was for the kids."

"With Iris, you get to maintain control over everything."

"No. I don't get to do that. I *do* get to be sure that when my family begins over again in a few days, there will be a nice place to live that's far from here, and there will be four of them: two kids, a father, and a mother. Nobody's missing, see? Nobody is going to run an easy search or publicize some easy lie and learn that a father and two kids the right ages showed up on this date and bought a new house. It's a family of four who have owned the place for four years. No woman who meets the family is going to see a slot that's open and decide she's the one to fill it. I don't have to worry that the Wicked Witch of the West is going to get the kids."

"You're not so worried about your husband, though. Why?"

"He's a grown-up. He has to do that much for himself."

"You're hedging, evading. Don't you care about him?"

"I'll miss him. Sure. He's a nice man."

"You didn't say you love him. Did you ever?"

"I was lonely. I missed having a relationship with a man. I like men. I like the feeling of security and someone to do the heavy lifting and reach the top shelf. Dennis asked me out, and we liked each other."

"Not enough."

"All right. The truth, then. Dennis was a father with two little kids. He wasn't too good at it, and he'd had no time to learn, but he was trying. He had the guts to try as hard as he could every single day. It appealed to me. I could see that he and the kids needed me, and that appealed to me even more. When I was young, I was one of those girls who took all the babysitting jobs I could get. I loved little kids—probably because I was an only child—and I got really good at taking care of them. When I met Dennis, I had just spent over a year doing nothing but thinking about myself and hiding from everybody else. I needed somebody who needed me, so when I saw three of them, I was willing to do what was necessary. That meant getting married."

Till said carefully, "If only you could think of something that would lead us to the man who's trying to have you killed, you could go back."

"If I could have done it, I would have long ago."

Till noticed that a car was slowly, steadily moving up behind them. Just as the headlights in the rear window began to be noticeable, the car dropped back. It allowed another car to pass it and pull in ahead, and then another.

Till said, "That one came close enough to take a look at us."

"What do I do?"

"Keep going at the same speed, but don't pass anybody. What

we're going to do is take the next exit. Don't let yourself slow down to prepare for it, and don't signal. When we get there, just veer off and coast down the exit ramp. At the bottom, turn right. Pull into the first parking lot, whatever it is. If there's a building, stop on the far side of it and turn off the lights. I want to see if anybody follows."

"What are you going to do if it's the people who killed Louanda?"

"Try to get a good look at them. I'd love to catch them, but our main concern right now is to get you to Los Angeles safely."

"There's an exit coming up. Half a mile," she said.

"Good." He watched the speedometer for a few seconds. "That's right. Same speed. Nothing to give away what you're going to do."

"A quarter mile."

He looked back along the line of headlights to pick out the ones he wanted to watch. "Keep it steady."

"Here we are." The exit ramp carried them off down a slight incline. They were moving too fast, and Ann Donnelly had to brake hard at the bottom of the ramp to make the right turn. Till kept his eyes on the road behind them as the car made its second right and bumped up a drive into a parking lot.

Ann Donnelly could see the lot belonged to a 1950s-style fast-food restaurant that seemed to be called Good Food Good Times, and she swung around the building and into a space behind it.

Till said, "Wait here," and then was out of the car and trotting along the side of the building toward the front. He stopped there and looked. There were lots of cars going past, and any of them could have come off the freeway while he was behind the building. None of the drivers seemed to be scanning the parking lots looking for a particular car. Two cars pulled into the strip mall just past the restaurant, and they both parked by the Laundromat. But a woman got out of the first car with a basket of clothes. Another car went by and stopped at the gas station farther down the road.

Ann sat in the car with the motor running. She lowered the window beside her so she could hear, but there was only the steady, dull sound of cars passing unseen on the street in front of the restaurant, and beyond that the occasional whine of a truck flashing past up on the elevated freeway.

After a long time, Jack Till came back and leaned on the roof of the car beside her. "If they followed us off the ramp, I didn't see them."

He got into the car, took out his cell phone and dialed a number. The phone rang several times before someone answered. "Jay?" he said. "Yeah. I know it is. I thought I should call now, before you go to sleep. I've got her with me." There was a pause. "Soledad. It's a couple of hours south of San Francisco. We're driving in." He listened for several seconds, then said, "We should be there tonight. I want to take her to your office in the morning. From there it's an easy drive to the DA's. Can you be there to let us in about seven A.M.?" He listened. "Thanks. And Jay? Don't tell anybody we're coming, even if it's your favorite cop or your lifelong friend in the DA's office." He listened. "I know you're not stupid, but I had to say it. Thanks." He put away the phone.

"Who was that?"

"Eric's lawyer. He's been with me on this. He wanted me to tell you that he's grateful that you're coming with me."

"How about Eric? Have you talked to him?"

"I was there when he got out on bail. He was happy to hear that you were alive, but he doesn't know that I've found you. Jay will try to keep it quiet until you're there."

"Will I see him?"

"I don't know. If you want to, we can try to arrange something."

"Maybe it's not such a good idea. I'll think about it."

"Ready to let me drive for a while?"

"Okay." As she got out and began to walk around to the passenger side of the car, there was the loud growl of an engine near the front of the building. Ann instinctively ducked low and crouched in front of the grille. Till had been getting out of the passenger seat, and he kept going and left the door open for Ann. He stepped to the next parked car and stood sideways with his hand inside his coat.

The car's tires squealed as it came into the lot and past them, came to a quick stop and rocked forward on its shock absorbers. The doors swung open and four young girls got out, laughing loudly at something that had been said inside the car. A moment later a second car's tires squealed as it made the turn into the lot and then stopped beside the first car. This one's doors opened and three boys got out.

Jack Till stood close to Ann Donnelly, guided her into the car and slammed the door shut. As he did, he heard another car's engine come to life on the far side of the building and accelerate onto the street.

Till got into the driver's side and pulled the car to the edge of the lot. He noticed a sign on the street, placed so that drivers would see it after they took the exit from Highway 101. It said G15. Under it was King City, 12. He pulled out to the right.

"Why are you going that way?"

"If somebody *is* following us, it's time to make them show themselves."

26

I CAN'T BELIEVE IT," Sylvie exclaimed. "She was actually out of the car, standing up where I could see her perfectly, and I couldn't get a shot at her."

"We can't open up with two carloads of kids standing around watching us do it. We've got to have them someplace where there aren't witnesses."

"I know that, Paul."

Paul refused even to look at her. His eyes were on the rearview mirror. She sensed that she had made a mistake.

"There," he said. "Duck down."

She slid on the seat so her head was below the window. Paul leaned to the side over her to stay low. After a few seconds, he sat up, fastened his seat belt, and pulled away from the Laundromat where he had parked, and onto the street. "This is good," he said. "I thought he'd turn the other way to get back on the freeway."

"Well, he's not. Where's he going?"

"He's taking the back roads. Get ready and maybe there will be a stretch where we can take them before King City."

Sylvie pulled her hair back into a ponytail and put a rubber band on it to keep it from blowing around if she opened a window. She took her pistol out of her purse and set it on her lap, then began to prepare herself.

This stupid job was turning into an endurance test. It made her cranky and made Paul silent and withdrawn. This was all just temporary, an unpleasant few days. Now maybe she could end it. If she could just get a clear shot at that woman, the job would be over. Paul would drive away, find a place where they could ditch this car, and then take her home.

She leaned close to Paul and stared at the dashboard. "Do you think you can catch them here?"

"We've got twelve minutes, maybe only ten if we're going to speed up to catch them on this stretch of road. Let's hope it's dark and empty ahead." Paul seemed absorbed in his driving, moving beyond the glow of light from the gas stations and the street lamps, and into the dark countryside. They passed a few houses set at increasing intervals, each one slightly smaller than the last, until they passed a couple that had sides of gray weathered boards and windows that had been broken out years ago. The land in this part of the state had once been divided into small farms, but farms were enormous now, all owned by corporations instead of people.

Sylvie gazed ahead at the red taillights in the distance, then looked back for headlights. "There doesn't seem to be anybody behind us."

Paul didn't respond to the hint. He stared ahead at the taillights, but she could detect no increase in his speed.

She held her gun the way he had taught her, with her finger alongside the trigger guard and her thumb where it could feel the safety. She flicked it off, then on again. "Honey, I'd like to take them on this highway. I'm ready to do it now."

"So am I. But I don't want them to see us coming. I've got to stay back while the road is straight and try to catch them on the curves, where they can't see us."

"Come on. If we catch them, then they'll be dead, and it won't matter if they saw us."

"They'll speed up."

"Then they'll be more likely to lose control and die."

"So will we."

"I'm willing to bet my life on you. I've done it before."

Paul turned to look at her, and his expression was amused—not exactly fooled by the flattery, but enjoying it. "All right. We'll give it a try."

She could feel the car begin to accelerate, and she pressed her back against the backrest as they built up speed. When the car went over a slight rise in the road, it became almost airborne for a second, rising up on its springs and then sitting down again. When there was a dip, the car skipped over the first part and bounced into the upward incline. Sylvie watched the broken yellow line in the center of the road, the dashes looking shorter and quicker every second, until they looked almost solid.

Sylvie stared ahead as the other car went into a curve to the left, and she was glad she had coaxed Paul into making a move. The timing was just about the way he had wanted: He could speed toward them unseen on the curve, and come out practically on top of them. "I'm ready," she said.

They went into the curve to the left, and Paul held the car to the inside of the lane, his left tires over the dividing line. Sylvie could feel the centrifugal force trying to push the car outward into the black stands of trees to her right. Her seat belt tightened on her and kept her from sliding into the door.

Paul brought the car well into the curve, but then Sylvie saw light ahead on the trees. "Someone's coming the other way."

She only had time to say it when she saw the headlights coming at them, and then they flashed past, and she heard a long blare of the horn, the Doppler effect taking it higher on the scale as the two speeding cars diverged. "God!" she muttered. The curve seemed to her to become more severe, but then they were out of it again, going straight. The taillights of Till's rental car were directly ahead, only a couple of hundred feet away. "Beautiful, baby," she said.

Paul was still gaining. "All set?"

"Yes. Just tell me when."

"I'll get him to pull into the right lane to let me pass. As soon as we're beside their car, fire into Till's head."

"Okay." She pushed the button on the door's armrest to lower her window. The wind that came in was incredibly strong, brushing her right cheek and making it hard to keep her eyes open. She kept blinking, then held her left forearm up to divert its direct force. She turned to see how it was affecting Paul.

His hair was only a couple of inches long, but it was fluttering wildly, as though he were in a hurricane. She could still see his jaw set, see both his hands gripping the wheel, and feel the car accelerating.

Paul flashed his high-beam headlights at the other car, signaling that he wanted to pass, but Till hugged the left side of the road. "He knows," Paul said.

"What?"

"He knows. He's not letting me pass. He would let me pass him, like any normal person, if he didn't know we were trying to get them."

"Are you going to back off?"

"We're committed. He's seen this car. We'd have to ditch it, and we're a long way from home. I'll try to get closer, but you'll just have to take the shots you have, and hope he's hit or makes a mistake."

Sylvie held the gun out the window and rested her arm on the door to fire, but at this speed every tiny bump in the road bounced her arm upward. Twice when her arm came down, the door was on the way up to hit her elbow. The jolt almost made her drop the gun. As she tried to sight the pistol, it bobbed and slid over Till's image, and she couldn't seem to hold it steady on target. "A little closer," she said.

Paul kept the car accelerating, and it seemed to Sylvie that he was testing it, bringing the speed up an increment at a time and then holding it there for a few seconds to see if the wheels wobbled or the engine overheated. Paul moved to the left into the oncoming lane to give Sylvie a better angle. She extended her arm, held the sight on the speeding car ahead of them, and fired. The shot kicked her arm upward, but she fought it back down against the wind and fired again.

This time the rear window of the car ahead of them turned milky and then blew out of its frame, falling like a curtain of ice onto the trunk and sliding off onto the road. Some of the pieces, glittering in the glare of Paul's headlights, blew into the air and ticked against the windshield and grille of Paul and Sylvie's car. Sylvie ducked back inside to avoid being hit.

"Keep firing."

Sylvie leaned out again and aimed, and this time she could see the two headrests clearly. She aimed at the one on the left where Jack Till's head was, and fired twice, then a rapid volley of four shots. She had no way of knowing how many of her shots had missed Till's car entirely, but she could see two holes in the trunk, and the safety glass of the windshield had a white impact splash of pulverized glass in the upper-left corner.

Sylvie released the gun's empty magazine and dropped it in her purse while Paul pulled back into the right lane. A car, then two more, flashed past in the oncoming lane. Sylvie fished in her purse for the spare magazine.

Jack Till's car made an unexpected move to the left as though he were unable to keep it straight. It drifted to the left into the oncoming lane. Paul said, "Look! You must have hit him."

Till's car veered across the left lane, off the pavement at an angle. As it crossed the shoulder, it kicked up gravel and a cloud of dust that made it hard for Sylvie to see. She listened for a crash, then looked for red taillights. When she found them, they were off the road in the field beside it, bouncing up and down wildly in the darkness.

Paul turned his car and crossed the road to the left shoulder, and Sylvie said, "No, you're not—" But he was already on the shoulder by then and following Till's car. As they left the road, Sylvie could hear the steady swish of weeds on the underside and rocker panels. The car hit a rut and bounced, aiming the headlights up into the sky, then down again. She could see that Paul was driving into a field of weeds that had probably belonged to a farm long ago. Everything on both sides was night-black emptiness, but ahead under the headlights she could see the dry yellow-brown weeds, and the swath that Jack Till had marked, pressed down flat where the tires had touched, and only half-down in the middle where the undercarriage had passed and bent them over.

She said, "I'm not sure I even hit him. Maybe I didn't. He can still drive."

"Keep trying."

With difficulty, she braced herself against the car's bouncing, drew the full magazine from her purse and inserted it into the pistol. She pushed it home with the heel of her hand, and tugged back the slide to cycle the first round into the chamber. She held the gun out the window, gripped her elbow with her left hand to steady it, and fired again.

This time she was sure her shot had gone high. She tried again, but her correction looked low. It was much harder to aim now than it had been on the road. The two cars were bucking and rocking as they crossed the field, but they were still going at least forty miles an hour. "Get him. Get closer," she said. "We've got to be closer."

Paul was wrestling with the steering wheel. When the tires hit uneven ground, he had to wrench the wheel back to correct it, then wrench it the other way. But he didn't argue with her, and she felt the car speeding up a bit. The next jolt brought her up off her seat, so the seat belt tightened painfully across her chest and shoulders.

Till's car reached the end of the flat field and bobbed down an incline, then went up a hill on the far side. Sylvie could see that this was pastureland, where the native short bushes, live oaks and dry grass reasserted themselves. She could see rocky outcroppings in a few places, and then Till's car climbed a ridge and disappeared over the top.

Paul coasted to the edge of the field and stopped.

"What's wrong?"

"We can't drive up there."

"He did."

"He's taking us off into the woods where there's cover, and I can't see a damned thing. It's an ambush. He's going to lie down in the right place, aim his gun, and wait for us to come creeping along at five miles an hour. Besides, if we wreck a wheel or something and get stuck out here, we're finished."

She was relieved. She sensed that she would be in a stronger position if she didn't exactly agree, but only acquiesced. "Okay." Men didn't really want consensus. They wanted to be obeyed.

Paul turned the car in a slow, wide circle until the headlights illuminated the path of flattened weeds he had followed to get here. Sylvie could look up the path to the end of the headlights' beam where the weeds faded into the dark. Till had led them far from the road.

"ARE YOU ALL RIGHT?"

"Yes."

Till's rental car was tilted to one side in a creek bed. The only sound was a trickle of water a few inches wide that ran out from under the car and meandered among the stones into the dark. After a few seconds, Ann Donnelly realized the water was probably from a puncture in the car's radiator.

Jack Till switched off the headlights, pushed his door open against gravity until it stayed, and pulled himself up and out. Then he held on to the side of the car and walked around to Ann Donnelly's door. "Come on. We've got to get away from the car." He opened her door, reached across her and released her seat belt, then held her to keep her from sliding out too quickly. She put her feet down and found her footing.

They climbed up the far bank of the creek together. In the moonlight Till could see taller vegetation along the creek. He conducted her to a spot about fifty feet downstream where the brush was thick. He said softly, "We'll wait here for them to catch up."

Ann sat down beside the thick bushes. She looked closely at the leaves and realized they were probably young oak trees competing for space and light at the edge of the creek. Even in the dark, she could tell the back of the car was a mess. Besides the blown-out rear window and the holes punched in the trunk, there were dents and scratches along one side and one of the wheels had been knocked askew by the rock Jack had hit when the car went into the creek bed.

They waited for a long time without speaking or moving. Finally Ann Donnelly was more uncomfortable than afraid. She wanted to lie down on the bed of leaves where she was sitting, but the darkness was deep enough to let her imagine snakes and poisonous spiders. Just as her imaginary spiders had become scorpions, Jack touched her arm and whispered, "I don't think they're coming for us."

"No?"

"No. We need cops, but calling them from here probably won't help. They'd take hours to find us. Let's walk out to the highway and call."

"Okay. Should I take my suitcase?"

"No. If we make it out, we can get our stuff when they tow the car."

They began to walk. Till led her farther down the creek bed to a place where it was dry and wide and the slopes were gradual, and then up onto the empty field. She said, "You were right. They seem to have left."

"Yes. It's kind of a mixed outcome. I was hoping that what I did to our rental car would happen to their car, too."

"I'll bet you're wondering how you get involved in things like this."

"I don't wonder. I know why I do."

"Why?"

He didn't answer because he had his telephone to his ear. "Yes. My name is Jack Till. A few minutes ago, two people in a car ran me off Highway G15. They fired a few shots at me and hit my rental car. They were in a green Toyota, late model, one of the bigger ones, probably a Camry or an Avalon."

He listened for a moment. "My friend and I are stranded, but we're not hurt. I can't give you the exact location, but it's a big field of weeds on the east side of the road about halfway between Soledad and King City. We're walking back from a dry arroyo where our car got stuck. We'll be near the road in a few minutes watching for a police car. Can you ask them to run their warning lights for us? I want to be sure the car I flag down isn't the one that was chasing me. Thanks."

Till disconnected and kept walking. "The cops will be coming along the road pretty soon. Probably by the time we can walk there." He thought about what Ann Donnelly had asked—why he got involved in things like this. He had told her the truth. He did know exactly why, and it was a secret he had been living with and lying about for so long that the secret was a part of him. He never thought about it anymore except when something reminded him.

Till had graduated from UCLA at twenty-two with a major in history and no job, found temporary work as a clerk in a liquor store during the day, and waited tables in the evenings. A week after his roommates had moved on, Till found his own apartment in Hollywood, where rents were cheaper in the older buildings.

Two young cops named Johnny and José would visit the liquor store about once a week. The store was on their regular rounds because there were some street characters in the neighborhood who acted as snitches for them, and snitches didn't like to be seen outdoors chatting with a pair of cops. Sometimes while they were waiting, Johnny and José would talk to Till. Late that fall, one of them said to him, "You're a smart kid, Jack. You should be a cop." He had laughed and said, "Not me, man. I'm a lover, not a fighter."

He remembered the words later because that was the night when the girl picked him out. He was in the Cobra Club, standing in a fluid crowd of people who were gradually making their way to the bar when she had simply appeared at his shoulder. He glanced down and noticed her long, dark hair, and then found that her brown eyes were already fixed on him. He had the presence of mind to smile and dispel the discomfort.

She smiled, too. "Hi," she said. "Do we know each other?"

"No. I wish we did, though. Can I buy you a drink?"

"Sure. White wine." The meeting had been that quick and simple, as they always were when two people wanted to meet. She had stood with him and they had talked while they waited their turn at the bar. She said she had never been to this club before, but liked it, and he told her that he had heard of it a year ago but had never gotten around to a visit. Three times other men emerged from the crowd to ask her to dance, but she had turned a dimmer version of her smile on them and said, "No, thank you." He had wondered if he was supposed to get rid of them for her, but he couldn't see what that could accomplish other than a bar brawl that would scare her off.

He bought their drinks and they made an attempt to dance on the crowded floor, and then moved farther from the music until they could hear each other. He said he was Jack Till, and she said she was Nicole. He knew they were going to leave together and so did she, so he wondered why she didn't want him to know her last name.

At one-thirty, she asked him to follow her home in his car. He was parked very close to the Cobra Club. When he had arrived after work at eleven-thirty, another car had just been pulling out of a prime space, so he had pulled in. He drove her to her car, and they kissed before she got out. He watched her step to her car, a little red Honda Civic, and felt astonished at his good fortune. She was extremely appealing, and they seemed to have formed an instant attraction. He was already aware that women often made their final decisions about men within a few seconds, but still wondered at her interest in him. As he drove east on Hollywood Boulevard, then north to follow her into the curving streets into the hills, he had misgivings. She was too pretty for him. Why had she picked him out among all of those men?

Had she made a bet with a girlfriend that she could pick up a guy before the girlfriend could? No. Men did that kind of thing, not women. Had she seen someone in the club she wanted to avoid? Maybe one of those guys who had hit on her while she was at the bar with him?

When Nicole arrived at her apartment building, pulled into the driveway, and waited for the barred gate to rise and let her drive down under the building to park in her assigned space, Till stopped his car at the curb across the street and watched. He half-expected her to go upstairs on the inner staircase and lock her door. Instead, she walked across the street and stood beside his car until he got out, then took his hand and said, "I didn't see you behind me. I was afraid I lost you on one of those turns."

"No, but if you were hoping you had, there won't be any hard feelings."

"I invited you."

"But you might have changed your mind on the way."

"You're going to have to stop that."

"What?"

"Asking me if I really mean the opposite of what I say."

"Sorry."

Jack followed Nicole into the building, up the carpeted steps and through her door. Her apartment was newer, cleaner and larger than his. She had a real living room with matching furniture and pictures on the wall like respectable adults had, and not an ill-assorted collection of garage-sale castoffs and dubious bargains like the furnishings in Till's studio. A few minutes later, he discovered that she also had matching sheets and pillowcases that didn't clash with the bedspread. After that he didn't see much of the decor because he was devoting all of his attention to her. It was very late when she said, "Jack, I'm afraid you've got to go home now. I need to sleep before work."

He memorized her telephone number and address, then read her full name off her mailbox on his way out: Nicole Kelleher. He got into his car and began to drive. As he retraced the route back out of the hills toward Hollywood, he was surprised to see that there was another car behind him taking the same turns.

He ignored the car at first, but then he began to wonder if Nicole was trying to catch him because he had forgotten something. He pulled over to the curb, left his motor running and his lights on, and looked into the rearview mirror to watch the other car overtake him. It didn't. The car simply pulled to the curb a half block away and turned off its lights. Jack pulled away from the curb and the car followed. He felt the hairs on the back of his neck rising. As an experiment, he took a turn to the left, away from the predictable route into Hollywood. The second car followed.

Jack made more turns, trying to see what the other car looked like under lighted streetlamps at intersections. He determined that it was a year-old BMW, and there was only one person in it. It was after four o'clock in the morning, and it was clear that the car's presence wasn't a coincidence. In his experience, nobody who could afford a BMW needed to rob Jack Till, but he wasn't willing to bet his life on it. He watched the driver's behavior, and gradually limited the possibilities to one: The driver was trying to follow him home. Till made a few turns, crossed Hollywood Boulevard to the south, and kept going. He began to form a picture in his mind of the right place to stop, and then searched for it as he drove.

Finally, after fifteen minutes of driving, he turned abruptly into a dark street, then into a driveway that led into a loading dock at the back of some kind of business. The other car went past the driveway, and Till could see the driver staring after him. The driver was a white male about his age, wearing a yellow hooded windbreaker. Till quickly backed out of the driveway, but instead of turning around and going the other way, he drove after the BMW.

The BMW stopped abruptly in the middle of the street. When Till pulled forward to pass, the BMW moved in the same direction to block him. Till tried going to the right, but the BMW pulled to the right and cut him off. The door of the BMW flew open and the driver emerged, running toward Till. Till's headlights revealed that the man had something in his right hand, but there was no time to see what it was. The man swung his arm and hit Till's side window. It shattered, the glass flying against Till's chest and into his lap.

The man raised his arm for a second swing, and Till pushed his door open as hard as he could into the man, his whole body behind it as he emerged from the car. He heard the man grunt and saw him stagger backward. Till could see that what the man was holding was a claw hammer, like the ones carpenters used. Till said, "What the hell are you doing? I don't even know you."

"Well, *I* know *you*, asshole!" The man's face was contorted with rage, his teeth bared and his eyes squinted in hatred. "You were with Nicole."

"What's it got to do with you? Are you an old boyfriend or something?"

The man lunged toward him, taking a wide swing with the hammer. Till dodged it, and the man's swing of the heavy hammer brought his arm across his body so he was momentarily off balance and defenseless. Till delivered a hard punch to the middle of his face, into his nose and upper teeth, that rocked him back and made him fall to the pavement. Till said, "Leave the hammer on the ground and we'll talk."

The man rose and sprang at Till again, but Till dodged and hit him as he went past. The punch connected with the added force of the man's momentum, and Till felt it all the way to his shoulder. He relaxed for a moment because he was sure the fight was over, but this time the man's recovery was a genuine surprise. The man should have gone down, but he pivoted and swung the hammer again, and this time he didn't miss.

The hammer hit Till's side, just below his rib cage. The hammer's head had turned in the man's hand, so the injury was more painful than damaging. Till instantly spun to face the man, and as his body reacted to protect itself, it took his mind with it. Till was wild with hurt and anger as he charged the man. He hit him just as he was trying to get a better grip on the hammer, and knocked it to the pavement. As the man reached for it, Till punched him four or five times in a combination, driving him back out of reach of the hammer. Till kept coming, knocked him down, threw himself on him, and hit him three more times. Each of his punches drove the man's head into the pavement. He stared down at the man and waited for the next move, the next trick, his right arm drawn back to hit him again.

But this time the man didn't move. His eyes were closed. His mouth was now bloody, his nose broken and out of line. His face had acquired a flat, loose look, as though the muscles weren't under his control anymore. He seemed to be unconscious. Till stood up and took a step backward, waiting for the man's next move: a kick to trip him and bring him down, another weapon, a sudden tackle. There was no movement. Till gave the man's leg a kick. There was no reaction, no twitch of an eyelid. The man's head was cocked to the side a little. Fine. Let the son of a bitch be knocked out, Till thought. He can wake up in a few minutes and think about what a fool he is.

Till picked up the hammer, got into his car, turned around, and drove back the way he had come. As he prepared to make the first turn to the west toward Hollywood, he looked into the rearview mirror. The man lay on the pavement just as Till had left him, his car parked in the middle of the street above him.

Till turned and drove away.

A few hours later, when Till's alarm woke him for his job at the liquor store, he turned on the television. The reporter was saying, "Sometime in the early hours of the morning, Steven Winslow of La Canada was beaten to death in a quiet neighborhood near the center of the city. Police say the body of Winslow, who was twenty-six years old, was found at seven A.M. in the two-hundred block of Pilcher Avenue. He appears to have been killed in an attempted robbery of some kind, possibly a carjacking. The street was apparently chosen because it is in an industrial block where businesses had been closed for hours, and is partially obscured by the sound-stages of a small movie studio. No one reported hearing the victim's cries. Police are asking that anyone who has any information about the crime, or who saw Mr. Winslow at any time last evening, call the Rampart Station."

Till remembered the moment when he had straddled Steven Winslow, his fist raised, waiting for any movement. He had, at that moment, been ready to kill him—he had thrown off all compunction. He realized now that Winslow probably had already been dead, but that hardly mattered.

He called in sick to the liquor store and watched television as long as there were reports, then went out to buy the afternoon edition of the papers. He read about the crime and waited for the police to come and knock on his door. There was no question what was going to happen then. His car window was shattered. His hands were scraped, and his right knuckle had a deep cut where he had hit

Winslow's teeth. He had snatched the hammer off the street before he had left, and it was still on the floor of his car. When the police began to ask questions, they would learn that he had picked up Winslow's girlfriend at a club, and spent the night at her apartment. They would look at the crime scene again and realize that Winslow had died in a fight. Who else would he have been fighting with, and what else would he have been fighting about? Nicole would tell them what had happened between them and who he was.

He waited all day for the police to come. The next day he went to work, and when he came home he read in the *Times* that Winslow's fiancée, Nicole Kelleher, twenty-one, had been interviewed. She said she could not imagine why such a tragedy had occurred, because Winslow was one of those people who had never had any enemies: "Everyone just loved Steve." She and Winslow had been planning to be married in about a year, but had not yet set a date. They had dated exclusively for nearly three years, but had been engaged for only four weeks.

Even while Till was consumed with guilt and regret for what he had done, part of his mind was mulling over the evening with Nicole and remembering the sensation that something was wrong. When he looked at the photograph of the girl in the newspaper and read her statements to the reporters, he realized what it was.

She must have known that Steven was spying on her. Till wasn't sure what had been going through her mind at the time, but he knew she had been aware he was watching and she had staged their liaison. Now that he thought about it, she had behaved as though she was trying to make sure Steven kept watching and following.

All kinds of small observations that had puzzled Till now made sense, beginning with her choice of him at the Cobra Club. Till had not been the sort of man this girl would pick. She was bait for the ex-prom-kings and the boys home from Princeton for the summer. At twenty-two, Till was tall and lean, with a face that had already taken a few punches. He made no sense as her partner in a summer one-night stand. But he was a perfect choice as an adversary for somebody like Steven.

She had definitely wanted to be seen. She had approached Till in the middle of the dance floor of the club, and stood right there under the lights talking to him for a long time, even though she kept attracting other men and turning them down. When Till and Nicole had left together, she had made a point of getting into his car with him right in front of the club, and having him drive her the short distance to where her car was parked instead of walking her there. She had kissed him before she got out of the car, and he remembered that she had opened the door so the dome light went on while she was still kissing him.

She had asked him to follow her car to her apartment. She had driven slowly and waited at traffic signals to make it easy for him to follow and, he knew now, for Steven to follow. She had parked in her space and then come back out, standing in the center of the street with him as though she wanted to be seen. He remembered her looking down the street, almost furtively. She had probably been verifying that Steven's car had arrived, and was parked there with its lights off.

Nicole Kelleher and Steven Winslow had changed his life. What had made Till feel that he had to perform some kind of public service was killing Steven Winslow. What had made him know he should be a detective was Nicole Kelleher.

Years later, after he had made Homicide, he took a look at the murder book that the detectives of the time had made for the death of Steven Winslow. He opened the single looseleaf notebook and found that there was nothing much in it—no interviews with eye-witnesses, no motive, no suspects, not even a reliable time of death. The cause of death had been blunt trauma to the back of the head. Jack Till was surprised to learn that the blood found at the scene had all belonged to Steven Winslow, because he remembered his own bleeding hands. It was clear that the technicians had taken samples at a number of places at the scene, and had simply missed whatever drops had belonged to Till. Since those days, the search for DNA evidence at crime scenes had grown feverish, but at the time the blood had merely been sampled and typed.

He read with intense interest the police interviews with Nicole Kelleher. She had shown the detectives only the grieving young wife-to-be. She had been planning to see Steve at noon that day. He had told her they were going to look for a present for her, and she thought he was planning to take her to pick out her engagement ring. They were that kind of couple. Steve would never have bought her a ring in advance and slipped it on her finger when she had said yes to his proposal. In families like theirs, the ring would be a lifetime investment and cost a lot of money, so the shopping was a serious task.

Winslow's father, Steve Senior, was the owner of a company that sold protective clothing for people who handled toxic substances, and he had done well. His son Steve would have taken over when he retired. Nobody in the family had anything helpful to say about Steve's associates, his activities, or his habits. The detectives had left notes to indicate that Steve had been charged with assaulting a woman at the age of seventeen, but the charges had been dropped when the victim changed her mind about testifying. It was clear to Till that the father had paid off the victim. There had also been a record of speeding tickets, two disorderly conducts, and a DUI. The father said those were all just the result of high spirits, that Steve was a great source of pride, and that Nicole would always be considered a member of the Winslow family.

By then Till had learned a few more lessons about human behavior, and the assault charge and the disorderly conducts had made him consider the possibility that the reason Nicole had wanted Steven to meet Jack Till was that Steven had taken up hitting her when he was displeased. At that point, Till closed the murder book, returned it to the cold-case archives, and never looked at it again.

Jack Till and Ann Donnelly hiked across the derelict field toward the road. His legs were long, and he had moved a pace ahead of her, ostensibly so they could walk single file in the tire tracks instead of fighting through the tall weeds.

"Have you ever been married?" she asked.

"Not lately."

"What does that mean?"

"I wasn't very good at it."

"I don't think it's about skills. I think it's about attraction and connection. There's no skill to those things."

She walked on for a few steps, and Jack Till began to think she was satisfied for the moment. He was relieved. He had kept the story of Rose's leaving him a secret for so long because he felt he needed to protect Holly. The story seemed to belong to her, not to him.

"So why did you really decide to come and bring me back?"

"Because Eric Fuller was arrested for your murder. Maybe I felt some responsibility."

"And maybe you feel a connection with me."

"Maybe. Maybe I think that you and I share the responsibility." Lights were visible ahead, and Jack Till waved his arms over his head and trotted toward the highway. After a moment the police car stopped, and a bright spotlight swept the field and found him. He held his arms out from his sides, then half-turned to call to her. "Show him you have nothing in your hands. I don't want any doubts about who the good guys are."

HOURS LATER, Till stood by a tree on the edge of the dry creek bed and watched the oversized tow truck drag his rental car up the incline toward level ground. The winch tightened and he saw the hook slip and scrape the bottom of the car, but that hardly mattered. Somebody's insurance company was going to be paying the cost of a new car. There wasn't much glass left, the front end seemed to be cocked to the right, and there were bullet holes in the trunk and in some of the sheet metal at the rear of the car.

He turned away from the car when the older cop walked back to talk to him. Till could see that his partner was still sitting in the police car beside Ann Donnelly. The older cop said, "Well, she verified your crazy story in all its particulars. I guess that surprised me more than it surprises you."

"Maybe a little," Till agreed. "This has been pretty stressful for her."

"I checked you with the LAPD," the cop said. "It seems that maybe what I ought to be asking is just what we can do to help you."

Till held his eyes on him. "I was trying to drive her to the DA's office in Los Angeles without being spotted, but that didn't work out. So I would appreciate it if you would do a couple of things for us."

"What are they?"

"Get her fingerprints and take her picture—front and side mug shots ought to do it. That way, if for some reason we don't make it, then at least Eric Fuller won't get convicted of killing her."

"We'd be happy to do that," said the cop. "Just tell me where to send it."

"If you'll give me your notebook, I'll write it down for you."

The cop handed him a small notebook and a pen, and Till talked as he wrote. "Sergeant Max Poliakoff, Homicide Special. Here's his number, and the address at Parker Center."

The cop accepted the notebook and turned his flashlight on it. "You have a good memory."

"Not that good. It was my desk before it was his." Till looked over at the police car, where Ann Donnelly was still sitting with the other police officer, and turned away so she couldn't read his lips. "The other thing you can do is drive me to a place where I can rent another car. I want to find a quiet place where she and I can stay out of sight for a day or two, then take her into Los Angeles when I think the time is right. And I'd appreciate it if nobody writes down where we went. The man who's hiring these people won't give up while she's alive."

27

SYLVIE DROVE THE CAR up the long, steep, curving grade, past a convoy of slow trucks climbing toward Los Angeles. Even in the predawn darkness she could feel the change in climate. At the bottom was Camarillo, where the air was cool and damp from the ocean, but up here at the top was Thousand Oaks, where the air was dry, still heated up by yesterday's sunshine. She knew that if she could have stopped the car and put her hand on the pavement, it would feel warm. As she drove past the green sign at the Los Angeles County line, she hit an invisible wall of frustration.

They had failed. She said, "I assume you don't want me to drive this car to our house. Would you like to dump it someplace before the sun comes up?"

"In time," he said. "I figure checkout time at the hotel where we got the car is noon. The housekeeping people will go into the room and find the bodies around twelve-thirty or so. We'll be fine for now."

"If you say so." She drove past the eternal tie-up at the junction with the San Diego Freeway, and took the Van Nuys Boulevard exit.

Paul said, "Pull into the mall and let me out."

Sylvie pulled to the far end near the corner and sat there as though she were checking a road map while Paul walked the few blocks to their house and returned in the black BMW. He stepped close to Sylvie and handed her the keys. "I'll drive that one, and you follow me."

He drove the stolen car onto the 170 freeway to the Simi Freeway and up to Little Tujunga Road. He drove up into the dry hills for a couple of miles, then pulled over on a wide turnout, and Sylvie stopped behind him. Already Sylvie could detect a special quality to the air that was still not luminous, but was beginning to lose its darkness. She got out of the BMW and joined Paul at the stolen car with the rags and Windex that Paul had brought from home.

They sprayed and wiped off the handles, knobs and buttons, the trunk and the hood, the interior metal and plastic surfaces. They were efficient and quick because they had done this together before. The whole process took no more than five minutes. Then Paul went to the trunk of the BMW, took out the fire extinguisher, opened the passenger door of the stolen car, and sprayed the interior thoroughly with white foam to destroy any prints they had missed. Paul reached inside to shift the transmission into neutral, then pushed the stolen car to the edge of the turnout and let it roll down the steep hillside into the dense brush below. The car was difficult to see from the turnout, and it appeared no more important than any of the other abandoned cars in gullies around Los Angeles. It looked as though it could have been there for years.

A few minutes later, they were in their BMW on the Simi Freeway going seventy miles an hour toward home. It was half-light when they approached the driveway of the house that Sylvie had inherited from Darren McKee. The garage door rose, Paul pulled inside, and the garage door closed behind them.

Neither of them spoke as they got out, walked through the doorway into the house, and locked the door behind them. One of the things that Sylvie loved about being married was that little talk was necessary at times like this, when they were both exhausted and disappointed and dirty. Two single people would think they had to fill the air with bright, insincere chatter. Sylvie stopped at the front door, glanced into the box she had put under the mail slot to catch the mail, but didn't see anything that tempted her to look more closely. She walked to the master bedroom, opened the walk-in closet, stepped out of her clothes, took her robe off the hook, and went into the bathroom. In her peripheral vision she saw Paul doing something similar, and then heard him go two doors down the hall to the guest bathroom and close the door.

She stepped into the shower and turned it on. Usually Sylvie stood in the shower and passively let the water rush over her, but today she adjusted the temperature to be slightly hotter than usual, covered herself with soap, and scrubbed her skin. She washed her hair, then got out and ran the bath, settled into it, and lay there soaking. When she felt cleansed of the whole experience of the past few days she stood up, dried herself with a big, fluffy bath towel, and went back into the bedroom.

Paul had kept the blinds and curtains closed, so the room was dim and felt cool. Maybe he had turned on the air conditioning. He was lying in the bed with his back to her. She took off the robe and slipped under the covers beside him. She slid close to him, but she didn't touch him. She closed her eyes.

When Sylvie awoke the room was still dark. She rolled over so she could see her clock radio. The red digits said 1:22. She reached behind her to verify the emptiness where Paul should have been. She lay there waking up. She smelled coffee. She caught a small sound in another part of the house that located him in her mind. She got up and went into the bathroom to brush her teeth.

As she passed the big mirror, she looked at her reflection, then took a step back to look again. Usually she saw only flaws, but today it seemed to her that she looked good naked. She brushed her teeth, then picked up a brush and began brushing out her hair in front of the big mirror instead of the makeup mirror as she normally did. She wasn't twenty-five anymore, but she looked better than most women did at thirty, she assured herself. She finished her hair, splashed water on her face and patted it dry, then stepped to the makeup mirror and put on light daytime makeup, giving special attention to her eyes today because she had been sleeping, and then studied the effect. She looked even better. She looked terrific.

Sylvie decided to heighten the effect. Why not? She put on the eyeliner and mascara, and added eye shadow. Then she went into the closet and opened the lingerie drawers until she found what she had been picturing. She put on a sheer black lace baby-doll night-gown that had a bit of a push-up to emphasize her breasts. She turned in front of the mirror and looked at herself critically. The lace came down just to the spot where her legs reached her bottom, but didn't quite cover her.

She and Paul had just spent too much time jammed into cars together, tracking that stupid woman and her private detective. It was time to remind Paul that she wasn't just some partner, some other man who was a buddy of his. She was his wife. She took one last look and then walked out of the closet and let her senses guide her to him. He was in the kitchen cleaning guns.

She stopped in the living room so he could just catch sight of her in the corner of his eye, then moved toward the big leather couch along the far wall in front of the bookcases. She heard a sound—the scrape of his chair, then heard him get up, his feet coming across the kitchen floor, through the dining room, then onto the carpet. She kept her back to him, as though she had heard nothing.

"Wow," he said.

She looked over her shoulder at him, smiled, and gave her bottom a comical little wiggle. "Oh, Mr. Turner," she said in a fake southern-belle voice. "What *can* you be thinking?"

He seemed to swoop, coming across the room without sound, or enough time elapsing, and he had his arms around her. She enjoyed the powerful effect she had on him. He never spoke again, he simply made love to her. There was never anything routine or perfunctory about the way Paul Turner was with her, but this time he was irresistible. At times he was tender, gentle, and then he would be ardent and passionate, almost too physical, so she felt small and weak. It wasn't that he seemed to be taking her against her will, but that her will was irrelevant because when she felt this way, he could make her want to do anything.

When it was over, she lay still, her muscles all relaxing, letting her heartbeat slow. She opened her eyes and was mildly surprised to remember that they had never left the living room. He was on his side, leaning on his elbow and looking down at her.

"What were you doing before I came in here to distract you?" she said.

"I was cleaning rifles. That pair of .308s we bought last year in South Carolina."

"I had forgotten we even had those. I remember we sighted them in on the range, and never fired them again. Why did they need cleaning?"

"They didn't, actually. It was just something to do while you were asleep. I'm glad you decided to get up." A small self-satisfied proprietary smile formed on his lips.

She forgave him for the smile, even though she deserved every bit of the credit and considerable gratitude for what had just happened. That, she supposed, was another aspect of long marriages. When they had first found each other years ago, she had not been able to read that smile, could not have detected that mixed with the admiration was pride of ownership and self-satisfaction.

Sylvie got up and walked into the bedroom suite. She tossed the skimpy nightgown into the bin for delicate wash and stepped into the shower. She hummed, then sang in a quiet voice, because she was happy.

When she was out of the shower, she pulled on a pair of comfortable jeans and a T-shirt. She walked into the kitchen, and poured herself a cup of coffee. Paul was just reassembling the second rifle, and she could see why she had forgotten he had bought this pair. She and Paul had at least two other pairs built on the Remington Model 7 pattern, all with dull gray synthetic stocks that wouldn't reflect light or hold a fingerprint. There were a pair in .30-06 and identical ones in .22, so they could practice without spending tons of money for high-powered, deafening ammunition that made the gun kick her shoulder until it was bruised and sore.

She and Paul tried to get in lots of practice sessions. The thought reminded her that when she and Paul had gotten together she used to call it "rehearsal," and he used to laugh at her. She watched him as he picked up the two guns and carried them toward the spare bedroom he used as an office, to lock them in the gun safe. She supposed there were things about her that annoyed him, but he almost never mentioned any of them. Maybe that was why she had bouts of free-ranging anxiety: She would notice signs in his face and body that signaled irritation, but since he hadn't said anything, she had no way to limit what she imagined might be bothering him. It could be anything about her—or even everything—so she became defensive.

When Paul came back into the kitchen, she put her arms around his neck and gave him a kiss. "Well, what can I make you for breakfast?"

"Nothing. I'll take you out to breakfast."

"No, thanks. I want to be in my own house for a while and bask in blissful domesticity. How about some eggs and bacon?"

He shrugged. "Sounds good."

She went to the refrigerator and took out the eggs, butter, and bacon while he cleared the table of his cleaning rods, patches, gun oil, and rags, and began to set it for breakfast.

She broke one egg, then another into the pan, dropped the shells into the sink and looked back at him. "Before you answer the next question, I would like you to take a minute to think, okay?"

"Okay."

"Do we really have to collect on Wendy Harper?"

He sat quietly for about five seconds, then said, "Yes. We pretty much do."

"Pretty much?"

"That means yes. It's a lot of money. We spend a lot, so we need to make a lot. And it's a job for Michael Densmore. He's been our best source of jobs for the past seven or eight years."

"That's true, but think about it a minute." Her spatula lifted the eggs expertly and slid them onto a plate without breaking the yolks. "Do we actually need this money? We own this house free and clear. We paid cash for both cars. We each had savings from before we met. We have the money we've saved together, and we still have all of the money Darren left me about fifteen years ago, don't we?"

"Yeah."

"That's got to add up."

"Of course. We could quit now, and probably live a very comfortable life until we die." He grinned. "Or until *I* die, anyway, which is all I need to worry about."

"You're so sweet." His toast popped up, and she plucked it out of the toaster, dropped it on the plate, and set it in front of him.

"Seriously, we're probably fine, as long as nobody gets sick, there's no unforeseeable disaster, and all that. We have some investment income that we've been reinvesting for years. If you don't like working, I'd be willing to stop after this job's done."

"Why not before? Why not today?"

"Because we took this job. Once we've met with the middleman and heard the whole story, we're in. We're obligated. We know too much to walk away."

"Densmore knows us. He knows we won't tell anybody anything. We killed that black girl, and the cop south of San Francisco, and the couple in the hotel. If we spilled everything, he might get ten years, but we'd get the death penalty. That's his insurance."

"His point of view would be, we've fucked up the job so far, and therefore we ought to clean up the mess."

"Can we at least try to talk to Densmore?"

"Let's think about it before we do that. What if he insists that we finish it? Is it possible we'll alienate him and still have to finish the job? And don't forget: He's just a lawyer, a go-between. We don't know anything about the actual client. Do we want to give the client the idea that we're not reliable, and that maybe he has to worry about us?"

"Since we don't know him, we can't do him any harm," she said. "And since he doesn't know us, *he* can't do *us* any harm. What's to stop him from calling somebody else?"

"It would have to be somebody who could drop whatever he was doing, get here, and go right to work. He'd never have seen Wendy Harper or Jack Till. And it has to be done now—in the next day or two—while she's in the open. All she's got to do is see the DA, and she's gone again forever."

"Okay," Sylvie said. "We're not doing this because we care if she lives or dies, right? We're in it for money. They hired us because we're professionals."

"Sure."

"So let's just say politely that we believe we've been spotted, and we've killed a few bystanders, so it's our professional opinion that the client would be better off having somebody else finish up. If Densmore says we're letting him down, we say we're sorry, but we know best. If his client gets all pissed off, we say we're sorry about that, too. But Densmore can't do anything to us. And if the client could, he wouldn't need to hire us in the first place. As soon as we hang up, we pack our bags and go to Spain. We can study flamenco. We've been talking about it for years. It's the height of tourist season now, but in a few weeks the off-season begins, and September is hot as hell here. We can come back after somebody else gets Wendy Harper."

"Spain sounds pretty appealing to me right now," Paul said. "From the moment when we heard Jack Till was getting ready to leave L.A., the whole thing got to be a pain in the ass. I'm sick of it."

"That's exactly how I feel. I've been afraid to tell you how much I hated it. I'm so glad you do, too."

"We agree on that, but it still doesn't get us out of the job. We gave our word to a man we've been working with for eight years. Changing our minds and pulling out isn't a small thing."

"If the relationship is worth anything at all, then we should be able to tell him honestly what's been going on and level with him about how we feel about it. He's a smart man. He may see the sense of it and tell us it's time to quit."

"That's true," Paul said.

"Should I get Densmore on the phone?"

"Hold it. We're still just thinking."

"Oh." She turned away and put the pan into the dishwasher. She had fooled herself, let herself believe he was taking her ideas seriously, but of course he wasn't. He didn't think of her as an equal. After all these years, she was still just somebody to fuck. If he had to keep her in a good mood by pretending to consider her stupid suggestions, he would do it.

He said, "I guess you're right. I hate to give up on anything, but this just isn't working out. Densmore likes to be consulted. Let's call him and see what he thinks."

She turned and studied his face. He was looking down into his coffee cup. Then he picked it up and stared at the rim from the side. He saw lipstick and realized he had picked her cup up by mistake, then stood to retrieve his from the counter. His posture indicated that he was completely unaware that she had been getting upset. He looked as guileless as a big animal. She said, "Do you want to do the talking?"

"I don't care who does it. It's up to you."

"I'll dial, you talk."

"Done."

She called Densmore's law office. When the receptionist answered, she said, "Hello. I have Paul Turner on the line for Mr. Densmore." She had such a professional assistant voice that she made the receptionist nervous. Paul smiled at her as she handed him the telephone.

Paul waited for a second, then said, "Michael, it's Paul. Is this your secure line? Good. No, it's not finished. Far from it, I'm afraid. What? No, the reason I called." He paused. "You're sure I can talk? All right. We've had some setbacks. In order to find out where she was living, we had to kill a friend of hers in Henderson, Nevada. After we found her and had her under surveillance, we got pulled over by a cop near the San Francisco airport. I was driving a car rented with a fake ID, so I had to shoot him, too."

Paul paused to listen for a few seconds. "Then a couple of hours south of there, we were just getting ready to make our move. We had her and Jack Till in a restaurant, and Sylvie was going into the ladies' room to pop her, when another cop spotted our car outside. I saw him radioing for help. We had to slip into the hotel next door, con our way into a guest room, and kill a couple for their car." He stopped to listen for a few seconds, then winked at Sylvie. "No. That still didn't stop us. We followed Till and Wendy and tried to pull their car over just north of King City. Know where that is? I pulled up behind and Sylvie emptied a whole clip into their car— blew the rear window out, and Till drove the car off the road into a field."

Paul put his arm around Sylvie and held the telephone so she could hear Densmore saying, "Didn't you follow him?"

"About a half a mile through weeds in the dark. Then he made it over a hill and into some woody country where he could see us coming. He was setting up for an ambush. The guy's a retired cop. You can't assume a man like that can't defend himself."

Paul stood and listened, his face beginning to have a flat, tired look. Then he began to pace. "We're pretty sure we've used up our value, Michael. Somebody got our license number when we shot the cop. People saw us rent that car. There may even be security tape. Till had plenty of chances to see us when we made our move. He knows who to look for. We tried our damnedest, but from here on, anything we could do would be no surprise. We'll charge you zero for the effort and call it even." He stopped talking and pacing, and listened.

Paul looked at Sylvie and she knew. The look was only a glance, a flick of the eye to her face and away from it, but it told her. It was the sort of look someone gave involuntarily when he wished the other person wasn't close enough to hear the phone conversation.

She knew that Michael Densmore was saying something that Paul was not prepared to refute. Paul had charged all the way to the top of the hill, but he was being slowly pushed back down to where he had started. She could see that the heavy weight of Densmore's argument was growing. Paul was straining to resist. "More money isn't the issue, Michael. It's that the risk for us has become worse than the risk for someone—anyone—who hasn't been seen." He had to listen for a moment. "The price doesn't matter. We want out. Today. There's not much point in hanging around if we can't get close enough to do the job."

He listened again, and it seemed to Sylvie that he was being flattered. "Thanks, Michael. It's good to hear that. But—" Densmore interrupted him, and he waited, then tried to cut off the pitch. "We've liked working with you, too." He was talking more loudly, trying to talk over Densmore, but Sylvie knew it would not be possible. "I've just told you that the risk—to us, to everyone in this—is huge now, and growing the longer we're involved."

Paul paced back and forth for a long time, and Sylvie saw the glance again. She decided not to watch his humiliation. She turned and walked from the kitchen through the living room to the other wing of the house. There was no reason to stay. She knew.

From the bed she could barely hear Paul's voice coming from the kitchen, just a faint male droning without any of the words. After the call was over, she heard his heavy feet as he wandered through the house searching for her. She knew when he had found her because the footsteps stopped for a few seconds in the hallway outside the bedroom, then receded again. She got off the bed and walked to the guest bedroom.

He was taking two suitcases down from the closet shelf. She could see that the gun safe was open again, and he had returned the two Remington Model 7s to the rack.

She said, "Are we going somewhere?"

"Yes."

She considered acting as though she thought he was going to take her to Spain, so he would have to admit his defeat. But she kept herself from being cruel. "He wouldn't let us out of it, huh?"

"No. He used the stick and carrot on us."

"What's the carrot?"

"Our price for getting Wendy Harper just doubled."

"What's the stick?"

"Well, the client knows our names."

"So Densmore lied. He said he never told *any* client who we are."

"He said this was a special case. There was no way to avoid it, and the client is somebody who would never be foolish enough to tell the police or anyone else about us."

"That's not the stick. What's the stick?"

"The client has power. He's had people looking all over the place for six years, nonstop. Now that we've used the bloody shirt and the bat to draw her out, he has no way of finding her again. We've used up his only chance. Densmore thinks that if we fail—let alone quit—the client will kill him and us, too."

28

IT WAS ALREADY afternoon when Jack Till awoke. He kept his eyes closed and oriented himself. He knew he was in a hotel bed in Morro Bay. He had driven from King City into Morro Bay in the night and found a hotel on a low ridge above the harbor. The hotel was big enough to have a night clerk on duty who was capable of finding a vacancy for a pair of tired travelers, particularly a pair who were willing to pay summer rates for an expensive set of adjoining rooms for a minimum of three days. He had gone back outside to park their new rental car among the others in the back of the hotel where it would not be seen from the street. This time he had chosen a blue Buick Park Avenue that didn't resemble the cars he had driven before. Moving the car gave him a chance to circle the lot and sweep the surrounding area with his headlights to search for parked vehicles that still had people in them.

When he had returned to his room, he had found Ann Donnelly placing a chair to hold the door between the two rooms open. She said, "Whatever else happens, I don't want to die and have you not know about it."

"We'll be okay. We're pretty far from where they lost us." Till had locked and chained his door and hers, then moved a chair in front of each to give him an extra second or two if the door opened. She sat on her bed and watched his preparations without revealing anything, but she did not seem especially comforted. He put his pistol in its holster on the bedside table. Then he turned off the light in his room before he undressed and got under the covers. For a time, he could hear Ann Donnelly moving around and see the flickering bluish glow of her television set on the white cottage cheese ceiling of her room.

Till closed his eyes and let the events of the day repeat themselves in his mind, from the time when he had reached Ann Donnelly's house in San Rafael before noon, through the sight of the car's headlights growing steadily in his rearview mirror and then the shots. He saw again the car veering to the left to try to pull up beside him, and remembered trying to block its movement and stay ahead. His body relived the feeling of speed, the sensation of rising in his seat whenever the car went over the top of a hill and started down, and his ears felt the shock of the bullet pounding through the rear window and spraying broken glass everywhere.

He had moved the car from side to side each time the car behind him moved, trying to anticipate the other driver's intentions and block them without losing control. Then the shots had come again, some of them making an amplified bang because what he was hearing was the bullet punching through the steel of his car's trunk.

Everything had happened so quickly that he had acted without deciding, not even contemplating the events until now, hours later, as he lay in bed. He remembered looking ahead at the windshield and seeing the bullet hole in it, the aura of powdered glass around it just above eye level and to the left, and knowing that the bullet must have missed his head by two inches. That sight had goaded him to act, and he had let the car fly off into the empty field because the road wasn't working and the shots were too close.

"I can't sleep in there."

He opened his eyes and dimly saw the shape of her standing beside his bed. She was wearing a pair of pajama pants and an oversized T-shirt. "Why not?"

"Because today I lost my best friend, abandoned my children, my husband, my home, my name, and then got shot at and driven into a ravine."

Till slid to the far side of the king bed and pulled back the covers to admit her. "Reason enough."

She climbed in beside him and rested her head on the pillow. "I'm sorry. I'm not used to sleeping alone anymore."

"You were married for three years?"

"Almost four." She was quiet for a few seconds, and Till thought she was falling asleep, but she said, "That's not a long time. It's just long enough so you get used to the illusion that things will always be the same."

"Never sleeping alone?"

"You don't think you'll ever have to lie in bed in a dark room at night alone. You will, of course. People go on business trips and things. Then you find yourself—by accident or on purpose—with your face in the other person's pillow, smelling his smell."

"So you loved him. When you were talking before it sounded as though you didn't."

"I don't know. It's hard to say what relationships are really about, other than not wanting to be alone. Mad, romantic love isn't necessary. All you have to feel is that you'd rather be with that person and all his faults than be alone. And you don't have to feel even that much all day, every day. You only have to feel it once each time you're ready to file for divorce and put it off. If that's what love is, then I loved Dennis."

"That sounds pretty grim."

"It's not meant to be. I was in disguise, living as a person I wasn't, remember? I knew the person I invented would be safer married than single. If your whole life is a lie, why draw the line at one more that will give you an extra layer of security? When a woman marries, not only does she get a bigger, stronger companion who will try to protect her, but she takes on his name, his whole history, whatever credit and credibility he's built up, friends of his who will swear she's legitimate. And I didn't lie to Dennis. Everyone else in San Rafael, but not him."

"Why did you think that he could protect you from the guys who were after you? Did you tell him what to look for, or describe them to him?"

"My disguise was being Mrs. Dennis Donnelly. It's a lot easier to stay in character if you can find things to like. I knew Dennis loved me, and for a woman, that's a bigger part of the equation than men know. I like him. I may regret that I married him, but I'm grateful to him. Now that's over."

Till had been asking for information about the killers, not her husband. Her answer surprised him. "You're sure?"

"God, if I wasn't before today, I would be now."

"Because they found you?""

She turned toward him in bed. He could see her big eyes reflecting the faint light of the clock. "If I had been with Dennis when they found me, I would be dead tonight. I'm not, because I was with you. And he's not dead, and the kids have their father."

He glanced at the red numbers glowing on the nightstand. "It's four-fifteen A.M. on your first night since you found out you were in trouble. For a while tonight, we were hanging by spit. Maybe you ought to put off thinking about the big things until you recover from that."

"Maybe."

"Good night." He turned to face away from her, and closed his eyes. After a few seconds he felt her move closer to him, so she was touching his back.

"Jack?"

"Yeah?"

"Thanks for letting me sleep with you."

"You're welcome." He lay in the bed staring into the darkness. Her voice had come from very close, almost the back of his neck, and he could feel that she was curled against him. Her touch, which she probably didn't think he could even feel, was the biggest phenomenon in the room. He squeezed his eyes closed, forcing out thoughts of her, and let his tired, overactive mind rest, as it often did at night, on the thought of Holly sleeping peacefully in her room at Garden House.

It was no longer morning when his eyes opened. He sat up in the bed, and he realized he must have been hearing daytime sounds for hours, because when he heard someone walking along the hallway outside the door of his room, the sound was a continuation, not a beginning. He looked at the clock on the nightstand. The numbers said 2:20.

Ann was still asleep. He got out of the bed quietly, took his cell phone off the nightstand, and walked into her room, closed the door, and pushed the curtain open a few inches. The afternoon was bright, and people were walking below the hotel along the street to the harbor. Beyond the docks, restaurants, and shops, a few hundred yards out into the ocean, was the bulbous shape of Morro Rock, with tiny white birds circling above it and launching themselves from its peak to plummet a couple hundred feet toward the water. He wondered what it would be like to live here, where there was a single feature, a shape that dwarfed everything and seemed to be everywhere he looked. He supposed that people must become experts on the way it looked at different times of day and in different weather.

Till opened his cell phone and dialed. After a moment he heard, "Hello?"

"Hi, sweetie."

"Hi, Dad. Checking up on me?"

"I guess so. I hope you don't mind."

"Not me. Where are you?"

He sighed. "I'm in a hotel."

"By yourself?"

"Checking up on me?"

"I guess so. Do you mind?"

"Not me. I'm alone at the moment. I was missing you, and I wanted to hear your voice and I wanted to tell you I love you. So here I am. I love you."

"I love you, too. Do you know when you're coming home yet?"

"It should be in a few days. Things are going pretty much as I expected, so I'm hoping I'll be there in time for the weekend. But I'll call and let you know."

"Good."

"Holly, do you remember what I said about this job the day I left?"

"I don't know."

"I said it was a job where people were going to know who I was. Remember?"

"Oh, yeah. That."

"I really hope you've been doing what I said."

"I have. The only places I've been are work and home. I stopped wearing my name tag at the store. I've been wearing one that used to belong to a girl who quit. The tag says 'Louise.'" She laughed. "Everybody keeps calling me Louise."

"Have you been keeping your eyes open?"

"Yes. No strange men, no cars parked at work or at home. Bobby and Marie and I go to work together and come home together. If I wake up at night, I check to see if something woke me up."

"That's good. Don't stop watching."

"Hey, you know what? Mrs. Fournier is waiting for me. We're going to pick up some paint for the walls in the back part of the store, and I can't keep her waiting for too long."

"Oh, sorry. You'd better get going, then. Nice to talk to you."

"It was. And Dad?"

"What?"

"Don't worry so much. Everybody here looks out for me."

"Good. Go back to work. Love you."

" 'Bye."

Till hung up and sat in Ann Donnelly's room, staring out the narrow gap in the curtain at the ocean. During his career as a cop, he had guarded against situations where Holly might be in danger. Right now he probably had even less to worry about. Holly hadn't lived with him in three years, and the phone at Garden House wasn't in her name. He had sold his house when he'd retired.

Till was accustomed to living with a constant low-level anxiety about Holly. Letting her out of his sight was an act of trust and confidence that he had not felt when she was four, and did not feel now. Every time he turned his back on her, his mind was crowded with images of Holly being careless or confused or victimized.

"Good morning."

He turned and saw Ann Donnelly standing in the doorway between the rooms. "Hi." He felt an unexpected hollow in his stomach, a feeling that he might have let something precious and important slip away. He told himself that it would have been out of place and unethical to make some romantic overture to her last night, but now he could not help feeling a terrible suspicion that she had been telling him to try. She looked appealing, squinting in the beam of sunlight from the open curtain, running her long, thin fingers through her light hair, trying to search for tangles that weren't there.

"Did you just wake up, too?"

"Yes." He looked out the window again. "I was just checking to be sure nobody was standing on the rock watching our room with a pair of binoculars or something."

She stepped close to him, her body touching his as she opened the curtain a few more inches. "Holy shit. I didn't see it last night." She laughed. "I can't believe I actually didn't notice that huge thing."

He shrugged. "It was dark. I drove straight into town from the inland side."

She stretched her arms, brought them forward and bent her back and then arched like a cat. He felt the hollow in his stomach deepening into regret, and looked away. She seemed to see his unhappiness. Did she guess what he was thinking? He said, "Let's get showered and dressed. We can find a place for—what time is it? Lunch, I guess it would be."

"Great. I'm starving."

He went back to his room and closed the connecting door behind him, but before he was two steps from it, the door opened again. She looked at him apologetically. "I'm sorry, Jack, but would you mind if we still left it open? Having it closed gives me the creeps."

"No, not at all." Of course she was afraid—not stupidly afraid of shadows, but realistically afraid of genuine danger—and she thought he had the remedy, or maybe *was* the remedy.

But fear was not affection.

29

JACK TILL WALKED Ann Donnelly to a small restaurant at the harbor with white wooden walls where the smell of food overpowered the smell of the sea air, and made them both even hungrier. He talked about neutral things that seemed to calm her. He praised the food and the sights at Morro Bay, and talked about the other places where tourists usually went around here—Cambria, San Simeon, Pismo Beach. All the time Till watched her face, wondering what he could do to make her tell him the parts of the story she was hiding.

When she seemed to be revived, Till said, "Let's go for a walk." He watched her for a time as she surveyed the windows of shops that sold beach clothes or exotic seashells. She was quiet and her eyes seemed not to focus for long on anything, so he judged it was time. When they reached the beach and the other people were too far away to overhear, he said, "What are you thinking about— being scared?"

"Yes. And no. I'm still so scared that I keep looking in window reflections to see who might be sneaking up on us. But what I'm trying to do is hold on to reality and not get hysterical."

"You seem pretty calm to me."

"I keep going over everything and finding lots of things I did wrong, misinterpreted, or ignored, but what I can't find is anything I did right."

"You did quite a few things right, or you would have been dead for six years."

"Before that. I was thinking far back, to the start."

"Tell me about the start. What was it?"

"It started with a girl named Olivia Kent. I hired her as the very first waitress at Banque, before we even opened. She was a great waitress. Beautiful, too. She had long brown hair and blue eyes, and the figure I wish I had. She had a quick sense of humor, probably from a lifetime of being hit on and turning guys down without hurting their feelings. She liked people and they felt it when she talked to them, but she was fast and efficient, so they didn't notice she was manipulating them into ordering quickly and clearing her table for the next customer."

"How old was she when she was killed?"

"She wasn't. She's not the one. You asked me where the trouble started, and it started with her."

He guided her along the shoreline. "Let's walk out to the rock. There's a long spit of land that leads out there, and you can tell me while we walk."

"All right."

"So place me in time and space. You and Eric were about twenty-three when you started the restaurant."

"Twenty-five. Olivia was twenty-one. I remember because when she applied for the job, she came in with recommendations from her last two jobs, two years and one year at restaurants in Cleveland when she was in college. Twenty-one meant she could serve alcohol, which was essential."

"Okay. You and Eric were twenty-five, and she was twenty-one."

"Yes. The whole staff was young. Eric had become a very good chef by then. He was precocious. Nobody gets to be a three-star chef after working in kitchens for seven years, half of it part-time. You can't get enough hours in the kitchen, enough instruction, enough years of tasting and screwing up and redoing. But he was very good. He had worked up a menu of twelve entrées with a few variations, all of them superb, and six appetizers that relied on small dabs of expensive ingredients arranged beautifully on a plate. That way, after a helper had assisted him a few times, he could make one himself. Even I could do it after a while if we were rushed."

"You said everybody was young. What were the rest of them like?"

"Like us. The waitstaff were all women, my age or younger. There were six of them to start, all with some experience. I picked the ones I did because I understood them, and they seemed to understand me. Until six months before we opened, I had been a waitress, and I still had the blisters, the burns, and the aching wrists to prove it. I didn't notice at first that they were so similar. But now I realize that I was so inexperienced that I could only evaluate people who were like me."

"You were still a waitress until six months before you opened Banque?"

"It was one of my jobs. I worked as a stockbroker during the day, starting at five A.M. before the New York markets open. I got home at three, then worked at Bernard's in the Biltmore from five until ten. Eric had lots of jobs, too. He was head chef at Désirée, and he also wrote food articles for a few gourmet magazines, and catered."

"Catered what?"

"People would come to Désirée and ask him to cook for private parties—mostly studio people. It helped him to build a clientele. If those people had a party, they wanted everybody there to know that they hadn't just had it catered, they'd hired the head chef from Désirée. Getting to know people was a big part of getting started. I think almost everybody we hired was somebody we met in the restaurants where we worked, and most of the customers at first were people who knew us from jobs. The big thing was money, of course. We saved everything—my tips, Eric's magazine checks and extra pay, even money people sent him from home as birthday presents. We spent nothing. The only time either of us was in a restaurant was for a paycheck. On Fridays I would deposit our checks at lunch, and I'd have most of the money invested by four, so we wouldn't be tempted to touch it. Then the weekend would come and we'd work all day and late in the evening, so there would have been no time to spend it anyway."

"All that was for the restaurant?"

"When you start up, you have to be prepared to lose money for a couple of years." She smiled. "I figured everything out in advance. We would run out of money and credit on April 26. For a while, we were all calling the place Le Vingt-six Avril."

"How did you get past April?"

"Dumb luck and lots of help. All of the people who worked for us took a cut in pay from their last jobs. They shared tips, and we were lucky with the waitresses. They were all young and shameless about coaxing big tips out of the customers. Whenever we had some windfall profit—we did a few wedding receptions, a few after-hours parties—the money would help us stagger through another week or two."

"When did Banque catch on?"

"We started pretty well and grew steadily. The big factor was that Eric had a following. There were some articles and reviews, and then we had to hold on tight."

"But you did, obviously."

"It was hard work for everybody. You have to maintain the quality of the food when you can barely cook it fast enough, preserving friendliness and efficiency when the staff are practically sprinting in and out of the kitchen for a whole shift. Every restaurant in history started with owners asking employees to kill themselves to get it going, and then never sharing the wealth. If you're smart, you start sharing after your first good week. We did that."

"So you managed to keep everybody friendly."

"That's a laugh." She shook her head as she walked along. "Banque was way too friendly. We had this great place where all these friends of ours were regulars, and at least a couple of times a night some celebrity would arrive. It felt glamorous, and the money started coming in. The bartenders and waitresses and all the kitchen staff were young and unattached, and worked long hours. They didn't just get along. The restaurant started to be a scene, and it took over their personal lives. After a couple of months, there was no way to keep up with who was with whom, and there were friends of both sexes from outside who would get drawn into the mix."

"So the employees were all very social. What about you?"

"I was the one who had her eye on the bottom line—the only one who did. It was what I studied to do in college, and managing the place was my only contribution. I tried to keep everybody paying attention."

"What about Eric?"

"I don't know if you've ever seen a great chef at work, but it's hard to describe. He was tuned in. He had his eyes on everything that went on behind the kitchen door, cooking with seven or eight timers going in his mind at once. If a new molecule had entered the kitchen, he would have known it. He was always sweating, moving from burner to burner to plating table to mixing bowl. We talked about all the pairing off, but the social dynamics of the restaurant were my problem, not his. He said, 'Who's not doing his job?' I said, 'Everybody is.' He said, 'Then what's there to worry about?'"

"So you both felt like outsiders?"

"Eric and I were in the center of it, but not part of it. We had hired people we found pleasant, and the consequence was that we ended up with young people who found each other pleasant. The atmosphere was charged. If there had been such a thing as a pheromone detector, it would have burned up."

"I think you made a good decision. You stay out of people's personal lives until somebody asks for your advice."

"Well, anyway." She looked away for a second. "That was the place, the atmosphere. We were there seven days a week, and working hard. People came in and out when the restaurant was closed, making deliveries or fixing stuff, cleaning and restocking. It was always active, always alive. We were surrounded with people. The business was charmed. We were making so much money that I paid off our start-up loans in a year. When I renegotiated the lease to buy the building, the landlord wanted to carry the mortgage himself. In the third year, we were making enough so that Eric and I bought a house with a big down payment. Around that time, he asked me to marry him. That was the beginning of the end."

"Because you said no?"

"I said yes. It was a surprise, but not in the way you might think. When he asked, it reminded me that we weren't already married. It was, 'Oh. That's right. We're not officially related, are we?' That kind of detail had been my job, usually—to keep us on the right side of the laws and solvent and secure. I knew that marriage was a necessary part of that, like liability insurance and fire coverage and a business permit. It was just a chore I had neglected."

"Girls are always planning their weddings. Why do you suppose the idea of marriage wasn't on your mind?"

"Yes, that's probably why. I didn't let myself suspect it, of course. I didn't want to delve into how I felt about my parents or what they'd shown me about marriage. But even more, I didn't want to spend time thinking about Eric and what I felt about him—or didn't feel. He was like a relative, my only one."

"I remember you said your mother had died when you were young. What about your father? He was an artist, right?"

She knitted her brows and shook her head. "That's right. When my mother left him, he didn't notice for a week or so that she had left me there, too, because his studio was always a gathering place for women—models, artists, dealers, buyers—and one of them took care of me. Her name was Margaret, and she was a rich woman who had come to learn to paint like Moss Harper. It took her a couple of years to realize that she never could, and she left, too."

"Moss Harper? I didn't realize that's who your father was."

"The great Moss Harper. When Margaret left, she took me with her. We went to her house in Poughkeepsie, and she was the one who raised me."

"Just like that? Nobody signed any papers?"

"That only happens when there's a possibility of a disagreement. He seemed to feel that taking care of children was the responsibility of the nearest woman, so when she left, he thought it was only natural that she took me with her."

"Were you in touch with him?"

"I saw him once, for two days, when I was in college. I went to New York to his studio. It was like going to visit a person who had donated an organ to you. The excuse for going was to thank the person, but the real motive was curiosity, and that part was more egotism than interest in him. I was seeing one of the factors that had contributed to the making of the glorious twenty-year-old me. There was no connection, really. He didn't care about me, and even my curiosity wasn't reciprocated. He had seen a million twenty-year-old girls, and I didn't strike him as one of the most interesting." She walked along the dirt path on the spit that led them toward the looming rock. "No, my father wasn't close to me. After Margaret died, only Eric was."

"That's why you agreed to marry Eric?"

"Of course. We told ourselves and each other that not marrying before was a small, amusing oversight. We didn't make a big deal out of the engagement, or even mention it at the restaurant. I noticed something I hadn't known before. Not being married was okay because some people assumed we were, and others thought we would be, but had some political objection to official marriage. Telling anyone we were going to get married would have weakened my position because Eric was the one who was indispensable, not me. As long as we seemed unbreakably tied together, I had authority. If I was just the boss's girlfriend with wedding plans, it would be different. There would be a period of time when he was still up for grabs."

Jack Till wondered why these were the details she was choosing to tell him, but he could see that she was choosing, so he waited.

"It became a problem. I knew that beneath all of the automatic stuff that was happening—like saying 'I love you' at all the right times, but hearing it sound like 'God bless you' or 'You're welcome,' instead of 'I think about you all the time and you make my knees weak,' there was something missing. We both felt that way, I think, but we didn't want to admit it even to ourselves."

"What did you say to him?"

"Nothing. What could I say?"

"And Eric?"

"Now we're getting close to the sad part. It makes me sad to remember it, anyway. Maybe I'm just feeling sorry for myself because my life is a mess."

"I can make your life better if you can just give me some hard information about the men who are after you or the girl who was killed. Anything might help. Even her name could do it."

"I'm getting to it. Today I'm finding that I can talk about it only by talking around it first. And only after I've stamped down all the weeds around it can I go to the center. The next thing that happened was Olivia."

"Oh, yes. Olivia."

"Yes. Olivia Kent was where I started, so I've completed the circle, walked all around the truth." She took a deep breath and let it out. "Eric cheated on me with Olivia."

"I'm sorry. It must have hurt." He had to be careful to keep the response simple and sympathetic. If she detected a false tone, it might make her see him as a manipulator and shut down.

"It was pretty much what I said earlier. He was in an atmosphere that was like a slow-motion orgy, where people changed partners over a period of months, making the rounds of the place in a couple of years. But there was always looking and flirting, always an undercurrent. Olivia Kent was the only one, at first, who knew that Eric and I had just decided to get married, and understood that the period leading up to it was an opportunity for her."

Till decided to follow the story she wanted to tell him, and hope that it led to what he wanted to know. "An opportunity to have a fling with Eric, or take your place permanently?"

"It's hard for me to say what she was thinking. She had been with us for a long time, and she liked Eric. Maybe all that time she had been developing a hopeless crush on him, and unexpectedly learned that the crush wasn't hopeless—was only *getting* hopeless, and that she had to make a move right then. It could have been more than a crush. But there are also women who get a thrill out of seducing men just before their weddings, and she may have been one of them. I had been her boss for almost four years, and maybe she had been building up resentment. I suppose it could have been all of those feelings in some proportion, because people are too complicated to do things for one reason."

"So she used her opportunity."

"Right. Eric proposed, I said yes, and we set the date for six months later. We said it was so we could do it during our least busy season, after New Year's. That gave Olivia plenty of time to work, but she started the affair right away. She made a move and Eric didn't hesitate."

"How did you find out he was seeing Olivia?"

"I figured out that something was going on. A lot of women say that a woman always knows, but it's not true. We don't. Eric was just about the same. Olivia wasn't."

"How was she different?"

"She started being sort of cold and snippy to me. I recognized the attitude. Sometimes when somebody is doing something to hurt you, she has to convince herself that you already deserved it. That was the way it was with Olivia and me, and pretty soon I began to suspect what the reason might be. One night when I left work, I just drove to Olivia's apartment, parked, and waited. It wasn't more than a few minutes before they showed up in Eric's car. They both went in, and an hour or so later, Eric came out. The prosecution rests."

"Did you tell him you knew?"

"I turned my car around so I wouldn't have to drive past him in the street, and then drove as fast as I dared to beat him home. I needed to think about the whole thing. At first I was horribly hurt and angry. Then I noticed that my own impulse wasn't to break up with him. I didn't hate him. In an odd sort of way, I understood him and felt sympathy for him."

"So you did nothing at all?"

"Olivia had a sort of on-again, off-again boyfriend. His name was David."

"Oh. Revenge sex."

"Well, not quite. I got him alone one night and kissed him, and I thought I was prepared to go through with it. But when he kissed me back, I wasn't, so I didn't. I said, 'I'm sorry, David, but I just realized why I was doing this, and it's not a good reason, or a good idea.' He was very nice and understanding about it. But then, he didn't keep his mouth shut. That was part of the claustrophobic atmosphere around there, too: Everybody was always telling each other secrets, leaving out no intimate details. He had a confessional relationship with Olivia's best friend, Kit, so he told her."

"Kit as in Katherine?"

"Maybe. Or Kathleen, or Katerina, or a hundred other names. She was just called Kit."

"Was she one of the other waitresses?"

"She waited sometimes. Primarily she was Olivia's friend. When Olivia had been with us for a few months, Kit just showed up. She was very striking, with bright red hair that was helped along only a little bit by the stylist's dye, to tone it darker and make it shinier, and big green eyes. She had freckles, but she was really good with make-up, so her skin looked clear and white, except for a blush under the cheekbones. She would come in and sit at the bar, sometimes with another girl or two, just drinking and waiting for Olivia. When she was with a man, she might have dinner. At some point, she started acting as Olivia's substitute. Olivia came to me and asked if I could arrange it when she had to go home to Ohio for some family thing. I was a little skeptical the first time, but after that I wasn't. She clearly had worked in a formal restaurant before, and learned to be profes-sional. She was fast and hardworking and knowledgeable. She knew the Banque menu by heart and could discuss it with customers. Then Olivia would come back from wherever she had been this time, and Kit would go back to being a bar ornament. When she wasn't filling in for Olivia, she acted like a rich girl who could barely bring herself to work hard enough to get drunk. And maybe she was. The arrangement was that we would pay Olivia for the time. I don't know what arrangement they made about Kit's tips, but at Banque those were bigger than salaries." Wendy glanced at Jack Till, and he could tell she was trying to see whether he knew.

He said, "She's the one?"

"She's the one."

"You're sure she never made it onto your payroll?"

"Positive."

"Too bad. A Social Security number would have given us a leg up. Even a full name." He needed to coax her, but he didn't want to distract her from her recollections. He had to keep her talking. "So Kit told her best friend Olivia that you had flirted with David."

"More than that. I was emotional about the whole situation right then. When I was with David, I was crying and saying far too much. I told him that Eric was fooling around with Olivia, and that it was making me crazy, and that was why I had made a fool of myself with him."

"And he told Kit, and Kit told Olivia."

"Kit told Olivia that I knew she was sleeping with my fiancé, that I was going mad with jealousy, and that I had slept with her boyfriend David."

"Really?"

"Yes. She had decided to give me a little revenge that I hadn't actually earned."

"Did it make you angry?"

"Not exactly. It was funny, really, because only David and I knew for sure what had gone on. I was denying everything, which people assumed I would do no matter what. He was denying it, too, but of course, Olivia would never believe him." She looked happy, wistful, but only for a second. "Kit and I became friends after that." She seemed to remember something and corrected herself. "Sort of. She was still primarily Olivia's friend, and so was I, but we had a secret that Olivia didn't know."

"Wait. You were still friends with Olivia?"

"Not right away. I still hated her then. The first thing was that Olivia told Eric that I knew all about it. I left the restaurant as usual one night and found Eric had followed me home. I had seen him getting ready to leave, but I had assumed he was going to Olivia's. Instead he pulled into the driveway right after I did. We sat in the living room of our new house that we had bought and furnished together, and talked about why we shouldn't marry each other, and what we should do about our predicament."

"Was it a fight, or were you both too sad for that?" He couldn't help remembering the breakup with his wife, Rose, when he had simply come home and found the note telling him that she was going away for a while, and which friend had agreed to watch Holly until he got home from work.

"We talked for a long time, and we both cried and held each other, then opened a bottle of really good cognac that we were saving for some big occasion, and got drunk and cried and hugged some more. I don't think we made any decisions except to announce to each other that we weren't in love. We still had Banque. Either of us could have walked away from the restaurant if it had been a failure, but it was a roaring, screaming success. We had named it Banque because it was in an old bank building, but after four years, it might as well have been a real bank. The place had become so valuable that neither of us could have bought the other out, and everything was leveraged. We had bought the building, so it had a mortgage. We had bought our new house, and that had a mortgage. There wasn't a way that Eric could leave, because he was the big attraction. We had never separated our interests in any legal way, just agreed that everything was ours together. So everything had changed, but nothing looked different."

"You mean because you stayed in the house and the restaurant." She was getting close to the part she had kept secret, so Till only prompted her.

"Yes. Eric moved into the second big bedroom. And half the time he didn't come home anyway, or came home when it was just about morning and I was ready to get up. We still worked at the restaurant, of course, but not together. A lot of the work I did was daytime stuff—taking deliveries, balancing the books, doing bills, payroll and taxes, and supervising the daytime crew. When Eric came in, he went straight to the kitchen. Sometimes he even entered through the delivery door in back near the pantry. It's possible we were even better workers than we had been—I was, certainly, because I had nothing else anymore. Then the drama kind of seeped away. It's amazing what you can get used to if you're busy enough to keep your mind turned outward all the time. The restaurant kept thriving, the money came in, and the days went by. Before long, Eric and I grew close again. We were still business partners and best friends."

"Eric had Olivia to occupy him. What was your social life like?"

"I went out after work with Kit, and after Olivia and Eric broke up, we took Olivia back, too. We went to late-night clubs, danced, drank, had fun. I had a few dates with men I shouldn't have, but most of the time I went out with the girls. I told you what the two of them looked like. It was great to be out with them. We walked into a club, and men just began to move toward them, as though they couldn't help it. Every night was New Year's Eve for about five months. And I was the one who didn't want to go home, the one who would slip the DJ a couple hundred bucks to keep the music going a little longer. Then Kit met a man and stopped hanging out with us."

"Did that stop you?"

"No. I went out, sometimes with Olivia, and sometimes with other women we knew. I went to parties. The whole period is kind of a blur, partly because I was drinking a lot for the first time in my life, and partly because I was moving fast, trying to jump back a few years and live the time that I had wasted on Eric. I wanted to be where the loud music was."

"Did you have some kind of plan for the future? What were you thinking at that time?"

"From the time when Eric and I had gotten together, I had begun to make plans, killing myself to reach certain goals and set our lives up in the best, most solid and predictable ways. When I was twenty-one, I could have told you what I was going to be doing at forty-one or sixty-one. I realized that I had been insane, so I was trying to develop a new strategy. I remember the day when I had planned to marry Eric, I was out with Olivia, and we ran into Kit."

"Where?"

"It was Darkest Peru, off Sunset. It was Olivia and me, and there might have been one of the other girls from Banque. We hadn't seen Kit for at least a month. We walked into the ladies' room and there she was, in front of the mirror fixing her makeup. As soon as I walked in, I spotted her. Who else could it be with that hair? She seemed really happy to see us. She said she was with her boyfriend. They were just getting ready to leave, and he was waiting for her, but she wanted us to meet him. We went out of the ladies' room and she took us to a table. There were five chairs, but just one young guy sitting there with a glass of cola. He was big, wearing a dark sport coat that looked tight because it was thin summer-weight cloth, and you could see arm muscles. He saw us coming, and stood up. I thought he was good looking, except for his thick neck. And I wasn't wild about the knit shirt with the coat. I smiled at him, but he didn't smile back, and she didn't introduce us. She just said to him, 'Where is he?' She said it kind of angrily, because she seemed to be embarrassed in front of us. I realized the guy was a bodyguard. He said, 'He went out to the car. He needed to make some calls. Come on.' If that wasn't exactly what he said, it was close. I could tell the bodyguard had been assigned to wait for Kit and bring her along when she came out of the ladies' room. Kit hesitated, kind of putting one hand on her hip and frowning. Then she decided, for whatever reason, that she wasn't going to push it. She said to us, 'Well, I guess he's in a big hurry now. I'll have to arrange a get-together when he's not feeling so fucking important.' She went with the bodyguard, though."

Till knew she was on the edge of telling him the things he wanted to know. "What did you make of the bodyguard? Were you afraid of him?"

"No. We had a lot of show-business customers at Banque, so I was used to them. Bodyguards had been *the* accessory for Holly-wood types since silent films. And people were even more likely to bring bodyguards to the late-night clubs. There was a kind of bad-boy ambience to those places, and it fit."

"What happened after that night?"

"I kind of forgot about it. After all, it was a nonevent, a meeting that never happened. I got distracted, and didn't think about it for a while."

"Distracted by what?"

"A big mistake. I got into a relationship with one of the owners of an art gallery. It was the gallery that hung paintings on the walls in Banque. His name was Matthew. At the moment I was looking for something to turn everything upside down, so the excitement seemed to be just what I needed. It wasn't."

"How did the relationship end?" Till was sensing that there was something about this period that she considered the cause of her problems. There was the language of excuses: heavy drinking, distraction, bad relationships.

"I know it's not exactly a surprise to anyone to say it, but there's just a hint of fraudulence about everything having to do with art."

Till studied her. "What exactly was the fraudulence in Matthew? Was it something to do with your being Moss Harper's daughter?"

"Wow. Did somebody tell you that, or did you figure it out?"

"Just a guess."

"I went to an opening at his gallery. Matthew was working the crowd, trying to make some sales. The crowd included a few artists who were there because Matthew was powerful and could help them, but mostly they were a bunch of rich people who had figured out that buying art was a chance to be part of a scene without having talent or personality or being attractive. I found myself standing there beside a very tall, chubby guy who was drinking and eating while he talked, and he looked like the spoiled son of a Roman emperor. He kept staring down at me as though he knew some guilty secret about me. Finally, he leaned uncomfortably close and said, practically in my ear, "Matthew tells me you're Moss Harper's daughter. Are you?" It was one of those moments when a dozen things that had all seemed just slightly off clicked into place at once. I had never told Matthew who my father was. It had never come up. Matthew had been using me for status. I was a curiosity."

"What did you do?"

"I dropped him and worked harder. For me, the restaurant had soured the night I caught Eric fooling around, but I didn't have anything else to do. Restaurants were the only business I knew. Eric was the only one I could really talk to. Everything I had was tied up in Banque. So I stayed. The only big changes were the ones I had made when Eric and I broke the engagement. I had split the long-term bank accounts into thirds—his, mine, and the restaurant's—and stopped putting any new money into the restaurant. I paid us each one-half of the net profits at the end of each week. So by this time, I had a growing backlog of money, most of which was still in cash in the safe in the basement of our house. It wasn't happiness, but it was a way to live. Then one night at the beginning of August, I saw him for the first time, and everything started to change."

"Do you mean Kit's boyfriend?"

She nodded.

Till waited, but she didn't go on. He said, "You're right to be scared. But the only way to end this is to remember and tell everything, and keep searching for things you didn't recall until now."

She was silent for a few steps as they walked together along the gravel path. The gulls from the rock were circling above them. "The restaurant had been packed all evening. Eric liked to close the kitchen at ten-thirty or eleven, but that night he didn't stop cooking until one. I went by the bar a while later, and there was Kit, in her favorite seat, talking to all the men, as she always did. I hadn't seen her in a long time. I might have seen her once after the night in Darkest Peru, but if so we didn't actually speak—just hugged and hurried off in different directions. But this time I joined her and we chatted for a minute or two. I remember she said that she hadn't been out much because her boyfriend had taken a summer place at the beach, so coming in to Banque had seemed like too much work. I might have said, 'You should make him bring you here more often.' But then she told me that she had come by herself while he was out, and she had called him after she had arrived, so he might come by later. That was it. I got called away because somebody else wanted to talk to me, so I moved on."

"Did you see her again that night?"

"Only from a distance. The place was like a big cocktail party that night. Everybody had a story to tell you, or a friend to introduce, or somebody who had asked to be remembered or something. I may have looked around for her later on and seen that she was in the middle of a conversation. I went into the kitchen to see if Eric and his crew had already buttoned up and gone. The busboys and dishwashers and the floor man were still there, but Eric and the cooks had left. I took my time, chatted for a while, and then went out the back of the building to head for my car. I always parked at the far end of the lot in the daytime, before the valet attendants arrived. The place had nearly cleared out while I was dawdling, so the whole lot was nearly empty. As I was walking, a car arrived. I thought it was odd, because it was so late, but then I looked at it and I thought it must be a limo picking somebody up. It was a big black American car, like the cars you rented yesterday to bring me back. It came into the lot and then stopped, swung around to face out near the exit, and turned off its lights, but the motor was still running, and I could see the green lights on the dashboard were on. The back door opened and a man got out and just stood there."

"What did he look like?"

"Just a man. Maybe five feet eight or nine. White. In his middle thirties."

"Close your eyes and think about him. Pretend you're seeing him again now. Do you feel anything about him—uneasiness, maybe fear?"

"No, irritation. I'd had enough of the whole restaurant scene, not only trying to get through that year after the engagement collapsed, but that night specifically. The way he carried himself, standing beside his chauffeured car that was half-blocking the exit, he seemed to be the epitome of what was wrong with L.A."

"So you stared at him and felt annoyed."

"Yes. He was wearing a pair of jeans and a jacket that I could tell even at a distance of forty feet or so in dim light was good, because of the way it fit him. He had dark brown hair, short. He was trim and had good proportions and I just knew he had a personal trainer and a nutritionist and all of that, but he wasn't like a young man. He acted older, kind of cranky and impatient. There was just something about his posture at first, kind of slouching there, looking mad."

"He was looking at something. Was he looking at you?"

"No. Not yet. He'd seen me but I was just part of the landscape. He was looking toward the restaurant. From where he was, he could probably see the front door, or certainly the front corner of the building where people came to pick up their cars."

"So you could see his face. What was it like?"

"That was part of the impression I had that he was not as young as he looked. It was the way the skin lay over the bone structure of his face. There was no fat, so the skin seemed thinner the way it does in middle-aged people. He was clean-shaven, sort of artificially tanned, although I don't know how I could tell that. I can see him now, staring in the direction of the front door, waiting."

"Tell me everything you saw, everything you thought."

"The front door of the restaurant opened—I heard voices, maybe the sound of the busboys clearing a table near the front, the dishes clattering in the bin, saw more light for a few seconds—and I could see his face better for a moment. There was laughter from the street. I heard a woman, then another, a couple of deeper voices. Some of the people went the other way on the sidewalk, away from the lot, so I didn't see them. Only one came around the corner of the building to the parking lot: Kit. She walked up to the man from the black car, sauntering a little as though she were teasing him. He put his hand on her arm. It wasn't a nice touch, you know? He gripped her arm, and the way she held it, a little away from her body, I could tell he was hurting her. But she didn't try to pull it away from him. She just stood there, and it reminded me of the way a child stands who's done something bad and the parent takes him by the arm. She just stood looking down and listened. He was saying something to her in a low voice, and he put his face really close to her ear. The way his mouth was opening wide while he was talking but not getting loud, I could tell he was angry."

"Did she answer him?"

"No. She just looked down, waiting for him to finish, when he hit her. It surprised her as much as it did me because it came from nowhere. He held her arm with his left hand, and his right came up and slapped her. She dropped her purse and put her hand to her cheek, and that seemed to make him madder. I yelled, 'Hey!' and started toward her. She saw me and yelled, 'It's okay, Wendy. I'm okay.' The man opened the back door of the limo and pushed her in, then turned for a second to look in my direction. The bodyguard, the same one I had seen the other time, got out, picked up her purse, found her car keys in it, trotted to her car, got in, and drove out the exit. The boyfriend got into the black car and followed him out."

Till was listening to her words, to her tone, to her hesitations, trying to detect the places where she was unsure, and the places where she was leaving something out. "What did you do?"

"I went back into the restaurant and called the police. I told them who I was and what had happened, and they began to ask questions that I couldn't answer. I didn't know the man or where he lived. I didn't know where Kit lived. I knew her last name was Stoddard. I hadn't gotten the license number of the car. I sent somebody to look for Olivia, but she had gone home. The police said they'd send a car, and I hung up. I called Olivia, and I told her what had happened. She sounded scared, but she didn't know the name of the man, either. By the time the cops arrived, it was at least a half hour later, and I had to tell them the whole story over again before they told me there wasn't much they could do. They radioed in to ask that other cops take a close look at black limos that seemed to have a man and a redhead in them. So I went home and tried to sleep."

"Did you call them the next morning to see if anything had turned up?"

"Yes. I ended up having to tell the whole story a third time because the cop on duty seemed not to have heard of it. He said he would check and see if anyone had found out anything, and call the restaurant if there was news."

"I take it he didn't call."

"No. I called Olivia again after that. It was around ten, and she came in, and we compared notes. She had called Kit a dozen times and gotten no answer. Finally she took me to Kit's apartment, which was in an old stucco building off Franklin that had been repaired. You know, it was one of those twenties buildings that have high, narrow doors and lots of arches, but it wasn't restored, just painted and held together. I remember the name on the mailbox wasn't Kit's. It was another girl's name, and Olivia said it was because the other girl had moved out and the landlord would raise the rent if he knew. We rang the bell and knocked on the door, but she wasn't home. Neither of us had a key, so we couldn't get in at first, but the lock looked really cheesy, so Olivia tried slipping a credit card between the door and the jamb, and it opened. The place had about a month of dust and smelled stale. The food in the refrigerator was all old, and about half of her plants were dead from lack of water. I looked in her closet and a lot of clothes were in there, but not the outfit I had seen the night before. Olivia and I tried to re-member other outfits she owned that were favorites, and all of them were missing."

"What did you think that meant?"

"That she had moved in with the boyfriend. That was what she had implied when we had talked to her. So we waited. Nothing hap-pened. After a few days of calling and leaving messages on her voice mail, we went over there again. We got into the apartment with Olivia's credit card again. As soon as we opened the door, I knew something had changed. It was the smell."

"What kind of smell?"

"Cleanser. Chlorine bleach. Then there was the ammonia smell of window cleaner, and some kind of pine-smelling floor wash. It was all mixed together in those four little rooms. Boy, was it clean. All of Kit's stuff had been moved out, and the place had been scrubbed. There wasn't so much as a piece of paper in the whole place. I know because I looked, and because there was nothing it could have been in or under. The furniture, which Olivia was sure had come with the apartment, was gone. There was nothing left. The only objects anywhere in the apartment were a couple of cans of white paint, a roller and a brush, and a blue plastic tarp."

"Did you see any stains or marks that they were trying to cover up with the paint?"

"Nothing. The paint made Olivia scared because she thought somebody must have left it there and gone back for the ladder. She expected to see them any second."

"And you?"

"Well, there's nothing as contagious as fear. It made me want to leave, but it also made me want to see if the cleaning crew had missed anything. You could see that this wasn't a building where that kind of cleaning usually happened. The entryway had old copies of *LA Weekly* lying in a pile. The halls hadn't been painted for a long time. After all, the reason we could see it at all was that the lock was too cheap to keep out the two of us for ten seconds. So I made Olivia help me search everything: kitchen drawers, cabinets, the space behind the bottom drawers where things sometimes fall. Nothing had been left. We went out to the back of the building to see if there was a conspicuous load of trash out there."

"Why were you so thorough?"

"Because it wasn't like Kit to do that kind of cleaning. Olivia kept saying that. Kit was the kind of person who never got back a cleaning deposit on an apartment. She just walked away from whatever she didn't feel like taking with her. I thought maybe she had stopped paying rent and the landlord had dumped everything to get the place ready for the next tenant."

"It sounds right. What did you find?"

"Zero. We had been in the apartment just a week or so before, and so we looked for familiar things: the clothes she had left in the closet, the pots from the dead plants, the magnetic calendar from her refrigerator. All gone. I went back into the building to talk to the manager. He wasn't the owner. He was like a lot of them are, an actor who spent most of his days going out on open casting calls or classes. Managing the building wasn't much effort, and it covered half his rent. He had known Kit by sight, but he had thought of her as Carolyn Styles, the name on the mailbox and the lease. She had been there when he moved in, and he didn't know anything about a sublet agreement. He gave me the name and number of the owner. He was a businessman from Korea who was very nice. He had no forwarding address for Carolyn Styles, but he did have a previous address and a few referrals from old landlords."

"You're good. It's what I've done a hundred times."

"Well, I hope you had better luck at it than I did. What I ended up with, after talking to everybody I'd ever met who knew Kit, was this: Kit Stoddard was not her real name. It was a name that she'd worked out with a casting agent named Marti Cole about the day after she'd arrived in Los Angeles. She had wanted to be an actress, so she needed a name like Kit Stoddard. The agent's office was where she met Carolyn Styles."

"A false name, too."

"Yep."

"It sounds as though the agent used names from a phone book—STO, STY."

"No, because neither of them was listed. I tracked Marti Cole down, though. She had gone out of business and was working as an assistant to a casting director at Southern Star Pictures. She said she'd closed her office because she couldn't afford health insurance—it had brought home to her that she wasn't making it. She hadn't seen either Kit or Carolyn Styles in two years, and no longer had any memory of what their real names were."

"You gave up at that point?"

"No. I just felt that I couldn't do that until I knew she was all right. I kept talking to people every night at the restaurant. I would check the reservation book for the names of people who had known Kit. At night I would check the bar for people I'd seen drinking with her. I asked them everything I could think of. Her real name, where she was from, any other addresses or phone numbers, anything about the boyfriend. Had she ever worked a real job. What I really wanted most was just somebody who had seen her that day, or anytime since that night in the parking lot."

"Get anything?"

"Not much. Everybody seemed to have the same relationship with Kit that Olivia had. They'd met her at a club or a restaurant or a party. She had always seemed to them to be close friends with somebody else, and then when I talked to the other person, that one didn't know much about her, either. A few of them knew she had wanted to be an actress, but none of them could remember her being in anything. Some thought she was a model. I knew a photographer named Jimmy Shannon. I called him, and he had one of his assistants check with the agencies. None of them ever heard of her, and I had already checked with the Screen Actors Guild. After all that work, I never found anybody who knew more than Olivia had told me the first day."

"What was Olivia doing all this time? Was she helping you?"

"At first she was. We even spent days and days driving the beach cities from Ventura to Newport, looking at beach houses, condos, and apartment buildings. We were looking for her red hair or his black car. Of course it was impossible. Then Olivia was gone."

"Gone?"

"Yes. She left."

"Why did she leave? Did she talk about it?"

"Well, Olivia was still working at Banque. She and Eric were through. David, her old boyfriend, was still interested, but not in any serious way. He just liked sleeping with her once in a while. The restaurant scene was getting to her, just as it was getting to me. And she was scared. We had started out the first night with the fear that Kit's story wasn't going to have a happy ending. As time went on, we were sure of it. We went to the police again, but you can imagine how far we got."

"Sure. A pretty young woman moved to L.A. hoping to be an actress. She changed her name, dated rich men, and then moved away and left her apartment clean."

"Well, the police didn't exactly issue an alert. It got to Olivia."

"How?"

"She got more and more afraid. She regretted leaving all of those messages on Kit's voice mail. She thought the boyfriend would find us and kill us to shut us up."

"Did she tell other people, or take precautions of any kind?"

"She was always looking over her shoulder, and she wouldn't leave the restaurant alone anymore. Then one night when I was expecting her to work, she called the restaurant. She said she was calling from the airport. She was leaving because she was tired of being afraid."

"Did it occur to you that she might have been forced to call you and say she was leaving?"

"Of course. By then I was as paranoid as she was. But I heard announcements being made in the background—gibberish about flights boarding, and not leaving bags unattended. She sounded calm, maybe even happy she was leaving. So I figured she was okay."

"All right. So you were on your own."

"Right. It was more than that. Eric was on his third girlfriend right then, and so he wasn't around very much to talk to me. My weeks of investigating and asking about Kit kept me away from the restaurant. I began to feel that the whole Banque scene was over. It wasn't just that Kit, who had become a friend, and Olivia, who had been with us from the beginning, were gone. It was noticing that what had been going on had not been real. Everybody was an actor or a model. What we actually spent our time doing was waiting on tables and tending bar, but we had all agreed to pretend that wasn't true. For a while Eric and I were protected because we had our own fantasy. It still worked for Eric, because he was a real chef, but it didn't work for me anymore. If I wasn't with Eric, I was just a twenty-nine-year-old woman who had worked eighteen hours a day for ten years in a job that would never get any easier or give me any chance at a life."

She was moving close to the night when she had been attacked, and Till needed to get her there, but he sensed that she was skipping something that had happened. "Did you do anything about it?"

"What do you mean?"

"Look into the job market, or think about other cities to move to, or call friends in other parts of the country."

"I didn't get the chance. About a week after that, I came home from the restaurant one night, and the man was waiting for me with a baseball bat."

"And you had never seen him before?"

She paused, looked away from him for a second. "I *had* seen him. I lied before about that. He was the bodyguard who had been waiting at the table in the club when we were with Kit."

Till had to keep himself from showing either his excitement at her admission or the fact that he had known from the first description that the bodyguard might be her attacker. Finally she was beginning to tell the truth. "Did he speak?"

"I spoke. I said, 'What do you want?' He said nothing."

"And then?"

"He started beating me, and then got scared off. Eric arrived, and right behind him there was another car. The fact that it was two cars was what saved me, I think. It seemed like a lot of cars, maybe a lot of people."

"Who was in the other car?"

"That's the best part of the joke, I guess. Just Eric's latest girlfriend. She had arrived at the restaurant to go home with him for the night, but she needed to have her own car available in the morning. She saved my life. I had been hit a few times, and I was down. I knew I couldn't run or fight anymore. Then all of a sudden there were all these headlights, and he ran."

She walked ahead toward the rock, and now they were near the foot of it, but she stayed ahead a couple of paces, and Till couldn't talk to her with all of the other tourists so close. Their conversation had not ended, only paused for an indeterminate period, and they both knew it. She had already made the first crucial admission: that she had lied when she said she knew nothing about the attacker. Now it was essential for Till to keep her confidence and find a way to make her tell him the rest.

He continued with their walk, and then spent the afternoon walking through the shops with her. He watched her closely all day, waiting for her to resume their conversation, but she did not do it. Once, as they were walking on the street far from other pedestrians, he said, "Ann?"

"I'm not Ann anymore."

"Who are you?"

"I have no choice right now. I have to be Wendy."

While she pretended to shop to keep him from interrogating her, Till used the time to think about the other part of the problem. He had to keep her alive. When they came back to their rooms in the hotel, he waited until she was in the other room and then used his cell phone. He dialed a number he knew very well, then said, "Sergeant Poliakoff, please."

30

PAUL INCHED the rental car along the freeway in the heavy traffic toward the cluster of tall buildings downtown. It was only four o'clock, but it seemed that rush hour started earlier and earlier. Paul turned his head away from the road in front of him and looked at Sylvie. She was quiet today. He wished that the reason she was not giving him an argument was that she understood the uncomfortable situation he was in, and not because she was thinking of all the ways he had disappointed her. He was almost sure that she was saving up the complete list of his offenses and trying out in her mind different ways of saying them so they would inflict the maximum pain. It was possible—even easy—for Paul to ignore the opinions of most people, but he was vulnerable to Sylvie. After being on the most intimate terms with a woman for fifteen years, it was difficult for a man to tell himself she didn't know much about him.

He tried to distract her, to get her to think about the present, the things they had to accomplish. "At least we've had a chance to stop at home and get some sleep. We're coming rested and prepared. This could even turn out to be easy."

"Don't worry. I'm not blaming you for this. You'll still get laid."

He laughed, more relieved than amused. She could be uncomfortably perceptive about the ridiculousness of the relationship between men and women. He tried to make the feeling of affection grow. "Well, I'm sorry anyway. It's not what I would have chosen to do. I'd like to be taking you to the airport to get on the plane to Madrid—that Air France/Delta flight that leaves around dinnertime."

She stared at him in silence for a couple of seconds. "I know."

"Maybe we can do it as soon as this is over."

"Maybe we'll have to."

"Don't worry. The situation may not be good, but *we're* good."

She said carefully, "I'll do my best to make this whole thing end the way it's supposed to. But after this, we'll have to be more careful what we agree to do, and for whom."

"We will. This is a special case. Densmore—"

"Is what I'm worried about," she said sharply. "I understand how we got into the position of having to finish this job for him. But the thing to remember is that he didn't tell us the truth."

"He's paying us twice the original price."

"He's making us do something we don't want to do." She stared at Paul again, her eyes not moving from his face. "Isn't he?"

Paul saw the trap and was almost grateful to her for placing it in the open where he could see it. "Well, yeah."

"I'm not going to be Densmore's underling."

"When this job is done and we collect our pay, it will be the last thing we do for Densmore."

"I hope so."

"It will be." He knew from her tone that she would remember and hold him to it. He didn't like losing Densmore, who had been the perfect middleman for eight years. Densmore had kept the clients at a distance from Paul and Sylvie, collected their money, and kept them frightened so that none of them had ever talked to the police. It was a shame to have to lose Densmore, but Sylvie had a point. Densmore had begun to presume too much. This time he had told the client who Paul and Sylvie were. His excuse was that this was a client who would never talk to the police under any circumstances. But the long-standing arrangement was not that the client wouldn't talk, it was that the client couldn't, because he didn't know anything.

Paul drove along Temple Street past the fortresslike structure of Our Lady of the Angels Cathedral and then the Superior Court building. He could see the gleaming stainless-steel curves of the Disney Concert Hall. "All right. Here it comes," he said. "That building coming up is 210 West Temple. The offices of the Assistant DAs working on this case are upstairs, but what we want to study are the approaches and openings."

"I am." Sylvie looked carefully at everything she could see from the car. It was difficult to assess the security of a building like this one, because the whole neighborhood was part of the court complex. The court buildings were full of bailiffs and marshals and deputy sheriffs. There were guards in all the lobbies to be sure nobody came in armed, but there were probably other security people who weren't visible. The biggest danger would be that there were so many armed cops coming and going on various kinds of legal business in a normal day, a lot of them in plainclothes. The building slid by her window, and Paul turned at the next corner.

She could see the twenty-story white rectangle of the New Otani Hotel a block away. It was a feature of the downtown skyline. Downtown was a difficult place to do the kind of business that Paul and Sylvie did. During the day it was lively, and there were lots of pedestrians around the courthouse complex, the cathedral, the Museum of Modern Art, the Disney Concert Hall, the plaza outside the Dorothy Chandler Pavilion. But an hour after the evening's events, very few people remained. The big hotels—the Biltmore, the Bonaventure, the Otani—were full, but no life spilled out into the surrounding blocks. People parked underground or in structures, so there weren't even many cars on the streets. Few people lived down here. There were a few new condominiums and a lot of talk about building lofts in old buildings, but she had not seen any change yet.

She sat quietly while Paul drove up to the entrance of the New Otani. A bellman appeared with a cart and lifted their luggage onto it, and the parking attendant took their car away. She walked inside with Paul, and sat on a couch in the lobby while he checked in.

Sylvie had made the reservations using her best secretary voice, and gotten them the special Attorney Rate. The hotel Web site promised them accommodations within walking distance of state and federal courts, "affording your legal team a productive workplace" and "war rooms" that included conference tables, fax machines, workstations, copiers, and shredders. Today Paul was attorney Peter Harkin, and Sylvie was his wife, Sarah Harkin. They were from Charlotte, North Carolina. Peter had a distinguished-looking head of graying hair and a matching mustache, and Sarah had blond hair of the type that was just light enough to look as though its color had a genetic component.

Sylvie had selected their clothes and wigs to be especially misleading from above, where most surveillance cameras were mounted. Her blond wig was already feeling tight and uncomfortable. It reminded her of a movie Cherie Will had made called *Blond-sided*. She and three other actresses had all supposedly been cheerleaders who arrived from Texas for the Rose Bowl and missed their team bus. She and two of the others had needed to wear blond wigs, and she had hated it. Whenever Cherie had an idea for a movie, it didn't matter if it meant actors had to be run over by a truck, as long as it was quick and cheap.

Sylvie distracted herself by looking at the lobby. The space was large, with lots of long angles and a mezzanine above, all in beige. There was a lounge that consisted of a long marble counter with tables and chairs along both sides of it, and at either end, an enormous arrangement of flowers exploding upward in various tones of bright red.

Paul stepped away from the front desk and Sylvie joined him on the way to the elevator. She said, "Any problem about the room?"

He shook his head. Then the bellman caught up with them and they had to wait to speak again. She had specified that the room be on the north side, high enough for a good view of the city. She had not dared to be more specific than that. There were over four hundred rooms in the hotel, so at there were at least eighty that would do.

They rode the elevator to the fifteenth floor. Paul and Sylvie both followed the bellman, looking down at the carpet as they walked, as though they were trying to be sure their luggage didn't fall off the bellman's cart. This kept their faces away from the lenses of the surveillance cameras in the hallway. At their room, the bellman unlocked the door and they had to endure his standard tour. When he began his recitation of the hotel's amenities, Paul put a bill in his hand and said, "Thanks, but we've been here before." He left.

Sylvie locked the door, then stood beside it and listened. When she heard the sound of the luggage cart clanking off the carpet onto the bare floor of the elevator, she took off the blond wig, then the hairnet, and shook out her own hair. "Oh, man," she muttered. "Feel my neck."

Paul touched the nape of her neck dutifully. "Sweaty." He kissed it.

She shivered. The nape of her neck had always been sensitive, even ticklish. She had been surprised again by the intensity of the feeling. She rubbed the spot with her hand as she watched Paul lift the two heavy suitcases to the bed.

She waited until he had opened the suitcases, then lifted out the folded clothes and set them on the bed so they would be out of Paul's way while he removed the two dismantled rifles. He reassembled the first rifle. He had decided to use the .308 Remington Model 7s he had cleaned yesterday. Paul had always said that .308 was the government-certified man-killing caliber because the FBI snipers used .308 rifles. She and Paul were hoping to put only one bullet through one small woman.

Paul was setting up the spotting scope on the table beside the window. He looked into the eyepiece. "It's just about perfect," he said. "I can see the curb, the sidewalk, the front steps, the door, and a hundred feet on either side. I can see in the windows. Take a look."

She stepped to the table and took his place. "Great view. There's a guy sitting on the bus-stop bench, and I can see the crow's-feet wrinkles by his eyes." She paused. "Oops. Not now. He's putting on sunglasses." She straightened and stepped to the window for an un-magnified look.

"If you stay back from the window a few feet, you'll be harder to see."

She retreated. He was right, of course, but she wished he had not spoken. That need that men had to assert, to insist, to instruct, was infuriating. She stepped to the bed, unfolded the few clothes they had brought, and hung them in the closet. Then she picked up one of the rifles, raised it to her shoulder, and looked through the scope at the District Attorney's building. The scope was a new Weaver V16 Classic that was adjustable from four to sixteen power. She settled the crosshairs on the front entrance and decided the scope was just right for this long shot.

Paul was busy placing the night-vision scope on the other rifle. The nightscope was harder to use, harder to line up, and made everything glow with a green luminescence. They would use the nightscope only if the girl arrived at night, but why on earth wouldn't she? It would be foolish of her to come any other time, and she would be foolish not to disguise herself. If the police brought her, they would treat her like a protected witness. She would arrive with three big cops, all of them wearing bulletproof vests and oversized jackets. They would surround her and hustle her into the building.

Paul's preparations had been meticulous, partly because he was trying to overcome the jinx that seemed to have followed them in this job. Being careful was also the rational reaction to a risky time and place for killing someone. Sylvie played with the telescopic sight, staring at the silent street so far below her. She placed the crosshairs on the man on the bus bench, but then a bus pulled into her line of fire and obliterated her view. The bus had an advertisement on the side, and she moved the crosshairs to the oversized front tooth of the reclining actress. "Coming August 12," she said aloud. "Bang." The bus pulled away and he was still there, sitting on the bench as before. The man was big, with broad shoulders and a suspicion of a belly. He lifted a newspaper and appeared to be reading it. As she watched him, she moved the crosshairs on his body, placing them on the small metal bridge between the lenses of his sunglasses, across his nose, then up to his forehead. From this angle, she could hardly take her eyes off his widow's peak. The hair jutted down to a point, with shiny receding spaces on either side of it that reflected the late-afternoon sunlight. She said, "Doesn't that man on the bus bench look like a cop?"

Paul said, "The guy in the sport coat?"

"Yes. See him?"

Paul made a tiny adjustment to the spotting scope. "With this thing I can read his mind. Yeah." Paul stared at him for a few more seconds. "He could be one. I mean, what the hell is he doing there? Guys like him don't ride buses, they drive."

"Maybe he can't," she said. "He's right outside the DA's office. Maybe he's had his license pulled for a DUI."

"I don't know," said Paul. "Come here and watch him through the spotting scope."

She set the rifle down on the couch and stepped to the table beside the window. She looked into the eyepiece. "What are you doing?"

"I want to get everything ready. Can you see anything on him? A radio, or a bulge in his coat that shouldn't be there?"

"How about a big gold badge?" she teased. "Nothing that I can see. He isn't wearing body armor, because I can see his gut. No earpiece."

"Check his shoes."

"Good idea." She overadjusted the elevation of the scope, and he disappeared. She brought the scope back up a bit and studied the man's shoes. "I don't think they're cop shoes. They look more like those walking shoes you have."

"Then he's probably not a cop. Those things cost me three hundred bucks."

"You never told me."

"An oversight."

"Sure. When I spend that much on shoes you sound like you've been stabbed."

"They're therapeutic. They prevent plantar fasciitis and shin splints."

"Are you ready?"

"The guns are both lined up and loaded. If that guy down there is the lookout and they come now, we'll at least get a shot. Keep watching him. If he does anything, it could be the all clear to signal them in."

"He's looking at his watch. Now he's standing up. He's walking." She was quiet for a few seconds. "Nothing else is happening. I guess it's a false alarm."

"Good. Can you still keep watch for a little longer? I want to get the other stuff all ready to go."

"Sure."

She sat at the table and watched the front of the building. She was aware of Paul moving around in her peripheral vision, taking two folded police uniforms out of their suitcases. He laid them on the bed and examined them. The badge was pinned over the left pocket of each one, the nameplate pinned over the right pocket. Paul set the black leather utility belts beside them. They were bulky, with handcuffs, pepper spray, ammunition clips, sidearm. He put the black shoes on the floor at the foot of the bed. Paul was much neater than she was. She had years ago given up the pretense that she was as neat as he was, and since then concentrated on keeping her things out of his way. "There's another one," she said.

"What?"

"The guy we were watching left. Now there's another guy in the same spot. He's wearing a sport coat, too, and a tie. He's not sitting. He's standing."

"Let me see." Paul stood over her and she leaned away from the table so he could look through the spotting scope. "That's odd. He doesn't look as though he's waiting for a bus, either. He's walking over toward the corner of the building. Now he's just standing there."

"You don't suppose it's some kind of national-security thing—protecting the court buildings from terrorists?"

"I sure as hell hope not, but it could be." He stared into the spotting scope. "I want to watch this guy for a while. You can take a break."

For the rest of the day, one of them was always at the table in front of the window, staring at the front entrance of the District Attorney's office below. They took two-hour shifts. Every time Sylvie returned to the window, she saw one of the two men in sport coats.

The men weren't on duty for longer than an hour, and they moved around, so she could not always find the one on guard immediately. She made a game out of searching. Sometimes the man would be around one corner of the building or the other, just far enough so he could face in a different direction and not appear to be staring at Temple Street. Once he disappeared, but she found him ten minutes later across Temple Street from the building, coming out of the doorway of another building where he had been watching the street from behind the glass doors.

At six she put on her wig and Sarah Harkin skirt to walk to a restaurant down the street and pick up a takeout dinner. There were five good restaurants in the hotel, but she didn't want to attract the attention of too many of the Otani Hotel's guests and staff, so she used a back elevator to get to the street. When she returned, she took the stairs up two flights before she emerged from the stairs and took the elevator the rest of the way.

During her first evening shift, she used the nightscope sparingly. The bright green glow gave her a headache after a few minutes, and she knew she didn't need it. A car pulling up in front of the building to let out passengers would be hard to miss.

Her rest periods were worse than the watch periods. Paul had sunk into his quiet mode, which made him no company at all, and she was afraid that watching television would light up the room and make Paul visible. Her eyes were tired anyway. At ten Paul lengthened the shifts to three hours, so she could sleep.

The bed was mostly taken up by the uniforms they had laid out, so Sylvie pulled back the covers and made a small space on the far edge. In the darkness and silence of the room, she went to sleep immediately. At one Paul gave her a small shake, and she managed to bring herself out of sleep and open her eyes. "I sure hope this is a one-day job," she said.

"Just do your best. Wake me up at four, unless something happens first. If you find you can't keep your eyes open, get me up."

"All right. I think I'm awake now. Where are the two men?" She put her feet on the floor and stretched.

"I don't know. I think they must be in the building or in a parked car somewhere. I haven't seen them since around midnight."

Sylvie kept herself awake by searching for the men for a time, and then by trying to use the nightscope to see into the cars that passed. The only pedestrians on the street were a couple of homeless men with shopping carts. It occurred to Sylvie that they could easily be cops, too, taking the night shift. She used the scope to study them, but could not reach a conclusion about them. Their clothes consisted of several layers to keep off the night chill, so it was impossible to tell if they were hiding weapons. She saw nobody else who interested her, and at four she woke Paul and went back to sleep.

When Sylvie awoke again, the light in the room was still dim. She looked in the direction of the window. Paul had it open, and she realized that the sound of his opening it was what had awakened her. He lifted the rifle to his shoulder.

"What is it?" she said.

"A car. Get up."

Sylvie threw off the covers and rushed to join him at the window, snatching up the other rifle. While she had been asleep, he had removed the nightscope and put on the other sixteen-power Weaver. Sylvie brought the rifle up, opened both eyes wide to rid herself of the filmy blur left over from sleep, then stared into the rifle sight.

A black SUV had pulled to the red curb in front of the building. Two doors on the far side swung open. Sylvie cycled the bolt of the rifle and aimed at a spot just past the rear door, where somebody was going to step out in a second.

"Hold your fire."

Something was wrong—she could hear it in Paul's voice. She looked wide of her scope, saw running figures approaching the SUV, and placed her crosshairs on one of them. "It's the man from yesterday. The one on the bus bench!"

Sylvie watched the man reach into his coat as he ran. His hand came out, holding a gun. There was a burst of fire from inside the car, but it was another volley of shots from somewhere else that caught him from behind and swept him forward onto his face on the pavement, where he lay with his arms out in a big embrace, blood pooling on the cement by his head.

There was another barrage of shots. Sylvie swung her rifle to her left to see, but Paul held her arm. "Put it down. We've got to go!"

She set the rifle on the table, her eyes still on the scene below. The second man she had seen yesterday was lying on the sidewalk, too. Three plain vans—white, blue, black—pulled up quickly and men and women in black nylon jackets began to pile out. Some of them knelt by the fallen men, while others spoke into radios. A couple of uniformed cops appeared a hundred feet down the street and tossed flares on the pavement to begin diverting traffic away from the scene.

"Did you see the girl?"

"I don't think she's even there." Paul wasn't even looking now. He was folding the legs of the spotter scope and putting it in a carry-bag. "It was an ambush, a decoy thing. It was set up for us. Help me collect our gear."

"But who were those two men they killed?"

"I think they were there to kill Wendy Harper, too. I think somebody has decided to hedge his bets by hiring another team."

"Without even telling us?"

She could see that Paul was concentrating hard, and that he was trying to keep his voice sounding calm. "I guess we never should have called Densmore and tried to back out."

"Are you saying this is *my* fault?"

"I'm not saying it's *anybody's* fault. I'm trying to tell you why we've got to get out of here. If the cops picked out those two, they must have been smart enough to check out the windows that over-look the entrance. Let's go."

"How?"

"We use the original plan."

He changed into the police uniform as quickly as he could, so she imitated him. As soon as she had her uniform on and the utility belt buckled, she stuffed their clothes into the black canvas bag, then the Peter and Sarah Harkin clothes and wigs. When she had finished, she pulled the covers tight on the bed again, and took a last look around the room to be sure they'd left nothing behind. They hurried out into the hallway, pulling their wheeled suitcases, and managed to get to the stairwell without seeing anyone. They took everything down two flights and left the empty suitcases on the landing. Now Sylvie had the black carryall bag slung over her shoulder, and she and Paul each carried a sniper rifle. Paul led the way down the stairs, prepared to fend off questions or open fire if they met police on their way up.

They made it to the ground floor of the building in a short time. They were near the back of the building, so Paul led them along a corridor of meeting rooms to a fire exit. He pushed open the door and stepped onto the blacktop just as a pair of police cruisers came up the side street and pulled to a stop. The whole area was full of uniformed police now, setting up to block off streets on all sides of the crime scene. The neighborhood seemed to be empty of people, except for police.

As the two police cars maneuvered nose-to-nose to block the street, Paul and Sylvie stepped past them, carrying the sniper rifles. A cop who was driving one of the cars looked at them curiously for a second, but Sylvie pointed at the parking structure where she had once parked when she was called for jury duty. She called, "We're setting up on the parking structure. Good view of Temple."

The cop nodded, and they trotted to the parking structure. When they had gotten into the car they had left the day before and Paul was driving down the ramp to the street, Sylvie said, "You know whose fault this is, don't you?"

"Yeah," he said. "I think I do."

31

YOUR IDEA brought us some surprises, Jack," Poliakoff said. "In fact, the plan worked *too* well. It went down around four this morning."

Jack Till held the cell phone to his mouth and spoke quietly because he didn't want Wendy in the next room to overhear. "What happened?"

"During the night, we deployed SWAT officers in buildings along the south side of Temple Street near the DA's office, just as you suggested. We had two black SUVs like the ones they use to deliver prisoners to court. When the two SUVs pulled up at the curb and opened their doors, two men came out of parked cars on both sides, apparently trying to get a shot at a female officer in the second vehicle. The SWAT guys had spotted them, so they each got about as far as pulling out a weapon."

"Is everybody all right?"

"Everybody but the two men. We would have liked to ask them some questions, but they were both DOA."

"Have you got IDs on them yet?"

"Not yet. When a guy has three driver's licenses on him, he may as well have none. The bodies have been fingerprinted, so we'll probably have names before long."

Till said, "I don't know what to say, except to thank you for doing this. If I had just pulled up in front of the DA's office and tried to take her in, we'd be dead."

"This is a win. Now that we've got those two out of the way, are you going to bring your client in to see the DA today?"

"I'll let you know when I've decided." He looked up and saw Wendy Harper standing in the open doorway between their rooms.

"Do that."

"Thanks again. I owe you." Till ended the call and put his cell phone into his pocket.

"What was that?" she asked.

"Good news. I asked a friend of mine who's still in the department to see what would happen if you and I were to drive up to the DA's office and try to walk in."

"What *did* happen?"

"Two guys with guns came out of parked cars. Both of them were killed."

"Oh, my God! Was anybody else hurt?"

"No. The cops are all fine."

She stepped closer until she stood over him, looking down into his eyes. "You didn't tell me."

"Tell you what?"

"That you were planning something like that."

"It wasn't my operation. It was Max Poliakoff's. He didn't tell me until just now, and it's been over for hours."

She looked at him closely. "Why didn't you tell me?"

"Same reason he didn't tell me. Until those two guys showed up, there was nothing to tell."

"Do you think they were the same two who killed Louanda?"

"The odds are they were, but we can't know that for sure. There may be prints or blood or something in her house in Nevada that ties them to the scene. We may have seen them at some point. They could have been in a crowd, or stopped at an intersection or something, and we'll remember the faces. But I never got a look at them when they were chasing us. Did you?"

"No. I saw their car, and I saw that there were two heads in it." She sat down beside him on the bed. "This is my fault. I should never have decided to leave Los Angeles. I was scared. I hated being scared, and I saw a way to fix it. I had started out okay, trying to find Kit Stoddard. But as soon as I got beat up, everything changed. I changed. I decided that I had already given enough to the memory of Kit. That was what I told myself she was by then—just a memory. And I had this belief that if I could just get away and stay away for a time, then her boyfriend would stop looking. I had the idea that my having done nothing to harm him would persuade him that I could never do anything, and he would realize that he should leave me alone. So I left."

"Look, Ann. I—"

"Wendy."

"What?"

"Wendy. I told you already, I can't be Ann Donnelly anymore. Yesterday, when I left, I gave that up. Using that name now doesn't help me. All it does is point out to everyone who doesn't already know it that there are people with that name who are connected with me. Being connected with me is dangerous."

"Less dangerous than it was yesterday."

"Does that mean it's over? We're going to Los Angeles now?"

"I don't think so."

"Why not? If the police shot the men who were following us, then what is it that you're worried about?"

"I'm not exactly worried, but I'm taking precautions. I'm resisting the flow of events. When you're trying to outsmart somebody, you shouldn't let a rhythm build up. We left San Francisco; they attacked us on the road. We lost them; they went to L.A. to wait for us. We set up our own ambush for them, and got two men. Now what? The logical, almost inevitable next move is to drive to L.A. now, today."

"So you're avoiding predictability."

"I'm not making the move that's called for at the moment when the rhythm demands it. What is the man who killed Kit Stoddard doing right now?"

"I don't know."

"He's scrambling, trying to scare up replacements for the two men who got killed. That's risky. Some of the people who do that kind of work are already in trouble. Their phones might be tapped, or they might decide that their best move isn't to take the job, but to turn him in and get credit for cooperating. He's probably going beyond his usual circle of acquaintances. All he has to do is miscalculate once—talk to somebody he thinks he can trust and be wrong. He's in a rush today because he thinks we're on the move."

"That's quite a detailed picture of somebody you don't know."

"The specifics don't even matter. Every minute he can't get to us means the cops might get to him first. The police are trying to find out who the dead men were. When they identify them, they'll search their houses and cars, talk to anybody who knew them. All kinds of things turn up when the cops begin to look closely."

"So we're doing nothing?"

"I'm giving him time to get unlucky, and time to make mistakes, and time to get betrayed. If his name turns up, we'll get a picture and you'll identify him."

"I don't know if that will help. Even if I'm sure he's Kit's old boyfriend, I can't prove he's behind everything."

"Things have changed. Six years ago, you had a theory that Kit Stoddard might have been a victim. This time we've got murders we can prove happened. This time if we find out who this guy is, he's got a problem."

She rested her hand on his shoulder and gave it an affectionate squeeze. "You're something, Jack. You always make things sound good. You give me strength." She stood and walked into her room.

Jack Till sat on his bed and closed his eyes. It had almost sounded as though she was telling him she cared about him. She was beautiful, and that made it difficult to interpret what she said. It was just as likely that she was telling him gently that she knew he was manipulating her. She knew that he had been a homicide detective, and she knew that he had spent a whole career getting people to tell him things that they didn't want to.

At six, she came in while he was talking to Poliakoff again. She sat down in the chair beside the window and waited until the call ended. Then she said, "Anything new?"

"A few things. The two men who were waiting for us at the courthouse have been identified. Their prints were in the NCIC database. One was either Ralph or Raphael DeLoza, depending upon which part of his rap sheet you're reading, age thirty-one. The other is Martin Osterwald, age twenty-nine. Have you heard either name before?"

"No."

"I didn't think you would have. They apparently weren't the kind of people who went to Banque. But eventually we'll look at their pictures, in case we saw them somewhere."

"Okay. When we're there, we can do that. Are you getting hungry?"

"I guess I am."

"Want to go out to dinner? I'll take you."

He hesitated. They both knew that whatever happened, she was very likely to be traveling soon, building another false identity and living on whatever cash she had managed to take with her until she was settled again. He didn't want her to pay for anything, but he didn't have a way to prevent her that would spare her feelings.

"If you're hoping for a better date to call up at the last minute, I'll understand."

"No, I've been waiting for you to offer. It must be at least an hour or two since lunch."

"You're a man of incredible self-discipline to keep from saying anything."

"Where would you like to go? What sort of place?"

"I've lost track of the restaurant scene over the years, but saw a restaurant in the tourist magazine in my room that I've heard of. And I liked the pictures." She handed him a sheet from the hotel's scratch pad with the word Aimee's and an address.

"Did they have a phone number?"

"They did, and they do. I already called it and made a reservation in the name of Harvey. Presumably you're Harvey. Now get showered and dressed. You could use a shave, too, Harvey."

"White tie and tails?"

"A clean shirt would be nice. It doesn't knock a girl off her feet, but you'll have to accept me *with* feet. I'll see you in about a half hour." She turned and walked into her room. After a moment, he heard the shower.

Till went to his closet to examine his options. He had a fresh sport coat. He looked in his suitcase and found that he still had a couple of clean dress shirts. He showered and shaved twice, making himself as well-groomed and appealing as he could.

He gave himself a last examination in the mirror. He was always startled when he saw that he no longer looked the way he felt. He supposed that he looked like what he was: a man in his forties who had spent his adult life carrying a gun for a living. His eyes looked cold and watchful, and the wrinkles at the corners and on his forehead were no longer faint crinkles, but sculpted lines.

He heard Wendy come into his room, so he stepped to the bathroom door and looked out at her. She was wearing a simple black cocktail dress that fit her perfectly and made her light skin look like porcelain.

"You look great."

"Thank you." She gave him a quick, perfunctory curtsy.

He stepped out, took his sport coat off the hanger, and put it on. He looked in the mirror and he adjusted his cuffs and collar, then shrugged to make the coat hang correctly over his gun. He glanced at her in the mirror. "Actually, you look beautiful."

"Thank you again. You look identifiably human."

"It's a step up. I can't believe that when you were throwing stuff into a suitcase to leave town, you brought a dress like that."

She looked down at it for a second. "It's funny how the mind works. I didn't think I was going to have to pack a bag again, yet at the same time I knew the things I had that I would put in it."

"In the bag you weren't going to pack?"

"Yes. I had in my mind an image of everything I would pack and knew just where it was. Does that make sense?"

"I guess it does. You knew what looked good."

"I don't know if that was it, exactly. I just had a sense of the things that would make me feel stronger, more able to go places. Maybe something inside me was reminding me that I had to be ready to move on. A little black cocktail dress takes up almost no space."

He opened the door to the hallway, leaned against it, and stayed there to hold it open for her while he looked up and down the hallway in both directions. Her eye caught his, and he realized that she had seen him scanning. When he spoke, it was to change the subject. "You said you picked this restaurant partly because of the pictures. What were they?"

She smiled. "The food looked believable."

"Believable?"

"Yes. You know—not a picture of three waiters in tuxedos and a sexy hostess grinning while they set a thirty-pound rib roast and a forty-pound world-record lobster on a table for two. This one had a picture of a nice room, an unassuming piece of grilled halibut, and a glass of wine. I can believe that if we walk in there, we'll get something not too far from that."

Till took a few seconds to scan the parking lot before he opened the door for her, but she didn't say anything about his precautions. He led her to a blue Cadillac.

"Where did you get this car?"

"Same place as the last one. Before we went for our walk I called the agency and had a guy drive this one here and take the other one back."

"Why?"

"Because I could." He opened her door for her.

She stopped without getting in. "Is this a bad idea?"

"Going out for dinner?"

"Yes."

"I don't think so. But you've been invisible for six years. I haven't. You tell me." He held his hand out toward the car seat, and she got in. He walked around the car, taking his time and turning to be sure he had surveyed the area in every direction, then got into the driver's seat and started the car. "No explosion."

"Yet."

He took out the piece of paper she had given him and read the address again, and she said, "Go up that road and turn right at the light."

"You know the area?"

"The ad had a map."

As he drove, she gave him the rest of the directions. The darkness of the roads once they were out of downtown Morro Bay made them feel anonymous and safe. The restaurant was beside a country club, so Till passed by it before he realized it must be the right place. He turned around in the road and came back. He was pleased to see that when he turned, there were no headlights coming toward him.

The restaurant was a long, low white building with gray trim. Till drove to the edge of the lot close to it. The brass plaque beside the door said Aimee's. He parked and they walked inside. As they approached the hostess, he whispered, "Is this the same as the picture?"

"Exactly."

The hostess seated them and the waiter arrived. Wendy ordered them each a martini. Till said, "How did you know I liked martinis?"

"I could say something witty and unkind, but I'll just tell the truth. I remembered from six years ago, when we were stuck in that hotel."

The waiter brought the drinks quickly. Till lifted his icy glass and said, "To better food."

She clinked her glass against his. "To old friends." She sipped her martini. "Wow. I forgot how good these taste. I haven't had a drink in about five years."

"Why not?"

"I don't know. I stayed out of restaurants at first, for obvious reasons. And nightclubs were a worse bet. Then, when you have young children, you forget there is such a thing as a martini."

Till's appreciation for the restaurant had nothing to do with aesthetics. The room was light with a single entrance, so there weren't places in the bar for unexpected people to sit without being seen clearly. The windows were all on the side of the building away from the road, a wall of glass overlooking a tee on the golf course. A long fairway stretched down and away into the darkness. He could see a glint of reflected moonlight somewhere out there, so he guessed there must be a lake. It was not impossible for someone to be out there watching the restaurant, but it was extremely unlikely.

He could tell that when Wendy read the menu, she saw more in it than he did. "Interesting." She pointed at a line of type. "This should be good, if you like warm salads, and I'd love to see what she does with this Thai-French chicken, but I've been thinking about paella."

"You order one, and I'll get the other."

"Thanks. I love a man who can take big fat hints."

"I'm only up to it if you speak slowly and look right at me."

When the food arrived, they shared the entrées. Wendy tasted the chicken and said, "This is a very nice variation on the sauce that Sybil Weitz used at Veritable in Chicago. I wonder if Aimee worked there." She sampled the paella and said, "Ooh, she's good. This looks like a big mishmash—clams, shrimp, lobster, mussels, chorizo, pork, chicken, all flavored with saffron, so how can you miss—but it's complicated to get it just right because the ingredients are all cooked and seasoned differently."

"I thought you didn't care about the cooking side of things."

"I don't anymore. But people don't forget everything they know."

"You seem to be feeling better about things tonight."

"You noticed."

"Yesterday was pretty awful. I guess it's good not to be scared."

"It is," she agreed. "I'd say that's a necessary condition—not to be actively scared. But you have to remember that I've learned to tolerate a certain level of insecurity in my life—just like you do."

"I'm sorry. I shouldn't start questioning the source of a good mood. It'll kill it."

"Not at all. I'm glad that you're watching me closely enough to notice it, and I'm glad you mentioned it because it forces me to confess."

"Confess?"

"Yes. I was smiling to myself because this is exactly the same as a fantasy I've had over the past six years."

"Really. Then I'm delighted to be at the table to see it." He looked around the room, as though in new appreciation.

"You're an essential part of it."

"I am?"

"Yes." She sipped her martini, but kept the glass up and studied him over the rim. "You don't think about having a beautiful evening by yourself. Somebody has to share it."

He met her gaze and understood. "I'm honored."

They ate in a leisurely way, each sampling the other's entrée. The waiter arrived to clear the table, brought the dessert menus and coffee, then returned with sweet berries and sorbet, all with a deliberate air of unhurried politeness.

As they shared their dessert and drank the coffee, Till had time to consider what he was about to do. It was going to complicate matters, it was unwise, and it was probably unethical. He waited through the elaborate ritual of the little leather folder. When Wendy paid the bill in cash, he nodded in approval. "Thank you for the wonderful dinner."

They walked to the car and Till opened the door for her, but she didn't get in at once. She put her arms around him and kissed him. The kiss began as a gentle, tentative peck, but when he responded, the kiss deepened and became passionate. She broke it off and ducked her head to get into the car.

He came around the back of the car and sat behind the steering wheel. "That was a nice surprise."

"It was very nice. But it wasn't a surprise."

"What do you mean?" Till started the car and drove slowly toward the exit from the lot.

"We're not teenagers, Jack. We both knew exactly what the kiss would be like. We've lived too much not to be able to imagine it perfectly. I'm sorry I didn't kiss you as soon as I saw you."

Till stopped at the end of the driveway and looked in both directions, preparing to pull onto the highway.

She said, "You're awfully quiet."

"I'm thinking."

"You're thinking about me."

"Yes."

Till drove back to the center of Morro Bay and down to the ocean, doubled back twice to be sure that they had not been spotted in the restaurant and followed, then parked the car in the hotel lot among the others. He and Wendy went up to the second floor, and he had her stay in the stairwell while he checked to be sure that they'd had no visitors in their rooms.

When he was certain it was safe, he went to the door and opened it. She was already stepping into his arms. She had not been quite right about knowing. She was exactly as he had known she would be—beautiful, pale, soft, fragrant—and yet his imagination had been unable to anticipate the way he felt. There was no hesitation between them because this decision had first been made six years ago, and even though they had denied it, the wish had not gone away. Tonight it was as though they had been given another chance to make the right choice, to live the images that had come into their minds in bitter regret and longing during the years since then.

Afterward they lay on the bed together, her head on his shoulder, and his hand caressing her naked back, moving slowly from the shoulder down to her narrow waist and along the curve of her hip. She sighed. "It sure took us a long time to get here. I'm so glad to stop waiting and wondering."

"I'm glad, too."

"I thought about you a lot after you left me at the airport. I don't mean that day. I mean from then until now."

"You were hurt and alone and scared. It's a natural reaction."

She raised herself up on her elbow and looked down at him. "Don't belittle this. It's not a weakness or a whim."

"I'm sorry," he said. "I thought about you a lot, too. I wondered about where you were, what you were doing."

"I dialed your number a few times. I even packed my bag twice."

"What stopped you?"

"Things that seem stupid to me now. At first I was still afraid. Then I didn't want anybody to think I was a failure who couldn't survive a month on my own—but mostly you, because you were the one who had taught me and helped me get away. I told myself that if I was gone for a year or so, you would think better of me.

After a year, it didn't seem enough. After a couple of years passed, it was too much time. I began to think that I had imagined that you felt anything for me. Neither of us had ever said a word. I thought that if I suddenly showed up at your office, you would probably say, 'Oh, yes. I remember your case. You relocated. How is that working out for you?' I would stand there with my suitcase in my hand and no place to go, and start to cry. Then I married Dennis Donnelly, and I didn't have the right to come to you anymore."

Till lay silent for a few seconds, not sure whether to say what he was thinking or not, but she knew the question was in the air.

"It's okay, Jack. Dennis knew it in advance. Ann Donnelly was a hiding place, and when it stopped fooling anybody, it was over." She hugged him and lay still. "If you and I were really young or one of us were really naïve, I would say that the marriage wasn't real, or that Dennis was such a bad man that it somehow didn't count. But he's a nice, ordinary guy, and the marriage was probably as real as most of them are. We told each other jokes, saved for our old age, and had sex. The only difference was that we both knew it might have to end suddenly. Now it has."

"Was yesterday really the end, or was tonight the end?"

"You have me figured out. Tonight was the end."

"It's a bit late to say that I didn't want to harm him."

"Want to give me back?"

"No."

"I haven't treated anyone as well as I wanted to—including him—but I told him the truth. I even told him about you. I didn't tell him your name, but I told him that it could end in two ways: if the killers came for me, or if you did."

"I've been wishing that this would happen since the first day six years ago. But I don't know what's after this."

"I don't, either. I've kind of given up on making that kind of prediction." She kissed him, her leg came across his belly, and she shifted her weight over him. She closed her eyes and gave a deep sigh. They made love again, this time slowly and gently, enjoying each other without the frantic uncertainty of a few hours ago.

It was after ten when they were lying in the bed in lazy silence again. She sat up abruptly, and he said, "Something wrong?"

"There's one more thing I wanted to say."

"What's that?"

"His name is Scott."

"Whose?"

"Kit's boyfriend. His name is Scott. I heard her say his name that night."

32

MICHAEL DENSMORE stepped out of his office carrying his briefcase. It was late—after ten o'clock—but he wore his suit coat with the middle button closed and his tie straight. He was disciplined about the way he presented himself, even when he was only taking the elevator down to the parking level where his car waited in its reserved space. Over the years, he had found that even if the only person he met on the way was a young secretary working late or a janitor on the night cleaning crew, his appearance gave him an advantage. His look made it clear that he was the boss, not just because he had good clothes, but because his standards were not a facade that he let down at five o'clock. When he was in his private office making telephone calls or reading legal files, he always hung his coat on a proper wooden hanger behind the door—or at least a chair—so it would not wrinkle, but he put it on before he gave his secretary permission to admit anyone he didn't know well. There was a padded hanger downstairs in the Mercedes that matched the interior of the car. He would use it to hang the coat behind him in the back seat while he drove.

He was a successful, wealthy man, and he wanted to look like one. He had been prosperous since he had become a partner in Dolan, Nyquist and Berne. He had saved money, and also, by degrees, broadened his offering of services, so his income had continued to grow. He had begun as a straight criminal-defense attorney specializing in white-collar crime. Then clients began to pay him for acting as negotiator or consultant in a few delicate business deals that needed legal adjustments to remain viable. A few times, it had meant drawing up papers for a limited partnership that did not list one of the partners because his name might attract the wrong kind of attention. There were a few deals in which getting the necessary permits and licenses had been expedited by his personal assurances and a few envelopes full of hundred-dollar bills. After that, he'd begun to arrange introductions, putting together people who had projects with people who had money to invest. Soon he was forming pools of investors who couldn't explain where their dollars had come from, and wanted profits without having their names written down. Now he earned more money making these arrangements for clients than defending them in court.

Densmore was largely satisfied with his public self, but there were still certain parts of his private life that shocked and disappointed him. He was approaching the end of his fourth marriage, and that period was always a depressing and dispiriting time. Lawyers learned a great deal about unpleasant corners of the human psyche, but there was nothing like divorce to complete their education.

Being divorce-prone was like having a bee-sting allergy. The first couple of breakups had hurt a little. The third had been severely painful because he'd had so much more to lose, and he had gone into shock. He didn't know how he was going to get through the fourth.

Densmore had met his current wife, Grace, five years ago, just as his third marriage had entered its guerrilla-warfare phase. His third wife, Chris, had begun sneaking around, looking at receipts and financial records. She had begun paying attorneys and private detectives to look into the size and shape of his fortune in preparation for her all-out attack.

Grace appeared in front of his eyes when he arrived at a charity event for arthritis at the Beverly Hills Hotel, and suddenly the divorce became urgent. Within a month, he had begun trying to expedite his divorce from Chris. He agreed to give in to some of her ridiculous demands just so he could get the process over, but appeasement was a foolish strategy. Chris and her lawyers became more greedy and inquisitive about what he was hiding. After a few months, their prying and spying alarmed a couple of Densmore's most difficult clients.

Densmore went to the house to meet with Chris, who had by then learned he was spending every night at the Peninsula Hotel with Grace and had stopped speaking to him. When he arrived, he listened tolerantly to a long, irrelevant diatribe about what a bad husband he had been. Then he approached his problem carefully and delicately. "As you know, I am an attorney specializing in the defense of people who are charged with criminal infractions. Many of these clients are innocent. Others have, at some point or other, made serious mistakes, and I must guide them in their dealings with the legal system. My arrangements with them are, by law, privileged and confidential. Your snooping into my professional affairs in search of hidden money is upsetting some very important clients."

"You know what, Michael? I find that I no longer give a shit about your problems. My detectives have already found four or five accounts that you absentmindedly forgot to mention in your settlement papers. My lawyers tell me I could get you in big trouble."

"If your people think they've found anything like that, they're mistaken," he retorted. "Accounts that don't belong to me sometimes have my name on them because I have power of attorney, or I'm holding funds in escrow. I don't own them."

"Bullshit!"

"Look, Chris. I've never talked to you about the details of my law practice, so you'll have to trust me. If I lose these clients, it will cut into the value of my practice and the value of my personal assets. That means I will lose half and *you* will lose half."

"Trust you?" Her expression was unspeakable, a mixture of revulsion and ugliness. "I trusted you not to humiliate me."

When he saw that expression, he almost lost hope, but he didn't dare to give up. "I haven't humiliated you, Chris. If it takes a goddamned detective to find out about it, then I'm being discreet."

"Not discreet enough, I can tell you."

"Chris, the reason I came here is that several clients in question are upset. In addition, any one of them is capable of being paranoid, angry and defensive about being investigated. Any one of them could react in very scary ways."

Her eyes narrowed. "Are you threatening me?"

"No, I'm not, Chris, *they* are. I'm trying to stave off a fucking disaster, and you don't seem to be capable of listening to reason."

"This discussion is over." She stood up, turned, and stomped off into the bedroom. When he followed her, he discovered that it had been fitted with a deadbolt.

Two days later, Chris's lawyer, Alvin Holstein, was found dead. His office had been gutted. Files, computers, disks, tapes, and even scratch pads had been loaded into a truck during the night and carted away. Pieces of the private detective Chris had hired were found over the course of a week along Interstate 15 between Barstow and Baker.

Chris became hysterical. She threatened to tell the police that Densmore had arranged for one of his clients to kill her lawyer and detective, but he pointed out to her that his legal defense would likely cost most of their joint assets.

He got out of the elevator on level B-1 and walked toward his reserved parking space. He was thinking about Grace now. She was his present wife, and she would be more difficult than Chris had been. Her smoldering hostility had not reached the explosive stage, but he could see that the time was coming. He had much more money now, and she knew it.

He felt the hands on him before he saw anything. He tried to turn to face the man, but the grip prevented him. Then Sylvie Turner stepped from behind a tall SUV parked in front of him and pulled her right hand out of her jacket pocket just far enough to show him the gun.

He smiled at her in relief, even though the grip on his arm was painful. "Sylvie. How are you?"

"You need to come with us."

"I've been trying to get in touch with you two."

"Get in the car." This time it was Paul. He was already pushing Densmore toward the rear of the SUV.

Densmore said, "Good idea," but he was sweating and his eyes were darting around above his smile because he couldn't keep them on any one object. He could see that the windows were tinted and the license plate had a plastic cover that was nearly opaque. People like the Turners used covers like that to make the plates unreadable on surveillance tapes. He had to keep talking, keep it friendly. "I like to be inside a car and moving when I have a personal discussion."

He heard the lock button pop up and he opened the door behind the driver's seat. Paul didn't move away. He stayed right behind Densmore as he stepped up and sat on the back seat, then climbed in after him.

Sylvie got in the front and drove. The vehicle was moving before Densmore noticed the empty place on the door panel where the handle had been. They had made sure he couldn't open the door from the inside. He said, "It's a pleasure to work with professionals who understand that it's dangerous to be overheard. Now, the reason I've been trying so hard to get in touch with you is that I heard something that worried me."

"What was that?" Sylvie's voice was flat and uninterested. It was like listening to Grace.

"Well, as I warned you on the phone a few days ago, the client has been getting more and more impatient and eager for results. Now I understand he's gone around us." Densmore was pleased with that locution because if he "understood," it implied he had only heard a hint from someone without knowing anything directly.

But Paul had caught the word, too, and didn't like it. "You *understand* that, do you?"

"Yes. This is the kind of thing that I advise clients against doing. If you want help, I'll give you help, but you have to put yourself in my hands. That's what I say to them. And if it's necessary to hire specialists, consultants, or experts, then I'll be the one to find them, hire them, and communicate with them. That's the way it has to be. If you want to handle your problem yourself, you're welcome to go off and do it, and I wish you Godspeed. But if you want me to take you on, I'm in charge." He was sure he had managed to get them past their irritation at him by now. He had learned from speaking to juries that enough words would slide people past an unpleasant discovery. The main thing was to keep talking and be sure they didn't fix all of their attention on one small bit of information and cling to it.

"You're off the subject," Sylvie said. "We want to hear what you were so anxious to tell *us*, not the client."

"What I wanted to tell you is that he went *around* me. He hired a couple of people of his own to go after Wendy Harper. Now, that's bad enough. But it gets worse. The two men he hired were told that Till would have to bring Wendy Harper to the DA's office to get the charges dropped. So they stationed themselves outside the building and lay in wait. Last night they managed to open fire on an unmarked police vehicle, and the outcome was pretty much what you might expect. They both got shot down on the street. I'm so glad to see you. I was really afraid that you might have been nearby and gotten scooped up in a sweep of the district."

"And what did you do to get in touch with us to warn us?"

"I called your house. I called about twenty times over the past day or two. You were never home."

"Did you even try to leave a message?"

"Of course I didn't. If the police ever found a message like that on your phone, then you'd have problems. Those men were after Wendy Harper, and you were after Wendy Harper. All the police would need is a phone call to prove you were part of a conspiracy. Since the cops killed those two in the attempted commission of your common crime, you would be charged with felony murder in their deaths. As your attorney, I don't see how we could beat the charge."

"Did you consider just leaving a message for us to call you?"

Tonight Densmore's professional skill at fast talk and obfuscation seemed to be failing him. Paul and Sylvie seemed to accept nothing he said. "That would have been even worse. It would give you absolutely no information, but it would make you keep calling me. I was in court for the past two days, so you would have had to wait for hours. In the process you might leave a message that could incriminate you. And all I wanted to say was what I just told you: that there might be another team around to get in your way. Might be. And in the end, it didn't happen, anyway."

"Didn't it?" Paul said.

"You mean something happened?" Densmore was sweating. His body didn't seem to be able to take in enough oxygen, and he felt dizzy. He looked at Paul's eyes, remembering an article he had read. The amygdala, an almond-shaped part of the brain, had evolved to detect the signs of fear in another human being. Paul's amygdala must be overdeveloped and trained to do that—probably what made him love killing. For him the sensation wasn't like feeling the other person's fear, it was like tasting it. Paul certainly knew Densmore was afraid, and that had made him stop listening to what Densmore said.

"Something happened," Paul said. "We were all set up in a room with windows overlooking the DA's office building. We spotted those two guys five minutes after we got there, and we watched them all night. We thought they were cops."

"Well, then, if you saw them so easily, what's the problem?"

Paul reached for his gun so quickly that it looked to Densmore as though it had been under his hand all along. He tugged the slide back to allow a round into the chamber, and moved his wrist slightly to aim at Densmore's belly.

Densmore's imagination became godlike. He could see the way the bullet would burst through his skin, through the wall of muscle and plow into the tissues of organs, the shock turning them into blood-soaked pulp, and then out again. He could actually feel a premonition of the pain: the blow, the bullet mushrooming and tearing a path that became an arc through his body, the burning. "If you're wondering whether that scares me, it does."

Sylvie gave a pitiless laugh. "You have a lot to be scared of."

Densmore discovered a surprising reservoir of hatred for Sylvie. Until now he had thought he had a weakness for her.

Paul said, "You told your client who we are. You betrayed us, didn't you?"

"I—"

"Before you answer that, think. If you open your mouth again and an avalanche of bullshit pours out, you won't make it."

"You would do that to me? After eight years?"

"*Especially* after eight years," Sylvie said. "Answer him."

"I had to tell this client who you were. I didn't intend to make you feel more vulnerable. It was a special situation—a unique predicament. He said he wanted me to hire a team to kill Wendy Harper. It had to be the best people, the very best. He offered a high price, but he said he had to be sure of you before the deal was struck. He had to know I wasn't taking a huge fee and giving a couple of bikers a thousand each. So I complied. It was a considered business decision. This client was not some dry cleaner in the Valley who was pissed off at the guy who owned the mini-mall. He had been a client for years, he was a substantial man, and he had a way to lure Wendy Harper back to Los Angeles. So I made a one-time exception to our policy about how much information we share with clients. Should I have talked to you first and explained what I was going to do and why? In retrospect, I suppose I should have done that. But I knew that if I did, there would be a lot of discussion and soul-searching, and you would eventually come to the conclusion that I had. I knew it was the right decision for everyone—for the client, for you, and for me."

Sylvie laughed. "Mostly for you, though, huh?"

Densmore was beginning to focus on Sylvie now, and his hatred was consuming a huge part of his consciousness. Paul Turner was pointing a gun at his stomach, and he should be paying attention to him—to preventing his index finger from tightening on the trigger to exert a two-pound pressure. But Sylvie's contemptuous tone was infuriating. "For all of us," he said. "I've been your advocate in this from the start. I received a very generous offer and selected you for the job instead of someone else. I improved the offer by telling the client about your abilities and accomplishments. Later, when you didn't finish the job on the first try, it reflected on me and put me in potential danger. Did I blame you or sell you out to the client? No. I made excuses for you and raised the ante, offered you even more money to finish the job."

Sylvie said, "I'm still stuck thinking about why you thought telling your client about us was the right decision for you. It could get you killed."

Densmore recognized in her voice the kind of grim amusement that he had heard only in the voices of killers talking about their victims. He was terrified. How could his fate have fallen into the hands of this violence-addicted whore? How could Michael Densmore, the consummate attorney, be failing so miserably to manipulate a woman who had let herself be penetrated every imaginable way by hundreds of men on the theory that it would make her a movie star? He turned his eyes away from her. "Paul, be reasonable. I've worked with you for eight years. No client I've brought you has ever known a thing about you, or ever been able to utter an incriminating word. I admit I've made a mistake. Now what can I do to make this right?"

Paul looked a bit uncertain. "To start, you could make us even. You told the client about us. Who is the client?"

Densmore would not have considered answering the question only a few hours ago, and he might not have done it now if he had been talking only to Paul. But he had heard Sylvie, and he knew that things were worse than he had suspected. If Paul hesitated, Sylvie would goad him into pulling the trigger.

In the instant required to draw in a breath to reply, he formulated a plan for the next few months. He would separate Paul from Sylvie. It would require some care because she had an animal cunning that he had not noticed before, but his strategy was obvious. He would find another woman for Paul. And Paul would never risk stepping into a divorce court with Sylvie. She was too crazy, too likely to say something that would incriminate both of them. She might even try to kill him if he replaced her. So Paul would kill her.

Densmore could hardly wait.

Densmore had to talk quickly now. "Of course, Paul. The client is Scott Schelling."

"What is he?" It was Sylvie again.

He wanted to ignore her, to speak only to Paul, but he couldn't let one of her questions hang in the air for fear it would seem to be a refusal to answer. He also couldn't let her suspect that he hated her. "He's the president of Crosswinds Records."

"A music executive?" Sylvie exclaimed. "You sold us out to some little record salesman?"

"I don't feel that I sold you out, and he isn't a little record salesman. He's barely forty now, and he's already being talked about as a possible contender for CEO of Aggregate Electronics Industries when Ray Klein retires. That's movies, television, cable companies, and God knows what else. Scott Schelling is a powerful man, and he's getting more important every day."

"Well, *I* never heard of him."

Densmore had to grit his teeth to keep from making a sarcastic retort. "Scott has always had an understated style, and that's contributed to his success. The entertainment industry is made up of lunatics and bureaucrats. If you're smart, you want to be on the side of the people without talent, the bureaucrats. Singers and actors come and go, but executives are forever. He knows that. He's stayed in the office and out of the spotlight. I think the reason he's so concerned about Wendy Harper now is that he knows he's reaching the point where he can't be invisible anymore. Power and money create celebrity."

"Why would a man like that be stupid enough to kill his girlfriend?"

"I don't know. He's never told me what happened. Six years ago nobody knew or cared about him. He was a third-rank talent manager in a fourth-rate company. Since then Aggregate Electronics bought Crosswinds and fired the president. Then the second in command got a face-saving offer from another company, and here's young Scott Schelling, the meek inheriting the earth. Only he wasn't meek. He had great influence with certain elements of the music business. I'm referring to the talent that came out of street gangs and jails. Crosswinds is hugely profitable."

Paul said, "Scott Schelling."

"Yes. What we're doing is erasing the last evidence of a youthful indiscretion for a rich man who will only get richer. He's into having power over people. Maybe six years ago he overdid it with some girl. Wendy Harper is the only one left who knows it, and he's willing to pay big to end the threat. And I guarantee he will have problems of the same sort in the future. Men like him always do.

Then you can be sure I'll get a call to have you come and solve his problem."

"Interesting," said Paul.

"Yes, interesting," Sylvie echoed. "It's interesting that you gave our names to a man who loves having power over people, and surrounds himself with thugs. Thanks."

Densmore's breath caught for a second. While he had been talking she had driven up the Golden State Freeway almost to the foothills. They passed under a big green sign that said "14—Antelope Valley Freeway." Densmore had made so many mistakes. He hadn't needed to stay in his office this late. He just had not wanted to go home and face Grace's resentment. The whole office had cleared out long ago. For that matter, he could have paid for bodyguards—the thugs that Sylvie seemed to be so afraid of. She was driving him up into the mountains. He hated her. He felt such contempt for her that it was making him stupid.

He had to appeal to Paul. "Paul, think about this. You and I have had a good working relationship. We've made money. We've lived well."

"Pretty well."

"And this time, when things got tough, did I question your competence or insult you? No. I offered to pay four times—" Densmore saw the expression on Paul's face too late. Paul must have been keeping this from her. He closed his mouth, but too many words had already come out.

The gun roared in the confined space of the car, fulfilling Densmore's premonition: The bullet burned through his belly. He bent double, not even in reaction to the pain, but as though the bullet had forced the muscles to spasm. Then he felt the hot muzzle of Paul's gun against the back of his head.

Darkness came.

33

TILL AWOKE AND LOOKED at the clock beside the bed. It was seven in the morning. He inhaled slowly and smelled Wendy's scent on the pillow, then turned to face her. Her facial muscles relaxed during sleep, so her face looked smooth and untroubled.

He took his cell phone, slipped into Wendy's room, then into her bathroom, closed the door and called Max Poliakoff. He got Poliakoff's voice mail. "Max," he said. "This is Till. The man who is after Wendy Harper is named Scott. I don't know if it's a first name or a last name. But now you know what I know. I'll talk to you later."

He called Holly's number, but her phone was turned off. He said, "It's just me, your early-bird father. I love you. Have a great day." He disconnected, and went to Wendy's window to look outside. As always, the sidewalks and the path to the rock were full of tourists—men wearing baggy shorts and women in unflattering hats. He studied them, and after a minute he had satisfied himself that there was no sign of suspicious activity, so he closed the curtain again.

He went back to his room, and when he stepped in, he saw that Wendy's eyes were open, looking at him, and he smiled.

"Good," she said.

"What?"

"When you saw me, you didn't frown and think, 'What the hell have I done?'"

"I didn't want to wake you up. I'm sorry if I made noise."

"You didn't," she said. "But it was time to get up and get moving. I'm feeling energetic today."

"Why? What happened?"

"You know what happened." She smiled. "Don't start pretending you weren't in your right mind or something." She stood up, threw her arms around him, and held him.

They embraced for a long time, and kissed. Then he pulled back a bit. "Do you think you're up to going the rest of the way to L.A.? I think it's time to go finish what we started."

They stood there together for a few seconds, and then she said, "I think you're right. Let's do it."

They went about packing, showering, and dressing without speaking. The silence was new. There was an intimacy to it, a change that came over them because they had slept together, but there was also an element of dread. As Jack packed his suitcase, he thought about the trip to Los Angeles, and about the man named Scott.

The telephone on the nightstand rang, and startled him. He supposed she had probably asked for a wake-up call. He picked it up. "Yes?"

"Mr. Till?"

"Yes."

"This is Rob Sheffield of the Cheapcars rental company, San Luis Obispo office. I hate to bother you, but I understood from the police that you were staying here, and if you could spare me a few minutes, we could get the accident report out of the way for the car you rented in San Francisco."

Till said, "Do you already have the police report?"

"That's been received at the San Francisco office, but I don't have a copy with me at the moment. I was out when I got the call, so I'm in the lobby, and I thought maybe you would come down to speak with me for a few minutes."

"All right. I'll be down as soon as I can." Till hung up.

Wendy appeared at the connecting door. "Who was that?"

"There's a guy downstairs who wants to talk to me. Just a second." He went to the desk where he had left his belongings, and found the papers for his rental car. He dialed a number from the back sheet. "Hello," he said. "My name is Jack Till. I'm a customer, and I was wondering if you could tell me if you have a Mr. Sheffield at your office. You do? Is he in the office today? No, that's okay. Thanks. I'll talk to him later."

"What's wrong?" Wendy asked.

"Just a precaution. The other night, the cop promised he wasn't going to write down where we were staying. Maybe he forgot to tell his partner. There's a workout room off the back hallway on the ground floor. You know—treadmills and weight benches and stuff. I saw it when I came in the back door a couple of nights ago. Go in there and wait for me."

She nodded. "Okay. Are we in trouble?"

"Sorry. It's just another precaution. If this isn't about you, then there's no reason for him to know about you. I'll come for you when I'm done."

"Fine," she said.

He opened the door and they walked down the hall to the stairwell. They descended to the first floor and he led her to the door of the gym, looked through the small window to see who was inside, and opened the door for her. "Nobody there. See you in a little while."

"Right."

He returned to the stairwell, ran up the stairs and along the hall to the elevator, then took it to the lobby. As Till stepped out into the lobby, he saw the man who was waiting for him. He was tall, about forty years old, wearing a gray sport coat, white shirt, and a red tie. He looked like a former high-school athlete who already had the bad knees and the slight belly, and would probably have the heart attack in a few more years.

The man stepped forward and held out his hand. "Mr. Till? Rob Sheffield. Thanks for setting aside the time to talk to me."

Till shook his hand. "No problem. What do we need to do?"

"You tell me the whole story of what happened to the car, I go back to the office and fill out the forms, and the company takes care of getting it appraised and sending it to the shop."

"All right. By the way, how did you find out where I was staying?"

Sheffield smiled. "The rental papers, I imagine."

Till didn't smile. "I didn't know where I was staying when I rented the car."

"Then I suppose it must have come from the police report after the accident. I really don't know. I was out and the office called me and asked me to stop by. Maybe I can find out for you later." He took a small notebook and a pen from his coat. "Would you like to begin by answering a few quick questions? First one, your full name."

"John Robert Till."

"And the car. What was the make and model, if you can remember?"

Till stood up. "I've got the rental papers upstairs. I'll be right back."

Sheffield held up his hand. "That's not necessary. I just—"

But Till was walking quickly to the elevator and could not be stopped. He saw that one of the two was empty with its door open, so he punched the button and rode it up to the second floor.

He hurried up the hall, stopped at the door to his room, and confirmed his suspicion. The woodwork was gouged and compressed beside the lock, as though the door had been pried open with a crowbar. He pushed the door open gingerly, then stepped inside and quietly moved into Wendy's room. There was no sign of the intruder, and his suitcase and Wendy's were where they had left them, apparently undisturbed. The intruder had not been interested in them. He had come for Wendy.

Till picked up the two suitcases, hurried down the hall to the stairwell, and descended to the first floor. He set the suitcases down, then went out the door to the hall, stepped to the gym door and looked in the window, but there was no sign of Wendy. Instead there was a short, stocky man in his thirties in a navy suit and a tie. The man walked across the exercise room toward the locker rooms. As Till watched, he walked to the door marked "Ladies," opened it, and stepped in.

Till moved quickly into the exercise room, opened the door of the women's locker room, slipped inside and kept the door from swinging to, then eased it shut. From somewhere around a corner, he could hear a slow drip of water.

Till waited.

When he heard a set of hard-soled shoes step onto a tiled floor, he moved toward the sound. He came to the corner of the entry and saw two rows of blue lockers with wooden benches in front of them. As he sighted along the row, he heard a faint shuffling sound on the tiles behind him. He turned and saw the man, already in motion, his arm swinging downward toward Till's head, a short iron pry-bar gripped in his hand.

Till ducked so the swing missed his head and struck a glancing blow off his right shoulder. He threw a quick left hook into the bridge of the man's nose, then a hard punch to the man's stomach. The man bent over and the bar clanged onto the tile floor. His left hand clutched his bloody nose.

Till saw that the man was using the crouch as a way to hide the movement of his right hand into his coat. Till squatted, snatched the pry-bar, and swung it in one motion. It hit the man's shin and buckled his left leg. Then he swung again quickly and hit the man's right forearm just as the gun appeared. Till's blow knocked the arm aside, but the man maintained his grip on the gun. Till popped up and swung the pry-bar once more, this time into the side of the man's head.

The man fell onto his side and lay motionless. Till lifted the man's gun out of his hand, pocketed it, took a deep breath and said in a normal voice that sounded loud in the empty locker room, "Wendy? It's me, Jack. Wendy!"

He heard a metallic clank on the other side of the first row of lockers, and came around the end in time to see one of them open. He came closer, and watched Wendy sidestep out of the locker. She saw him. "Jack! I thought I heard—"

"You did. Come on! There's at least one more."

"Come where?"

"The car." He put the gun into his belt where his sport coat would hide it, and they hurried out the gym door and across the hall to the stairwell where he had left their suitcases. He pointed to hers. "Take whatever you can't replace, and we'll leave them."

She knelt and opened her suitcase, took a large stack of currency out and put it into her purse. Jack opened his suitcase, found his gun, slid a new magazine into it, and then pushed both suitcases into the dark space under the bottom flight of stairs.

He handed his gun to Wendy. The gun looked big and heavy in her small hand. "Put the gun in your purse. Keep it on top so you can reach it."

"Are you saying that I should shoot somebody?"

"I hope not. So far there's one other man—tall, in a gray sport coat and red tie. He was trying to keep me occupied while this one got you. But there could be more." He took out the gun he had taken from the man in the locker room, checked the load, and then slipped it back into his belt. "Now we've got to step out of here, walk to our car, and go. Ready?"

Wendy nodded.

They walked to the rear exit of the building at the end of the wall, and Till stopped to look through the glass door. He could see his rented blue Cadillac in the lot, about two hundred feet away. It was now the middle of the morning, so most of the cars that had been parked around his last night were already gone.

He said, "The tall guy is in the lobby, and I'm pretty sure he can see the car through the front windows if he looks. I'm going to walk toward it. You go out and inch to the left along the wall toward the end of the building. If I make it to the car, be ready to climb in. If something happens, get out of sight and I'll find you later."

"This is a crummy way to start a relationship," she said.

"After we get to the DA's office, we'll drive straight to counseling." He pulled her out the door with him and walked briskly across the lot toward the blue Cadillac.

Wendy began walking slowly along the side of the building toward the corner, but she kept moving her eyes to Jack Till to check on his progress.

She saw him approach the car, the key in his left hand, and she knew that meant he was keeping his right free to reach for the gun. Seeing him made her lift her purse in front of her and pretend to be searching for something with her right hand. The gun that had frightened her now seemed comforting. She kept her head down as though she were looking in the purse, but her eyes returned to Jack.

He was opening the door. He was in. She looked toward the front entrance of the hotel. A big beige car was moving across the parking lot, and she could see that there were two people in it. The driver seemed to be the man Jack had described, and the other was shorter and darker. They were driving toward Wendy.

Wendy turned away from them and began to walk quickly. She heard the car's engine grow louder, and she was sure they were going to try to run her down. She looked over her shoulder to judge how much time she had, ran for the first row of parked cars, and crouched between two of them. The car with the two men in it flashed past her, then accelerated into the turn so fast it fishtailed.

Till's Cadillac swung wide to come up at the end of the row of cars, glided down the aisle, and stopped beside her. Till got out and stood beside the open door with a gun in his hand, watching the two men in the beige car as they pulled out onto the street and drove off at a high speed. Till got into his car again and leaned over to push open the passenger door for Wendy. She got inside, and Till's foot stomped on the gas pedal so Wendy's body was thrown back against the seat by the sudden acceleration. He hit the exit from the lot at an angle so he didn't lose control trying to hold the car on the street, but he still swerved into the oncoming lane as he roared up the road after the beige car.

He took out his cell telephone, and she could see his thumb was dialing 911. He said, "My name is John R. Till. I'm a private detective. Two men just came to the Seawall Hotel to kidnap and kill my client, who is a key witness in a Los Angeles murder investigation."

Wendy could hear the woman's voice on the other end say, "Sir? You'll have—"

"They're driving eastward on Route 41 at high speed in a full-size beige sedan, possibly a Chevrolet. One man is short and heavy with dark brown hair, wearing a navy suit. The other is taller, over six feet, wearing a gray sport coat, red tie, charcoal pants. They're armed and dangerous."

He clicked off, then pressed the phone again with his thumb. This number was in the memory. "Max Poliakoff, please. Jack Till. Max? I've got another emergency. I'm on Route 41 heading east, trying to chase down a couple of guys who just tried to kill Wendy in the Seawall Hotel. I'm not having much luck. I can't see them. I just called the cops in Morro Bay. Can you call and tell them what you need to?" He listened. "Thanks." Poliakoff was saying something. Till listened for a few seconds, then said, "All right. Got to drive now. Talk to you later."

Wendy rose in her seat to watch the road ahead. "I still don't see them."

Till shrugged. "They're too far ahead of us." He let the car slow down, then pulled to the side of the road and made a U-turn.

"What are you doing?"

"We're not going to get close enough to see them. It's time to get you to Los Angeles."

34

SCOTT SCHELLING STRAINED to bench-press the weight, his arms trembling as he pushed the bar and straightened his elbows. "Three more, give me three more." Dale, his personal trainer, was shouting into his ear. "Three. Two. One." Schelling pressed the weight into the air above his face, the big hands appeared above Schelling's head and then the thick, hairy arms and the olive-drab T-shirt, and Dale guided the heavy weight bar onto the support above the bench. "Fair, Scott. Pretty fair. Now we still have time for a quick run."

Scott Schelling sat up, his arms limp, and looked at the clock on the wall of his exercise room. "I don't think so. I have a meeting in a few minutes. But I'll run tonight when I get back, and then take a swim."

Dale squinted. "I hope you get around to it, Scotty. You're in a good place now, and you've got to keep your heart pumping every day to get to the next level."

Schelling looked at Dale and nodded in solemn insincerity. He was comfortable lying to Dale Quinlan. Schelling had paid to have him investigated, and found that he really had been a marine, and he really had arrived in California as a physical-training instructor for recruits at Twenty-Nine Palms. Dale had a tattoo of the eagle, anchor, and globe on his left arm, a bristly whitewall haircut, and a brusque, strutting manner. But Schelling knew that he had gotten the tattoo and the haircut only after he had been out of the marines for a year or two, trying to break into the personal-training business. People who had money felt they needed a big jarhead shouting at them as though they were going to war instead of losing five pounds of flab.

Scott Schelling took a towel off the pile and wiped the sweat off his face and neck. "I'll see you tomorrow."

"Right, Scotty. I'll be here at six. Be ready to work." He walked to the door, where he had left his gym bag, and then he was out in the corridor. Schelling watched him check his complicated-looking military watch, turn his cell phone on, and start along the glass wall up the corridor toward the front of the house. In a few moments, he would be outside, driving to his next appointment.

Schelling walked into his shower room, adjusted the array of showerheads, and let himself be sprayed with hot water from four angles for a few minutes. Then he stepped out, dried himself on two more towels, and walked through the bathroom into his closet, a huge square room with clothes hanging along two walls and drawers and cabinets along the others. He could see that Kimberly, his personal assistant, had selected and laid out his clothes on the long, padded island in the middle of the room. He was color-blind, but he could see well enough to tell that the tie and handkerchief were not a match, and he knew that whatever colors she had chosen for them and the shirt were the most fashionable for this day in Los Angeles. His shoes gave off the proper shine, and the gently laundered condition of the socks and underwear she had chosen did not escape him.

He did not raise his voice. He said, "Kimberly," and she came in from the desk in the bedroom. She was wearing a headset with a microphone, which meant she was already in a telephone conversation with Tiffany in the office. She held a clipboard, taking notes as she listened, making no acknowledgment that Scott was naked.

"We're on with Scott," she said to Tiffany. To Scott she said, "Some of the people for your meeting have begun to arrive. Quentin, Ali, and Tara."

As he dressed, he said, "Treat them as well as you can, Tiffany," as though he were speaking into the telephone. Kimberly repeated his words exactly as he said them. "Are they in my meeting room?"

"Not yet."

Schelling liked the way Kimberly and Tiffany connected to become a single intelligence. They conveyed things to each other, asked each other questions in advance because they knew he would want to know. But they weren't presumptuous. Neither of them ever said no. Everything was "not yet," which was only a variation on "yes." "Put them in my office, then, on the couches. Patch me into the room so I can talk to them while you bring them drinks."

While Kimberly repeated his words she was unclipping the telephone from her belt. He continued dressing, and when Tiffany was ready, Kimberly disconnected the cord to her earpiece and handed the telephone to Scott.

His voice was smooth and unconcerned. "Tara, Ali, Quentin. Thanks so much for doing me the kindness of coming to my office and the courtesy of being on time. I'm apologizing for not being there to greet you, but I had an unexpected delay and I'm on my way. Tiffany will give you copies of the release schedule I've worked out. I want all of you to take a look at the projects you're running and see how the schedule meshes with your progress. If there are differences, I want to hear them. I'd also appreciate it if you would explain what's up to the others as they arrive, so everybody can be ready when I get there. Thanks."

He handed the phone to Kimberly and stepped into his pants. She reattached herself to the telephone, clipped it to her waistband, listened to Tiffany, and took notes. After a few seconds, she said, "They took it well, Scotty. They're getting over being there before the others. Now they're studying the schedule and working trades so they can move up the releases that are ready now and hold back others."

"Good. Keep watching them. What else?"

"Good. Keep watching them," she repeated. To Scott she said, "Ray Klein's party is tomorrow night at his house in Santa Fe."

"I remember."

"The limo will pick you up here and take you to the airport at four P.M. When you arrive, you go to your hotel, the Eldorado. The party is at eight. Your present for Mrs. Klein is an antique map made by Herman Moll in 1719. It shows New Mexico, including Santa Fe, and California is still an island."

"What did that cost me?"

"Twenty-seven thousand, but you won't have to worry about her showing it off. The provenance is reliable and clean, and that's hardly ever true of rare maps. It's being professionally packed and shipped to their house to arrive at five P.M. tomorrow, so they will have had time to unwrap it and make some calls to find out how grateful to be."

"What else?"

"You have meetings at three and five with the groups Code 187 and Nine-One-One Bang. Your haircut and manicure are set for five forty-five in your office today. The drafts of the cover notes on next month's releases are on your desk now, so you can look them over between appointments. Also the sales figures for the week, and the proposals for ad budgets for next week."

"Fine. Put the demo tape for Code 187 on in the lounge while they're waiting for me, so everyone has heard it before I get there."

He stepped into his shoes, tied his necktie, and put on his coat. Kimberly was beside him, still repeating "before I get there" while her hands smoothed the coat on his shoulders and adjusted the back of his shirt collar so the tie was not rolled beneath it. They walked together through the master bedroom. "There was a call in to Mr. Densmore, but he hasn't returned it yet. His assistant says he's in court, but she's covering."

"When he returns the call, switch it to my cell," said Schelling.

They made their way down the long hallway, across the huge two-story living room, the two-way conversation between Tiffany and Schelling-Kimberly continuing all the way to Kimberly's office on the ground floor, and then out to the car in the cobblestone turnaround outside the main entrance. His dog King came trotting around the house to be petted. Scott scratched him under the chin once, and Kimberly held King's collar so he couldn't get dog hairs on Scott's suit.

Carl was waiting beside the car. He opened the door to admit Schelling and held it so Kimberly could slide in, but she shook her head, so he closed it and got into the driver's seat.

Schelling looked out his window while Carl put the car in gear. Kimberly was talking into her headphone again, and although her eyes were on Schelling, they were blank, unseeing. The car slid forward around the turnaround to the driveway, and Carl hit the button to open the gate.

Schelling was pleased with Kimberly and Tiffany. Together they were doing an excellent job, but even with their sharp understanding of detail and information, he could not have kept them around if they had not been decorative, too. He was in a business where death stalked people who weren't fashionable.

The two assistants also were participating in one of his experiments. He'd had sex with Tiffany only once, a year after she had come to work for him. It had been late at night, after everyone had gone and the office had been locked up. It had been a droit de seigneur kind of sex: He had merely been claiming her as a member of his staff. He had left her alone after that. He had wanted her to wonder whether it was going to happen again, and then to wonder why it had not. Right now, he knew, she was trying to form theories about whether it would be more to her advantage if it did or didn't, and how to accomplish one or the other.

With Kimberly he had decided to behave differently. Since she had come to work for him, he had treated her as a sexless personal servant, maybe even an appliance. He paid no attention to her, or to what she might be thinking. Today and for the past few months, he had summoned her into the dressing room while he was still naked, as though she were his valet, and begun their work while he was getting dressed. He knew that the two assistants spoke to each other all day long every day.

He also knew that both of the assistants were supplementing their income and preparing the way for promotion by sharing his schedule and the substance of his business activities with his boss, Ray Klein, the CEO of Aggregate Industries. He didn't mind that at all, because it gave him two extra ways to feed Klein what he wanted him to know.

As the car moved along the street toward Sunset he said, "Carl, what's the situation on Densmore?"

"Those two guys he hired to hang out at the DA's office had more balls than brains."

"I know that." People weren't supposed to tell Schelling things that he already knew.

"Sorry, Scotty. Kaprilow and Stevens are watching his house and his office this morning. His Mercedes was in its spot at his office before they got there, and the engine wasn't warm. His wife is at his house, and she doesn't seem to be doing anything. She's not packing to run off and meet him in Brazil or something. She hasn't left the house yet."

"Any signs of police at his house or his office?"

"Not yet."

"Let me know right away if anything like that turns up."

"Will do."

"You're doing a good job, Carl." Schelling had made a decision to say that long before he had left the house. Carl was not doing an especially good job, but he could be made to work harder and smarter with a few words of encouragement, and he would turn sullen if he felt unappreciated. He paid Carl very well, but no amount of money was enough to keep a man like Carl absolutely loyal. His best interests had to be exactly the same as Scott Schelling's. To keep the connection strong, Schelling sometimes reminisced with Carl about things that they'd done together, but he couldn't face that today.

In the old days, Carl had often scouted the fashionable bars and clubs to find women for Scott. Schelling had been a young music-company executive, barely out of business school. He had already discovered he could make surprisingly good money in the music business, but he had not been very successful at attracting women.

Carl procured an introduction to Kit Stoddard at the bar in Gazebo at around midnight one night, and called Scott immediately. Schelling had been getting ready to leave for a business party, but he had already had enough experience with Carl to know that he should come when Carl called. While Carl was waiting for Schelling to arrive, he started a conversation to stall for time. Carl was a muscular, athletic-looking man in his mid-twenties, with lots of wavy black hair, strong, sculpted features, and a tanning-salon tan. Scott Schelling had never, even now, met a man who looked that way and was intelligent. It was some obscure law of genetics that prevented anyone from having every advantage at once.

Carl kept Kit and her companions amused with his patter. Schelling had heard enough of it on other occasions to know what he must have said. "You're actresses, aren't you? I thought you had to be. How do I know? It's just a look, like a glow. Either a woman has it, or she doesn't, and you do. And besides, what are the chances that three such amazing women would be together unless they were acting, or they were triplets? You're not triplets, right? Am I disappointed? No. I'll admit triplets are a fantasy, but I have so many others I have to get through first. I'm still working on things I promised myself at age fourteen. Anyway, let's be honest. I'm not in your league. A woman like you deserves to be with a man who can buy you things and take you places. Who? My boss, for instance. He's barely thirty and he's a gazillionaire. He's in the music business."

In those days, Scott had not been comfortable trying to meet women. He was small-boned, narrow-shouldered, and wore thick glasses. He had a New York accent, and had been out of the city long enough to know that women in the rest of the world found it a cause for suspicion.

Whenever Carl managed to get him successfully connected with a new woman, he had given Carl a bonus with his next paycheck. As Scott sat in the car thinking about it, he remembered that Nancy Russo and Carol Peters, the two before Kit, had each earned Carl ten thousand dollars. Carl must have made at least fifty thousand in bonuses that year. But Carl seemed to get more out of these services than money. It occurred to Schelling that Carl enjoyed some vicarious sexual titillation, too, because he was the one who had accomplished the initial seduction.

When Scott walked into Gazebo that night he was aware of the importance of first impressions. He had worn a dark Armani suit that had been altered beautifully to fit him, a pair of handmade Italian shoes, and his most expensive Rolex. When a woman looked at him, she didn't see the prematurely middle-aged slouch. She saw the suit. She didn't see the dull brown hair that had already begun to thin on top and still looked unruly after a two-hundred–dollar haircut. She saw the two-hundred–dollar haircut.

Schelling watched Kit Stoddard sitting at the bar and lifting her graceful, long-fingered hand to touch her shining red hair, pushing it out of her eyes, not so the eyes could see him, but so he could see the eyes and add them to his appraisal of her. Scott invited her to come to the party with him. She shrugged, looked at her two friends, and agreed.

He took her to the party at the new house in the Hollywood Hills that Mechanismo had bought with the signing bonus he'd received from Bulletproof Records. Scott walked with Kit through the faux Tuscan villa, looked at the things that all young musicians bought that year: a huge flat-screen television set, a saltwater aquarium with a couple of sharks in it, a couple of bad portraits of themselves. They crossed the broad veranda, and went down the widening steps to the lawn, where Scott had seen Artie Bains from Bulletproof Records trying to be part of a gaggle of recording artists. Scott stepped close to Bains and said, "When are you putting him on the road?"

Bains said, "The new CD isn't finished yet, but the week it comes out. He hasn't thought as far ahead as tomorrow, so don't say anything."

"Professional courtesy," Scott agreed.

"I'll explain it to him in a couple of days, when he's sober, and then we'll start booking dates. I'll call you to see if we can avoid conflicts." He saw Kit Stoddard and held out his hand. "Hello," he said. "I'm Artie Bains, from Bulletproof. I know I would remember if Scotty had ever had a friend as beautiful as you."

"Thank you." Kit had never heard of Artie Bains, but she had certainly heard of Bulletproof.

Scott steered her out of Bains's reach. "Good luck with the tour."

Bains understood his good wishes. It wasn't quite a threat, just a reminder that he had just given Scott information that Scott could use to make his next few days more difficult.

Kit saw the party exactly as Scott had wanted her to. He introduced her to the members of Los Federales and The Scheme, both of them groups he had signed. She met Marsha Steele in the powder room and then watched her come out, pick up a guitar, and give an impromptu performance of two of the songs on her next CD.

At around two-thirty, Little Nancy's limousine pulled up at the front of the house, and Little Nancy made an entrance wearing so much diamond jewelry that she was weighed down by it. Before she went down the lawn to disappear among the group there Little Nancy stopped and embraced Scott Schelling.

Later still, as they walked past the people at the buffet tables and milling around the three bars, toward the driveway where the valet attendants would bring his car, Kit said, "It's amazing how anybody can make this much money."

Scott said, "Mechanismo's not only broke, but he already owes more money than he's made in his life. He just doesn't know it yet."

"He is? After one CD?"

"He's good. If he holds up, he'll work his way out of debt some-day. But he's going to be on tour a lot, and the second CD had better hit."

"Why is he in debt?"

"Because he's new. He doesn't know yet that there's a difference between money and credit, and it wasn't in Artie's interest to tell him. I think Mechanismo's signing bonus was two million. He put a million or so down on this house, which means he owes the bank about ten. If he got two, the government wants the rest, and they want it yesterday. He's spent a lot on cars, jewelry, and parties. To-morrow or the next day, Artie will sit down with him, add up the figures, and explain to him how money works. Then he'll tell him what he has to do to get more."

"Do you do that, too?"

"Do what?"

"Get them into debt to control them."

"Of course not. Whenever I see this kind of thing coming, I try to head it off. I'm in this business because I love music and I want to find wonderful artists and help them create. Along the way, they make money, and the company I work for makes money."

After only a few of those parties, Kit had begun to hear comments about Scott from people she met. She repeated the words to him with a worried look, as though she were bringing news to him that would break his heart. "Scotty, I think you've got to try to let more people know who you really are and what you're like, and not be so aloof and invisible. Tonight I heard this person call you the Prince of Darkness."

He grinned and shrugged. "If your competitors say you're the worst, then you're the best."

Scott had become infatuated with Kit. He began referring to her as his girlfriend, and treated her generously. He let her buy expensive clothes in the boutiques along Montana Avenue with his credit card. He went off to work each morning at five-thirty and left her in charge of a big, luxurious house until eight P.M. or later. He took her to the best parties in town.

But eventually the relationship began to lose its freshness. Kit said she was bored and that she missed her friends. He did not want to meet her girlfriends, or let Kit take a car to the clubs. He ordered Carl to drive her to a restaurant where she had agreed to meet her friends, and then pick her up at a prearranged time and place. Scott didn't want to have all of her friends, family, and acquaintances invading his life. He wanted her—the long red hair, the white skin, the soft lips. He wanted to see himself through her deep green eyes and feel her appreciation, her admiration, her arousal.

They had begun to issue short, cold, sarcastic comments, sometimes not answered, like solitary blows. One night he came home from work expecting to take her out to dinner, and found her in the bedroom getting ready to go out with her friends. He kept himself from speaking because he did not want to blurt out some jealous, angry remark that he would instantly regret. She noticed his dark mood and said he was pouting. He knew that if he spoke, she would react only by tormenting him intentionally, and then he would lose his temper, so he went off to the pool to swim while Carl drove her to her meeting place.

While she was gone, he found himself consumed by loneliness and longing. He had always been very gentle and patient with her, but now the feeling was different. He began to pace. At two A.M., he was waiting for her at the door, let her in and locked it, stripped her clothes off in the foyer and took her. When it was done, she kissed him over and over for a long time without speaking, and they went to bed and fell asleep in each other's arms.

From then on, whenever she went out without him, he would lie in wait for her, thinking about her until she appeared. He would make love to her on the carpeted bedroom floor, or on the couch in the media room, or the big overstuffed chair near the door.

She enjoyed the game—the fact that she aroused him so much that he couldn't control himself, or the power she had to make him wait by the door for her, staring out the window and listening. He thought about her during the day, caught himself daydreaming about her during meetings or when he was listening to CD cuts, trying to make a decision about the fate of a performer.

One night was worse than before. She came home much later from one of her evenings with the girls. When she came into the bedroom, he undressed her roughly. She resisted, and he snatched up the silk necktie he had taken off and hung from a knob on a dresser, and used it to bind her arms behind her, then pushed her to the bed and forced her. From her movements and sounds, he could tell that she was more excited than she had ever been. After it was over, they lay still for a minute, and then she said, "Untie my wrists, Scott."

He could tell from the stern, cold way she said it that she was serious now. He untied the knot, and she sat up and faced him. "That can never happen again." At first he thought he had misunderstood her—that she had actually hated it and wanted him to stop—but he studied her face in the dim moonlight, and knew that he had not.

She was not angry. She was frightened because she had begun to see what he had already seen: Each time they had sex, it had become rougher, more violent. Each time they came together like this, they had to go a little bit farther. She said, "This has gone too far."

"Okay. We won't do that again."

"I don't mean the necktie. It's being rough. Hurting me."

"You liked it."

"I don't think this is good for us. For me, or for you."

"So we'll do something else next time. We'll be gentle and slow. We can take a long, hot bath and I'll give you a massage."

"I think I should leave."

"It's almost three. Where would you go?"

"Home. I have an apartment, remember? I want to go back to my own bed and sleep. I think we need to take a break from each other."

"Come on, Kit. This wasn't a big deal. It's just a little game, and pretty tame by most people's standards."

"I need time to think."

He lay back on the bed staring at the ceiling while she went through the closet and the bathroom, dressing. It took only a moment to realize that she was rushing, as though she couldn't wait to get away from him. She wasn't saying that she was breaking up with him, but Scott knew she was. As soon as she was dressed, she was going to hurry downstairs, get in her car, and drive away. Once she was out of his house, away from him and on the telephone where he could not reach her and she did not have to look into his eyes, her tone would change. Maybe she would not even answer his calls.

Scott tried to lie back calmly and get used to the idea that she was no longer his. He took deep breaths and concentrated on making his muscles lose their tension. She was dressed now. She came into the bedroom and stopped. "I'll call you."

He lay there, paralyzed with sadness. She was lying to him. She would never call him, never want to talk to him. He had been so kind to her, so generous. She had probably been trying to use him from the beginning, using his influence, his contacts, his access. He sat up as she was going past him. "Kit, wait!"

"I'm going. I don't want to talk."

Something in him shifted, some undiscovered switch turned on. He was out of the bed, still naked, and he was charging toward her. He half-tackled, half-threw her to the floor. He yanked the belt out of the pants he had left there, looped it around her neck and through the buckle, and held her there.

SUDDENLY HE HEARD Carl's cell phone ring, and it jarred him back to the present. He lifted his eyes and squinted into the glaring sunshine. He was breathless, sweating in the air-conditioned car. Kit had actually died. He really had killed her.

"Yeah?" Carl said. After a moment, Carl said, "Scotty?"

"What?"

"They just found Densmore's body. It was in a field up near Santa Clarita this morning." He kept whoever had called on the line and waited, driving along in the slow traffic on Sunset toward the turn into the Canyon at Crescent Heights.

Scott Schelling sat in the back of the car, staring out the window. "Damn. That's a problem. Who is watching the District Attorney's office?"

"We can move Kaprilow and Stevens. Neither of them is really cut out for—"

"Do it. No. Just tell Stevens to watch the building entrance for the moment. He isn't to do anything. We just want a phone call the second he sees Wendy."

He listened as Carl repeated what he had said to the person on the telephone and ended the call. Then Scott said, "And the first two shooters. The Turners. Get in touch with them so they know that we're still here and the contract is good. We don't want them to panic just because Densmore isn't around. We still want them out looking for Wendy Harper."

Carl was feeling good. He was always amazed when Scott Schelling moved into action. Densmore's body had barely hit the ground. Scott had heard about it when? Ten seconds ago? And he was taking steps to reestablish order and communications, get the new chain of command in place, and make everybody feel safe. For the fiftieth time, he wished he were younger and smarter—maybe just more ambitious—so he could be learning how to be successful from the master. These lessons must be worth all the business-school degrees in the world, but Carl knew he would never take advantage of them.

"And Carl?"

"Yes?"

"When you talk to them, keep in mind that what probably happened to Densmore was that they killed him. Don't make them feel uncomfortable. We need to get this Wendy Harper thing done."

35

WHILE SYLVIE PACKED their suitcases in the bedroom, she could hear Paul in the kitchen and the living room and the office collecting things. Paul was good at picking out his own clothes, as men who were narcissists all seemed to be. Paul chose clothes that emphasized how tall and slim he was: pants with pronounced waistbands and narrow legs, tight pullover casual shirts, dress shirts with vertical stripes, sport coats that he wore buttoned to show off his thin waist.

She could tell from the sounds that Paul was collecting money from the various places where he had hidden cash. It was foolish to use credit cards when it wasn't necessary, so as soon as they landed, they would use false names and start changing small numbers of dollars into euros as they needed them. There was no way to be completely anonymous, but there was no sense making yourself accessible to amateurs and incompetents. Paul had also called the bank this morning to let them know that sometime over the next few months, they might order an electronic transfer to a foreign bank. It was always best to smooth the way and know the latest procedures before you were on the other side of the earth and talking to a banker long-distance.

Sylvie had fretted while she was trying to decide what to pack for such a long and unpredictable trip, but Paul had said, "There are two suitcases, thirty by twenty-four inches. If something doesn't fit in there, it's not going. We'll shop there and dress like locals." She loved Paul's ability to settle her. He spoke with a quiet, untroubled voice and rested his strong, gentle hands on her shoulders and held her still, grounding her, the way an expert rider calmed a skittish horse. Afterward, she didn't know what had made her feel so anxious. Of course they didn't need to bring everything in their closets. They could shop for anything they needed after they were out of the country.

It was ridiculous to be frantic and agitated: Densmore was dead. That had ended that stupid job they should never have taken in the first place. They would take a nice vacation, make it last a few months, and then come home long after everyone had forgotten about Wendy Harper and Eric Fuller.

She had known for a long time that Densmore was dangerous because he took so much trouble to be the sort of person nobody thought was dangerous. He'd had that smooth, soft way of speaking that could only be false. She had suspected that if he gained too much power over them, he would show a different side.

She went over in her mind the items she had put in the suitcases to be sure she had done her best with the time and space she had been allowed. Then she closed the suitcases and lifted hers tentatively off the bed, then Paul's. They were both heavy, but she could carry either one if she had to, and Paul could carry them both. She looked inside again, and verified that she had put in the right variety of garments for late summer in Europe. Then she sat on the bed to think of anything else she needed.

She heard Paul moving along the hallway from the living room, and a slight feeling of worry crept into her mind. Last night, Michael Densmore had said, "I paid you four times—" and right then Paul had pulled the trigger and killed him. It had sounded as though Densmore might have been about to say, "I paid you four times the original price." Paul had told her two days earlier that

Densmore had offered to double the price, not quadruple it. She replayed the conversation in her memory, trying to intuit from the tone of Densmore's voice what the rest of the sentence would have been. As she ran it through her mind again, she realized that she had the phrase wrong. What Densmore had said was "I offered to pay you four times—" That was important: offered, not paid.

It was entirely possible that Densmore, addled by cowardice, had simply misspoken, saying "four times" instead of "twice." Or he may have been, in a clumsy, frightened way, trying to double his offer a second time to make up for his disloyalty in revealing their identities to a client and hiring a rival team without warning them. Densmore had denied hiring those men, but she had no doubt he had done it, and the more he had railed against the client for doing it, the more certain she had become. Redoubling the offer would not have been a bad strategy at that point. But that point was precisely the moment when Paul had shot him. She had to face the possibility that Paul had killed him to keep him from blurting out the *real* size of the deal in front of Sylvie. Could Paul have been planning to skim half the price of the job and hide it from her?

The question was delicate and unpleasant. They had gone to the parking structure without an agreement to kill Michael Densmore. Sylvie had secretly hoped that was what would happen, but she had professed to agree with Paul when he had said, "We ought to get him in a quiet place, ask him a few searching questions, and see what we think of his answers." Sylvie had been afraid of Densmore. Paul did not seem to have noticed, but Densmore had been too attentive to her in the wrong way: opened doors for her, but didn't leave enough space for her to get past without brushing against him; leaned over her too close when he had pulled out her chair. He had appeared overly polite and respectful when they had all been together talking about business, and had deferred to her as though he accepted her as Paul's equal. But as soon as Paul stepped out of the room, or even looked away for a few seconds, Densmore's eyes had changed. He had stared frankly and openly at her body, or looked into her eyes with a smirk. But he had never done anything that would give her a chance to say to Paul, "Look. See what he's doing?"

She had not been completely sure what Paul's reaction would have been if she had said something to Paul. She knew Paul would say, "Did he touch you? What exactly did he say? What did he do?" If she tried to explain, she was afraid he might say, "Sylvie, you're suddenly shy about the way men look at you? The star of *Honeymoon Ranch Two* and *Three*?"

She had been cautious, but she had known that the last thing she wanted was to find herself in Michael Densmore's power. Last night she had actually wanted to kill Densmore, but the way Paul had done it, in such a hurry as though he had intended to shut him up, made her wonder.

Suppose Densmore had actually offered more money on the phone a few days ago than Paul had said. That might not matter, either. Paul might have been saving the real figure to surprise her later. In either case, the money was only hypothetical: They had not killed Wendy Harper, and so they had not received payment.

Still, Sylvie was not satisfied. Maybe Paul had received an advance and kept it from her. Maybe Paul had demanded more after their failure up north. Maybe Paul had been hiding money from her for a long time, and Densmore had known and played along. That would provide an entirely different—but not necessarily better—meaning to the way he had looked at her all those times in his office. She shifted, and the sound of the floor creaking under her foot startled her. She caught her reflection in the mirror over her dresser.

To her horror, she saw a woman who had become middle-aged. She had wrinkles, breasts that were beginning to sag even though she had worked tirelessly to maintain her muscle tone. Of course Paul was hiding money from her, using it to pay for affairs with younger women. Good hotels were expensive, even if he used them for only three hours in the middle of the day.

Sylvie felt angry at herself, humiliated. She had to get through the next few minutes, to avoid Paul. She looked around, saw the bathroom door, hurried through it into the bathroom and turned on the water in the big tub. She wasn't sure why she was doing it, except that this was a familiar, simple act, she was alone, and the sound of the water was a kind of privacy, too.

The doorbell. How could there be anybody at the door? She turned off the water, rushed back into the bedroom, and looked through the window to see if there were cops moving through the yard. No. She could see the pool, the trees, the wall at the back of the property. She opened the cabinet and snatched a stack of clean towels, took her pistol out of the nightstand, stuck it between the top two, and carried them toward the living room.

When she came into the living room, she saw Paul on the opposite side of it, hurrying in from the kitchen, putting a pistol into the back of his pants, and covering it with his shirttail. He waved his hand toward the door and pantomimed turning a knob. She nodded and went to the front door just as the bell rang again. She looked through the peephole and saw a man standing on the front steps.

"Who is it?" she called.

"My name is Carl Zacca, Mrs. Turner. I represent the man who's been dealing with you through Mr. Densmore."

Sylvie turned to Paul. "Shit!" she whispered.

"We've got to let him in," Paul said. "He knows we're home."

She glared at him and shook her head, but Paul brushed past her, opened the door, and stepped back.

The man who stood in the doorway was handsome, with thick black hair and a genuine-looking smile. He held out his hand. "Carl Zacca, Mr. Turner. I'm really sorry to bother you, but would you mind if I came in?"

Paul stepped back. "Come in." When Carl Zacca was past the threshold, Paul swung the door shut. He had his hand behind him, on the gun in the back of his belt. "Sit down over here on the couch."

Carl Zacca sat on the white couch in the conversation area facing the front of the room. Sylvie kept her hand on the gun under the towels and planned the shots she would take through the back of the couch so she could kill him quickly.

As though he'd had the same thought, Zacca turned his head and looked over his shoulder at her. She said, "Hello, Mr. Zacca."

"Carl. Please call me Carl. And the guns aren't really necessary. I'm a friend."

"Fine," Paul said. "Tell me again. Who do you work for? What's his name?"

He answered without hesitation, "Scott Schelling." He smiled and watched Paul and Sylvie exchange a glance. "The reason I came was—I don't know, you may have heard already—that Michael Densmore has died. Did you know?"

"No," said Paul. "How did that happen?"

The expression on Paul Turner's face answered that question, thought Carl. They had killed him. "I don't know. Somebody shot him, I heard. As soon as we knew, Mr. Schelling sent me here to establish contact with you. Densmore said that you prefer not to work directly with customers, but we didn't know what else to do. We don't have a go-between anymore, and we're in the middle of a crisis. I hope you don't mind."

He looked at Sylvie, but she said nothing. She didn't remove her hand from the stack of towels. He looked at Paul.

"No," Paul said.

"Good, because every minute counts now. We're only going to have a brief period when Wendy Harper is in sight. She's like a rabbit. We've seen her pop out of her hiding place, but she's running, and what she's running for is the next rabbit hole. If she makes it, we're through."

Paul said, "We appreciate your coming all the way over here, and we respect you for being straight about who you work for and not trying to lie about it. But you guys already exercised your right to choice when you hired a pair of amateurs to take over for us. We watched those two die while we were staring through rifle sights, waiting for our shot."

"We didn't hire them; that was Densmore."

Paul glanced at Sylvie again. She was watchful, her face conveying nothing of what she might be thinking or feeling. Paul said, "When we got replaced, we came home. We're out. We haven't been paid anything, so we don't owe you anything."

"I can understand why you thought that, but I'm here to tell you everything's okay. You can go finish the contact."

"We're out."

"Then we'd like you to come back in."

"What are you offering?"

"Paul." It was Sylvie's voice, and he could see in his peripheral vision that she was shaking her head, but he ignored her.

"We'll pay in full what Densmore promised you."

"Densmore's dead."

Carl studied Paul for a moment. He saw that Paul was not returning his gaze as a man might who was bluffing. Carl said, "I get the feeling that we started out wrong. I'm just trying to build an easy, open relationship so we can handle this situation efficiently. Mr. Schelling didn't want you to worry when you heard Densmore was dead. We're still around, and we're still interested. You'll get paid. We'll live up to our end of the agreement."

"The only agreement we had was with Densmore," said Paul. "He's dead, so there is no agreement."

Carl wondered what strange thing he had done in some earlier lifetime to put him in a house in Van Nuys between two professional killers, each of them with one hand hidden so it could hold a gun. "I'll tell you what. You give me a figure that will bring you back in, and I'll call Mr. Schelling and see if it's acceptable to him."

"A million dollars." It was Sylvie's voice—a number called out in urgency, like an auction bid.

The two men turned to look at Sylvie. She stared back at them defiantly, letting the words hang in the room.

Carl spoke. "I don't understand. You're joking?"

"No," she said. "This wasn't a regular job from the beginning. From the minute we planted the bat and the bloody rag in Eric Fuller's yard, everybody who mattered knew we were luring Wendy Harper into the open to kill her. Now the cops know it, too. They're waiting for somebody to try again. If you think *you* can do it, go ahead."

Carl Zacca looked at Paul Turner. "I'm going to reach into my pocket for my phone. Okay?"

"Okay."

Carl moved his right hand slowly inside his coat pocket. His hand almost involuntarily moved to touch the handgrips of his gun. Verifying its presence was like touching a good-luck charm. He removed his hand, transferred the cell phone to his left, but kept his posture the same: sitting on the edge of the couch, bent forward slightly so his coat was pushed away from his body and the inner pocket was easy to reach. He pushed the button to dial Scott's number and put the phone to his left ear.

After a few seconds, he said, "It's Carl. I've met our two friends and we've been having a nice talk, but they want more money, and I need to run their offer past you. Is that something you can do now?"

He heard Scott Schelling say, "Is this figure a holdup?"

"Yes."

"Just say yes or no. Is it a million?"

"Yes."

"Take a very good look around you. See every security mechanism, where the furniture is, the alarm system, and so on. I'll want you to draw a picture of it from memory the minute you get out of there. Can you do that?"

"Uh-huh."

"Okay. Then I'll give you some time to look. Give the phone to Paul Turner."

"Yes, sir." He held the telephone out toward Paul. "He would like to talk to you."

"Me?"

"Yes. He's waiting."

Paul took three steps forward and accepted the telephone. Carl noticed that he, too, held it to his left ear. His right hand moved to the back of his shirt. "This is Turner."

"Paul, this is Scott Schelling. I've heard a lot of good things about you and your wife. I really sent my friend Carl over there just to make sure you didn't feel you were abandoned and on your own now. We want you with us. You're the only ones who have seen her in six years, and I can't find somebody else now. She'll be in Los Angeles in three or four hours. Carl tells me that it will take more money. How much?"

"A million bucks."

"That's a lot of money."

"The only reason to *do* this is for a lot of money."

"I suppose. But getting that much in cash on short notice is not easy."

"If you want to let it go or have somebody else do it cheaper, we'll never reveal anything we know about it. But if you want us, that's what it will cost—in cash, as soon as it's done."

"All right. It's a high price, but no hard feelings. I'll have the money ready. You can get to work."

"Then we're in."

"Paul!" It was Sylvie's voice. Paul jerked his head to look at the man on the couch, then at her, but she had not been warning him of danger.

"What?" The phone had gone dead.

She was angry. "We need to talk."

"We can talk while we're getting ready. She has to be done today." He tossed the phone back to Carl Zacca. "Carl, it's been pleasant, but time is passing."

Carl put the phone away and stood up. "Well, then, we'll see you later with your money. You made a hell of a deal on this."

"We'll see." Paul followed Carl to the door, closed and locked it behind him.

"Paul, have you lost your mind?"

"Sssh." He had the gun in his hand, prepared to fire through the door as he squinted through the peephole. After a few more seconds, they heard a car moving off. Then he turned to her. "He's gone. I haven't lost my mind, and neither have you. That million-dollar thing was quick thinking. It made everything kind of crystallize." He stepped close and hugged her, then kissed her cheek and released her. He hurried toward the bedroom, and she pursued him.

"What the hell are you doing?"

"You named the price, and he met it."

"But that was just—"

"Brilliant."

"You can't possibly think this music guy is planning to hand us a million bucks."

"No, I don't."

"Then what are you doing? We're all packed. We have reservations. We could be gone already."

"We *will* be. It will just be a few days later before we get to Europe, that's all. Pack the passports and shove the money I've been collecting into the suitcases. When the doorbell rang, I stashed it in the refrigerator."

"What are you saying? We can't leave now." Her voice was a wail of frustration. "You just agreed to a job."

"I'm not talking about running. We'll do the job. We'll get a million bucks."

"I only said that to make him go away. And he only agreed because he expects to have somebody kill us afterward."

Paul held Sylvie's shoulders and looked at her as though he were trying to hypnotize her. "Sylvie, think about this guy. Six years ago, he made a mistake. So what did he do? He spent the next six years trying to find the woman who knows about it, even though she hasn't told anybody. He's a maniac about being careful."

"That's not reassuring. That scares the shit out of me. He'll kill us, too."

Paul grinned. "I know he doesn't intend to pay us. I could have asked for New Jersey, and he would have agreed. But he's also smart enough to know that no matter what precautions he takes, there is at least a slight possibility that he might find himself alone with us after we kill Wendy. He knows that if we show up to get paid and he isn't ready to hand us a suitcase full of money, he's dead. What do you think he's going to do?"

36

JACK TILL DROVE south on the Golden State Freeway in the bright afternoon sun, keeping his car to the left, away from the big tractor-trailer trucks on the right making their way down from northern California and Oregon to Los Angeles. On the long up-slopes, the heavy trucks all geared down and labored to climb, the weight of the trailers heating their engines and making transmissions whine. Now and then, one with a lighter load would pull out into the next lane to pass, and Till would have to swerve to avoid it. Poliakoff had not called to let him know that the two men in Morro Bay had been caught, and that meant that they might be on the road behind him, pushing the speed limit, too.

He kept turning his head to pretend to look in the right mirror, but really to look at Wendy in profile. He was going to have to keep her safe.

She turned to him. "Do you think that tomorrow at this time we'll be alive?"

"That's the plan."

"There's been a lot of death, a lot of loss in a short time. Do you wonder about things like that? Have you ever thought that maybe the best thing to do would have been nothing?"

"Sometimes. But when I was a homicide cop, most days I had the opposite problem. There was a body, usually a person who wasn't very big or strong or rich or anything. Somebody had wanted something he had, or got into an argument with him and got so mad they killed him. And I would look around for the giant structure of law and sanity that I was brought up to believe takes care of these things, and realize that it's a fraud. It doesn't exist. There was only me. The body was a person, and I was his only advocate. So I'd try to do something."

"That was the way I felt about Kit, but now Louanda has died because of me."

"Not because of you. Because of this Scott, the boyfriend. You're just the victim who survived."

If Till could take the name "Scott," the description of the car, and the new information about Kit Stoddard, and develop them into a full identification, then Wendy's six-year ordeal would end. Till knew that with the danger gone, things would look very different to her. He'd had clients infatuated with him before. Most likely she would have a gentle, quiet talk with him about how important he would always be to her, and how glad she was that they had met. And then she would get on the flight that would take her back to San Rafael.

Till kept watching the road, pushing his speed. He had taken the Golden State Freeway with the notion that any chasers would make assumptions: Because he had taken Highway 101 all the way from San Rafael, he would simply turn back onto it, or maybe because it was closer, he might take the Pacific Coast Highway out of Morro Bay and meet the 101 again at San Luis Obispo or Arroyo Grande or Orcutt. Instead, he had gone inland to the Golden State. It was a gamble because there was no way to change his course now if he was pursued.

Whenever he looked in the rearview mirror and saw a car that appeared to be gaining on him, he sped up enough to give himself time to study it. Each time, he saw something that persuaded him that the car was just a speeder: the wrong kind of car, the wrong kind of face behind the windshield.

He kept on past the Bakersfield exits. As he drove, he thought as far ahead as he could. In his memory, he studied the rest of the highway, the city streets beyond, and picked a route that would bring Wendy safely to the end of the trip. He drove with his left hand, and then felt her slip her small hand into his right and hold it. The feeling made him think about Holly. She was at work now, and probably by the time Till reached Los Angeles, she would be on her afternoon break. Maybe he would call her then.

"I'm scared," Wendy said.

"Don't be ashamed of it. I'll do my best to be sure nothing bad happens to you."

"Maybe it's better this way. Dying might be better than hiding someplace, living an imitation of a life with a false identity."

"Was it that bad?"

"Not day to day. That was part of the problem. After a year, my biggest fear was not that I'd get caught. It was that I wouldn't. I'd live to be sixty or so, and suddenly realize that I'd thrown away my chance for a real life. I would be perfectly safe. I would just have let my life go by, waiting for somebody to tell me I could come out."

"Wendy..."

"I know. After this, I'll have to go into hiding again. This is only one day, but it's my day. I get to do something."

He kept up his speed, and welcomed the approach of the Grapevine, the long climb up to Tejon Pass at over four thousand feet. His rental Cadillac had a big overpowered engine that could do it without slowing, and he hoped that any chasers would not be as fast.

Till kept rehearsing the route ahead, driving it once in his mind and then doing it again as he came to it. He left the Golden State Freeway for the Hollywood Freeway just past Osborne Street, got off at Victory, took Laurel Canyon Boulevard to Burbank Boulevard, turned right and came to Woodman Avenue, and took it down into Sherman Oaks. Till turned onto a quiet street lined by houses.

Wendy said, "What's this? What are we doing here?"

Till pointed at a house. "That's where we're going." The house was a small pale yellow colonial with clapboards and shutters in a neighborhood full of neat, pleasant-looking houses with carefully tended yards. He drove past slowly to read the house number, then kept going around the block, and pulled to the curb in the shade of a purple-blooming jacaranda tree.

"Be patient. I just have to make a couple of quick calls." He dialed his cell phone. "Hi. It's me. Where we agreed. Yes. I'd appreciate it if you could get here right away. Thanks, Max." He disconnected and called another number. "Jay? It's me. I'm there. You ready? Good." He put the telephone away.

"Now what?"

"Now we move again and come back in half an hour. If anything in this neighborhood looks different, we keep going. If it doesn't, we get this business over with."

"You mean we're meeting here?"

"That's right. After those two men attacked the car in front of the DA's office, I managed to get them to agree to a different plan. That little yellow house with the shutters back there belongs to Linda Gordon."

"Who's that?"

"The Assistant DA who's prosecuting Eric Fuller for killing you."

"I can hardly wait to meet her."

Till drove out of the tangle of shady residential streets to Ventura Boulevard and cruised to the east from stoplight to stoplight.

Wendy said, "Ventura Boulevard. In the old days, I always planned that we would open a second location of Banque in the Valley, along Ventura."

"What stopped you?"

"At first, it was the obvious thing. We didn't have the money. By the time it might have been feasible, we weren't building anything anymore. We were breaking up, and taking money out of the business instead of plowing it back in. It's sad when things end, isn't it?"

"Not everything is pleasant."

"No, but even when something is mostly bad, when it ends you think, 'Well, that's that. I'll never be here again.' That part of your life is over, and can't be gotten back. There are no do-overs."

"I guess not." He saw a Starbucks in Studio City, turned off Ventura, and parked the car on a side street. They went inside, bought cups of coffee, and then walked back to the car. Till kept scanning though the whole process, but the tables outside the coffee shop were inhabited only by a group of young people slouching over their coffee and talking while their lazy dogs slept at their feet. The pedestrians on the street were mothers and nannies with strollers, joggers, shoppers.

Till drove back along Ventura, studying the mirrors to be sure there was nobody he had missed following him, and returned to Sherman Oaks. "Look around," he said. "Anything that's different is important."

When they approached Linda Gordon's house, Wendy said, "There's a car in the driveway. And I see a car in front of the house that wasn't there before. See? It looks like a cop car."

"That's Poliakoff. And across the street, that red Saab is Jay Chernoff's. It looks as though everybody is already inside." He drove around the block once, but saw no other signs of change. When he came around again, he parked, and they walked together to the front door. Till stayed close to shield Wendy with his body. Poliakoff opened the door for them, his eyes scanning the street. He closed the door as soon as they were inside, and went to the front window to check for any activity on the block.

Jack Till said, "If there was ever a time for introductions, I think it's come. The lady with me is Wendy Harper."

Poliakoff moved from the window, and shook Wendy's hand. "I'm Sergeant Max Poliakoff. I'm pleased to meet you. Thanks for coming out for this." Then he shook Till's, much harder. "Hi, Jack." He turned and pointed to a man in his early thirties with light hair. "This is Officer Tim Fallon, from Forensics."

Fallon muttered something to Wendy about it being a pleasure as Jack saw Jay Chernoff standing in the entrance to the kitchen with Linda Gordon.

Till said, "This is Jay Chernoff, Eric's lawyer, and the lady is our hostess, Assistant District Attorney Linda Gordon."

Linda Gordon had been staring intently at Wendy since she came in the door. Now she nodded, but did not smile. "Good afternoon."

"Good to see you, Jack." Chernoff came forward to shake Wendy's hand. "And Miss Harper. I'm honored to meet you."

Linda Gordon's eyes narrowed. She turned to Chernoff. "Shall we get on with this?"

Chernoff raised his voice. "Let's get started, if we may. Miss Harper, what we need is to ask your cooperation so that we can establish positively and officially that you are who Jack says you are."

"I'm willing," she said. "What do I do?"

"Officer Fallon is here because he's an expert in collecting and interpreting evidence. He'll take over the next phase of this."

Fallon stepped to the end of the living room, where he had a big briefcase and a metal toolbox. He opened the metal box and approached Wendy. "We'll start by taking a couple of head shots, if you don't mind, Miss Harper."

"Okay."

"You may or may not look exactly the same as you did six years ago, but the biometrics will be the same. Your eyes will be the same distance apart, have the same flecks in them, and so on."

"I understand," she said.

Fallon was uncomfortable working with so many people watching him, and he performed each task with exaggerated care. He asked Wendy to stand by a plain white wall, then took four digital photographs of her from the front and four from the side. He held a tape measure up beside her and muttered, "Same height," apparently to himself. He used a counter in the kitchen to lay out his fingerprint equipment, then inked her fingers and pressed her prints onto a card. Then he had Wendy sit at the kitchen table while he drew three small vials of blood and scraped two cotton swabs on the inside of her mouth. When he had finished, he packed up all of his samples.

"Well?" Chernoff said. "When will we have the results so we can get an official concession from the DA's office that what we can see with our own eyes is accurate?"

"It should be a faster identification than usual," Fallon said. "Our own print people are backed up for months. But Miss Harper has been in the federal system for six years as a missing person, and the FBI Fingerprint Identification Records System can probably do an online match today. The DNA gets sent to two private labs, both of which have analyzed other samples of Miss Harper's DNA during the earlier parts of this investigation. The National DNA Index System has it, too, and they may be faster. We'll have a positive answer within a couple of weeks."

"You took photographs," said Chernoff. "When can you analyze those?"

"Right now, if you'd like."

"Then please do it."

Fallon took a laptop computer out of his briefcase and turned it on, then connected his digital camera to it and transferred the pictures he had taken.

Wendy stepped close to Linda Gordon and said, "I really *am* Wendy Harper."

Linda Gordon only turned her head to look at her long enough to say, "We'll see," then turned away again. As Till watched the exchange, it occurred to him that the argument for Wendy's identity might have seemed stronger to Linda Gordon if the two women had not looked so similar. They were both in their thirties, about the same shape, and blond.

Fallon's screen was changing. "Okay. This photograph was taken at the DMV when she renewed her driver's license the last time six years ago, and here's the one four years before that, when she first moved to California."

"For Christ's sake, look at that!" Chernoff said triumphantly. He pointed at the screen, then at Wendy Harper.

Linda Gordon said nothing.

Fallon continued, as though he had not heard. "I'm putting the first picture I took today beside the most recent DMV photo. Now I'm superimposing the two. What we can see right away is that the general shapes are identical. We can see the measurement from chin to crown is the same, the eyes and nose are the same size and in the same positions. We'll do much more scientific measurements and comparisons when we're at the lab."

"Come on," Chernoff said. "You'd have to be blind not to see it's the same person." He turned to Linda Gordon. "Can't you drop the charges on the strength of these pictures?"

Linda Gordon said, "Your client was granted bail the day after he was arrested. Waiting to be certain of the evidence imposes no hardship on him."

"But it's an obvious injustice. Eric Fuller is accused of killing a woman who is standing here in front of us. What could possibly be the point of prolonging this?"

"She *looks* like Wendy Harper. We all knew that from the minute she walked in the door. Do you imagine that if someone wanted to bring in an impostor, they would bring in someone who *didn't* look like Wendy Harper?"

"I *am* Wendy Harper. Who would be crazy enough to impersonate me? People are trying as hard as they can to kill me."

Linda Gordon turned to Wendy. "You think you can stroll in here, say you're Wendy Harper, and the whole criminal-justice system will move instantly to do your bidding? Well, it's not quite that easy. The system works on its own time, after all the evidence is in. When we hear what the FBI's experts have to say about the fingerprints and the DNA, then we'll know who you are."

Till said, "This isn't fair. Miss Harper came here voluntarily because you said her presence was the only proof you would accept to prove she hadn't been murdered. There was an assurance that if she took that risk, the charges would be dropped."

"Who assured her it would all happen in ten minutes?"

"The whole point of framing Eric Fuller was to get her to Los Angeles. Every minute that she's here, the danger increases." He turned to Fallon. "What more can we give you?"

"I think I've got everything I need," he said.

Till looked at Linda Gordon. "Then I'll take Miss Harper out of here, and someday we can all hear officially what we already know."

"Don't leave Los Angeles," said Linda Gordon. "And make sure my office knows exactly where you are at every moment."

"What?" said Wendy.

"You heard me. If you *aren't* Wendy Harper, then what you've just done is an obstruction of justice, for starters. Mr. Till will be your codefendant. If you *are* Wendy Harper, then there are other things that you need to talk about with the police. We understand you have been withholding information about a possible homicide that occurred six years ago. You also may be charged with grand theft in connection with a fraudulent life-insurance claim. I'm being very casual about this because you came on your own. But don't test me."

"Excuse me," Chernoff broke in. "Since this isn't over, we might as well get a few more things on the record. Don't anyone leave just yet."

Till said, "All right, Jay. What is it?"

"Give me a few more minutes." He took out his cell phone and dialed. "Okay. Pull up ahead of my car and come in. We're expecting you."

Linda Gordon turned to stare at Chernoff. "What are you doing? This isn't the time for the kind of antics you pull in the courtroom. We all have other things to do."

"Nothing as important as this," Chernoff said.

"This is ridiculous," she said. "Your client isn't sitting in a cell surrounded by psychopaths. He's in his very expensive house or his famous restaurant."

"His reputation is priceless, and his arrest has been all over the press. He deserves to be exonerated as quickly as possible. And when it's appropriate, as visibly as possible."

There was the sound of a car's tires scraping the curb across the street, then a car door slamming, then another. Poliakoff pushed the curtain aside a few inches to look out the front window, then stepped to the door and opened it.

The first person in the door was a pretty woman about thirty years old with long brown hair and blue eyes. "Wendy!" She rushed to throw her arms around Wendy Harper. "Where have you been?"

Wendy said, "Olivia. Did you come back just for this?"

"No," she said. "I've been back for three years. I still work at Banque."

A man in the doorway came forward. "Wendy, it's really good to see you again." He took his turn to hug Wendy, but there was a self-conscious, reserved quality to the embrace. "We were all afraid you were dead."

Wendy said, "It's nice to see you too, David. Are you still at the restaurant, too?"

"No," he said. "Except once in a while if somebody is sick. I've been getting work as an actor. Olivia and I are married."

Olivia held her left hand out to Wendy, and Wendy said, "Wow, look at that rock!"

Olivia said, "David got an airline commercial. He makes a cute pilot."

Till watched Wendy as a third person came in the door, and her eyes began to fill with tears. "Eric!"

He stepped forward, looking tired and shaken, and said, "Do I get one of those hugs, too?"

"Try and stop me." She threw her arms around his neck and they embraced hard. "I missed you so much." After a few seconds, she pulled back to look at him. "You look good for a condemned man."

"Thank God you came back," he said. "I've heard what you've had to go through to get here. Why did you ever leave in the first place?"

"I was just so scared, and I had to get away. I never imagined you could be accused of killing me." Her eyes drifted to Jack Till. "I came back because this whole nightmare has got to end." She hugged Eric again and then, after a few seconds, they parted.

Linda Gordon turned to Chernoff. "Do you want to tell me the purpose of all this?"

"Depositions," Chernoff said. "You and I and Sergeant Poliakoff and Officer Fallon can go into your kitchen and take some official statements." He turned to the newcomers. "I assume you can all swear on pain of perjury that this woman is the same Wendy Harper you knew six years ago?"

"Of course," Olivia said. "Let's get it over with so we can catch up on things."

"I don't see any point in deposing anyone," Linda Gordon said. "We'll have irrefutable scientific evidence in a couple of weeks, and it will make witnesses irrelevant."

Jack Till said, "You weren't shy about taking an official statement from me when I went to see you the first time. It doesn't matter if you won't take a statement from them, though. Sergeant Poliakoff is the detective in charge of a murder investigation. He can interview anyone he pleases, tape-record their statements, or take his own notes."

"You came to me and offered to give me your statement voluntarily, so I took it," Linda Gordon said. "But this is no longer a matter for the opinions of witnesses. Either she is Wendy Harper, or she isn't."

Poliakoff had made a decision. "Tim, take a few pictures of everyone here."

"What's that for?" Linda Gordon asked.

"It will help me identify them later."

She turned to stare at Chernoff, who seemed uncharacteristically silent. "You're planning to call me in front of the judge, aren't you? You'll put me under oath and force me to say that all of these people recognized each other."

"I don't want to do anything theatrical."

"Do you honestly not understand why I feel it's best to wait until the positive scientific evidence is in?"

"I don't."

"All right, then. We'll take depositions."

Chernoff said, "Olivia? Would you like to go first?"

"Yes." And she walked into the kitchen ahead of the others. The two lawyers swore her in and explained perjury to her. Then each of them asked her questions. "How long did you know Wendy Harper?"

"Ten years."

"Don't count the six when she was missing."

"Four years, then."

"How often did you see her?"

"Every day."

Her husband David said, "I knew her for four years at the

restaurant. Olivia was the first person hired to work at Banque, and then she persuaded Wendy to hire me."

"*Wendy* hired you, not Eric?"

"Wendy ran the dining room and the bar. I was a bartender."

"How well did you know her?"

"Extremely well."

"What do you mean by that?"

"She and I, um, dated once."

Jack Till was the last one in the kitchen. Linda Gordon began, "Do you swear that the woman you brought here today is the same Wendy Harper you helped to disappear six years ago?" Then: "Did you ever reveal to anyone what you had done?"

"Not until the day I read in the paper that Eric Fuller had been charged with her murder."

"But otherwise you didn't reveal it to anyone?"

"No."

"You know that there was a large life insurance policy on Miss Harper that Eric Fuller collected on?"

"I've heard that. You'll have to ask him."

"You know you're guilty of assisting him in a life-insurance fraud?"

"No, I'm not," Till said.

Chernoff said, "Hold it, Miss Gordon. I need to interrupt this for a moment." He turned off the tape recorder.

"Is there a problem?"

"Yes. I see you're searching for a pretext to try to detain either Miss Harper or Mr. Till. The reason I stopped the tape was to save you from going on the record with something that would have terrible consequences for you. I assure you that any charges will be dropped, and you'll spend the rest of your career fighting to keep from being fired and disbarred."

"Are you threatening me?"

"Of course it's a threat. My God, are you listening at all?"

"This meeting is over," she said. "You can all leave my house now."

"I'm happy to do that," Chernoff said. "I'll be petitioning the judge to dismiss the charges against Eric Fuller before the end of the afternoon. If I were you, I'd try to get in first to drop the charges before then. But you suit yourself."

Chernoff crossed the room in ten quick paces, opened the door and stopped only long enough to say, "Eric, I'll call you later when the charges are dismissed." Then he was out the door.

Eric nodded, then looked at Wendy. "Do you think we could talk?"

Wendy looked at Eric, then at Till. Jack Till hid his instinctive feeling of jealousy and his more reasoned dread of loss. He said, "I don't think Miss Gordon wants us here, and I don't want you standing around on a street in plain sight. Wendy, you can ride with Eric, and I can follow you to the police station. Eric, do you know how to get there?"

"Unfortunately, I do," Eric said.

Linda Gordon came out of the kitchen, and she seemed to be propelled toward the door. She hurried past them, flung the front door open, and stepped out onto the porch. Jay Chernoff's red Saab was just pulling away from the curb as she shouted, "Mr. Chernoff!" She waved her arm frantically. "Mr. Chernoff!"

Jack Till saw her do a quick half-turn and then fall sideways on the porch before he heard the distant report of the gun. He and Poliakoff dropped to their knees on opposite sides of Linda Gordon's fallen body. Each of them grasped an arm to drag her inside. Till kicked the door shut, and then he and Poliakoff were up and at the windows, trying to locate the shooter.

"Rifle," Till said.

"A sound delay," said Poliakoff. "At least half a second."

"Six or seven hundred feet."

"The hill at the end of the street."

"There's an empty lot, and I think there's a road up above, so it could have been one of the back yards. Call it in."

Poliakoff took a hand radio out of his pocket. "This is Sergeant Poliakoff. I am under sniper fire at 5605 Greenbelt Street, Sherman Oaks. There's a gunshot victim here, and I need an ambulance. I think the sniper is at the south end of Greenbelt on the hillside. It's three blocks south of Ventura, four blocks west of Coldwater. I'll stand by."

Till was back on the floor with Linda Gordon. "Wendy," he said. "Get a couple of blankets and a pillow off her bed." To Linda Gordon, he said, "You're going to be just fine. You got clipped in the shoulder, but it went right through. We're going to make you comfortable, and the ambulance will be here in a minute."

Wendy knelt beside Jack with the blankets and pillow. Till gently lifted Linda Gordon's head and slipped the pillow under, then covered her with the blankets. As Wendy bent over her, he noticed how closely Wendy's long blond hair matched the color of Linda Gordon's.

37

PAUL TURNER RAN down the hill with long strides that his momentum lengthened into jumps and landings, and then he was off the hill and into the car. "Got her," he said. "High on the left side, maybe the heart."

Sylvie looked into the rearview mirror and pulled the car away from the curb, then continued up Valley Vista. "You're sure it was fatal?"

"I can't give you a firm medical prognosis through a rifle scope," he said. "All I can do is hit her with a .308 and clear my calendar in case there's a funeral."

"I suppose," she said. The road skirted the low hills in winding curves toward the west. She couldn't drive as fast as she wanted to because this was a suburban residential area, with stop signs and streets coming in on the right every two hundred feet or so. A few of the curves were blind, and this was not a time when they could afford to risk an accident. Paul opened his window. She said, "Can you close your window?"

"Why?"

"It's creating a vacuum or something and it's hurting my ears."

"I'm listening for sirens."

"We won't have any trouble hearing them. If you drive with your window open, people think you're drunk or smoking pot."

He sighed, pressed the button, and watched the window slide up. "I can't believe how great this feels."

"I guess I'm still a little bit behind you," she said. "Everything about this job has been hard until two minutes ago. I need to get used to the idea that Wendy Harper is finally dead, and we can take a vacation."

Paul was grinning. "It's great. I knew the thing to do was follow Eric Fuller. I knew damned well that wherever she was, he would turn up."

"You get full credit." At the time when they had been planning, Sylvie had been about to suggest the same thing, but she had wisely decided to let his idea be the one they chose. She had seen nothing objectionable in it, and she had known that if it turned out to be a mistake, she would rather blame him than be blamed. She had also decided that it was a good strategy to accept his idea without a murmur because her acquiescence would give him confidence. Killing was mostly psychology. Paul had followed Eric Fuller to the safe house easily and bagged Wendy Harper with a single shot from two hundred yards out, so obviously Sylvie had been right. She congratulated herself silently. "You're the best," she said.

He said, "I knew that no matter what else she did, as soon as she hit town, they would see each other. He could hardly have her come all the way down here after six years to save his ass and not even thank her. It just wouldn't be natural. And from our point of view, I knew he was going to be perfect. The one you want to shadow isn't some cop who follows people for a living, and is perfectly capable of noticing you and getting you arrested. It's the sorry bastard who spends his time in a restaurant chopping onions."

Sylvie kept herself from speaking. At times she felt amazement at how egocentric men were. It had not yet occurred to him that he owed her a share in the congratulations. Killing Wendy Harper had not been a matter of following a lovesick chef from La Cienega to Greenbelt Street and sitting behind a bush waiting for a chance to pop an unsuspecting woman. There had been plenty of effort and frustration for Sylvie, too.

Paul seemed to notice that she wasn't seconding everything he said anymore. "But I can't take all the credit. You did a great job on this, too, Sylvie. Really."

She detected in herself a perverse urge to bait him, to say, "Oh? What did I do?" She knew by now that he would say something patronizing: "What? Oh, a lot. You were with me all the way." She forced herself to forgo the opportunity to make herself irritated and miserable. That was another skill she had picked up during a long marriage. She could see quarrels coming from a great distance, could play them out in her mind to confirm that there was nothing for her to gain, and then decline them. "You're sweet, Paul."

She swerved into the turn at Beverly Glen, crossed the intersection at the Cadillac dealership onto Tyrone, and kept going north toward home. She moved up the back streets until she came to Vanowen, and then followed it west nearly to their house. She was thinking ahead. In less than a day, they could be on their way to Madrid.

She drove up to the house and pulled into the driveway. It was late afternoon now, and other people in the neighborhood would be getting home soon. That felt good. She loved living a secret life while appearing to be doing exactly what other people did. She pushed the button on the opener and watched the garage door roll up. She drove in, turned off the engine, and closed the door behind them. "We finally killed the bitch, and now we're home free. I love it, and I love you." She leaned over and kissed Paul's cheek.

"I love you, too," Paul said. "Just one more thing, and we'll be on our vacation."

They got out and Sylvie went to unlock the kitchen door. Paul brought the rifle and ammunition in. He said, "All we really have to do is go pick up our million bucks."

"You don't mean now, tonight?"

"Sure I do. We did the job, and he said he'd collect the money and have it waiting. That was the arrangement."

"But we don't need to have a million dollars in cash tonight. It's silly. I wouldn't even know where to put it all. We've already got so much cash for the trip that I'm worried about it."

"It's not important where we put it," Paul said. "We'll shove it under the bed, or in the oven or something until we can put it into safe-deposit boxes. That isn't the point. We go to pick it up tonight because we don't want to give Scott Schelling a few days to dream up a way to keep us from collecting. We don't have to be rude about it, or anything—just cool and businesslike. We show up and say, 'We did what you asked, and here we are. Time to pay. Bye-bye.'"

Sylvie nodded. "Okay. Give me a chance to change."

"I've got to get this rifle ready to dump before we go see Schelling."

"Okay." Sylvie went off to take another shower and dress. She knew that they were going to be out late tonight, so she selected a pair of black pants and a black pullover and black shoes. Black was always right in these ambiguous evening situations, and she looked good in black.

When she came out of the shower, Paul was in the bedroom already dressed in a pair of nicely pressed gray pants, a dark blue shirt, and a black jacket.

"You don't need to get dressed. You look incredible." He plucked the towel off her, then put his arms around her and held her there.

"I'm cold. Cut it out. I want to get dressed. This isn't the time." She held herself rigid, her back hunched over.

He kept his arms around her for two more seconds, as though she might relent, then let her go. "I suppose it's not." He turned and walked out of the bedroom. She felt relieved for a few seconds because he intended to leave her in peace. She knew she had hurt his feelings, and knew that she shouldn't have been quite so insensitive to his mood. He was still feeling manic about their difficult victory, their sudden freedom from that awful job.

She should have been flirtatious and teasing, and made him go away feeling good about her. Instead she had fended him off clumsily, so she had looked unattractive, and actually stood there like a statue, like a symbol of frigidity. As she dressed, she cursed herself for being so slow to think. It was just that she had been forcing herself to face her tension about Scott Schelling, and fear was not an aphrodisiac.

Sylvie finished dressing, then did her makeup and hair, unable to stop thinking about her foolish miscalculation. She went out looking for Paul. She found him in the kitchen wearing a pair of surgical rubber gloves, dismantling the rifle he had used on Wendy Harper this afternoon. The scope, the ammunition and the magazine had been removed and put away, probably in the gun safe. He had the barrel off, the bolt and the receiver out, and he had dismantled the action so the trigger, sear and spring were on the table.

She came up behind him and kissed the back of his neck. He didn't move. "I'm sorry, Paul. I'm in love with you. I didn't mean to be unfriendly." She had her hands on his shoulders. She kept them there and leaned down to kiss his cheek. She could feel his jaw muscle working, and it frightened her. He was beyond feeling upset and unappreciated, he was angry. She walked around him, knelt on the kitchen floor in front of him and spoke softly, her hands on his knees and moving upward. "Don't be hurt." She looked up at him. "Oh. I just thought of something that might make you feel better." She undid his belt.

Later, when it was over, Paul seemed happy and relaxed again. She watched him take the pieces of the rifle and put them in a plastic trash bag so he could drop them in a Dumpster on the way to see Scott Schelling. Sylvie was feeling confident. She had been very foolish before, but at least she'd had the presence of mind to fix things. Letting Paul stay angry would have been a mistake.

She walked around the house checking to be sure everything was locked or turned off. When she had verified that things were as she wanted them, she joined Paul in the garage, watched him engage the deadbolt, and got into the car.

As Paul backed the car out of the garage, she said, "So we're off. Do we know where we're going?"

"Yes. We're going to his office first. If he isn't there, he'll be at home."

"Where is Crosswinds Records?"

"Burbank, on Riverside. You know where all those other companies are—Warner Records, the Disney Channel and DIC and all that stuff? It's right along there in one of those buildings."

He drove eastward on the Ventura Freeway to the 134 Freeway and got off on Buena Vista, then parked the car off Riverside in the lot beneath Dalt's Restaurant. Instead of taking the elevator into the restaurant, they walked up the entrance ramp to the street. They kept going along Riverside until they came to one of the tall buildings of reflective glass that had sprouted oddly on the island between Alameda and Riverside, like a mirage in the midst of the old one-story stores and restaurants. "This is the one," Paul said. "Let's look around."

Sylvie understood. Looking around meant assessing the security. It was nearly dark, and the street lamps had come on, but it was easy to stay in the dimmer spaces away from them. The building was like the others, all glass and steel and hard corners, set right on the sidewalk a few feet from the curb. When they walked past the front door, she could see into the lobby, where two men sat behind a counter. Above them was a sign that said, "Please check in," and the counter was situated so nobody could reach the elevators in the alcove beyond without being seen. Sylvie said, "This isn't looking simple, is it?"

"It's not impossible. Let's try the easy way first. Keep walking." Paul took out his cell phone and a piece of paper, and dialed the number on it. "Hello," he said. "I'd like to speak with Mr. Schelling, please."

The woman on the other end had a silky, calm voice of the sort that made people put up with more delay and neglect than they had believed they could. "May I ask what this refers to?"

She had lost him. He said, "It's a personal call, and he's expecting it. I'm a friend of his, and my name is Paul."

"One moment, please." There was a delay so long that he wondered if she had answered another line and forgotten about him. Just as he considered ending the call and starting over again, she was back. "I'm afraid he can't speak with you right now, but he asked if you could meet him after he finishes his conference."

"Where does he want to meet?"

"He suggested Harlan's, just down the street from the Crosswinds offices. Do you know where that is?"

"Yes. What time?"

"Can you be there in thirty minutes?"

"Tell him I'll be there."

"He'll meet you at the back entrance by the parking lot."

Paul disconnected and kept walking beside Sylvie. "His secretary says he wants to meet us at that restaurant down the street— Harlan's. She says he'll come in the back door in a half hour."

Sylvie shrugged. "It's sort of a dark place inside. It's got booths, and it's probably not such a bad place to hand over some money."

"Maybe not. I don't like letting him choose the place, though. Let's go check it out before he gets there."

"Do you want to bring the car?"

"No, let's keep it out of sight."

They walked up Riverside past Bob's Big Boy, a forties-era burger restaurant with a huge chubby-cheeked boy in front. On Friday nights the parking lot of Bob's was full of people who had brought customized antique cars for other aficionados to admire. At the next block, they turned and began to walk along the alley behind the stores and restaurants on the north side of Riverside. To their left were the back entrances, and on the right were the parking lots.

Harlan's was a low wooden building that looked as though it belonged on a wharf. Paul said, "He'll be here in about twenty-five minutes. What do you think of the place?"

"I don't know. There are a lot of people making a lot of noise down the street and in the front, but it's pretty deserted back here. I don't like it."

"Neither do I. What do you want to do?"

"Anything. I'll be perfectly happy to write off the money, get in the car, and head for the airport."

"We may have to do that yet. Let's go across the street to Marie Callender's and watch the parking-lot entrance from there. If he drives in, we'll see him."

"All right." They walked back along the alley a few steps, and a big beige Chevrolet sedan swung into the lot from the other end, its front end bobbing upward at the bump and then down, the headlights flashing in Sylvie's eyes. The car stopped ahead of them, idling. When Sylvie shaded her eyes, she could see the driver was a tall man wearing a red tie and sport coat. A shorter, darker man sat in the passenger seat. The driver opened his door and got out. "Mr. and Mrs. Turner?"

Sylvie whispered to Paul, "Get ready."

Paul called back to the man, "What can I do for you?"

"Would you come with us, please? We're here to take you to the meeting."

Paul and Sylvie had already begun sidestepping apart. "That's not the arrangement."

"It's a precaution. All you have to do is get in the car."

Sylvie had her gun in her hand inside the jacket pocket. She glanced at Paul, and she could see that his longer legs had carried him to the other side of the car. His right hand was at his belt, and his knees were slightly bent. Sylvie selected her targets. She would fire first at the man who had gotten out, then at the shorter, dark-haired man in the passenger seat, who seemed to have a bandaged head. Sylvie would have little time to react, so she moved her eyes from one to the other, practicing.

Paul said, "I'm not comfortable with this. Call him and tell him."

The man who was standing beside the car said, "We're police officers, and you're going to have to come with us." He opened his coat to reach for a gun, and Sylvie caught sight of a badge. The man in the passenger seat flung the door open on the other side of the car.

Sylvie shot the man who was holding his coat open, then dropped to her knees and fired into the passenger seat at the dark-haired man while Paul fired into the windshield.

The short, dark man was wounded, but he managed to slide into the driver's seat and step on the gas pedal. The car lurched ahead at Paul, but he jumped aside and fired three more rounds. The car coasted a few feet, then bumped into a fence made of steel cables strung between poles, and stopped at the edge of the parking lot.

Paul yanked the driver's door open, dragged the dead man out onto the ground, and took his place. Sylvie climbed into the back seat. Paul drove the car down the alley, up Riverside for a couple of blocks, and then turned to the side street and drove until they were back on the street behind Dalt's. He pulled to the curb and wiped off the steering wheel and door handles. They climbed out and walked down the ramp to the parking lot beneath the building, and drove out in their black BMW.

They raced along Riverside to Barham, then past the Warner Brothers studios over the hill to the freeway entrance. Paul muttered, "Jesus. Fake cops. I can't believe I let him set us up like that."

"That's really about all I can take," Sylvie said. "This has been nothing but misery."

"Giving up?"

"No. But I'm not sure what I'm after is going to be money."

38

SCOTT SCHELLING felt his cell phone vibrate in his coat pocket. This was the third time tonight, and each time, he could feel his heartbeat quicken with excitement. The news was better and better each time. He glanced at the other end of the room. Ray Klein was about midway in his cocktail-party speech about the fully integrated electronics conglomerate, so there was plenty of time to answer the call.

He made his way through the vast living room slowly, careful not to look as though he was in a hurry. Doing business at these parties was considered rude. But he was anxious to return Tiffany's call. Her first call had been the most important one. She had conveyed the message from Paul that everything had gone as he had hoped. That meant that Wendy Harper was dead at last. Scott had been in a state of buoyant good spirits since that moment, which he recognized as a turning point in his life. For six years—the years when he had been working to build his reputation and gain power at Crosswinds Records—he had been afraid.

He had tried to be cautious about having his picture taken or being on television, but he still had to do his job and live his life, and they were the same. Work was social. Scott Schelling had always taken women to parties and used his business relationships with musicians to impress them. He had talked to women in the way he had talked to the musicians. He told each of them she was the very best, the one he wanted above all the others. He implied as clearly as he could that he would give them everything they could ever want, just because they were special. He would give the woman of the moment a sample, a taste of what was to come. It would be a watch or a bracelet, usually, something that had cost enough to let her know he was not the same as her old boyfriends.

Scott had been very generous about exposing the new woman to the talent right away, to demonstrate that he was an important man. He let her meet the stars, dance with them, drink with them, talk to them. But being with music celebrities was a mixed experience for a young woman. Many of the stars were wild and sloppy, drinking heavily, or disappearing for a few minutes and returning with a manic craziness and dilated pupils. Offstage, stars were often crude and boorish and even frightening. The woman could see the freak show, be dazzled and fascinated, but after a surprisingly short time, Scott would feel the woman clinging to his arm again, half-hiding herself behind his reassuring dark suit coat and his sobriety and reliability.

Scott stopped to say hello to Bill Calder, the Entertainment Division Comptroller, then eased by Calder's wife, confiding, "Excuse me, my phone is ringing," and out the open arch into the cactus garden. He liked Klein's Santa Fe house. It was adobe, with big timbers in the ceilings and every portal curved. When he was certain that nobody was near him, he took out his telephone, pressed Tiffany's number, and said, "It's me."

"Scotty, it's both of us—Tiffany and Kimberly—on a conference line. We wanted to be positive you wouldn't be needing us any more tonight."

"Did you have someone meet the gentleman who called earlier?"

"Do you mean Paul?"

"Yes," he said.

"I called the number you left me."

"Good. If everything's taken care of, there's no reason to hang around. Just reconfirm the time of my flight tomorrow morning and turn out the lights. And make sure somebody remembers to feed my dog tomorrow."

"Thanks, Scotty," Tiffany said. "See you Monday morning."

He hung up. He inhaled, and as his lungs expanded he felt even happier. He felt a crazy, impulsive wish to do something for those two, like give them both a huge raise. But he couldn't do that every time he felt happy. And Bill Calder, who was no more than fifty feet away from him right now, would see the raise and want to know the justification. Maybe Scott would take them with him on a trip. There was one scheduled for later next month to France and Germany for some conference or other.

He put away his phone and made his way back to the party. The people at this party were alien to Scott Schelling. The presidents of all the other subsidiaries were married, and they brought their wives—all blond and tall and twenty to thirty years younger than their husbands, but all showing face-lifts and teeth with the whiteness of a porcelain sink. He was never sure what to make of these women because there was no way to read their expressions.

Their husbands were slightly easier for him, because he could recognize the hostility and suspicion when he talked to them. As he stepped inside from the desert garden, he saw that Taylor Gaines had been watching him. Gaines was the head of the finance subsidiary of the parent company, the one that used the profits from each of the divisions to make loans. Gaines said, "Hello, Scott. Got to keep on top of the trends even while you're here, don't you?"

"That's right, Taylor. If you're not ahead, you're behind."

Scott hurried down the hallway and noticed he was moving past framed antique drawings and maps from the Spanish era. His girls had done their job beautifully when they had bought an old map as a present for Jill Klein. As he had the thought, he remembered that they had not needed to strain much to accomplish it. Ray Klein had probably told them what to buy.

Everything that happened seemed to be controlled by Ray Klein. Ray Klein wanted the girls to please Scott Schelling with their efficiency so Scott would keep them on his staff. That way they could keep feeding Ray Klein information. Klein wanted Scott to feel good about his relationship with him, to feel that he had done well and Klein appreciated and liked him. Klein wanted his wife, Jill, to have a nice addition to her collection so she could feel involved and admired, and not have as much brain space to observe her husband's relations with Martha Rodall, vice president of the Public Relations Division. All this was what Ray Klein was famous for: managing his people.

Scott slipped past white-shirted waiters serving tiny blue-corn tamales, ahi tuna on small beds of rice, and cocktails, and into the center of the party, just close enough to Ray Klein to be sure that Klein included him in any mental roll-call he was taking, but not close enough to be an obstruction or a distraction. Scott made sure he had been seen, and then smiled and shook hands with Sam Hardesty, the head of the Aerospace Electronics Division. "Hi, Sam. Scott Schelling, Crosswinds Records. How are you tonight?"

"Fine. Yourself?" Hardesty was nearly seventy with white hair and the build of the retired general he was.

"Great," said Schelling. "It's such a beautiful night, and I find getting out of Los Angeles this time of year a treat. Hell, just getting out of the office is a treat. How are your numbers going to come in this quarter?"

Hardesty flinched at the directness of the question. "I'm afraid that's not a number I can give out just yet."

"Oh? Classified?"

"No. But it's inside information. You work in a different company, even though we own it. It's against SEC rules for me to tell you."

"Well, then, good luck with it," Scott said. He moved deeper into the room toward the next set of executives, a pair of computer-hardware nerds from Syn-Final Microsystems, when he felt something touch his arm. As he began to turn he saw the hand. On one of the fingers was a bean-sized emerald with diamonds around it. He lifted his eyes to see Jill Klein's face close to his.

"Scotty," she said, her voice low and conspiratorial. "I just had to take you aside and tell you how much I love the map." From this close, he could see that her face showed signs of surgical procedures. The skin above the cheekbones had been tightened from the sides so her oversized eyes looked permanently startled. She leaned close and kissed his cheek with pillowy lips. "It's really gorgeous." She smiled. "Sometimes a thank-you note just isn't enough."

"*I* should thank *you*. I'd rather have a kiss than a note any day."

"Would you like to see where I've hung it?"

"Sure."

She walked him out to the fringes of the party, along a wide hallway toward the back of the house. He could hear the sounds of caterers working in a restaurant-size kitchen beyond the big doors at the end of the hall. As he walked, he tried to remember the description that Kimberly and Tiffany had recited to him so he would recognize it when he saw it. He remembered something about California being an island. The kitchen sounds made him sure they were near the dining room. Maybe she had hung it there, where the other guests would have to look at it and envy his taste and thoughtfulness.

But she turned in the other direction, up a narrow staircase that led to the second floor. She took a few steps and opened a door. "This is my personal suite." There was a large sitting room decorated with kachina dolls and Navajo rugs, furnished with couches and a heavy antique desk of dark wood. Above it he could see several old documents framed, but not a map.

"This is really a beautiful room," he said.

"Oh, yes. It's quiet and private." She opened a door beyond the desk, and led him into a bedroom. There was a maid in the room, busy arranging something in the drawers of a dresser. "Here it is." She pointed to the inner wall of the room. The map was larger than Schelling had imagined, a folio-sized sheet in a thin black frame hung on the uneven faux-adobe surface.

"It looks very authentic there," he said. He was relieved that he didn't have to pick it out of a whole row of nearly identical maps.

Jill Klein turned to the maid. "Consuelo, make sure we're not disturbed."

Consuelo scuttled out of the room. He heard the sound of a lock clicking, then, a few seconds later, another.

She said, "When I'm thanking someone, I think the old ways are best, don't you?" She put her arms around his neck and kissed him on the lips.

Schelling was shocked, alarmed. He had no response ready. "I don't think this is smart," he said. "Your husband is—"

"Downstairs at the party with his mistress." She took his hands and put them around her waist. "Just be quick, so nobody gets embarrassed."

The telephone in Scott's coat began to vibrate again. In the silence it gave an audible buzz, and he jumped as though they had been caught.

"Turn that thing off."

He dug the phone out and flipped it open. "Yes?"

It was Tiffany's voice. "Scotty, I'm sorry to call again, but I'm in my car, and the news is saying that the two men you were asking about have been shot to death."

"Are you sure?"

"The description is the same. And it's the parking lot behind Harlan's, where I told them to meet Paul."

"All right. Thanks."

"What do you want me to do?"

"Go home. Do nothing. Say nothing. I'll see you Monday morning." He disconnected.

Jill Klein had turned away from him, and now she was walking toward the door. He said, "Jill. Please wait."

She stopped and looked over her shoulder as she reached for the doorknob. "Jill? To you I'm Mrs. Klein. I'll always be Mrs. Klein." She opened the door. He could see that in the office Consuelo had been sitting on the couch in near-darkness, probably so nobody would see light under the door. She stood up quickly, turned on the light, and unbolted the door so Jill Klein did not have to break her stride on the way out.

Schelling walked through the sitting room past Consuelo, but she did not meet his gaze. As far as he could tell, her eyes had never moved to his face. She was obviously paid never to see or hear.

As Schelling walked to the back stairwell, he saw Jill Klein far ahead of him near the front of the building, turning to go down a different staircase. She looked in his direction, but it was only for a second, and her face was utterly blank. She was timing her descent to coincide with his so it was not possible for anyone downstairs to see them both.

Schelling went downstairs, skirted the group in the living room, went outside to the garden again, and dialed his phone. He heard the voice of Dale, his personal trainer. "Dale here."

"Hi. It's Scotty. Are you alone? Can you talk?"

"Sure. I'm at home doing my own workout. What's wrong, Scotty?"

"I'm in Santa Fe, and I've only got a minute or two to talk. You really were a marine, right?"

"Yes."

"You were trained to kill people?"

"Well, yeah, I guess so. I mean, that's what it boils down to. That's what war is. It's for your country, for the rest of the people, but they train you to fight."

"Have you ever killed anybody?"

"Me? No. When I was in Desert Storm, they kept me in Kuwait, making newly arrived National Guardsmen do push-ups and squat-thrusts while they got used to the heat. I was sent to Haiti and Liberia, and I didn't get even that close. Most of that time I was on a ship outside the harbor."

"But you knew how. And you were ready, right?"

"Sure, but I don't get why you're asking."

"I need a huge favor."

"Wait a minute."

"I'll make it worthwhile."

"Scotty—"

"Look, I'm in terrible trouble. I'm in Santa Fe tonight on business, but tomorrow I have to get on a plane and go back home. These people have already killed some people who work for me. I'm in danger. It's a self-defense situation. It's self-defense."

"Have you talked to the police about this?"

"Dale, this is way beyond that stage, and I don't have time to explain it all."

He heard a deep sigh. "Scotty, I can't help you on something like this."

"Please."

"What?"

"I said please. If you can't do it, then give me a name. I can take it from there. If you don't want to have me use your name, I won't."

"I'm sorry. I don't do that kind of work, and I don't know people who do."

Scott laughed. He decided the sound was no more false than

any other laugh he had given. There was silence on the other end, so he said, "Got you! It was just a joke, Dale. I was just yanking your chain. You fell for it, though. Admit it."

"Scotty, if you're in some kind of trouble, I think you've got to go to the authorities. If you're not, and this really is a joke, then your sense of humor is really sick."

"I'm sorry, buddy. I was just calling to tell you I won't be back in time for our workout session tomorrow, and the idea came to me, so I went with it. If it wasn't funny, I apologize. It seemed funny at the time."

"Are you sure you're telling me the truth now?"

"Of course I am. Look, I'm in a hurry right now, but I'll give you a call when I'm free to slip a workout into my schedule. Take care, Dale."

"All right. Call me."

Scott Schelling stood motionless for a moment with the dead phone in his hand, every muscle rigid with fear and regret and humiliation. What if he hadn't convinced Dale that he'd been joking? No, he decided. He had to stop that train of thought now. He couldn't spend any time worrying about Dale. What was he going to do—hire somebody else to kill Dale? He had to keep from getting crazy.

As he let his brain concentrate on the problem of the Turners, he fought his fear and anxiety and forced himself to think about what he was going to do. He had hired the Turners, promised them a million dollars in cash to kill Wendy Harper. When they had succeeded, he had tried to have them killed, but the Turners had survived. The only person he had left that he could trust was Carl, and Carl couldn't fix this alone. But Scott still had one other asset—the million dollars. It was in a suitcase in the trunk of his car in Los Angeles.

He heard music, and looked back through the French doors into the hallway and the living room. There was a group of mariachis at the edge of the cocktail party, strumming instruments and singing. There were no signs the guests were going in to dinner yet. He punched Carl's number into his cell phone.

"Hello?"

"Carl. It's me. The two jerks who met with the Turners got killed."

"Holy shit! When?"

"A little while ago, but Tiffany says it's already on the radio. I want you to talk to the Turners. Tell them I want to pay them what I owe them, but I'm out of town until tomorrow. Tell them those two were trying to turn on me, kill the Turners, and keep the money for themselves. Got it?"

"Yes. I'll try to reach them."

"Carl, this isn't a time when you give it a try and see what you can do. You have to succeed. I'm trusting you with my life here."

"Okay, Scotty, okay. I didn't mean it like that. You know I'll do whatever it takes."

"Thanks, Carl. I've got to go now." He hung up and looked inside again. He was ashamed that he had panicked and tried to hire Dale to kill the Turners. Carl would use money to succeed with the Turners. Nobody wanted a half-second of revenge more than they wanted a million dollars. Once Carl paid them off, then he would be safer than he had been at any time in the last six years.

But there was one more problem that was nagging at him: the terrible mistake he'd made upstairs. He couldn't have Jill Klein as an enemy. She was his boss's wife, even if his boss slept with somebody else now and then. She could sour Scott's reputation with the board of directors of Aggregate, who were virtually all presidents of other big companies. She could squash somebody like Scott Schelling in a week.

He slipped indoors and began to search for her. He moved through the crowd, looking in every direction until he spotted her. She was at the far end of the big living room, standing with another lady and laughing at something the woman had said, her head back and her too-perfect teeth on display. Her eyes were always rolling to see how people around her were looking at her, but when she saw Scott Schelling, her laugh lost its energy and died.

He stood patiently a few feet off until she had to notice him or risk causing a scene. She nodded and stepped away, and he moved to intercept her. "Hello, Mrs. Klein." He held out his hand to her. "I don't know if you remember, but I'm Scott Schelling, Crosswinds Records. We met at the party a few months ago when Aggregate bought us up."

She stared at him with narrowed eyes. "Schelling? Yes, I believe I do remember. Nice to see you." She took a step to his right, to move past him.

"I sent you a small present, and I wondered if you had opened it."

Her eyes moved from side to side to be sure nobody was listening. She whispered, "What are you trying to do?"

"I'm trying to start over. I want to apologize for answering my telephone. It's a line I use only for emergencies. My mother has been hospitalized for over a week with a stroke, and the hospital wouldn't connect me with her room earlier. My secretary was calling to tell me she got through and my mother's doing better."

"Oh," she said. "I'm very sorry she's been ill."

"Thank you, Mrs. Klein."

"Jill. Please call me Jill."

"Jill, then. I wondered if you would be willing to show me where you've hung the map."

She looked around with the alertness of a deer. "There's not enough time now. I told the caterers to call everyone in to dinner in five minutes. Where are you staying?"

"The Eldorado. Room 362."

"Expect me at one." She turned and disappeared into the crowd, then reemerged on the other side of the room near her husband and Martha Rodall.

Schelling used up a few minutes trying to have conversations with the wives of two executives in the Legal Division. They were well trained in talking to men, but they seemed to be under the impression that all men wanted to talk about golf.

When dinner was announced, he filed into the dining room with the others and took his seat near the foot of the table among the executives from other minor subsidiaries of the parent company. It was like being one of the youngest children in a big, complicated family.

But tonight he didn't mind. He had just saved himself from destruction. Maybe he had even found the secret back stairway to the next level of success.

39

AFTER DARK, Jack Till walked along the sidewalk away from the hill and headed back toward Linda Gordon's house. He had watched the men and women beyond the yellow POLICE LINE DO NOT CROSS tape, searching for the brass casing from the rifle or any impression left on the dirt by the shooter's shoes, but Till had been forced to keep his distance. The police would stay at the scene for a while trying to get everything that there was, but he had known for hours that there was nothing left to find.

He walked back to the house. There were two cops still working the front yard, looking for the bullet that had passed through Linda Gordon's shoulder. They had a faint hope that it had gone into a tree trunk or a fence or the next house. He could see that others were finishing their door-to-door interviews in the neighborhood with the usual hopeless questions: "Did you happen to see?" "Did you happen to hear?" "Will you please call us right away if you hear of someone else who did?"

He went in the door and saw that Max Poliakoff was back inside, using the small kitchen table as his headquarters while the other cops searched. Till said, "Max, can I talk to you for a minute?"

"Sure."

"Have you found out anything about Kit Stoddard yet?"

"Hell, Jack. One crisis at a time. You gave me the name yesterday, and I've got a man on it. There was such a person, but the name probably was an alias, as you thought. She's not on any list that he's checked yet. Nobody he's talked to knows where she went."

"What about Scott?"

"Well, yeah, that's the important one, isn't it? He's even harder to find because we don't know where to begin. Apparently nobody knew anything about him even at the time when he was dating Kit Stoddard, including his last name—if Scott was his first name. He could have been from out of town—out of the country, even. He was seeing Kit, but none of her friends met him."

"I have a feeling," said Till.

"What's your feeling?"

"Ever since I went to talk to Linda Gordon a couple of months ago, I've thought there was something odd about her. She seemed to have an abnormal interest in how this case came out. She didn't want to hear that the victim was alive, she wanted Eric Fuller to go to trial. Did she strike you the same way?"

Poliakoff looked down at the table for a moment. "Yeah, actually, she did. I asked around, talked to some people in the department, and then a couple of contacts I have in the DA's office. The word is that she's always a competitor. But she really likes these cases where some guy victimizes a woman. It seems to inspire her, to make her feel like she's fighting for something. It makes her tough to beat in front of a jury. So the head deputy DA assigns a lot of them to her."

"You're telling me that what we saw here today was normal?"

Poliakoff shrugged. "What's normal?"

"If you hadn't thought she was behaving strangely, then you wouldn't have asked around about her."

"All right. That's true. But I can believe she just got carried away. Everybody here must have seemed like they were on the other side, trying to push her into rushing her decision. Maybe she felt cornered."

"There were four witnesses who had known Wendy Harper six years ago, and a police forensics technician who as good as told her that the picture he took of Wendy today matched her old driver's license. But she wanted to try to keep Wendy in town and vulnerable. You heard her trying to dream up charges to file to keep her here."

Poliakoff held up his hands. "What do you want from me, Jack? She's the prosecutor in the case."

"She just got shot."

"She got shot because all that blond hair made her look from a distance like Wendy Harper, and no other reason."

"She's an attempted murder victim, and it happened right here. This house is a crime scene. It's got her blood splattered on the front of it."

"You're telling me to search her house? What's the probable cause?"

"You don't need a warrant. You were already inside when the crime was committed, and the scene belongs to the detective in charge until he releases it."

"What the hell would I even be looking for?"

"What I'd be looking for is something that proves she knows a man named Scott."

"Scott? That's a stretch. There's no evidence that she's anything but overeager and suspicious."

"So look for some, and you might find it," Till said.

Poliakoff looked at him for a moment. "Wendy is waiting for you. Do you want to drive her to the station, or do you want us to do it?"

"*I* will. Is she alone?"

"She's out back talking to Eric Fuller."

Till walked to the front door, stepped carefully past the dried pool of Linda Gordon's blood, and then out onto the porch. He took a deep breath of the night air, then walked up the driveway to the corner of the house and stopped to compose himself. As he came around the corner, he saw Eric and Wendy sitting on a porch swing together. Were they holding hands? He couldn't tell from here.

Till stopped walking and said, "Hello. I'm sorry to interrupt."

Wendy turned toward Till and he advanced. He could see that she had been crying. She didn't rise, nor did Eric. Instead, she turned away from Till toward Eric and said, "I don't ever want to lose touch with you again."

Eric stood up and shook Till's hand. "I suppose you have to take her somewhere, right?"

Till nodded. "They want her at the station."

Eric said, "All right, then. It's the middle of dinner, and my sous-chefs and cooks have been making my new lobster risotto without me. I'd better show up and give them a hand." Eric's eyes were moving, staying away from anyone else's eyes. He turned, walked around the house, and up the driveway.

Till saw that Wendy was still crying. He tried to think of something to say.

She caught him looking at her. "I told him what I had been doing since we last saw each other."

"Oh," Till said. "Sometimes I think honesty is overrated."

"I think I knew that once, but forgot. Well, where are we going to go now? To the police station?"

"That's the second stop. First, St. Joseph's Hospital."

"Why?"

"Because that's where the ambulance took Linda Gordon."

They got into Till's rental car. He drove up the street a few yards, turned around, and headed out toward Ventura Boulevard, then turned east toward Burbank. They were quiet for a time, and then Wendy said, "We saved Eric. We accomplished what we had to do. Has it occurred to you yet that maybe what we ought to do next is get the hell out of here?"

"This isn't six years ago. Last time there didn't seem to be much choice, but this time, you aren't the only one who thinks that this Scott guy is a killer. If the cops keep at it, they'll get him, and this will be over forever."

"Then why don't we leave town and let them have at it?"

"Because I believe that for now you'll be safer here than running. And if I'm here, I can push some leads that I don't think the cops can follow."

"At the hospital?"

"To start."

"You're going to get in to see her by pretending you're still a cop, aren't you?"

"Maybe. I'm pretty good at it."

"Jack, even if you fool everybody and get in, she's not going to talk to you. She hates you. She hates *me*."

"Right now I'll bet she hates the man who shot her even more."

Till drove from Ventura Boulevard up Vineland. When he turned right onto Riverside for the last few blocks toward the hospital, he could see the lights of several police cars and a couple of ambulances blinking on Riverside. There were other emergency vehicles parked on the left side of the street. "There's something up ahead," he said.

Till drove up to the area, and found that the police were waving cars on, keeping them moving. He pulled off Riverside at Ponca, parked, and got out. "Come on. I don't want you alone in the car."

They walked across the street, and made their way through the crowd of people who had gathered. There was more police tape, and there were police officers busy working the area as a crime scene. There were two bodies lying in different parts of the alley. Till asked the man beside him, "What happened?"

"Those guys got shot a while ago. See?" He pointed at the bodies.

"What was it, a robbery?"

"I don't really know. I heard it was a carjacking."

Till edged closer to the nearest body. The police forensic people were kneeling on the rough pavement beside it, trying to measure angles and examine the ground for evidence. Till took Wendy's arm. "Look at this."

"I don't want to."

He pulled her closer. "Look."

She said, "My God! It's that guy. The one in Morro Bay."

Till pointed down the alley, where other officers were working beside a second body. "There's the man from the locker room." He took Wendy's arm. "Start walking." They began to walk toward the street. "I don't know who did this to them, but he didn't do it for us."

40

PAUL AND SYLVIE TURNER were already over the six-foot fence and walking on Scott Schelling's smooth, level green lawn. It was pleasant walking here because even at night it was easy to tell that nobody but the men who cut and rolled it had ever walked here, and because the fence was lined with taller hedges that made it safe for even Paul and Sylvie to stand erect as they made their way across the lawn. The two strolled toward the house, then stopped a distance from it and circled it slowly.

Their first stop was the garage. Paul took a small Maglite out of his pocket and shone it through the window at the side. He whispered, "There's a sports car, and a Lincoln Town Car."

"Good. He's probably home."

Paul nodded, and they resumed their walk. There were a number of procedures that they followed without discussion. They stayed ten or twelve feet away from the house while they studied it, so they were outside the range of motion detectors that could trigger floodlights. They checked the eaves and peaks of the house for surveillance cameras, although they didn't matter so much at this hour because nobody would be awake to watch the monitors. They examined the shrubs and perennials for signs of electrical wiring, checked the window screens for conductive mesh and the glass for silver wire. The doors were sturdy, well-made, and equipped with heavy gleaming hardware.

When they went around the corner, there was a metallic jingling, and then the sound of quick footsteps as a dog bounded across the lawn toward them. He was big, a retriever of some kind, and in a moment he was on them, panting and jumping. Paul petted him, then patted his shoulder, hard, whispering, "Good boy. Good boy," as he took out his gun. He held the silencer a few inches behind the dog's head and fired, then watched the dog fall to the grass and held the gun closer to fire a second round. Paul grasped the dog's hind foot and dragged it into a clump of bushes.

"The dog's our way in," Sylvie whispered. "I'll bet there's a doggy door."

"Let's take a look."

They continued their circuit until they came to the kitchen door in the back of the house, where there was a pet entrance cut into the lower panel. Paul and Sylvie knelt on the back steps to examine it.

"This has got to work. The alarm system is all pretty well wired," said Sylvie.

"And there are video cameras," said Paul. "We'll have to find the deck and erase the tapes or take the chips later."

Sylvie reached out and tested the pet door. "I'm sure I can fit through."

"It won't be wired, but we have to be careful about noise."

"Of course. And internal traps and electric eyes. You're sweet to worry."

"What are you going to do when you're in?"

"Wake him up, make him turn off the alarm, and let you in."

"Good. Warn him what happens if he pushes a call-the-cops code." He leaned close and kissed her cheek. "I love you, baby."

Paul put on his thin kidskin gloves while Sylvie did the same.

Paul lifted the clear plastic flap away from the dog door, held it up and whispered, "Good luck, baby."

"Thanks." Sylvie slipped her arms through the opening, shrugged to get her head and shoulders in, turned to the side to get her hips in, then turned the rest of the way to sit and pull her legs and feet in.

The kitchen was dark and quiet. She listened to the sounds of the building while her eyes accustomed themselves to the dark. Then she got up, took out her gun, and began to explore.

She found a dining room with a crystal chandelier and a long formal table and antique sideboards that didn't seem contemporary enough for a music executive. The living room was divided into two carpeted areas with two separate sets of white furniture, with a clear space of marble floor down the center, which told her that Scott Schelling passed through the room only on his way to and from the front door. She followed a corridor off the living room and found a large den, a media room with thick leather theater seats, a huge flat-screen television set, smaller monitors, and lots of speakers and control boxes for various interlocking sound systems. She made her way back down the long corridor past the living room and into a small gym. It had many of the machines and pieces of equipment that Sylvie's first husband, Darren, had bought her, but the set of weights was bigger and heavier than hers.

She had reached the private areas of the house, so she knew she must be coming closer to the bedrooms. The gym had a door that led to a shower room, and on the far end of it was a door to a conventional bathroom, and then another door to a large walk-in closet and dressing room. She could see built-in dressers and cabinets and rows of men's suits on hangers, rows of shoes on shelves.

Sylvie edged close to the next door, her gun ready, and stepped out suddenly, the gun aimed at the bed. But the bed was still made, the covers perfectly smooth. There was a desk to her right near the wall, so she came close. There was nothing on its surface—no papers, no wallet or keys, no sunglasses or coins he might have left there when he went to bed. She looked at her watch. It was very late—after two. He should be home, if he was coming.

Maybe he slept in another bedroom. She made her way out the door and down the hall, looking in each bedroom. When she had seen them all, she walked back toward the kitchen. On the far side of it was a separate corridor she had missed the first time; it led to a suite for a maid. She opened the door carefully and explored it. The closet had a woman's clothes in it, and there were Spanish novellas on the bookshelves, but the bed had not been slept in. In the maid's bathroom, Sylvie studied the louvered window above the shower for a moment, then returned to the kitchen and knelt by the dog door. "Paul."

"What did you find?"

"Not him. He's not here. There's nobody in the house. The maid seems to get the weekend off. I've been in every room. Time for you to come in."

"How? I'll never fit."

"Come around to the end of the house by the garage. I'll show you."

Paul went around the house to the far end, and when he arrived, Sylvie was already taking the strips of glass out of the louvered window. He pushed the last three out, handed them in to Sylvie, and climbed through the empty window frame into the shower. They replaced the glass and stepped out of the shower.

"Where should we start?" he said.

"The kitchen's right down here." She led him down a short corridor into the kitchen.

He shone his flashlight on the long granite counters, the copper pots hanging on the walls, the giant sinks and stove. "Nice."

"Let's find the money," she said.

The kitchen was rich in places for hiding things: the refrigerator, inside pots and pans, in the removable backs of electronic devices, in cabinets and drawers. They found nothing, and moved to the next room. Paul stood on the dining-room table to see if anything could be hidden in the chandelier. They looked underneath tables and sideboards. In the living room, they pulled back runners and moved paintings to search for secret compartments, took out drawers. They checked inside the piano, then moved on.

It was nearly dawn before they finished. They had found seven thousand dollars in cash, a few thousand dollars' worth of watches and other jewelry, two loaded pistols, and a short-barreled pump shotgun. They had not found the million dollars that Scott Schelling had promised them.

"What do you think?" Sylvie asked. "Do we give up and go?"

"He's not going to get Wendy Harper for free. He made an arrangement, and he's going to pay us."

41

WHILE THEY HAD a drink in Scott Schelling's suite, Jill Klein introduced Scott to a whole set of grievances against her husband. Fifteen years ago, Jill had been a young, extremely pretty woman who worked for a subsidiary called Carbondale Industries in Chicago. Ray Klein told her he had come to the moment in his life when he wanted only to step back from running the conglomerate and enjoy life with a woman like her. He told her he would always cherish her and be faithful to her. Every one of his statements had been a deliberate lie.

"Now he's got another new girl—about the hundredth one—but this one is much worse. He's promoted her to vice president and travels with her, like a corporate wife. It's the most public humiliation yet. I hate him." Then it was as though she remembered something she had forgotten to do. She put down her drink, stood up, and began to take off her clothes.

When they were in bed, he saw that what she was doing was avenging her humiliation. Anger made her passionate and eager. She wanted to be more excited, more enthralled by Scott than she had ever been with Ray Klein because that was part of her revenge: to show some impartial, invisible universal arbiter that Ray was not as good at making love as the first man she picked out at a party. And there was another comparison at work in her mind, too. Her sex had to be wilder, more erotic than the illicit sex that Ray had with Martha Rodall. And Scott could tell there were other feelings, too, ones that Scott did not have enough experience or enough empathy to interpret.

Scott had been afraid of Ray Klein, terrified of the power that Ray Klein had over him. But tonight Scott was in a hotel room having sex with Ray Klein's beautiful wife. It was the antidote to the cowardice and the shame and resentment, and it was intoxicating. He and Jill had become complicit in deceiving Ray Klein—not just in fooling him, but in dishonoring him, mocking Ray Klein's brute power over them. What could Ray Klein ever do to Scott that compared with this? While they were in bed, Scott already knew that the next time he was forced to defer to Ray Klein, to tolerate his dominance, Scott would be thinking, I fucked your wife. And he knew that Jill was looking forward to having thoughts on the same topic.

While Jill dressed, he said, "Am I going to see you again?"

"You must know I'll see you again." Her tone was peculiar. It was not affectionate, not even warm. There was an edge to it, and his ear caught the tone.

"When?"

"When I can."

"I want it to be soon." He could hardly believe he had said that, but he meant it. He wanted not just to have one night with Jill Klein. He wanted to be able to repeat this night as often as possible. He wanted her to belong to him.

She touched his face, leaned close and looked at him, but did not kiss him. "If I have a chance to do this again, believe me, I will."

"Let me give you a phone number." He took a piece of hotel stationery and wrote while he talked. "This is the cell I carry. It's a number almost nobody has because I use it only for emergencies. Call when you think you might be able to see me."

She took it, folded it and put it in her purse. "Fine. Now I've got to get out of here."

At nearly three A.M., Scott Schelling escorted Jill Klein out of his room and down the hotel hallway to the elevators. When he pressed the button, the nearest elevator opened immediately, they stepped inside and the doors closed with a quiet, rolling sound. Jill Klein gave one of her semaphore smiles, embraced Scott and kissed him. Scott knew that hotel elevators usually had cameras in the ceilings, but he decided it was best to acquiesce. The mouth-breathers who looked at the tapes certainly wouldn't know who Scott Schelling was.

Scott didn't want to seem timid to Jill Klein. Everything she did was flagrant. While she kissed him, her hands moved below his belt, and he had to break off the kiss. "If you do that, I can't very well walk back through the lobby with you."

She laughed. "I'll be good."

"I just mean right now, not in the future."

"No? Then next time I see you, I think I'll be as bad as I can possibly be."

"When will that be?"

"I'll try to call you tomorrow. If I don't, then find an excuse to skip the European conference in a couple of weeks. I'll fly to L.A."

"Good. You have my cell-phone number, right?"

"How could I lose it this soon?"

The elevator stopped and the doors slid open. The lobby was nearly deserted at this hour. A uniformed man with an electric machine buffed the floor, but he paid no attention to them. A night clerk looked up as they passed the main desk at a distance of seventy feet, and then returned his eyes to the magazine he was reading.

Schelling and Jill Klein went out the main entrance, and Schelling's eyes were already sweeping the parking lot and the street beyond to spot anyone who might be watching them. As far as Schelling could tell, tonight he was in luck: There were no visible watchers. The valet-parking attendant and the doorman were sitting on a bench a few paces away beside the cabinet full of keys. The parking attendant jumped up eagerly and took the chit from Jill, then ran down the ramp under the building and came back up with her car. Scott had asked him to park the car below, even though there had been spaces in the open lot when she had arrived. He handed the attendant a ten-dollar bill.

He opened Jill's door so she could slip behind the steering wheel, then leaned in to kiss her.

She turned away. "Don't be stupid. I'll see you soon enough." She drove out of the lot and turned toward the central square in front of the old Palace of the Governors. After two blocks he saw the lights of her car turning north toward the road to the Klein house.

Back in his room, Scott caught a faint scent of Jill's perfume. The twisted upper sheet thrown back from the bed and the scattered pillows brought back the surprise Jill Klein had been. He had expected the night to be only a couple of hours of diplomacy to pacify an aging beauty, but this had been a night of new emotions. Now he was alone again. As he took off his sport coat and hung it in the closet, he took his cell phone out of the pocket and pressed the menu for Tiffany's line at the office. He got her voice mail. "Hello, Tiffany. I'm going to stay longer in Santa Fe. I'll cancel my own flight and make another reservation. Coordinate with Kimberly."

He disconnected, put the phone on his nightstand, brushed his teeth and lay on the bed. He had another reason for not going home in a few hours. Carl had not yet called to tell him that he had solved the problem of the Turners. Maybe Carl had found he needed to kill them. If so, then it was a good idea for Scott to stay away until it was over. Occupying a hotel room in another state wasn't the best alibi, but it wasn't the worst, either. He reached for the house telephone. When the clerk answered, he said, "This is Mr. Schelling in 362. I'd like to stay an extra day. Can you arrange that for me?"

"One moment, please, while I check." After a moment she said, "Yes, sir. I've extended your reservation an extra day. Is there anything else I can do for you?"

"No, thank you." He hung up. It struck Scott Schelling that a subtle shift had taken place in the universe yesterday afternoon, and now the purpose of the whole world was to say "Yes, sir" to Scott Schelling.

42

O N SATURDAY AFTERNOON, Carl drove up to the gate of Scott Schelling's house. He pressed the remote-control unit he carried in his car and watched the electric motor slide the gate along its track and out of his path. He pulled up to his usual spot at the end of the row of six visitors' spaces near the right side of the house. Carl was pleased to see that his was the only car.

Scott Schelling was a demanding employer. He worked long hours, and he wanted everybody available until he quit for the day around eight. Carl sometimes worked long after that. On the occasions when Scott went out of town, the office girls tried to give the staff a break. Kimberly wasn't in, even though it was Saturday afternoon. Sonya the maid was gone, too, so Carl had volunteered to feed the dog.

Carl was eager to get inside. He had guessed that if he came over here he would be alone, but he had been mentally prepared for the possibility that one of the others might show up after all.

Carl had not slept well last night, thinking about today. Scott had never really been fair to him, but in the past few days, things had gotten worse. At the start of the relationship, he had liked the job. He and Scott had been two young guys, and on many nights they would be out looking for women together. The only real difference between them had been their bank accounts. They each had assets.

Scott Schelling may have had more money and status, but Carl had a handsome face, good hair and teeth, a muscular body, and a sense of humor. In the early years, Carl had practically invented Scott Schelling's personal life. He had taken him to clubs, found his women for him, and talked them into being interested in Scott.

But things between Carl and Scott Schelling had changed six years ago. Carl had been out at a club late one night when Scott called. Carl could have had his phone off, he could have let it ring and listened to the message, but he had answered. It had been Scott, telling him that he needed him right away.

When Carl arrived at the house, Scott was wearing only a pair of jeans, pacing back and forth in the driveway in his bare feet. Scott was wild-eyed and scared, like a kid. Carl said, "What's the problem?" and Scott shook his head and pulled Carl inside. Once the door was shut, Scott said, "Carl, I'm in trouble. Kit died."

"What do you mean, 'died'? Of what?"

"Come on." Scott hurried him along the corridor past the workout room and into the big master bedroom. There was Kit, lying on the carpet with a belt tightened around her neck.

Carl had felt revulsion, but his strongest impression now was how scared Scott had been. Scott swore through clenched teeth at his bad luck, and then blamed Kit for making him do this to her. He paced, looking in every direction but at the body. Then he collapsed on the bed, sobbing at the fact that he could go to jail for life.

Repelled and disgusted, Carl felt ashamed to be there. But he had known Scott for years by then, and he couldn't help having some concern for him. Scott was usually so definite and decisive, so sure of himself; but here he was, whining and swearing, yet absolutely helpless.

Carl had looked at the clock on the nightstand. "Scotty, it's going to be light in three or four hours. Call the cops and tell them you killed her, and it was an accident."

Scott said, "I can't call the cops. What can I say—that I thought she was an intruder, so I strangled her with my belt? Please. You've got to help me get rid of the body."

Carl had resisted. "You've got no record. If you call them, maybe it was just a fight and you lost your temper."

But Scott had kept after him, begging and pleading, offering money and eternal gratitude. Finally it had gotten to be too much to listen to anymore. "All right," said Carl. "I'll help you. There's an old tarp in the garage. We'll wrap her in that for now, and get her out of the house." Carl took over and told Scott what to do. He made Scott put on some shoes and a hooded sweatshirt. They rolled Kit in the tarp, dragged her along the hall, and out to the garage. Then they lifted her into the trunk of the Town Car. Carl set two shovels and a case of bottled water in with her.

Scott asked, "Why use the Town Car?"

"It's got a big trunk. She won't fit in the Maserati."

Carl drove them out into the hills to an area above the San Gabriel Reservoir. Carl drove the car off the road into a stand of big trees, and then kept driving as far as he dared. After he stopped, he took a shovel, handed the other to Scott, and said, "Dig." Scott was not accustomed to doing physical work, but he had been lifting weights and doing machine workouts, so he was better at it than Carl had expected. They were still digging when the woods around them began to come out of the deep dark. By then the hole was so deep that Carl's shoulders were below ground level, and the pile of dirt was high above their heads.

They climbed out, lifted the body from the trunk, unrolled the tarp, and set the body at the edge of the grave. Carl said, "Okay, undress her."

"What?"

"Take off her clothes in case she's found. If it's just her, she's a Jane Doe, probably forever. They can trace clothes and jewelry."

Scott nodded. He knelt beside the body and unbuttoned her blouse. His hands shook. "Shit," he said. "I can't do this."

"You have to."

But in the end, it had been Carl who stripped the body. He took her clothes, the watch and rings, and put them into the trunk. Then he rolled the body into the grave and began to shovel dirt over her. After he had been shoveling by himself for a few minutes, Scott came up behind him and took a cautious peek into the hole. When he had verified that she was no longer visible, he joined in and shoveled the dirt so quickly that Carl had needed to step back to avoid having loose dirt tossed onto his shoes and pants.

Carl smoothed over the dirt and shoveled some leaves and debris and rocks over it to make the spot hard to distinguish from any other in the area. After that, he put Scott in the back seat to wait while he dragged his shovel over the ground to get rid of footprints. Finally he backed the car out to the road and drove Scott home in the early-morning sunshine.

It took Carl three more full days to get rid of every sign that Kit had ever existed. Kit's clothes had to be taken out and burned, along with the clothes Carl and Scott had worn to bury her. The car had to be washed at home, then rewashed at a car wash and detailed. Next Carl had to take it to get four new tires. The shovels had to be washed, and the tarp thrown into a Dumpster sixty miles away. Even Scott's bedroom furniture and carpets were replaced.

A week later, he and Scott had become aware of the problem of Wendy Harper's curiosity. She and her friend Olivia had been to Kit's apartment at least twice, and she had asked numerous people for any and all information they had about her. It was as though she were trying to prepare a case against Scott. Carl had listened in disbelief to what Scott proposed.

"You use a bat. You hit her once on the legs to knock her down. Then hit her once on the head. One line drive, and she's dead. That's all it takes. The cops will think it was a mugging, or a pervert, because who else would do a woman like that?"

Carl answered, "Not me," but Scott kept talking. "Is it money?

You know I'll take care of you. What do you want—a house? I'll give you enough for two houses and a car to put in the garage. Think about it."

"I'll think about it."

"I don't mean a long time, I mean right now."

"I'm thinking. No."

"You've got to do this, Carl. You're vulnerable. Regardless of how she died, just moving and hiding a body like that will put us both away until we're old. A house free and clear, Carl. You'll be able to buy a house, a car, and get a year's pay for starters."

Carl had listened more closely to Scott's warnings than to his promises, and slowly he began to be afraid. Wendy Harper knew too much already, and she kept prying and searching and questioning. He had waited for Wendy outside her house late one night, and he had hit her with the bat. The first swing had knocked her flat, but she had gotten up and tried to run. He had dropped the bat, grabbed her by the sleeve of her blouse, and thrown her to the ground, but the blouse had ripped off in his hands. Then he had snatched up the bat and swung for her skull, but had missed her out of nervousness. The truth was that he had closed his eyes at the last second. He had not wanted to see this woman's head smashed open, so he had shut his eyes. The bat had hit the sidewalk with a hollow sound and sent a sting like an electric shock from his palms to his elbows. He could see that he had hit her head on the bounce, and it was bleeding.

Then there had been bright headlights on the dark, quiet street—first one set, and then another behind it. He could see nothing beyond the blinding glare, and there was no way to hide the woman at his feet—she seemed all white blouse, white skin, blond hair that glowed with reflected light—so he ran. He ran through back yards and over fences, out to the next street and around the corner to the alley where his car was parked.

Carl had reached the car before he looked down and noticed

that he still held half of her white blouse in his left hand with the bat. He wrapped the bloody bat in it so it wouldn't stain the carpet in his car, and then drove.

That night changed Carl's job completely. He was no longer a driver, he was an accomplice posing as a driver. Driving was just a cover, a plausible reason for Scott and Carl to go places together and talk alone in the car with no chance to be overheard. Carl had needed to find the kind of people who would search for Wendy Harper, then hire and supervise them. Scott had acted as though that kind of thing would be easy for Carl, but it wasn't. Killers didn't take his orders easily. They seemed to sense instantly that he was afraid of them, and they spoke to him with a patronizing tone, an affection that didn't include respect. It was the way some people talked to children.

For six years he had acted as paymaster and go-between. He had done it all, without ever keeping a dime of the money. As he thought about it, he realized that Scott Schelling would never have done that. Scott would have found a way to steal a little. That was simply another of the differences between them.

As soon as Densmore was dead, Scott had decided that he and Carl would handle the whole problem themselves. Carl had known it was madness: Neither Carl nor Scott had any business trying to manipulate and fool people like the Turners. There were just some people who were too mean and crazy to fuck around with. Now Scott had finally figured that out, too, so he was planning to pay them a million dollars in cash, just as he had promised.

Carl knew exactly what the amount would consist of. It had to be in hundreds because smaller bills made a bigger package. Even in hundreds, it meant ten thousand hundred-dollar bills. There would be a suitcase full of money. Scott would never walk into Crosswinds Records carrying a suitcase full of cash. For one thing, it meant that later the Turners would have to walk out of Crosswinds carrying a suitcase full of cash. They could be stopped, and he could find himself having to explain it. Scott had to have hidden it where he could control it, and where he could come and get it at will. It had to be somewhere in his house.

As Carl walked toward the house, he took out his keys. His mind was already running an inventory of the best places in the house to hide a suitcase. The place he planned to look first was in the row of suitcases Scott stored in the closet of the second best guest bedroom. Carl unlocked the front door, stepped to the alarm keypad on the wall, punched in the alarm code, then ENTER, then OFF, then ENTER.

He stepped inside, and as he closed the door, his eye caught movement. He turned. There stood the Turners. They had been watching him come in, waiting at the right side of the stairs. They had guns in their hands, so he kept his hands in sight, far out from his sides. "Paul. Sylvie. Wow! You scared me. Is Scott home already?"

"No, he's not here," Paul said. "Do you know where he is?"

"That's why I didn't expect to see anybody here. He's been out of town since Friday for a weekend conference with a bunch of other bigwigs. He was supposed to be back this morning, but he got held over. It's just one of the problems that come up when you deal with important people—they're busy. You'll get used to it."

"Where's our money, Carl?" Sylvie asked.

"Scott has it. I'm sure he's got it ready for you, but I don't know where."

"Too bad," Paul said.

"Really bad," Sylvie echoed.

Carl held up his hands. "Wait. Let me call him and ask."

Paul said, "All right."

Carl took out his cell phone and pressed the autodial key for Scott's cell. He listened to the sound of a ring, then another, and another, his heart pounding. Then there was a tone, and Scott's voice came on and said, "Leave a message." Carl winced. He said, "Scott, this is Carl. Please give me a call right away. It's really important."

He disconnected, then pressed the key for the next number, the office number. It went right to Scott's voice mail. A recording of Tiffany's voice said, "Please leave a message," and Carl left the same message. He could see that Paul was watching him closely, his fingers flexing on the gun.

Carl said, "He seems to be out of range right now. He's in Santa Fe, so I guess it's not too surprising. But I have an idea as to where he might have left the money. Let's take a look."

Paul considered the suggestion for a moment. "Okay. We may as well try."

Carl trudged toward the staircase. He was almost certain that the money would be in the suitcase upstairs, and he was leading them to it. He had been hoping, imagining that he was going to end up with the million dollars, but he had been kidding himself. People like Carl Zacca didn't end up rich, they ended up driving cabs until they were seventy-five.

He was afraid, and he hated himself for being afraid. He was sure he knew where the money was, and he had a gun in his coat pocket, but it might as well be a pocketful of sand. He didn't have the courage to reach for it. He climbed the stairs, wishing that he had courage. He walked along the upstairs hallway and opened the guest-room door. He went to the closet, with Paul and Sylvie a step behind him on either side.

Suddenly Carl saw things clearly. He realized that he didn't have to reach for his gun and try to shoot it out with two people. If he were to lunge at Sylvie, he could grab her gun and turn it on Paul, using Sylvie as a shield. He reached toward the closet door, pivoted, and made a desperate grab for Sylvie.

Sylvie spun and jumped away at the same time. When her feet hit the floor, she was aiming her gun at him.

Carl felt the shots enter his torso, as though they were hitting him in specific places for target practice. There was something shameful in doing that to a person. He pulled his gun out of his coat, but he never got to fire it. He fell to the floor.

Paul kicked the gun away from Carl's hand, then opened the closet door. There were three black Tumi suitcases inside. He opened one, then the second, then the third. "Shit," he said. "Nothing in here but empty suitcases."

43

JACK TILL GAZED through the half-open door into the small office. Claire, the police sketch artist, lifted her right hand with the pencil in it and brushed back her long, natural gray hair, then returned the pencil to the big sketch pad. She listened to Olivia's description as she worked, made erasures and new lines with a methodical, imperturbable patience. Till stood looking at the sheet for only a few seconds, then walked on. It was enough to verify that Olivia's memory was producing a picture that matched the pictures from Wendy's and Eric's memories. Kit Stoddard's face stared out at him from the paper, and he felt Kit Stoddard was a real person.

Till walked along the hall past two more offices and into the Homicide bay. Wendy was still in there talking to Poliakoff, but when Poliakoff saw Till he beckoned. As Till approached, Poliakoff said, "Wendy, why don't you take a break? I want to talk to Jack for a minute."

"Fine with me. You going to be long?"

"No. You can both be out of here in ten minutes. There's fresh coffee in the break room."

She walked off toward the break room, and Poliakoff pointed to her chair. Till sat down.

Poliakoff said, "This afternoon I managed to keep Linda Gordon a female victim in her thirties, who will be identified after her family is notified that she's been hurt."

"Thanks for that, Max."

"Don't bother to thank me. A couple of reporters got the truth out of the DA's office, so as of the eleven-o'clock news tonight, the shooter will know he shot the wrong blonde."

"Shit," said Till. "So much for having the heat off."

Poliakoff studied him. "Why haven't you told me that you and Wendy were screwing?"

"My mother doesn't know yet."

"Your mother is deceased. And she isn't trying to conduct a homicide investigation. Why haven't you told me?"

"It's very recent. I'm not sure what to say about it yet."

"You two should talk more. She told me it's not recent. She says she was trying to interest you six years ago, but you wouldn't bite."

"She was a client who had hired me to get her out of town because people were trying to crush her skull with baseball bats. Somehow it didn't strike me as the right time to start a relationship."

"But now is the right time?"

"Maybe. It doesn't change anything about the case."

"Sure it doesn't. Why haven't you asked me what I found in Linda Gordon's house after you left?"

"You found nothing, or you wouldn't have been able to wait to tell me."

Poliakoff sighed. "You're close enough."

"Did you get to look?"

"No. The lieutenant showed up right after you left, and so I ran out of time."

Till noticed that Poliakoff was looking past him at the doorway, so he turned and saw Wendy there waiting for him. "Is there any reason why I can't get her out of sight before the eleven-o'clock news?"

Poliakoff said, "No reason I know of. As soon as you two leave,

I'm going over to St. Joseph's to see if I can interview Linda Gordon. Sometimes getting shot makes you rethink your alliances. Then I'll go home." He stared at Till for a moment. "It's too late to go back to Linda Gordon's house. I've already sent everybody there home for the night."

Till stared at him. "Thanks, Max."

AT TEN-THIRTY, Till pulled off the freeway at Coldwater, drove up Ventura Boulevard to the street where Linda Gordon lived, and cruised past her house. "The crime-scene people are finished, and the house is empty," he said. "Let's take a look around the neighborhood to see if we're alone." He drove up and down the streets in the neighborhood, satisfied himself that nobody was watching the house, and then parked up the block and took two flashlights and two pairs of gloves out of the trunk of his car.

"Gloves?"

"I forgot to tell you. Always wear gloves when you commit a felony."

"A felony? Are you any good at that?"

"I have some professional knowledge."

They walked around to the back of the house and stopped. She whispered, "How are we going to get in?"

"Foresight. Before I left, I flipped the latch on a window in the pantry." He put on his gloves and handed the other pair to Wendy.

"What about the alarm system?"

"There will still be cops coming and going for a day or two, so I'm betting they haven't turned it on." He walked to a window near the corner of the house, slid open the window, and climbed inside. He walked through the kitchen to the back door and opened it for Wendy.

When they were both inside, with the door closed, she said, "Now, tell me. Why are we back here tonight?"

"Because it's our chance to check out a suspicion I have."

"And the thing we're looking for is—?"

"I don't know what it is. Something to tell us who Scott is."

"Give me a hint."

Till turned on his flashlight. "Start by looking for an address book, or a list of phone numbers—anything like that. If you see a collection of letters or cards, check it. Some people keep business cards in one place. Look for the name 'Scott.'"

"You know, that's not a rare name.'

"I know. If she knows fifty or sixty Scotts, I'll check out all of them."

They searched the kitchen, then moved into a spare bedroom that had been in use as an office. Wendy found a Rolodex, put it on the floor so she could read it by the light of her flashlight without being seen from the windows, and went through it, card by card. Till went through drawers full of papers, scanning each one for the name.

Till found files related to investments and taxes, but no sums were mentioned that weren't the right size for an Assistant DA's salary. There were none of the signs of disorder in her life that Till had hoped for. There were no overdrafts or big withdrawals, no indications that she had suddenly come into money. "Any Scotts yet?"

"No. Maybe it isn't there. Maybe you're wrong about her."

"I don't think so. There's something off with her." They moved into the bedroom and began to search.

"You know, it doesn't seem strange to me that she charged Eric with murder on that evidence," Wendy said.

"Not weird at all. I didn't like her, but it never occurred to me that there was anything strange about her until the last few days. It was pretty clear to everyone that you were alive, but she still wouldn't drop the charges. When it seemed clear today that Jay Chernoff had enough evidence to get the judge to dismiss the charges without her, she changed her approach. She wanted to hold us for insurance fraud. She wanted to keep us in town, and to know exactly where we were."

"Maybe it was spite. My taking off years ago was what made her waste a lot of time and money charging Eric."

"Anything is possible. But if you're really going to prosecute somebody, you do it. DAs don't tell people who haven't been charged with anything that they're under some kind of house arrest. And she and Jay both seemed to know that she couldn't do it. So why was she trying to?"

"I don't know." She began to open drawers.

Till knelt beside the bed and ran his hand between the mattress and the springs. He touched something, lifted the mattresss and pulled it out, then turned on his flashlight. "Interesting," he said. "She must have just had time to hide this before we got here."

"What?"

"Look at this," he said. He held his flashlight on a photograph in a frame. It showed a man standing in a driveway beside a blue classic Maserati.

"Oh, my God!" she exclaimed.

"Who is he? Is that Scott?"

"No."

"Then who?"

"The one who beat me up. The one with the bat."

44

SCOTT SCHELLING SLOUCHED in the back seat of the taxicab, watching the buildings, the cars, the streets sliding past his window. He was in a state deeper than weariness. When he had come off the plane, he had turned on his phone, heard the message indicator chirping, and turned it off again, something he rarely did. He liked to know the latest, liked to be alert, liked to be taking in information, gobbling it and then sending it back changed, a solution to each problem, an answer to each question.

But tonight was different.

Wendy Harper was dead. He had endured the long period of fear and used it in intense, concentrated work, the quiet building of his power and knowledge. He had let other people share in the credit to make them into allies. He had always chosen carefully and consciously who these people would be: whom he would push into positions of prominence, and which adversaries he wanted them to weaken and defeat. He had studied and planned, and now he had found his way to Jill Klein. She was going to be—already was—important to him. This morning—Saturday morning—when Ray Klein had flown to New York to get back to running the conglomerate, Jill had returned to Scott's hotel room in Santa Fe, already full of ideas and plans for raising Scott's status.

Early in the morning she had actually begun taking thank-you calls for the dinner party from her friends, members of the board of directors and their wives, major shareholders. She had used this chance to mention how impressed this person or that person had been with Scott Schelling. She was far too clever to say she'd even spoken with Scott alone: She was only repeating the impressions other people had conveyed to her as hostess. By now she had built the impression of a consensus. Anyone who had not made it his business to get to know Scott Schelling, well, you simply had to wonder about anybody like that. It was a small step, but it was the right step, and it could only have been taken on this particular day, when many of the guests had seen Scott for the first time, and he could still be a topic. Jill's years as a corporate wife had given her a feel for what to do and when to do it, and Scott was her new beneficiary.

The houses were getting bigger and the cars newer and more expensive. The cab was entering his neighborhood now. The streets and sidewalks were clean, the trees tall and old, the lawns broad and green.

He would get a few hours' sleep and then go to the office and begin making things happen. He would set up a Sunday meeting with the heads of publicity and fan relations and get them going on the new project. They had done it a hundred times before, and now they would do it for him. He envisioned the whole campaign. There would be an article in a magazine: an exclusive interview with the modest genius of pop music, Scott Schelling of Crosswinds. It would be a campaign that built slowly and subtly. The publicity people could feed the reporter statements from all of the current Crosswinds talent about how brilliant he was. It would work because it always worked.

After that, he would be offered television appearances. His PR people would let the cable networks know that he was available to serve as a talking head about music, popular trends, and celebrities. There was no reason to worry about high visibility anymore: Wendy

Harper was dead. He would throw parties and invite the cream of the industry, then feed the fan magazines. Once photographs of stars taken "at Scott Schelling's party" began to appear regularly, he would become familiar to the hard-core fan demographic.

Scott stopped himself from thinking too far ahead. This wasn't the time, and it was not his job, anyway. Crosswinds had the best publicity people in the business, and they had actually improved since Aggregate had taken over. Scott had been able to get them more money to work with. Music was a business that was almost entirely a matter of creating stampedes, but his first bosses—the ones he had replaced—had been incredibly shortsighted and stingy about publicity. Ray Klein had a larger perspective, and he had not flinched at Scott's budget requests.

For about the tenth time in the past two days, Scott realized that he actually respected Ray Klein. He was a good businessman, and he wasn't really such a bad man to work for. Scott just didn't like a boss—any boss. Ray Klein held power over him and made him afraid of losing what he had. Ray Klein stood in the way of his getting more.

There was the house. The gate was open, and in the space near the side of the house he could see Carl's car. The cabdriver stopped outside the open gate, but Scott said, "Go on in. Let me off at the door."

The driver backed up a few feet and then drove up the long cobbled driveway to the broad, flat space at the front. Scott got out and handed the driver a fifty-dollar bill, which was at least a twenty-dollar tip he didn't deserve. "Keep it," he said. When he was in the public eye in the next few months, he didn't want cabdrivers giving interviews about how cheap he was. The driver lifted the suitcase out of his trunk, set it on the ground carefully, extended the handle for him, got into his car, and drove away.

Scott took a moment to look at his house. Carl had left the gate open for him, which meant that he must have called the hotel and found he'd checked out. Carl's presence here meant that everything must have gone well. He took out his keys and unlocked the door, pushed it open and pulled his suitcase into the dimly lighted foyer.

The first thing Scott saw was the silhouette of a woman. Could Jill have flown here instead of New York to surprise him? The woman stepped toward him and he saw the gun. The woman's voice was different from Jill's. It was harsh, unfriendly. "You must be Scott."

"That's right. Who are you?"

"I'm Sylvie Turner. And right behind you is Paul."

Paul was almost at Scott Schelling's ear when he spoke. "Pleased to meet you, Scott. Welcome home. On Friday night your secretary said you were in a meeting. She didn't say it was in another state."

"Yes. I had some business in Santa Fe."

"I guess you know what we're here for." Sylvie stepped closer. She was taller than Scott, and she looked down at him in an eager, predatory way that made Scott uncomfortable, but he didn't dare to step back.

"I would guess you're here to get paid," he said. Carl's car was parked outside. Where was Carl?

Paul spoke from behind him. "If you're ready to handle that now, we can take our money and be on our way."

Sylvie's face leaned closer, like the face of an apparition in a fun house. "You *do* have the money, don't you, Scotty?"

"Yes," he said. "Yes, I do. It's here at the house. I'll go get it right now." He began to turn and took a step.

"Stop!" Paul's voice was like a whip-crack. He said more quietly, "Hold it right there, Scott. Where are you going?"

"The money is outside. In the garage. I was going to get the opener."

Paul rested his left hand on Scott's shoulder, and Scott could feel the gun pressed under his right shoulder blade. "You've got to be careful around us right now, Scotty. I know you're used to having people trust you, but we don't. You were very definite on Friday that you wanted to pay us a million dollars for this job. Then that night your secretary sent us to meet you, and two guys tried to kill us."

"I'm sorry that happened," Scott said. "It wasn't anybody's fault. Those two were supposed to take you here, and I was going to call and tell them how to find the money to give you. I guess I over-estimated them. They must have wanted to rob me."

Sylvie said, "There's no need to go into all that now. We're only interested in collecting our money and going away."

"That's exactly what I want. What I'm planning to do now is walk outside to the garage, go in, and get your money. It's in a suitcase."

"I hope you don't mind our going with you," Paul said. "If we see what you're doing, neither one of us will be nervous and edgy."

"All right. Can I go now?"

"Go."

Scott resumed his walk into the hallway, picked up a remote-control unit, and pressed the button. They heard the hum and rattle of the garage door going up. He set the unit down, then said, "I'm reaching for my keys," and put his hand in his pocket.

He could see the two of them now. They were both tall, so they seemed in proportion to one another, the woman six or eight inches shorter than the man, but their heads came up almost to the tops of doorways and the bottoms of light fixtures, adding to the impression that they didn't belong here. Their presence was an invasion of his refuge, and their height seemed freakish. He was eager to be rid of them. "I'm going to walk out to the garage now. There's nothing out there that you aren't expecting. No guns or anything."

"Good," Paul said. "All we want is a clean deal."

Scott moved to the front door, stepped out and walked across the cobbled pavement. He could see Carl's car, and it occurred to him again to wonder about Carl. Maybe Carl had driven in, seen something odd, and decided not to go into the house. Maybe he had gone in, heard the Turners arrive, and hidden somewhere inside. Carl would not want to be stuck in the house with these two and not have the money to pay them.

As Scott thought about it, he realized that he had handled the whole matter badly. He should have made sure the Turners got their money as soon as Wendy Harper had died. In the end, that was what this was going to amount to, anyway, and he could have had Carl make the payoff quickly and efficiently on Friday and averted this mess: having people following him around aiming guns at his back. If one of them tripped on the stupid rustic, uneven cobblestones, Scott was likely to die.

That really had been an act of the old Scott, not the new one. The old Scott had been occupied with small, scuttling, ratlike maneuvers that would keep him safe and still preserve his million dollars. He'd had the film washed from his eyes since then. A million dollars had seemed like so much money a few days ago, but now he knew that it was a small investment that was already bringing him huge benefits. He had to think like a winner.

Scott Schelling went to the garage and stepped to the back of the blue antique Maserati. It was the only car he ever drove himself. Most of the time, he sat in the back of the Town Car and let Carl drive. He felt guilty now, but he had put the suitcase in the Maserati because he hadn't quite been able to trust Carl.

It wasn't that Carl had ever been disloyal or dishonest. But part of Carl's reliability was that Carl was an unimaginative and unambitious man. He was too inert and inactive to form an alliance with Scott's enemies or concoct some scheme to embezzle. But what if he had found the compact black Tumi suitcase and opened it up? Who knew what Carl's reaction would be to all of those crisp hundred-dollar bills? Carl was a blue-collar guy. One bill was a dinner for Carl and his blond girlfriend. She worked for the city, so she probably made less than he did. Two bills was a big night out. It was a lot of money to Carl, and it would be staring up at him from the suitcase. He might walk off with it without even taking a moment to think. So Scott had saved him from himself. He had simply put the money in the trunk of the Maserati, where Carl wouldn't stumble across it.

Scott found the key to the Maserati, inserted it, and unlocked the trunk. For a second, he felt a premonition, a sensation that things were not right. But there was the suitcase, in the middle of the trunk, exactly where he'd left it. He used his thumbs to slide the buttons to the side so the catches would snap open, then lifted the top of the suitcase to reveal neat stacks of hundreds.

He turned to give Paul and Sylvie a look of triumph.

Paul said, "Okay, close it."

Scott closed the suitcase.

"Bring it into the house."

Scott lifted the suitcase, closed the trunk and carried the suitcase across the parking area and through the front door into his house. He was disappointed in their reaction. Did they actually plan to sit in his living room counting all those banknotes?

He closed the front door and held out the suitcase so Paul would take it. There seemed to Scott to be a regal quality to a man who was paying anybody a million dollars for any purpose, a natural superiority. Paul took the suitcase, but set it down by his feet.

Scott said, "Look, I'm sure you know that I didn't count every bill myself. If a bank teller gave you a few hundred extra, keep it. If it's short, I'll make it good. You can count it at home."

"That seems reasonable," Sylvie said. With relief, Scott Schelling watched her step away from him toward the door.

Once Sylvie was clear, Paul fired into Scott Schelling's back where he thought the heart should be.

45

JACK TILL SAT in the back seat of the unmarked car beside Wendy as Max Poliakoff drove them along the quiet street toward Scott Schelling's house. Till said, "That house is 2908. Schelling's is 3206. It's going to be the third block up, on the right."

"I'm nervous," Wendy said.

Poliakoff half-turned in the driver's seat to look at her. "Don't be. We'll knock and ask to speak with him. We won't say who you are. If he's the one, all you have to do is nod, and we'll arrest him. If he's not the right Scott, then you shake your head, and I'll tell him some comforting nonsense about Neighborhood Watch."

"I guess it's just that I've spent so much time thinking about him. First Olivia and I kept searching the city for him so we could be sure Kit was all right. Then, after I got beat up, the last people in the world I wanted to see were him and the one with the bat."

"We'll get the one who hit you, anyway. He's as good as in the bag. Once we pick him up, we'll do a lineup and have you identify him formally. And then he's going away."

"You don't sound as though you're so sure about Scott," she said.

Till said, "That might take a bit longer, that's all. Nobody saw him do anything to Kit Stoddard. But there will be some connection between him and the others. We'll find it."

"We could even get something going this morning," Poliakoff

said. "I've got Horton waiting at the DA's office. If this is the right Scott, I'll make a call, and he'll walk a search warrant through for us. I mean, how can it not be the right Scott? The blue Maserati in the picture is registered to him."

They were quiet as they moved up the final block. Till could see that Schelling's house was different from most of the others in this stretch. His was a long, two-story house with white siding and tall windows set far back from the street. It was a style that seemed almost antique now because most of the others had been bulldozed recently and replaced with oversized Tuscan villas closer to the street but built on raised ground, so visitors had to climb wide ornamental steps to reach the entrances.

The unmarked car pulled through the open gate, up the driveway, and stopped at the front of the house. Till and Poliakoff got out, and Till leaned back into the car. "Wendy, if you feel frightened, you can stay in the car. You'll be able to see him through the window."

"No, I want him to see me." She got out and stood beside the car.

Till said, "Max."

"What?"

"The garage. The lights."

The garage door was open and there were two cars inside. The overhead lights in the garage were on, even though the morning sun was shining in through the open door. "Yeah," he said. "Odd."

Till stepped closer. "That's the Maserati in the picture we found." He turned around to see that the other two police cars had arrived. One had parked at the entrance to the driveway just inside the gate, and the other was now pulling up beside Poliakoff's car in front of the house. Two officers got out and followed Poliakoff to the front door.

Poliakoff rang the doorbell and waited, then rang it again. Next he grasped the heavy door knocker and rapped on the door loudly.

There was no response. The police officers looked at each other. Poliakoff took a small radio out of his coat pocket and said, "Dave, this is Max. Can you go to the gate and press the intercom button to let them know we're here?" There was a hollow "Roger" from the little box. From the door they could hear a telephone ringing inside the house, but there was no sign that anyone was going to answer the call from the gate.

Till walked to the nearest window along the front of the building. "Max?"

"Yeah?"

"I see somebody lying on the floor in the foyer. Take a look."

Poliakoff stepped up beside Till, held both hands beside his face to shade his eyes. "You're right." He turned to call to the other officers, "We've got to go in."

One of the uniformed officers went to his car and opened the trunk while the others moved toward the front of the house. Poliakoff stepped back onto the porch. As an afterthought, he tried the doorknob. "Hold it," he called. "No need to knock it down, it's unlocked." He turned the knob gingerly, then pushed the door open with his foot.

Till went inside with Poliakoff. After a moment Poliakoff came out to confer with the others, then went back inside. They seemed to be gone a long time, and then Till and Poliakoff emerged together. Poliakoff held two California driver's licenses. He set them both on the roof of his car, so Wendy could see them clearly.

Till said, "Do you recognize either of these men?"

She began to blink back tears. "It's them."

Till put his arms around her and said quietly, "Then as soon as you tell me the rest, it will be over."

She looked at him, then at Poliakoff, as though afraid he had heard.

Poliakoff said to Till, "If you want privacy, all I've got is my car."

"Thanks," Till said. He joined her in the back seat of the un-marked police car, and they sat still for a moment. Finally Till said, "How did you know him?"

"What do you mean? I didn't know him. I saw him once, and I told you all about that."

"You just saw a pair of driver's licenses six years later, and you said, 'It's them.' You got her into it, didn't you?"

Her eyes were wide with disbelief and anger. "What are you talking about?"

"*That* was why you felt responsible for Kit when she disap-peared. You felt as though it was your fault."

Her eyes were filling with tears. "I didn't know Scott Schelling at all. The one I had met was Carl. He was one of those good-looking guys who hang around clubs late at night. You see them a few times, and even though you don't really know them, you feel as though you do. One night he asked me about a couple of girls I knew, and Kit was one of them."

"How did he know you were in that business?"

"Oh, God," she said. Her body slumped into the seat, as though her muscles had gone limp. "That wasn't the way it was. It wasn't a business, it was just social. The first time, it was at Banque, and a man named Jerry asked me about Olivia. The man was a good customer, a lawyer, and we were joking around. He said he would give me a thousand dollars just to introduce him to Olivia. I thought he was nice, so I laughed and held out my hand, and he gave me the money—just like that. I stopped Olivia in the little space between the dining room and the kitchen, and I showed her the money and pointed him out. We laughed because it was a big compliment, and she went along with the joke. She went to his table and they talked, and she made a date with him." She shrugged. "The same thing happened later with Kit. Carl asked for an intro-duction, and then handed me some money. That was all."

"That *wasn't* all. This is me you're talking to."

"Yes. All right. There were others. A few times."

"And you took money from the men."

"Maybe once or twice. It sounds so sleazy, and it wasn't like that."

"Besides Jerry and Carl, who was there?"

"There was a businessman named Bryce, who was just a familiar face at first. He entertained clients from out of town and he asked me to scare up a few attractive friends to fill out a party."

"Just once?"

"Well, no. A few times. It wasn't a formal thing. He just didn't know anybody, and he needed a favor. I knew girls—some who worked for me, some I had met in other ways—who loved the chance to go out to a nice party and meet some new men. I went once myself. What I did for him was what any hostess does. I invited people I knew would be fun. What any of them chose to do afterward was her business."

"And the word got around."

"No. It wasn't like that, ever. There were only a few people, and it didn't go on for that long. Nobody knew, really."

"But Carl heard, and he paid you for an introduction to Kit."

She was crying, her eyes on his in a pleading look, but she didn't speak. He waited, and finally she said, "Yes."

"And that's why you lied to the police, and to me."

"It wasn't lying. Don't you see? If anyone heard that I had taken money, then they would get a completely wrong idea. All I did was keep them from thinking something that wasn't true."

"You were afraid of being embarrassed?"

"It's more than embarrassment, Jack. It would give the whole city the wrong idea about Banque, after we had worked so hard to make it the best kind of restaurant and attracted the very best patrons. Important men can't afford to be seen in a place where people pay for sex. And no woman wants to be suspected of selling herself. The money would have dried up. The critics would have dropped us. Then some reporter would have found out who my father was, and *I* would be the story. I had a right to avoid that."

"How much did Eric know?"

"None of it. This happened after our engagement was broken, and we didn't talk much about our social lives."

"What about Kit Stoddard? Who was she?"

"I don't know, exactly."

"Yes, you do."

"I think I do now, but I didn't at first. I thought Kit Stoddard was a real name. But I found some letters in her apartment when Olivia and I broke in. The envelopes said Katherine McGinnis, and the return addresses were in Canada. Hamilton, Ontario."

Till's anger was visible now, but his voice was calm, even. "Didn't you think it would help to tell the police that? Or to tell *me* that?"

"I wanted to. I would have, if it would have saved her. But at that point, I already knew she must be dead. Telling everything I knew after that would have made it all a hundred times worse. People would say she was a hooker, when she couldn't even defend herself, and that I had sent her to a psycho who killed her."

"So you were afraid of being prosecuted?"

"I don't know. I knew that some of the things I had done would sound much worse than they were."

"That was why Olivia ran away, too, wasn't it? She had taken money. She had been one of the women you set up with men."

"Yes. Neither of us ever knew what had happened to Kit, or why. Olivia was afraid to be alone, afraid to go to work. So she left. Then Carl came after me."

Till put his hand on the door handle. "Well, it's over now. You're safe."

She reached and grasped his wrist. "I did what I could."

"I'm not going to pretend that I'm buying your view of things. If you were afraid to tell the police, you still could have told me."

"I wish I had. I wanted to, and I'll always be ashamed that I didn't. But what I did was weak and stupid. It wasn't evil."

"That's what makes this such a waste. You knew that I had been a cop long enough to have seen everything. You should have known that what you had done wouldn't have struck me as anything but a mistake. But *not* telling was important. You lied to me."

She let go of his arm and held herself away. "What about you? Were you telling me the truth? For the past few days, what you were doing was interrogating me. You said and did anything that might make me care about you, just so I would tell you what you wanted. Well, congratulations, Jack. You didn't let me keep anything to myself. You're a hero."

"I was trying to help you do what you had to. The better I got to know you—the closer I got to you—the more certain I was that you had a secret."

"It was *my* secret, and *I* was the only one who was suffering for it. When I heard that it wasn't just me anymore, I did what I could." She sobbed. "And I was brave, damn it. I took risks. I wasn't doing what was right for me, just what was right."

"You were brave. I'll give you that."

Now she was angry. "Thank you very much. And you're a saint. You've made it clear that you'd rather cut off your arm than do anything unethical, but haven't you ever had a moment when you just didn't know what to do and guessed wrong? In all those years as a cop, haven't you had one conversation you wished you hadn't, or maybe wondered if you'd hit somebody too hard?"

Till stiffened, barely breathing. He sat in silence for a few seconds, looking ahead through the windshield. He could see Steven Winslow again—not the face contorted into a snarl as he swung the hammer at Till, but what he became after Till had hit him: a boy stretched out on the deserted street, dying alone in the dark. It had been more than twenty years, but Till was still able to see him. Till couldn't tell Wendy why forcing her to give up her secret had been so important to him, couldn't describe the self-hatred and shame he was trying to save her from. He became aware of her physical presence, the sound of her breathing, the smell of her soap, the closeness. He felt the seconds passing and made a decision. He swung the door open and got out.

She leaned toward the open door. "I think we've both known for a while that I'm not the perfect human being. I'm just the one who loves you. If I'm not worth salvaging, then I guess you should go."

He looked startled. "I wasn't walking away from you," he said. "You're right. I've been unfair, and I'm sorry. I was just going to tell Poliakoff we're leaving."

"Together?"

"Unless you don't want to anymore."

She shrugged. "I don't know what's going to happen to us. But I think we should let it."

"So do I. Come on."

She slid out of the police cruiser and stood beside him. She slipped her hand into his, and he let it stay there. They climbed the steps to the doorway, where Poliakoff was sketching the crime scene while two uniformed officers took measurements.

Till said, "Max, I left my car at the station. Can you spare the cop by the gate to drop us there?"

"Sure. I left him down there to keep these guys from running off," Poliakoff said. "Not much chance of that. Thank you both for your help. I'll call you."

As they walked down the cobbled driveway toward the patrol car idling near the gate, Till turned to Wendy. "There's somebody I have to see right away, and I'd like you to come, too. Her name is Holly."

46

PAUL AND SYLVIE TURNER stepped out of the taxicab in front of the Southwest Airlines terminal and watched the driver lift their suitcases from the trunk. Paul gave him a tip, and Sylvie turned and pulled her suitcase through the automatic glass doors into the terminal. Paul joined her and they stood for a half minute, until the driver had merged into the traffic and driven off. Then Paul and Sylvie pulled their suitcases out of the terminal and walked toward Bradley International Terminal. Paul had insisted that they appear to be going on a short flight to Las Vegas or San Francisco, not out of the country, just as he had insisted that they wait for the cab at a bus stop rather than at their house so the driver didn't know which house they'd left empty.

Sylvie was tired and irritable. To her the money that they had earned had begun to seem like a curse, a heavy weight. After a night and day in Scott Schelling's house, barely getting enough sleep, she'd had to come home, shower and dress, make cash deposits in four banks, pack as much money as they could into four safe-deposit boxes, and help Paul hide the rest of the money in their house.

The money didn't make up for all of the problems and risks and the sheer fatigue she had faced in getting through the job. At first the Wendy Harper business had sounded incredibly easy, but it had turned into a nightmare. The money they had finally taken from Scott Schelling was simply the reward for longevity, for being the last people standing. It was more like an unwanted inheritance than a payday.

Here they were, walking toward the international terminal to catch a flight to Spain, but she wasn't happy. She had been looking forward to Spain for weeks. There had been anticipation, then hard-won success, but the trip had been spoiled for her. All this money brought was insecurity. The additional money was contributing to the volatility of Paul's relations with her. For a week or two he had been giving all the signs that he either was cheating on her or would be shortly. Only during the period of hours when they had decided to abandon the job, fly to Madrid together, and forget the money, had their marriage seemed to heal. But while they were at home today getting dressed, he had been impatient with her. "Just put something on. Anything, just so we go." When they were driving around putting money in banks and safe-deposit boxes, he had been short with her. She had asked, "Which bank next?" and he had snapped, "Christ, Sylvie. I already told you. Pasadena." He had rolled his eyes at her and frowned when he'd lifted her suitcase. "What the fuck are you bringing—guns and ammo?" That had been particularly telling to her because he had lifted the bags before they had even gone after Scott Schelling, and they hadn't seemed so heavy to him then. What could have changed his feelings for her? It was the money.

They'd always had enough money before. The house she'd in-herited from Darren, her first husband—her house—was worth at least a couple million. Darren had left her bank accounts, stocks and bonds. And Paul had always saved most of their pay since then. But this money was dangerous. It was money that he didn't have to account for, or even count. He could use it to pursue love affairs. He could buy gifts for other women, take them places, and never risk Sylvie's noticing any bills.

Paul said, "You know, this whole Madrid thing feels like a bad idea. We're both exhausted, and we're leaving a house full of cash without a really adequate way to keep it safe. We have no plan for what we intend to do in Spain or when we'll come back, or anything."

"The house is fine. The lights will go on and off, the lawn will get sprinkled, and the gardeners will mow it. The pool man will clean the pool. The paper and mail were stopped days ago."

"Those are just incidentals. I don't even know why we're going," he said. "There's no reason to leave the country now."

"I'm going to Spain because it's one of the most beautiful places in the world, and I want to look at it and learn some new dances. You're going because you love me and want to make me happy. And also because I just suffered through a long and horrible job to make you happy. Okay?"

"I'm not denying any of that. I'm just saying it's inconvenient right now, and it's impractical."

"Women are an impractical thing to have, Paul. We're expensive, we pack too much, we're demanding. But going to Spain with me is not a lot to ask. It was your idea in the first place." She tugged her suitcase toward the distant terminal.

Now she had proof enough. There was at least one woman, and probably more than one. Certainly Mindy, the dance teacher, was one. He must have been screwing her for some time. There was simply no doubt, the way she had been acting toward Sylvie. Now Paul couldn't bear to leave town for a few months because he had it so good here in Los Angeles.

Sylvie had been fighting this realization for weeks, but there was no other explanation for his not wanting to go. The next level of understanding came to her suddenly. What Paul must really want wasn't to have her cancel the trip, it was to have her get on the plane to Madrid and let him stay behind. He would say "Adios" at the airport, go home and make the rounds of his sweethearts. Within a day or two, he would have them staying over at the house, sleeping on her side of the bed, one after another. She felt herself sinking into a dark and desperate mood.

The next few hours were going to be difficult for Sylvie. She couldn't let him start a fight now because that would allow him to storm off and refuse to get on the plane. Sylvie was going to have to force him to go with her to Spain. Once he was there with her, she would have to be decisive and act before he did. Getting a gun legally in Europe was probably impossible for a tourist. There were always knives, but she had no illusion that she could kill Paul that way. He would take it away from her and use it on her. It was going to have to be poison.

If it had to be poison, Europe was a better place to kill him than at home. The authorities there wouldn't care much about what happened to some American tourist, and wouldn't even bother to do a lot of tests on the body if the grieving widow didn't demand it. He could be buried abroad. No, cremated. She would have Paul cremated.

Paul caught up with her, and put his arm around her waist. "I'm just saying we could have a pretty good time right here with all that money."

She looked at him, her eyes wide and her smile comfortable and sure. "Spain is one of the most romantic countries in the world. I promise that I won't give you enough time to get homesick."

Paul grinned and kissed her behind the ear. "I love you."

It was absolutely no use trying to get her to abandon this trip. He would have to go to Spain and try to figure out the best way to kill her there without getting caught.

Turn the page to read the first chapter of
Thomas Perry's newest mystery,

FIDELITY

Available wherever books are sold.

1

PHIL **K**RAMER **WALKED** down the sidewalk under the big trees toward his car. It was quiet on this street, and the lights in the houses were almost all off. There was a strong, sweet scent of flowering vines that opened their blooms late on hot summer nights like this one—wisteria, he supposed, or some kind of jasmine. There was no way to limit it because there wasn't anything that wouldn't grow in Southern California. He supposed his senses were attuned to everything tonight. He had trained himself over the past twenty-five years to be intensely aware of his surroundings, particularly when he was alone at night. He knew there was a cat watching him from the safety of the porch railing to his right, and he knew there was a man walking along the sidewalk a half block behind him. He had seen him as he had turned the corner—not quite as tall as he was, but well built, and wearing a jacket on a night that was too warm for one. He could hear the footsteps just above the level of the cars swishing past on the boulevard.

He supposed the man could be the final attempt to make him feel uncomfortable—not a foolish attempt to scare him, but a way to remind him that he could be watched and followed and studied as easily as anyone else could. He could be fully known, and therefore vulnerable. The man might also be out walking for some reason that was completely unrelated to Phil Kramer's business.

Phil approached the spot where his car was parked—too near now to be stopped—and the man no longer mattered. He pressed the button on his key chain to unlock the locks, and the dome light came on. He swung the door open and sat in the driver's seat, then reached for the door to close it.

In the calm, warm night air he caught a sliding sound, with a faint squeak, and turned his head to find it. In one glance, he knew his mistake in all of its intricacies: He took in the van parked across the street from his car, the half-open window with the gun resting on it, and the bright muzzle-flash.

The bullet pounded into his skull, and the impact lit a thousand thoughts in an instant, burning and exploding them into nonbeing as synapses rapid-fired and went out. There was his brother Dan; a random instant in a baseball game, seeing the ground ball bounce up at his feet, feeling the sting in his palm as it smacked into his glove, even a flash of the white flannel of his uniform with tan dust; the pride and fear when he first saw his son; a composite, unbearably pleasant sensation of the women he had touched, amounting to a distilled impression of femaleness. Profound regret. Emily.

EMILY KRAMER AWOKE at five thirty, as she had for twenty-two years of mornings. The sun barely tinted the room a feeble blue, but Emily's chest already held a sense of alarm, and she couldn't expand her lungs in a full breath. She rolled to her left side to see, aware before she did it that the space was empty. It was a space that belonged to something, the big body of her husband, Phil. He was supposed to be there.

She sat up quickly, threw back the covers and swung her legs off the bed. She looked around the room noting other absences: his wallet and keys, his shoes, and the pants he always draped across the chair in the corner when he came to bed. He had not come to bed.

That was why she had slept so soundly. She always woke up when he came in, but she had slept through the night.

Emily had the sense that she was already behind, already late. Something had happened, and in each second, events were galloping on ahead of her, maybe moving out of reach. She hurried out of the bedroom along the hall to the top of the stairs and listened. There was no human sound, no noise to reassure her.

Emily knew her house so well that she could hear its emptiness. Phil's presence would have brought sound, would have changed the volume of the space and dampened the bright, sharp echoes. She went down the stairs as quickly as she could, trusting her bare feet to grip the steps. She ran through the living room to the dining room to the kitchen, looking for a sign.

She pulled open the back door, stepped to the garage, and peered in the window. Her white Volvo station wagon was gleaming in the dim light, but Phil's car was gone. No, it wasn't gone. It had never come back at all.

Emily turned, went back into the kitchen, and picked up the telephone. She dialed Phil's cell phone. A cool, distant voice said, "We're sorry, but the customer is out of the reception area at this time." That usually meant Phil had turned the phone off. She looked at the clock on the wall above the table.

It was too early to call anyone. Even as she was thinking that, she punched in the one number she knew by heart. It rang once, twice, three times, four times. His voice came on: "This is Ray Hall. Leave a message if you want." He must be sleeping, she thought. Of course he was sleeping. Every sane person on the planet was sleeping. She hoped she hadn't awakened him. She stood with the phone in her hand, feeling relieved that he didn't know who had been stupid enough to call at five thirty in the morning.

But that feeling reversed itself instantly. She wasn't glad she hadn't awakened him. She wasn't in the mood to think about why she cared what Ray Hall thought. She knew only that she shouldn't care, so she punched his phone number again. She waited through his message, then said, "Ray, this is Emily Kramer. Phil didn't come home last night. It's five thirty. If you could give me a call, I'd appreciate it." She hesitated, waiting for him to pick up the telephone, then realized she had nothing else to say. "Thanks." She hung up.

While she had been speaking, several new thoughts had occurred to her. She set the phone down on the counter and walked through the house again. She had no reason to think Phil would kill himself, but no reason to imagine he was immune to depression and disappointment, either. And bad things happened to people without their talking about it—especially people like Phil.

Emily walked cautiously through the living room again. She looked at the polished cherry table near the front door under the mirror, where they sometimes left notes for each other. She forced herself to walk into the downstairs guest bathroom and look in the tub. There was no body. She reminded herself she shouldn't be looking for his body. A man who carried a gun would shoot himself, and she had heard nothing. If he *did* kill himself, she was sure he would have left a note. She kept moving, into the small office where Phil paid bills and Emily made lists or used the computer, into the den, where they sat and watched television.

There was no note. She knew she had not missed it because she knew what the note would look like. It would be propped up vertically with a book or something, with em printed in big letters. For formal occasions like birthdays or anniversaries, he always used an envelope. Suicide would be one of the times for an envelope.

She walked back to the telephone and called the office. Phil's office line was an afterthought, but she knew she should have tried earlier. The telephone rang four times, and then clicked into voice mail. She recognized the soft, velvety voice of April Dougherty. It was an artificial phone voice, and Emily didn't like it. "You have reached the headquarters of Kramer Investigations. I'm sorry that there is no one able to take your call at the moment. For personal service, please call between the hours of nine A.M. and six P.M. weekdays. You may leave a message after the tone."

Emily had written that little speech and recorded it twenty-two years ago, and the moment came back to her sharply. She remembered thinking of calling the crummy walk-up on Reseda Boulevard the World Headquarters. Phil had hugged her and laughed aloud, and said even the word *headquarters* was stretching the truth enough.

Emily took the phone from her ear, punched in the voice-mail number and then the code to play back the messages. "We're sorry, but your code is invalid. Please try again." Emily stared at the phone and repeated the code. "We're sorry, but—" Emily disconnected. She considered calling back to leave a message telling Phil to call her, but she knew that idea was ridiculous. He could hardly *not* know that she was waiting to hear from him. She made a decision not to waste time thinking about the fact that Phil had changed the message-retrieval code. Maybe he hadn't even been the one to change the code. Maybe little April had put in a new code when she had recorded the new message. It would be just like Phil to not know that a new code would be something Emily would want to have, or that not telling her would hurt her feelings.

How could Ray Hall sleep through eight rings? Maybe he was with Phil. That was the first positive thought she'd had. Then she reminded herself that the ring sound was actually a signal, not a real sound. If Ray had turned off the ring, the phone company would still send that signal to Emily's phone.

She thought of Bill Przwalski. He was only about twenty-two years old—born about the time when she and Phil had gotten married and started the agency. He was trying to put in his two thousand hours a year for three years to get his private-investigator's license. Could he be out somewhere working with Phil? He got all the dull night-surveillance jobs and the assignments to follow somebody around town. She looked at the list in the drawer near the phone and tried his number, but got a message that sounded like a school kid reading aloud in class. "I am unable to come to the phone right now, but I will get back to you as soon as I can. Please wait for the beep, then leave me a message." She said, "Billy, this is Emily Kramer, Phil's wife. I'd like you to call us at home as soon as possible. Thank you." *Us?* She had said it without deciding to, getting caught by the reflex to protect herself from being so alone.

The next call was harder because she didn't know him as well as Ray, and he wasn't a trainee like Billy, but calling the others first had helped her to get past her shyness and reticence. She had already called Ray and Billy, so she had to call Dewey Burns. If she didn't call him, Dewey might feel strange, wondering if she had left him out just because he was black. She made the call, and there was only one ring.

"Yeah?"

"Dewey?"

"Yes."

"This is Emily Kramer. I'm sorry to call so early."

"It's all right. I'm up. What's happening?"

"I just woke up, and Phil isn't here. He never came home last night." She waited, but Dewey was waiting, too. Why didn't he say something? She prompted him: "I just started calling you guys to see if anybody knows where he is, and you're the first one who answered."

"I'm sorry, but I don't know where Phil is. He's had me working on a case by myself for a while, and he hasn't told me what he's doing. Have you called Ray yet?"

"Yes, and the office, and Billy. Nobody's up yet."

"It's early. But let me make a couple of calls and go to the office and look around. I'll call you from there."

"Thanks, Dewey."

"Talk to you in a little while." He hung up.

Emily stood holding the dead phone. His voice had sounded brusque, as though he were in a hurry to get rid of her. But maybe that terse manner had just been his time in the marines coming back to him—talk quickly and get going. He had been out for a couple of years, but he still stood so straight that he looked like he was guarding something, and still had a military haircut. Phil had told her he still did calisthenics and ran five miles a day, as though he was planning to go into battle. Still, he had sounded as though he wanted to get rid of her. And he had said he was going to make calls. Who was he going to call? Who else was there to call besides the men who worked for Phil?

She reminded herself that this was not the time to be jealous. Dewey might have numbers for Ray Hall and Bill Przwalski that she didn't—parents or girlfriends or someone. But what he had actually said was that he would make a couple of calls. What numbers would he have that he could call when Phil Kramer didn't come home one night? She hoped it meant Dewey had some idea of what was going on in Phil's latest investigation, or at least knew who the client was. But if he did, why had he said he didn't?

There was so much about Dewey that she didn't know, and she'd always had the feeling Phil must know more about him than he had said. Nobody seemed to know how Phil even knew Dewey. One day there was no Dewey Burns, and the next day there was. He and Phil always seemed to speak to each other in shorthand, in low tones, as though they had longer conversations when she wasn't around.

There was one more person to call. She looked at the sheet in the open drawer, dialed the number, and got a busy signal. She looked up at the clock on the wall. It said five forty. Had it stopped? Had all of this taken only ten minutes?

She hung up and redialed the number. This time the phone rang for an instant and was cut off. "What?" April Dougherty's voice was angry.

"April? This is Emily Kramer, Phil's wife. I'm sorry to call at this hour."

The voice turned small and meek. "That's okay."

"I'm calling everyone from the agency." Emily noticed that April didn't ask what was up. How could Emily not notice? She answered the question that April had not asked. "Phil didn't come home last night, and I'm trying to see if anybody knows where he is, or what he was working on, or if he's with someone."

"No," April said.

"No?"

"He didn't mention anything to me. I went home at six, and he was still at the office."

"Do you remember if Ray was there, or Billy?"

"Um, I think both of them were still there when I left. They were, in fact. But they were getting ready to leave, too."

"Do you remember what Phil was doing when you left? Did he have a case file, or was he packing a briefcase with surveillance gear or tape recorders, or anything?"

"I didn't notice. He could have. I mean, it's his office. He could have got anything he wanted after I left. I think he was sitting at his desk. Yes. He was."

"Was his computer turned on?"

"It's *always* on."

Emily was getting frustrated. "Look, April. I know it's early in the morning. I would never do this if I weren't worried sick. In twenty-two years, Phil has always managed to make it home, or at least call me and let me know where he is."

"I don't know why he didn't come home." April's voice was quiet and tense. "I'm sure there's a good reason."

Emily was shocked. She had not said anything critical of Phil, but here was this girl, defending him against her. Emily said, "If you hear from him, tell him to call home right away. I'm about to call the cops. If you know of any reason not to, I'd like to hear it."

"If I hear from him, I'll tell him."

"Thanks."

"'Bye." April hung up.

Emily dialed Phil's cell phone again, and listened to the message. "The customer you have called is not in the service area at this time." She put the phone back in its cradle. The chill on her feet reminded her that she was still barefoot, still wearing her nightgown. She picked up the telephone and hurried to the stairs to get dressed. On the way, she looked at the printed sticker on the phone and dialed the nonemergency number of the police.